Matty Brown was born in Reading, Engla   grow up in the West Country and scarred him with a lifelong attachment to Plymouth Argyle FC. His formative years were spent in easily-disgusted Tunbridge Wells, where he still lives. He teaches humanities in a nearby Sussex state comprehensive. *The Art of Skimming Stones* is his second book, the first being a travelogue that gave him the inspiration for this work – his debut novel.

The Art of Skimming Stones

Also by Matty Brown

The Lonely Penguin Tours – Travelogues of a Reluctant Adventurer

Matty Brown

The Art of Skimming Stones

Vanguard Press

VANGUARD PAPERBACK

© Copyright 2015
Matty Brown

A CIP catalogue record for this title is
available from the British Library.

ISBN: 978-1-84386-776-0

This is a work of fiction. Names, characters, businesses, places, events and
incidents are either the products of the author's imagination or used in a
fictitious manner. Any resemblance to actual persons, living or dead,
or actual events is purely coincidental.

*Vanguard Press is an imprint of
Pegasus Elliot Mackenzie Publishers Ltd.*

www.pegasuspublishers.com

First Published in 2015

**Vanguard Press
Sheraton House Castle Park
Cambridge England**

Printed & Bound in Great Britain

For the lovers and dreamers and smiley baristas

Acknowledgements:

Thank you, Annie, for your time and advice.

Contents

Ideal Skimming Locations – Reference

Key
*Fun and/or aesthetic reasons
**Competition reasons
*** Fun and/or aesthetic and competition reasons

Compliments of Mother Nature

When the conditions were perfect: the wind in the right direction and speed, the barometric readings at a certain pressure, through the open sash window on a cool summer's morning would drift the lowing of cattle.

It was an odd sound to dominate in this urban theatre for we were more than two miles from the edge of town and the first woodlands of the Weald, but the lowing seemed to drown out the familiar first light sounds of the summer birds: the screeching swifts taking to the air for a breakfast of foolishly early insects on wing high above; the chattering blackbirds nesting in the neighbours' leylandii; and the beautiful song of the unknown summer visitor who must have arrived only just last week.

I leant across to the window and pushed it up a few inches, trying to do so with difficulty from this angle and without waking her up. I took in the cool, damp but fresh air through my nostrils, full of the sweet smells of summer that the garden had exhaled through the night, it taking a welcome refuge and a consequent sigh of relief from yesterday's intense sun, the first real scorcher of the season. The honeysuckle hit me and the lowing cattle continued, an octave higher this time.

Turning my head back towards the room and the bed, I lost the sweet summer scents and became very aware of Anna. I could smell her, not in the room but on me still. It was an indescribable scent but one that made my heart skip, put a smile on my face and let me flirt with the idea of happiness. The smell would last for days, cling to my clothes, linger on my fingers stronger than any shower gel, soap, or perfume, and sometime in midweek it would mingle with the everyday grind of modern life and the bombardment of fragrances, sweat, and toil and would become mine and me. But for three days I could smell her, feel her and want her just by bringing my hand to my face, nonchalantly scratching my nose, taking a subtle deep breath and with it, enjoy the thought of her.

She was sleeping still, breathing steadily and slowly, the duvet moving slightly every few seconds to tell me that she was alive and that I hadn't smothered her in a sleepwalking nightmare. Often one to spoil the moment, my mind would create these macabre thoughts to shatter the illusion of happiness.

The sound of lowing reached me once more and I lay down next to her and considered the poor cattle, a waft of our own scent hitting me as I settled. I followed the sound out of the window and across the gardens of Dundee Road, soaring like the screeching swifts, and turned right up Marsh Lane to the corner and the grotty house with the wrecked cars used for scrap, up the hill and past the recreation ground and Infants school, across the busy Bell Road and all the way down Powder Mill Lane, past the new estates seen only last week on the regional news for the spate of arson attacks, and onto Reynolds Wood Nature Reserve, home to impromptu mountain bike tracks, burnt out bonfire pits and makeshift swings that seemed to have damaged the trees more than a herd of wild elephants on the rampage, and on across Badgers Pond, low and green and stinking at this time of the year. At the edge of the woods a stile led into a field, home to untendered clumps of rye grass, angry thistles and brambles at first, then opened out into an idyllic meadow where wild flowers bloomed, miraculously untrammelled by the hordes of kids that lived nearby and unpicked by the ramblers that came this way on a Sunday.

Walking towards me was the man again, heavyset figure and a shock of jet-black hair and the blackest of beards. He carried his lunchbox and a newspaper and strolled happily along the path as though he had not a care in world. He acknowledged me with a broad and welcoming smile and swung his arms a little more as he did so, causing the paper to flutter in his breeze.

Ever since I saw him last year on this path, I had wanted to be him; something about his demeanour, his very being, was so damn peaceful that I craved to feel the way he did, to have the peace of mind he seemed to possess. I could sense the control he had on his own life; I could smell it. But as I continued my walk, tracing his footsteps at a distance, the path led away from the field and onto a collection of brick barn buildings at the edge of the woods. I could hear the farm animals inside, the bleating of the lambs, the clattering of hooves on concrete and looked up at the wall of the first and oldest outhouse. 'Bailey's Abattoir' it read and I reeled at the rude interruption to my bucolic world. This seemingly satiated man must have worked here at the abattoir, and the animals I could hear would soon be mincemeat, literally.

Although not a vegetarian, I was still somewhat repulsed at the thought of what went on in there and I felt cheated at the discovery of the profession of my chosen role model. This happy and calm man had blood on his hands five days a week, forty-seven weeks of the year; this man was a killer and happily walked through this beautiful meadow to his killing fields.

My daydream today, as always, would only take me as far as the sign, to the meeting of the happy man and never any further. It was during this encounter of course, that I realised the occasional lowing that reached my window was in fact that of cattle facing imminent slaughter and that, on those rare days when the conditions were right, what you could hear were the poor creatures' last rites.

I came back to the room and looked at Anna: still she slept, blissfully unaware of the killing that would soon begin. I touched her slender left shoulder and felt the wonderfully smooth, baby-bottom skin, carefully nurtured to feel this way by bottles of moisturiser that she would unpack from her bag on the occasional days that she stayed over, less now than in the depths of winter. Her hair was short, not long and silken as it was when we first met, when I fell for her. I'm not sure I liked it, or the significance of this recent cut. She had told me on our very first fieldtrip together that she grew her hair long when happy but always had a drastically short cut when insecure or a great change was pending. Well, perhaps I was the guilty party there and my indecision the catalyst, but it still unsettled me nonetheless.

I touched her hair, lightly, and pushed a wayward clump of strands behind that beautifully elfin ear and leant in close to kiss her on the cheek, the heat and warmth that the snug of sleep produced radiating on to my lips. I just watched, waiting for that 'Emily' moment: a song that made me happy, made me believe that this is how love should feel 'For Emily, wherever I may find her' by Simon and Garfunkel played in my head. But I didn't love her any more, despite wanting to and Anna must have known this.

Sex last night was good, as it always seemed to be with Anna, even in my bedroom, me shushing her so as not to wake my housemate, Phil, an odd but charming British eccentric who had a prized collection of ethnic Barbie dolls that he proudly displayed on a shelving unit in his bedroom – not many girls came back again once they'd seen them. It was quite intense, the sex, and although it was dark, being a new moon and all, I could sense her big brown eyes looking into mine and waiting for me to utter those three words that men are so bloody scared of saying. And I couldn't.

"I want to tell you something," she gasped.

"Go on then," I replied. I'd still like to be loved, even if I wasn't going to reciprocate.

"I want to say it," she continued.

"Go on then."

"You say it first." She threw it back at me – an ace: a non-returnable, blistering first serve.

I resorted to the male security blanket of silence. We stopped making love (well, having sex), unfinished, and she climbed off, turned over and pretended to sleep. I went to the loo and sat there for a while wondering at what point my mad passionate love for her had slipped away.

She stirred now and turned to me and said, "Hi" with that Northern Irish brogue that I often disliked. It was a little harsh sometimes.

"I was dreaming," she said.

"Was I in it... naked?"

"No, it wasn't a nightmare." She tried to giggle. It was early and she'd probably begun to remember that we'd not left things at a good point last night.

"I was dreaming of a house we used to live in when I was... God, I must have only been two or three."

"Uh huh."

"It was weird. Mum and Dad were there but they were different somehow. It was really odd. It was kind of... kind of my first memory."

"Oh... right... what was that then?"

She sat up, rubbed her left eye with the knuckle of her index finger on her left hand and smiled sweetly.

"Mum and Dad were arguing and she was holding me. I was crying and so were they, I think? I remember so vividly looking out of the window and seeing a soldier walk past with a gun. I can still see his face."

"That's sad. That's a sad first memory to have."

"Yeah, I suppose it is, growing up during the Troubles..."

"No... yeah, sure, but the crying – that's sad."

"Oh, yeah..." she said and the sentence drifted off into an uncertain reverie.

I put my arm around her and pulled her in close. She was the only girl I'd slept with who still smelt good in the morning. Her skin seemed to be naturally perfumed and I drank in the scent.

"What's yours?" she asked.

"What, first memory? I'm sure I've told you before."

"Maybe, but I don't remember."

"Hmm, let's see. I have a couple, I think. One of them…" I laughed. "One of them is running around our house chasing my brother and I was wielding a yellow plastic Indian axe."

"Nothing's really changed has it? With your brother, I mean, not the axe. God, I hope not the axe!"

"That was in Scotland. I guess I must have been two or three as well."

"What's the second one? You said there were two."

"Well, I'm not sure if it is a real first memory or one triggered by Dad's infamous slideshows. You see, there's this beautiful photo of me and my two brothers standing ankle deep in the water – Loch Lomond – and throwing stones; well, skimming stones, or at least they were trying to. I was in the process of chucking a pebble badly, a little bit like you do."

She hit me, playfully but with some force.

"Ow!"

"Typical," she said, resting her head on my shoulder. "Your first memory is skimming bloody stones."

"Yeah, I know. But I really think it is a memory. I don't think I've invented it. I can feel the stone in my hand almost. I can feel the… happiness… I dunno… sheer joy of throwing the stone into the water: hearing the splash, the beautiful concentric rings, the sunshine, the dappled light across the water from behind the trees. I was really there. Yeah, it was definitely a memory."

"Bloody stones," she said, the slight movement of her body signifying an inward chuckle.

The family had lived for two years in Cardross, near Helensurgh, in Scotland. Dad would often take us across the B832 to the A82 to stop at Luss from where we'd walk along the shore of Loch Lomond to picnic. I always remembered it as sunny and warm but Mum recalls (not so fondly) that the sun shone rarely and that it was usually piddling it down, grey, cold and constantly damp.

I have not skimmed a stone (or 'skipped' as the Americans refer to it) on Loch Lomond, not since that early memory at least. The stones transported down the Luss Water along Glenn Luss, maybe originating from Old Shielings or Coille-eughain Hill, who knows, possibly Beinn Chaorach at 713 metres (or 2280 feet in Imperial), are most probably well-rounded and the local boulder clay and fluvio-glacial drift would mean that palm-sized pebbles would be abundant. The signs seem good for excellent skimming. I must go back to see how far I can throw one, and how many skips I can get.

(Location No.1 and 13, Luss, Loch Lomond, Scotland)

We both sat there and the lowing of the cattle drifted on in again, a bit louder this time.

"Cows?"

"Yep."

"Oh."

I didn't tell her they were screaming for their lives. Silence seemed the best option.

***

I can tell you the moment I fell in love with Anna; I can feel it, smell it, and taste it still. Ironic too, hey, that it would involve a stone, though a mightily bigger one than those that I would hunt for over the years in my search for happiness. This is really a story of geography, that glorious social science that takes the whole damn world and tries to explain it, reference it and so singularly fails to sell itself as the most important of all subjects, when clearly it is; everything we see is geography, everything we feel is geography and my quest for happiness is inextricably linked to it too.

This is a love story told through landscapes.

Part 1

In search of Anna

Chapter 1

Gently sinking into the depths

Mrs Cooper looked like a cartoon character, one that I couldn't place at first. It was only on the long road to southern France, via Dijon, sitting next to her in the front seat of the school minibus, that I realised who it was she reminded me of. It wasn't a cartoon character at all, but Beaker out of *The Muppets*. Indeed, the term 'Muppet' is perhaps more commonly used to describe what Mrs Cooper actually was: a Christian lady, with an avid love of the Liberal Democratic Party; she displayed nothing of what I would define as Christian values, always being the first to cast a stone, but her liberal tendencies made for a relaxing field trip nonetheless, both for me and the students.

She was remarkably ugly and the further we drove into France the more that silly mug and sour countenance began to wear on me. Anna was sitting up front too, to my left, and I alternated between driving and sharing her company at close quarters. When it was my stint at the wheel, Mrs Cooper, or Leslie, as she insisted we all call her, including the students, would drift off to sleep, leaning into Anna and dribbling a little, much to our amusement as we motored on through Champagne. Behind us were fourteen sixth formers, all of us on our way to Les Haute Alpes (High Alps) for a weeklong geography fieldtrip.

Anna had been at the school for just over a year now and I was her boss, her Head of Department or HOD, an acronym that Leslie liked to use when sarcastically referring to me. Technically, I was her boss too, but she pulled rank continuously through age and a tenuous Deputy-Head-of-Citizenship link. I taught a couple of lessons of what the kids called 'Citizen', due to it being too long a word to fit onto their printed timetables and Leslie was responsible for running the organisation of who taught this odd subject. Anyway, I'd made her cry once when clearing out her old cupboard-sized office, now in my tenure. It was so full of horded geographical detritus dating back to the last ice age it seemed, or at least the late Pleistocene era, that it was all I could do to dispense of a skip-load just to be able to turn around in it.

Regardless of our antipathy towards one another, Leslie was a vastly experienced geography teacher and although her odd and slapdash methods irritated the kids and me most of the time, she was excellent in the field. I had shared many a trip with her before the arrival of Anna and she had taught me a lot and I grudgingly appreciated it.

We'd been driving since six this morning, back in a rain-sodden Blighty, and it was nearly five o'clock now. We'd booked into the youth hostel in Dijon for the night and stopped a little way out in the beautiful medieval town of Beaunne, slap bang in the middle of Bourgogne, or Burgundy country, for a break before dusk. We parked in the town centre car park, me inching my way delicately in between two clapped-out old Citroëns, Anna directing me from just in front. As the kids jeered at my failure to hit any 'frog mobiles', as they so wonderfully put it, Anna smiled and winked at me. It wasn't one of those jokey 'well done mate' types of winks but a 'there's a definite possibility of sexual action between us at some point in the future' kind. However, it had a proviso, or so I read it as the right eyelid returned to parity, so beautifully accentuated by those long, calf-like lashes. The caveat was 'as long as you impress me, that is, tell me how gorgeous I am, how infatuated you are with me and how you will do battle valiantly with my big, bad boyfriend Mike', for big, bad Mike was getting the odd mention, noticeably not when we conversed, but when Leslie and Anna did, in those brief moments between dribbles.

The children had an hour to stretch their legs, hopefully not long enough to find a bar that would serve them and get drunk. Leslie went off to find a local wine merchants and Anna and I decamped to a cosy continental café for coffee and pastries where I impressed her with my schoolboy French; no mean feat as it was a good five years longer than I last studied French at school than she had. I was in the last cohorts of the O' Level educated and she the first few experimental years of the GCSEs, and did my superior knowledge of our neighbours' tongue represent the superior nature of the old exam system to the new? I doubt it; I was just better at French than she was. The café was cosy and welcoming and we sat by an open fire and chatted idly about fellow teachers, the ugliness of Mrs Cooper and the potential for romantic liaisons between our geography A' Level students.

"I'm not really looking forward to sharing a room with old sour puss," she complained.

"Shame," I said. "I'll just have to enjoy the luxury of a double room all to myself."

"Bastard. Maybe I'll come and join you if it all gets too much."

I chose silence as the most appropriate response here. It was to be a tactic returned to often in our odd, long drawn-out, hot-cold, on-off affair. I looked at my watch and reckoned it was time to be rounding up the troops.

"Come on, Miss Taylor; time to go and find the lost souls."

I rested my hand on her knee as I stood and left it there a little too long. She didn't react; neither bad nor good news, I supposed.

An hour later we had arrived at the Dijon Youth Hostel and I had a gang of helpers atop the bus undoing the maze of tangled ropes and elasticised grapple hooks that tentatively held the bags, suitcases and rucksacks of seventeen people in place on the roof-rack frame. It was dusk now, into the second week of October, and the neon lights of suburban Dijon lit up the puddles that were gradually being spat into again from a threatening continental sky.

"Come on, lads! Let's get the bags down before the rain."

The three most helpful boys, Josh, Scott and Neil, were up on top with me, all three already taller than me at sixteen, and I wasn't short. As the rain came down, heavier still, we passed the bags down to the waiting cold and weary travellers and off they trotted into the warmth of the hostel to be allocated rooms by fluent French speaking Mrs C.

In a show of unity, Anna waited in the rain until I had unpicked the last of the tattered cargo net that a parent had donated two years ago after the calamitous loss of two bags on the M54 on the way to Snowdonia. She loyally grabbed the ties and hooks I passed down and stood around whilst I locked up and tried in vain to make sense of the taco-graph readings we were supposed to be taking, EU rules and all.

"Ta for hanging around."

"That's okay. Anyway, the less time I spend with Mrs C the better."

Dinner was typically French fare with al dente vegetables and nearly-raw meat that all of the girls left and, after a Mrs C inspired briefing, we gave the students an hour off before bedtime. The games room in the basement was out-of-bounds, inconveniently, so we let them have a wander in the rain-sodden streets of the neighbourhood. We'd been here before and it was a safe area with very few bars so we could let them stretch their legs after a long day cooped up in the bus, take a break from us and return bored within half an hour hopefully. Anna and I followed the most likely candidates to do something silly, (the three boys who'd helped me earlier) down the damp leafy streets and lost them as they became aware of our mistrust and sprinted away once around the corner. We'd assumed they wanted to smoke, so didn't bother to follow. We decided to stroll back when the rain began hitting out a pretty rhythm on the damp plane tree leaves that littered our path.

"What you doing at half term?" I asked, a little desperate to break the silence.

"We're going back to Northern Ireland." 'We're' meaning big, bad Mike, I supposed. "Family thing."

"Oh."

"Yeah, I'm meeting my sister at Stansted on Saturday morning and we're flying off home."

"Great." Great, no mention of Mike: maybe they're splitting up.

"And you?"

"Oh, nothing much: home alone."

She stopped abruptly in the shelter of a large plane tree sprayed sepia by the glow of neon.

"I can't believe you're still single."

Blimey, where did that come from? "Why do you say that?"

"Well, you're clever, successful... fairly," she said play-punching me, "and quite good looking too."

"Quite?"

"Okay, a little bit more than quite good looking."

"Ta." Underneath the camouflage of the neon lights I was blushing and getting quite excited by this revelation. Should I respond?

"You're not so bad yourself."

A strange whooping sound came out of nowhere.

"What's that?" she said, moving a little closer, foolishly supposing I would be able to protect her. Something hit the wet ground near our feet and she moved closer still, this time grabbing my arm.

"What the f...!" and then I heard the tell tale giggles of what could only be our students pratting about somewhere nearby. Anna looked up and started to laugh. Up above in the balding plane trees sat the three suspects lounging around on the thick bough and branches like a troop of proboscis monkeys in the rainforest.

"Bloody idiots! Get down now before you kill yourselves or damage the tree."

"Sir, you swore, sir!" shouted Neil.

"I'll do more than bloody swear in a minute. Now get down!" I broke into a grin; couldn't help myself.

"You're laughing, Mr Jones. I can see it."

"No I'm not," this time barely unable to finish the sentence before breaking out into a big, broad smile.

"Look!" shouted Josh, grabbing a handful of dead brown leaves and helping them on their way to the dark suburban streets. "Xerophytic drought!"

"Oh God, they're talking geography now," I said to Anna.

"What are they saying?" she asked.

"Oh, nothing, just something I taught them in the Ecosystems module last week."

"Yes, xerophytic drought is why deciduous trees shed their leaves, isn't that right, Mr Jones?" Neil said, looking to me for affirmation.

"Don't be a nerd, Neil." The others laughed.

Regardless, Neil carried on quoting the definition from the text verbatim. "At least that's what Mr Waugh," (pronounced 'war') "says. So, trees drop their leaves in the winter to stop losing water and getting thirsty."

"Mr Waugh," (said as 'woff') "Neil, he likes it be pronounced 'woff'," I reminded him. David Waugh was the guru of school geography, writing text books for all the year groups and his book, which Neil had quoted from, called *Geography, An Integrated Approach* (published by Nelson) was the Bible for all A' Level students. I was secretly quite chuffed that Neil had memorised the definition of xerophyitc drought, although was slightly embarrassed for him too. He was clearly trying to show off to Miss Taylor.

"Get a life, Neil," I mocked.

"Just telling Miss what you taught us."

"I know, and I'm impressed, but when have you ever taken anything I taught you seriously?"

"True sir, but you gave us a challenge, remember?"

"Hey?" He was making me sound like an evangelical Hollywood-style educator who came to the slums to help the poor kids fulfil their potential and rise above the grizzly reality of drugs and shootings that was their everyday existence. True, Gravesham was rough in places, but these kids were soft and I never looked at teaching as a religious-style vocation. I enjoyed it (most of the time) but it was only a job, but a job that gave me thirteen weeks holiday a year and at the end of August I would receive a whole month's salary just for being on holiday.

"You know," continued Neil, "you said, '*Xerophytic*', *what a great word. I bet you can't use it in a conversation down the pub this weekend.*"

"And did you?" I asked.

"Yep. And guess what?"

"Erm… You met a doctor of dendrology and she was so impressed you went home with her."

"Well, almost," Neil replied, keen to impress me now with his attraction to the opposite sex. It was pretty obvious that he didn't have many problems in that field, being a tall, dark, handsome rugby player with a bit of a brain and a penchant for impertinence that charmed both the girls and female staff alike. Miss Taylor seemed to be no exception.

"Don't be silly, Neil," I said.

"What are you two talking about?" interrupted Anna at this point, feeling left out at this staff-student banter. It's a reality in teaching that we get jealous of each other's popularity with the kids and at times it slips shamefully into competition. No one perfected this art of popularity-by-grooming more than the PE department. At Christmas they would manufacture a student card and gift competition between themselves and would share out the spoils in a mercenary fashion in front of the rest of the staff at the end of term do. I was once foolishly cajoled into joining in and was shamed by my seeming unpopularity.

"Miss Taylor, are you quite aware of what Mr Jones talks to us about in class?"

"Don't listen to them," I pleaded playfully.

We were strolling slowly back now, the rain having stopped once more.

"He talks about you, miss."

"Shut up, Josh! Don't," I said pointing my finger at him and smiling, quite pleased at having my feelings about Anna confessed through a third party.

"And he often encourages us to go to the pub and chat up women."

"You don't need encouraging, Josh." He laughed.

"He does, miss," continued Neil. "Whenever we ask 'what's the point of learning about this?' he goes, '*You never know when you'll use this information. You could be in a pub one day and standing next to you will be a beautiful woman.*'"

"Yeah," interrupted Scott, pushing his way towards Anna. They surrounded her now, she being quite dwarfed by their big hulks. "And he goes that she'll turn out to be an expert in hydrology or something and when we talk to her about bi-furcation ratios she'll get turned on and we'll end up in bed with her!"

"I didn't quite say that," I defended myself. "I said that she'd be so impressed you might end up marrying her."

"He's lying, miss. He's a bad influence."

Anna was loving this now. It takes a while to be accepted by kids, especially the older ones, but she was in her element here surrounded by keen-to-impress young men.

We were soon back at the grey, industrial-sized hostel, a finer example of 1970s drab French architecture you could not hope to find, and the kids drifted off to their allocated rooms before the official lights-out and quiet-time of ten thirty. There have been occasions when the first night of school trips have often been the worst with antics abound that parents would wince at if only they really knew but, after a day cooped up in the minibus and an early start, the low, dark sky had drawn a blanket of melancholy over the kids and, heavy with sleep and the oppressive weather, they quietened down quickly and without a fuss.

Never one to underestimate the power of students to deceive, we patrolled the corridor, as was usual, until midnight. We told Mrs C not to worry about it for today; Anna and I would hold tonight's vigil. She listened outside the girls' rooms for signs of unruliness and I, the boys'. By 11.17 p.m., they were all quiet and we sat in the prison-like, grey-painted walled corridor and shared a mini bottle of wine from plastic glasses – a small perk after a long, hard day. We chatted and as the wine kicked in, not needing much to relax us in our present state of torpor, we giggled at the prospect of Anna having to share a room with the venerable Mrs C. She laid on her back on the grubby, hardwearing beige carpet and let out a loud sigh.

"Oh, God," she let out, in that harshly attractive provincial brogue. "I'll have to see her naked in the morning! We're sharing a bathroom," and giggled again.

The ruby red wine had stained her moist, full lips purple and her tainted teeth beneath that showed as the giggle turned into a full laugh, gave her the look of a freshly fed vampire. Little was I to know how much this Vampira would tear into my heart and rip it open in the next year or so. I think it began that very night, though I was still unaware; it would be two days before it hit me hard in the face.

"Time for bed," I said and offered my hand. Her clammy little right paw took it and I helped her up. "Night."

"Let's have a look at your room, Mr Jones? I can't face going back to mine just yet."

"Okay."

I opened the light blue door, paint scratched off in places across the panel in lines as though a wild animal had tried to break its way through, into a drab box room, devoid of any furniture and character save for a low single bed and wobbly desk and chair.

"Nice," she said sarcastically.

"Hmm."

We walked to the window and from the fifth floor looked out across the orange-lit city sparkling in the rain that was now beating against the small window again and crying tears down the pane.

"Shit, what's that?" I said, turning back to the room and spotting a huge insect on the wall directly above the headboard.

"Oh, no! A cockroach," she laughed.

"Get rid of it. Urgh, shit, get rid of it, Anna!"

"Seriously?"

"Seriously, yes. I can't stand them!"

"Ah, diddums," she said and went to the en-suite bathroom (of sorts), returning with a glass.

"Got any card?" she asked matter-of-factly.

"Card? Why?"

"To trap the little beauty in the glass with."

"Umm… I suppose we could use this." I rummaged in the box full of stationery, the odd textbook and worksheets, and pulled out a small laminated card that had 'Powers Roundness Index' printed on it, a waterproof method for a piece of information that the students would need to refer to whilst checking pebble shape and roundness in rivers.

"Great."

Calmly and quickly, she placed the glass over the top of the large creature and slid the card betwixt it and the wall. The little critter skipped as its ground changed, but then remained calm and still, as though accepting its fate with a cool compliance.

"Open the window."

I fiddled with the obsolete contraption of the latch and pushed hard, the window eventually giving way to weeks of being shut tight with a 'swoosh' and a puff of dust and peeled paint. And out went the cockroach, falling, almost dancing gracefully down into the murky depths until we lost sight of it.

"Ta," I said.

"No problems. You'd do the same for me if it were snakes, right?"

"Course, I'm not scared of them," I lied.

"Night," she said and went to the door.

"Have fun," I teased.

"Bastard," and she was gone.

* * *

The grey sky had lifted a tad the following morning and allowed us the opportunity of fixing the luggage to the roof in the dry, a laborious and fingernail-splitting task that took at least thirty minutes and left me out of breath and sweating like a pig as I took the passenger seat next to Anna and waited for the fan to clear my sweat-induced mist from the windscreen. Mrs C was on the first leg to Lyon on the A6 (the E21, or more beautifully known as the 'AutoRoute de soleil' and we prayed for some today), where after I'd take the stretch along the A43 (E70) to Grenoble, and then we'd fight for the fun section up into the high Alps on the N91.

The hair raising U-bends, disconcertingly narrow 1920s tunnels, thin enough to just about fit two mopeds abreast it seemed, and the joy of seeing the terror on the kids' faces, especially those seated on the right hand side as we drove along the Romanche Valley, hundreds of feet of precipitous drops straight down into the dammed reservoir of Barrage de Chandon, sapphire blue due to nearby quarry run-off, were the highlights of the day's drive. Here, the geography would begin with field sketches of glaciated valleys, rejuvenated 'v' shaped river valleys and impressive rock folding and faulting. We stopped at Vizelle to sketch the spectacular folds, a brief and unconvincing explanation of their origin from Mrs C with the help of a tattered and torn piece of A4, and the sun at last poked through the thinning clouds.

From here on in we followed the N91 up and up into the high alpine mountains with the faded graffiti of famous Tour de France riders' names white-washed all along the road ahead, as it first forked to the left to access Alpe d'Huez, and soon after to the right for Les Deux Alpes, both famed for the Tour and excellent skiing. Anna boasted of her expertise on skis after a February half term spent in these resorts earlier in the year, courtesy of Mike.

As we headed further into the Massif des Écrins, the clouds began to build again, the weather fickle at these lofted heights, and I soon found myself gingerly heading in and out of old road tunnels, trying not to skid on the now greasy road surfaces. Scars that pitted the road floor told of nasty rock falls from the sheer cliffs rising way above and I thanked the protection of the painstakingly tied on luggage above our heads – maybe it would soften the blow of a smaller landslide: no chance on a bigger one. The conversation faltered here, people tired after another day in the bus, a few reeling from the innumerable bends we had recently negotiated, and others a little nervous of the precarious nature of the Route National 91.

At the pretty and tiny ski resort of La Grave we stopped in the car park and stretched our legs, taking in a view down the deep valley of Combe de Malaval below and on up to La Meije, peaking at 3892 metres (or 12500 feet), which played host to a series of glaciers, the lowest of which, Glacier de Tabulet, we could just discern through the haze of drizzle here and snow up there. It was a shame, as on previous visits we had been afforded glorious views of the glaciers and would take a while completing field sketches and introducing the students to glaciation, and the small glaciers visible would help us explain the process of 'nivation' and the birth of these monster bulldozers made of ice.

We sat in the minibus after our brief enjoyment of the reduced vista and a short lecture from Mrs C and watched the drizzle turn to 'snizzle' as Jo called it, the temperature dropping further still and turning the drizzle into ice and making snow appear as if by magic from the mist. It was four o'clock and I was keen to top the Col du Lautaret, the highest point in the journey, before too much of the white stuff got in the way.

Soon after we headed up from La Grave we were plummeted into the old, dirty and frighteningly narrow Tunnel des Ardoisieres, where large trucks seemed to bear down right upon us and only at the last minute scraped past us to the left, me fearful of whacking the right wing mirror against the untidily chiselled rock of the tunnel wall. Emerging the other side at 1600 metres (5300 feet) brought us into a slushy grey alpine world and the kids whooped with joy at the prospect of an early season snowball fight. They'd forgotten their concern of precipitous drops, whilst the three teachers all looked at each other nervously, wary of the half an hour left on the loaded-to-full capacity bus on these increasingly treacherous mountain roads.

"Rather you than me," cajoled Mrs C, thoughtfully.

"Cheers," I said and laughed nervously. I'd won the right to drive this section.

The N91 curved ceaselessly upwards further into the white mist and the snow grew in size from flecks to fully-grown flakes and began to settle with intent on the road ahead. It was only mid-October and snow at this height and season was unusual, and we tried to convince ourselves that we were careful and cautious professionals having covered all bases on the health and safety front, and that we were just unlucky with this inclement weather. We scratched our heads as to what 'Plan B' might be if the road became too slippery for me to continue confidently. We were painfully so close and yet so far from our hotel, just a few miles across the Col as the crow flies, in the adjoining valley of Serre Chevalier.

In fifteen minutes, the good old reliable minibus, full to the brim, had ploughed its way to the top of the pass and we briefly stopped off in the car park of the Col du Lautaret at 2058 metres (6600 feet). I got out to have a stretch and to peel the tee shirt from my back, courtesy of a nervous sweat on the final ascent. Here at the pass, with a small collection of outbuildings and a hospice for shelter-seeking intrepid adventurers, the wet snow was two inches deep and the flakes that now fell were like full, thick lumps of cotton wool and I beckoned the kids off the bus to enjoy the freak snow storm and let off a bit of steam in a short, sharp and manic snowball fight. Passing car and lorry drivers smiled at the mad dogs and Englishmen and, thoroughly soaked through, we boarded the bus with broad grins, all except a clearly disapproving Mrs C.

I'd hit Anna full in the face with a snowball I'd aimed at her rump, but luckily the loose collection of giant flakes disintegrated on impact, leaving only a fat flake on the end of her red-raw nose that didn't melt until she was sitting next to me in the front of the bus.

"Sorry," I pleaded. "I didn't mean to…"

"Git!" she smiled, and as she did so it disappeared into a large dewdrop that collected on the end of her pretty little nose and was wiped away by a cold thumb before it could gather momentum and drip onto the gear stick. She looked at me, and I at her, and neither could think of anything to say. Mike, I thought and looked away, starting the engine as I did so.

Once gingerly through La Marionnaise tunnel, a hooded edifice enclosed to the left and above but open at intervals to the right between pillars, designed not as a tunnel to bore through impassable rock but to act as a guard against avalanches and landslides from above, the road began to straighten and head down the emerging valley of Serre Chevalier. The River Guisane that lived in its floor was a small mountain trickle here to the right and, as we gradually descended, the snow turned to cold drizzle and at the hamlet of l'Etrat stopped altogether.

Relieved, I encouraged the kids to look into the valley on the hunt for clues of recent glaciation and as they did so I joined them, glancing occasionally at the empty road ahead. Along the valley floor, still quite high here not far from the pass and Col du Lautaret, were dotted pale white and grey rocks that if they weren't stationary you could have mistaken for sheep. Indeed, these smoothed-over boulders, too hard for the glaciers to have worn away, are called 'roches moutonnées' in the textbooks; a glacial feature common here and therefore attributed the French name that literally means 'rock sheep', the animal they can so easily be mistaken for at a distance.

"See any roches moutonnées, kids?" I shouted above the sound of the engine.

"Roche what?" asked Sarah. She should have remembered.

"Roche moutonnée. It is a mass of more resistant rock. It has a smooth, rounded up-valley or stoss slope facing the direction of the ice flow, formed by abrasion, and a steep, jagged, down-valley or lee slope resulting from plucking." I was pleased with my textbook quote of the feature.

"Hey?" said Sarah. I didn't think she'd heard me over the engine and tinny fuzz emanating from earphones playing somewhere near the back.

"It is a…" I began again.

"Sir!" shouted Jo, a sweet, slightly buck-toothed girl, sitting just behind the front passenger seats. I looked ahead and saw a flash of grey and braked suddenly, or as suddenly as the brakes on this ageing machine would let me, skidded a few feet and came to a halt next to three grazing and oblivious mountain sheep, still tearing at the thin grass on the verge, blissfully unaware of the huge chunk of metal that had stopped no more than three feet in front of them.

A muffled clunk or thud had accompanied the skid and I prayed it was just some luggage movement atop the bus that could easily be fixed and not the sound of bumper on sheep, not so easily fixed I feared.

"You hit one!" screamed Jo.

"No I didn't," I hoped. "It was the luggage."

"No, no, I'm positive. You hit one."

"Jo, I didn't! Look, if I did, where is he… she?"

There was no traffic thankfully, so I pulled over onto the verge, wide enough to take the bus off the road, nudging the sheep forward like a shepherd's dog as I did so. I got out and checked for damage. I could see nothing, no injured sheep, so passed my attention to the roof rack and the potentially dislodged luggage. As I did so, I caught a glimpse of something stuck to the corner of the bumper on the driver's side, near to the indicator light. I looked closer and saw a small clump of what could only be wool. I took another look around and over the low metal barrier into the steep field and saw nothing but thin grass and boulders and the sheep-like roches moutonnées further down the valley near the Guisane River, still little more than a trickle at this height near to its source and the valley's watershed. Anna tapped on my shoulder from behind, silently taking me by surprise.

"What's that?" she asked, pointing to the tell tale clump of wool in my hand.

"Oh, nothing," I said, tossing it over the barrier and smiling.

She smiled too, leaned in and whispered, "Do you think you killed it?"

"No, of course not! I'm still not convinced I hit anything."

"But what about the…" she said, pointing in the general direction of the discarded wool.

"Could have picked that up anywhere, and these guys could've just brushed past it," I said, pointing to the ruminating sheep.

"Hmm." She wasn't convinced; nor was I.

Jo had come outside now, visibly upset at the prospect of me having hit a sheep.

"Where is it?" she asked agitatedly.

"What?" I knew what.

"The sheep you hit."

"I didn't. Look, can you see an injured or dead sheep anywhere?"

She scanned the immediate area. "Look! There!"

We turned in the direction she was pointing and on the other side of the road, about twenty metres up in amongst dying vegetation, possibly ferns, I couldn't tell, there lay a motionless sheep. Jo started off across the empty road, over the small metal barrier and was scrambling up the steep field towards it.

"Jo!" I shouted. "Wait!"

I followed, and by now two of the lads had got off the bus and were also in pursuit. We clambered on up but still couldn't get a clear view. Jo, a fit young thing and keen athlete, beat us all to the poor creature and up above I saw her, bizarrely, stand on top of it and burst into laughter. What a sick girl,

I thought and immediately realised that we'd been duped by glacial geography.

"A roche moutonnée, sir! I've found one." As she passed me, skipping back down the hill like a little shepherdess, she let out a gasping but jolly 'Sorry', and was soon on the bus.

Vindicated, I climbed on top of the minibus via the ladder attached to the back door and fiddled with the ropes and cargo net that held down the luggage of seventeen people, and it seemed as tight as when I'd left it in Dijon that morning. I got back in the driver's seat and started the engine.

"Sir?"

"Yes, Josh?"

"I was just about to tell you how impressed I was with your driving skills, what with the snow and that... but then you... like... killed a sheep!"

"I didn't k..."

They all burst out laughing, Anna too, and I pulled away, unimpressed with them ganging up on me. Mrs C was laughing too – cow. Anna looked across, and sitting so close, the three of us crammed in the front seats like sardines, whispered, "Good job they didn't see what I did."

"Hey?"

"The dead sheep, fifty yards back behind the bus."

"The what!"

She was laughing at me again.

"Git."

"Sheep killer."

***

Serre Chevalier is a beautiful, almost picture-perfect, Alpine valley that in the winter is home to huge volumes of skiers and in the summer plays host to outdoor activities, mainly hiking and mountain biking. However, the dead season is the autumn, and October and November, before the first major snows arrive in December, are the time for hoteliers to take a break, or for renovations and redecorations to take place. So, as we drove on down through the small hamlets of Le Lausset and Le Cassest, we saw nobody, it feeling like an early, wet November Sunday evening on Dartford High Street. Life was spotted briefly in Le Monetier-les-Bains, a small elderly lady crossing slowly and obliviously in front, dragging her half dead poodle-like pooch behind her.

The long valley, with the ever growing Guisane River always to our right, is surprisingly forested – unusual for such a popular ski resort – and eventually ends at the fortress town of Briançon, reputedly the highest in Europe; though this of course depends on the definition of a town and, indeed, Europe, so many people forgetting the tiny Caucasus' states which rise higher than the Alps at the south-eastern fringes of the continent.

At five o'clock, the gloomy, grey but dry skies above making it seem more like dusk (which would fall an hour or so later here), we arrived at the ski resort of La Salle-les-Alpes, and in the small district of Villeneuve surprisingly easily found our hotel, Le Petit Lapin or 'Little Rabbit'. It was, like so many here, a chalet-style four-storey building, the twee wooden-sculptured balconies more akin to Switzerland, and our host, English Rob and his pretty girlfriend Eileen, were waiting for us.

The only hotel open in Villeneuve, we were the only guests and had the whole place to ourselves and the fourteen kids were billeted in gender and friendship groups, as organised last night in Dijon. I was in a double en-suite room at the end of the boys' corridor on the second floor, directly below Anna and Mrs C's shared and identical bedroom, except they had twin beds, I suspected. If not, that would have been particularly funny and cruel.

The luxurious perk of our six day, 144 hours on duty fieldtrip was a plush, free hotel room and full board. The kids' parents had kindly paid for our stay here and we were very grateful for it. Once the rooms had been allocated I got the three lads atop the bus and, along with them, untied the soggy luggage and passed it down to the tired and waiting crew. We'd told them to pack their clothes and sundries in bin liners inside their bags and holdalls in case of rain but three of the lads had forgotten to and were presented with sodden clothing.

They had until five thirty p.m. to unpack and freshen up when we would meet in the bar-cum-dining room to get straight down to some geography. They were sent off in groups of threes and fours to complete an 'urban cognition' of Villeneuve and La Salle-les-Alpes, a forty-five minute task using the last of the light that slid into the valley to briefly map the land use, note the services and age and style of the buildings. It was an excuse to get them out and about after two days of driving and to make them realise that we meant business here: fun was sure to be had, but this was a working trip, and work they would.

Mrs C took the opportunity to have a nap, and Anna and I strolled the streets of the out-of-season ski resort, checking up on the kids and making our own notes about the place to help back-up their research. An old man of the mountains, a weather-beaten face and stereotypical beret atop his full head of wispy-white hair, stopped us outside the closed charcuterie. He spoke good English and, on hearing of our activities, proceeded with a potted history of this quaint place.

Away from Villeneuve and its télécabine lifts and new ski-service buildings and on up the slight rise on the opposite side of the town and valley, lay the old town of La Salle-les-Alpes and our gentleman friend, Sylvain, walked with us up to the church, pointing out renovated farm buildings and telling us a few stories as he did so. The holiday chalets here had spacious living rooms that led onto the narrow streets and cosy bedrooms upstairs with balconies. It wasn't so long ago, according to Sylvain, that these lower floors were barns holding the farm's cattle, goats and sheep in the depths of winter when it was too cold and snowy to use even the valley floor fields for grazing. The heat generated from the huddled beasts helped warm the living quarters above and, still remembering this himself, old, stale and rock-hard bread was hung on the rafters above the animals, using their body heat and steaming breath to soften it up for the morning. He bid us farewell at the old church and Anna and I walked slowly back to the hotel, passing the group of Jo, Lisa and Kimberley as we did so. They were studiously noting down the building style of a chalet, its occupancy and guessing its age, made slightly easier by the '1886' tacked to the beams of the overhanging balcony.

"Ooh…about a hundred and twenty years old, I reckon, girls."

"How do you know that, sir?" asked Jo, a little puzzled.

"The style, Jo, can't you tell?"

"No," she smiled, apologetically.

Kimberley raised her eyes to the sky, tutted and pushed Jo's writing arm as she noted down the age I'd just told her.

"Hey!"

"Look!" said Kimberley, taking her arm gently by the elbow and nodding towards the balcony.

"Oh!" She giggled.

Dinner was served at six forty-five p.m., affording us time to take a shower and change our clothes. The group would sit at a large pine table, the teachers at one end, plied with cheap French table wine inclusive of the charge (thanks kids), and the students spread out along it, jostling for social position and leaving poor David (one of two boys with the same name) at the far end ostracised as usual, though this was usually out of choice. I looked down the table, caught his eye and gave him the thumbs up. He smiled, briefly, back.

We were concerned for him, a slightly autistic lad who usually kept himself to himself, afraid to enter into long conversations, and most of the time playing on his Gameboy or phone. Out of the window the lights of the télécabine sparkled, halfway to the peak, from here, of Serre Chevalier, topping off at 2491 metres, just about 8000 feet. The candles that our generous English hosts placed on the table flickered from atop old wine bottles, the tears of candle wax that fell like stalactites evident of years of use, and I looked across at Anna, her brown eyes sparkling in the soft light. Her shoulder length, dark hair shone with a chestnut sheen and I so wanted to reach over and run my fingers through it. Instead, I just smiled, which she warmly returned.

Anna and Mrs C took the first study session after dinner, eight until ten o'clock, giving me the evening off as I'd done the majority of the driving, especially the hairy section across the Col du Lautaret. I lay on my bed and listened to music, got bored and went downstairs to the bar for a drink and to help the kids complete their colour-coded land use map and short essay on the changing function of La Salle. Anna was working hard, leaning in close across the boys' map, and pointing to something. They tried not to, but I saw them looking at her cleavage and ample breast and caught the eye of Josh. He smiled and I pointed accusingly at him as I sipped my beer. At ten o'clock, they packed away, half of them having finished the mini-essay, and we allowed them an alcoholic drink, courtesy of English Rob. The best way to stop the little buggers getting pissed was to offer them one or two small beers with us in the hotel: besides, nothing else was open. This way, they'd feel mature and not constricted and would be less likely to smuggle in contraband. Generally, the tactic worked well and it did so again tonight, the students sitting and chatting with us until eleven fifteen p.m. when we decided on bedtime.

Tomorrow would be a busy day. We were to drive all the way up La Clarée Valley from Briançon to the car park at the Refuge de Laval at 2030 metres. This picturesque valley ran almost parallel to ours but in terms of development was a hundred years behind. As such, it was a gem of a place and a quiet, undeveloped haven in this tourist-hungry region. The objective of the day was to map its land use, assess its tourist potential and make a decision as to whether it would be beneficial to build the long proposed, but long opposed, road improvement through the Col de l'Échelle, a tiny 'B' road that runs from the Clarée Valley through the small and hardly used pass at l'Échelle into Italy, and then soon joins the main road to Bardonecchia.

By eleven thirty p.m., all was quiet on the boys front and I settled down for a long awaited rest and, hopefully, interruption-free sleep. Just as I lay my head on the freshly laundered pillowcase, my phone buzzed. The incoming text read, 'Mrs c snoring. Am goin to kill her!'

Sleepily, and slowly, as was always the case with texting and me, I replied, 'All quiet on boys front. Am cosy in double bed.'

A short wait and a buzzed return. 'Git. Am mvin in wit u!'

'Plenty of room.' I slowly replied.

Buzz. 'If only...'

If only it weren't for Mike, it should have read. My reply was silence. Actually mentioning him would have been an admission of our infidelities – well, on the thought-front anyway. At this point it still felt like a game, nothing more, though of course I found her devilishly attractive.

Chapter 2

Render the landscape singularly beautiful

I took great pleasure in waking the boys at half seven, wrapping loudly on the thick wooden doors and shouting, "Wakey, wakey, rise and shine!" The room with Josh, Tom and Scott, the only threesome, took the longest to stir, unsurprisingly, and I loitered outside as they slowly did so, trying to detect traces of smoke or alcohol or both in the musky teenage-boy smell that emanated through the draughty gaps of the old door. I couldn't detect a thing, so gave them the 'five minutes 'til breakfast' warning. A muffled grunt was the reply.

After all the ranting and raving at the boys not to be late for our first eight o'clock breakfast, it was Anna who was down last, smelling of freshly washed and blow-dried hair as she squeezed past me into the empty place setting. Coconut shampoo, I guessed. She smelt like a sweet Bounty bar.

"Sorry everyone," she said, seemingly unembarrassed at her tardiness, obviously used to being the last to emerge, as is the wont of so many well-groomed and beautiful young things.

She was five years my junior and dressed as such in the cool, London twenty-something urban style that I'd missed, courtesy of age and small-town provincialism. God, she looked good in those tight-fitting combat-cum-walking trousers and indecipherable scrawled writing on a well-known, name-branded tee shirt, the likes of whom I'd never seen or heard of before. I pushed my chair further under the long table to hide my Millets summer-sale, cheap trousers and passed her the last of the French bread, not steamed soft with cattle breath these days.

"Ta," she said, smiling sweetly and looking at me from the corner of her eyes, to the left and slightly and coyly up, using those puppy-dog eyes and long lashes to make my heart skip a beat. I hated Mike. He didn't deserve her, or so I supposed. She smelt so good that I could have stayed there all day breathing her in and staring at those come-to-bed eyes. Mindful of the kids,

Mrs C and especially Josh's testament to our future dalliance, I took my eyes from Anna and engaged Mrs C in a conversation about today's activities.

By eight forty-five a.m., we had gathered back down in the cleared-up dining room and had begun our briefing for the day. At nine thirty-five, kitted out with worksheets, day-bags, packed-lunches, clipboards and cameras, we were on the road again. Mrs C was to drive the upward leg of the valley 'long profile', and I the return. We were soon skirting the lofted town of Briançon, the Cite Vauban (old town) and imposing Fort du Chateau proudly and menacingly protecting the entrance to the three valleys that met here, all having been carved by glaciers and now the home to the three rivers of Guisane, Durance and Clarée, thus giving the town its historical, political and commercial prominence. Tourist signposts told us that it was, allegedly, the highest town in Europe and that it boasted three-hundred-sunshine-days a year. Today, thankfully, was no exception, the beautiful golden autumn sunshine guiding our way eastwards, briefly following the Durance, a tributary of the mighty River Rhône.

The kids, sixteen and seventeen-year-olds, all screamed with delight as we passed the newly opened McDonald's restaurant and I promised them that we would not, at any cost, be making a visit. They moaned a little and I told them how sad they were to be so excited by such a commercial and ubiquitous behemoth, or words to that effect. They moaned again, and I realised that I was rapidly becoming their parent, and with it, my dad – every man's worst fear as he travels inexorably onwards through his thirties.

At the BP garage, just before the turn-off from the N94, the main road here that runs east into Italy, we stopped and the kids took a traffic count for five minutes so that we could compare the flow from Italy on the main route with that in the as yet undeveloped Clarée Valley, to get an idea of how much busier it might become if the long proposed road improvement to Italy and Bardonecchia was to go ahead. The N94 would soon rise into the Col de Montgenèvre, another Tour de France favourite, and would pass through the border town of Montgenèvre itself before entering Italy, but we turned off onto the D994 at La Vachette (Little Cow) to access one of the prettiest and most undeveloped valleys in the whole of the Alpine region.

The morning passed quickly doing the sampling activities through Le Rossier and the elongated linear Val-des-Prés with its beautifully pine-scented timber yard and 'fer', an ancient adobe-bricked communal oven, which, up until the 1970s, had seen villagers take it in turns to bake for the whole commune, two solid days per month inside the small outhouse – a job more comfortable in the bitter winter months I was sure. After pretty Val-des-Prés, the road straightened, heading directly north towards the Col de l'Échelle and Italy; though geography dictates Italy virtually surrounds us in all directions here, we were in the remotest corner of the French Republic. The D994 passed through thick larch forest (on the turn now, this unique deciduous pine yellows in a multitudinous marvel before the brown death of winter), the Clarée River dipping in and out of view, now to our left after having cut underneath us just outside of Val-des-Pres. Signposts along the road forbade campfires and warned of wild animals, most notably deer and goats. The sign resembled that of a springbok, and Lewis piped up from the back.

"What does that sign mean, sir?

"It says to watch out for springbok."

"Oh."

"You div, Lewy, springbok are African!" ribbed Josh.

"True," I continued, "but there is a wild population here."

"Really?" Josh said, not sure if I was pulling his leg or not.

"True," Anna said, supporting me.

"A landowner around here called Monsieur De Klerk lived in South Africa for many years and on his retirement brought back five springbok so he could see them in his garden to remind him of the great Highveld. Well, they escaped within three days of getting here and bred in the wild really quickly; the terrain and climate are quite similar to that of the Highveld. This was well over… oh, fifty years ago. Some estimates put the population at over four-hundred-and-fifty in this valley alone!"

"Will we see any?" asked Jo excitedly.

"Keep your eyes peeled. They're timid little things, but it's not unknown."

"They saw four last year," added Anna, grinning at me out of the sight of the kids.

I looked in the rear-view mirror and could see them all scouring the roadside bush, some with their cameras at the ready. A funny thing about teaching is that the kids often have such faith in your knowledge that they really will believe anything you tell them, within reason – even Mrs C cracked a smile.

We lunched near Plampinet, parking up on a bend in the road, just enough gravel to fashion a lay-by, and a skip and a jump led to a small river beach, boulder-strewn on top of a thin, light brown layer of sandy silt. The boys took up residence on the rocks touching the water's edge and the girls nearer us, a split of the sexes that was common during the day, the Montague and Capulet-like feud softening in the evening when the lovers emerged to forge treaties for the night: daytime would find the regiments reformed along gender lines.

The river was lively here, sparkling in the watery autumn sunshine and bubbling up, over and around giant boulders freshly fallen from the steep west-facing valley walls. We all tucked into large and relatively healthy French-stick sandwiches and enjoyed the sun on the back of our necks.

"Why are the rocks so large here, miss?" asked Jo. The question was directed at Leslie. Jo couldn't bring herself to address her in the first person. Leslie was busy chewing, so looked across to Anna to answer on her behalf.

"Why d'you think, Jo?"

"Umm... not sure. Tougher rock?"

"Nope."

"Umm... I dunno, miss," she said and laughed self-deprecatingly.

"Well, I'll give you a clue. It's to do with erosion and this slope," said Anna pointing way up above.

"Oh, I know, I know," said Jo, a look on her face that indicated a light being switched on deep inside her head somewhere. "The rocks have just fallen off the mountain!"

"Yep. Well done... and...?"

"And... umm... due to that freezer thing...Oh yeah, freeze-fraw," she giggled. "I mean theeze-fraw," giggled again and others started to laugh too. "No, no, stop it... Theeze-Fraw!" she said exactly, with a proud look on her face, not realising that she was still jumbled.

By now all the girls were laughing and Jo didn't know quite what to do.

"FREEZE-THAW!" she shouted triumphantly and the boys stopped their pebble chucking and watched Jo punch the air, slap her thighs, and Kimberley, in celebration.

"Ow!"

"And..." continued Jo, pushing away Kimberley's half-hearted retaliation attempt, "they haven't been in the river long enough to be eroded!"

"Very good!"

Further upstream, the boys had begun an adventure, skipping across the accessible boulders in a brave attempt to fully ford the river. We should have admonished them for breaking at least fifty-six health and safety rules, but the river, although lively, was not deep enough to cause any damage, other than that to pride, as I was convinced one would soon take a tumble and fall in.

We watched them having fun, a rare commodity in today's risk-assessment-obsessed world, but had to step in when boulders were picked up and hurled towards each other's feet, the intention not to maim but to cause tsunami-like splashes. Once reined in, they sat near the girls and ate their lunch in seconds, hurling orange peel and banana skins at each other instead of stones. Anna shouted at them to pick it all up, which they did despite their protestations.

"But, miss, it's biodegradable."

"It's still litter!"

"But…"

"But nothing. Oranges do not grow here and nor do bananas, so it is not natural litter is it?"

"Yeah, but…"

She had to say nothing further. She gave the stare; the stare that engendered fear in the hearts of the hardest students (and teachers) and would do so for the foreseeable future at our school. Anna was a petite lady with a satanic stare that could control the unruliest of kids across a whole-school assembly. I found the look quite a turn-on.

Back on the bus for only a couple of minutes before we decamped at Plampinet, the village at the turn of the valley, the river and road that ran along its bottom heading due-west hereafter. This beautiful place had an ancient church dating back to the twelfth century and we walked our lunch down along its medieval streets. A group picture, a photo that still hangs on my office wall today, was taken on the church steps and we walked back through the eerily empty streets, across the rickety old bridge to the bus. Up ahead, the D994 turned west and the D1 forked off to the right to soon head up and up and up to the Col de l'Échelle and into Italy. If a bigger road was to be bulldozed through it would be here, and the peace and quiet of perfect Plampinet would be lost to history, old photographs and recollections of it soon to fade and die respectively with time.

We motored on into the low-angled sun through the hamlet of Le Cros and parked up in Ville Basse. Leslie drove on, leaving us to stroll through the timber yards and partly renovated farm houses, the comforting domestic and busying sounds of drilling evidence that this was the off-season; time to take stock and make any alterations before the skiing season and the long, cold winter. The fire station here would be busy with the larch forests during the summer but was enjoying the slumber of autumn along with the village, and in the car park just outside, we caught up with Leslie.

From here, the D994 would start to climb and would not stop until we reached the Refuge de Laval at 2081 metres. So far the valley had been enchanting, transporting us back to 1896 and sometimes earlier it felt, but from now on the scenery would rival that of any in Western Europe. This was not the awe-inspiring glacial valleys of Les Écrins, but the unique, untouched and unspoilt iridescent larch-filled upper valley of La Clarée, a tentatively protected refuge for the Alpine 'ancienne' where the crisp and clear upper Clarée River tumbled over fairy-tale waterfalls, babbled between roches moutonnées scraped and polished clean by more recently receding glaciers, the relicts of which we would see on tomorrow's trip.

Up over la Basse Sausse, a short, sharp climb to a lip of rock, bolder and stronger than any other, so leaving it battle scarred but defiant at the head of the upper valley, and here we stopped to sketch the section below us. It was a grand view and the upper valley beyond took on an olde-worlde charm with scattered chalets once refuges for farmers and livestock caught out in the unpredictable late spring and occasional summer snowstorms, now holiday homes and an escape of dream-like quality where Anna and I would think of running away to and living a winter-long secluded life of love-making.

At Chalets de Lacha, a small collection of tumbledown farm buildings, still-working barns and a renovated holiday home, an elderly shepherd watched over a woolly flock, his ancient frame bent almost double over his hook, resembling Old Father Time himself it seemed, and we completed a field sketch as his dogs nipped at the heels of the sheep, moving them down to the river for a drink. We were mesmerised by this rural idyll, the valley's enchantment working its spell on Anna and I as we sat on a rock and looked at each other for a long time without feeling remotely uncomfortable. At the end of it we smiled and embraced the view and the sun on our faces. Even the most hostile and belligerent of the students was touched by this place.

A little further on a path led off from the gravel lay-by to the water's edge and to the right, and just out of sight, you could hear the thunderous roar of the Cascade de Fontcouverte. A tiny path, most likely created by rambling sheep, followed the river up and around the falls and afforded spectacular views from above. I slipped away, irresponsibly (or like a 'prat', as Anna so kindly put it later), to clamber up the side of the thirty-foot cascade whilst Leslie gave a brief seminar on waterfall geography. I was sure none of the kids had seen me but I just couldn't resist the childlike lure of the scramble up the slippery rocks to the sound of the crashing falls to my left.

Within a minute, I had topped the cascade and stood amongst the falling beech leaves, a confetti of pastel shades that caused the sunlight to flicker like a glitter ball at an eighties disco. I could see Leslie and the kids standing near the water's edge now and waved as they looked my way. Jo and Kimberley spotted me first and waved their arms vigorously, and the three lads rushed off to the path to follow my example. I'm not sure if I heard Leslie shout but I felt it through the rumble of the constant falls, knowing that her ire was as much for me and my irresponsible role-modelling as it was for their impetuous disregard for the basics of health and safety rules. Later on that day I would feel the rapier side of her tongue, quite rightly so – I was a team leader and should lead by good example.

I sheepishly strolled through the small riverside beech glade and across a huge slab of rock to await the group. This was the textbook perfect 'roche moutonnée' where I would try and get the students to join in a group hug, a close hand experience to be at one with nature and appreciate the power of the ice through the rock's polished surface and occasional deep scarring and scratching called 'striations'. These claw marks were made by small rocks stuck to the underside of the glacier that scraped along the outstanding tougher rocks that would become the roches moutonnées.

In preparation, I lay face down on the boulder and stretched out my arms, spreading my fingers wide to feel as much of nature's work as possible. The rock was not cold, still clinging on tenaciously to the last of the autumn heat graciously donated by the watery sun. There was a primeval draw to this slab of bedrock granite and I just lay there, clearing my mind to a state of Zen, where time and events ceased: just me and geology, all alone. I felt something touch the little finger on my left hand and, oddly, didn't react by jerking it away. A second later, a warm and slightly clammy hand lay intertwined with mine. It was a small hand and although unfamiliar, fitted perfectly and felt like an old glove.

In the pit of my stomach, where nerves would play havoc with my powers of control and concentration, there fluttered a new energy, uncomfortable in its novelty but thrilling in its intensity, and the more this hand enveloped mine, the greater this intensity became. I knew it was Anna. I knew, however briefly, that we were alone, and I knew that this was a connection between me and her and my rock that was as powerful as the force of nature that had created this landscape, and I knew that she would be in my thoughts from now until the very end: whether together or not, this girl would pass through my mind every day until the day I died.

I spoke softly.

"La vallée de la Clarée a conserve de nombreaux heritages de la dernière glaciation, notamment des roches moutonnées," and I lifted her hand and we patted the rock together.

"Where d'you get that from?"

"Étienne Cossart."

"I don't know who the hell Étienne Cossart is, but it sounds bloody sexy." She squeezed my hand gently.

"He's an academic."

"Oh. And what does it mean?" she asked.

"It means… I… oh, not a lot. Just something about this rock."

"Sh…" she whispered.

We held hands and kept our eyes closed and I smiled. I'm guessing she did too until we heard the first scrambling of kids just below, near enough to be heard through and over the thunderous roar of the falls and our hearts. Had I just felt love? When the three boys appeared over the top of the rock, they found me lying prone and stroking the surface in an over-the-top, theatrical manner. The smile was genuine.

"Hug the rocks, boys. Feel the force of nature."

"You're a freak, sir. No offence."

"None taken, Josh, but just lie down and feel the polished rock; feel how smooth it is."

I looked up and his quizzical countenance said it all – 'freak'.

The girls arrived and Jo squealed at the thought of hugging a rock, so she lay down and copied me, and now Anna did too. Jo's infectious giggles, as she drew imaginary angel wings on the roche moutonnée, encouraged the others to join in until the whole group, including a still-vexed Leslie, lay face down on this beautiful boulder and stroked the polished surface, searching out the thin scars of striations to trace them up and down. We lay on the rock as a group for a while, eventually the giggling and laughter and then chuckling grinding to a halt, and enjoyed this tryst with nature in silence. Somewhere beneath the veneer of our twenty-first century synthetic lifestyles was a desire to return to a primeval, natural existence and we all understood it – we all got it. It was a magical moment.

The path back to the bus was boggy from here and we treaded carefully, me leading, and the occasional hoot or moaning screech told of misplaced footing and a sodden trainer or two. I took over the driving for the last stint up to the car park at the refuge and apologised to Leslie for my irresponsible actions.

"No harm done, I suppose. We'll talk later!"

The road narrowed and we criss-crossed the shallow and sparkling Clarée River on wooden plank bridges, the rhythmic rumble playing out a dull-thudded xylophone beneath us. We were soon parked at the top and walked down to the river and the footbridge of Pont de Moutet, where we stood facing the sun and looked into the cool, clear waters. The stones here were surprisingly rounded and a few of the boys jumped down onto the river beach to pick up a handful of them and started to skim them across the shallow pools that clung to the bends of the subtle meanders. The small river cliffs stopped the better skims in their tracks and an average of two or three skips was hit.

"These are good stones," I told Anna.

"Hey?"

"For skimming. They're really good: quite rounded, palm-sized and a good weight. Almost the perfect skimmer."

"Oh… great!" she said in a deliberately exaggerated and sarcastic tone. I playfully pushed her, glad for an excuse for a bit of contact. Our eyes met and my heart skipped like a record-breaking stone on a never-ending, placid lake.

I joined the boys, looking up at Anna's golden, sun-drenched face and tried to think of anything to stop the stirrings in my groin grow into something noticeable and potentially embarrassing.

"Oh yes, nice one, Dave!"

Dave, mark II, was the perfect opposite of his namesake and roommate. A confident (perhaps too much at times) and handsome boy, he had skimmed his stone to the base of the shallow river-cliff and skipped it up and over and onto the grass bank that was sporadically dotted with thinning patches of ice, the remnants of yesterday's snow showers, no doubt. The next few minutes saw an intense game of skimming, the boys trying in vain to emulate Dave's neat trick. The distraction of the competition had rescued me from arousal and, a little reluctant to show off my skills on the skimming front to a group of hard-to-impress young lads, I nevertheless could not help but grab a stone from the shallows of the sparkling river beach and let it fly across the pool, two skips and a sudden jump to land gently in the middle of an icy patch next to Dave's resting stone.

"Cool, Jonesy!"

"Fluke!" shouted Dave.

I picked up another stone and let it take to the air, repeating the same feat with it landing just beyond the first, clapped my hands together as though brushing dust and dirt from them and said, "That should do it," and walked back to the bridge.

"Cool," said Tom again.

Anna tutted, but I'm sure I garnered a hint of her being impressed in that smile.

*(Location No.2, Pont de Moutet, Clarée Valley, France)

We'd all worked hard these last few hours, so I took an expeditionary group across the bridge and iced-to-firm marshland to join with an alpine hiking trail that led up the hill in large zigzags, eventually topping out at the 'cirque' of Lac des Beraudes. These 'cirques', or relict lakes, are the leftovers of nascent glaciers, their bases scarred deep into tough rock, the melting ice leaving dark, deep mysterious lakes called 'corries' in Scotland and 'cwms' in Wales. I took the four lads and Jo and Kimberley to the second 'zag' or 'zig', and we enjoyed the view back down to the river and patches of snow in shaded hollows that the others couldn't have been able to see from their height, and made a mental note of their location, planning an ambush on the way back to the bus.

We scouted back along the river, mindful to stay out of view and took position behind a roche moutonnée, the snow still fresh in the shadows of the jagged lee slope and, with Apache-like screams, came at the group from the top armed with freshly-packed balls and pelted them into a retreat. A mini-battle ensued and even Leslie joined in, and at times prisoners would be taken, a stumble allowing them to be tortured in the slushy patches, and the giggles rang around the empty upper valley and on up to dominant Mount Thabor and the Pont des Cerces at 3097 metres (9900 feet).

The dip of the sun below the mountains hurried us back to the bus, and I crossed the Pont du Moutet at the rear of the group and in the cool, clear waters saw a beautiful stone sparkling in the last of the sun as the shade crept across the Clarée. I jumped down to the water's edge and picked up the palm-sized stone and pocketed it, a small memento from the day I fell for pretty little Anna Taylor.

The kids were at the bus before me and I thought about pretending that I'd lost the keys, but didn't have the energy to keep up the pretence long enough to wind them up. So I took to the driver's seat, Anna close to my left, our arms brushing as I changed gear down the long and beautiful valley of the Clarée which chased us out, its long and creeping shadows nudging us towards the N94 and home.

The kids were set free for an hour to relax before we started to collate all of the day's information in the short session pre-dinner. Leslie sat in the dining room and marked some essays from the previous night (we took a third each), and I went upstairs for a quick shower and a daydream of Anna and me stuck in a snowbound chalet in the upper reaches of La Clarée Valley.

The hour soon passed and I jogged upstairs to call on Anna and drag her back to the reality of three more hours' work before the day was done. The door to her room was ajar and I stood just outside and peeked in. The nearer bed was empty and on the far side on the other one by the en-suite lay Anna, face down and unchanged as though she had just collapsed on the spot and hadn't moved for fully sixty minutes. The curve of her bottom seemed to fit her expensive trousers perfectly and the butterflies in my stomach were urging me on into the room to run my hand over those smooth curves and in between the legs, to run up to the belt and down under the fabric to the warm, delicate skin that would lie beneath imagined brightly-coloured cotton briefs, and at that point Anna would stir and help me by unbuttoning the trousers and loosening them to allow my hand more room to explore. My reverie had me adjust my midriff to allow for the movement that was now occurring there. I coughed quietly and rapped on the door.

"Excuse me, Anna? Wake up, lazy bones."

"Hey," she said, "what… what time is it?" She raised her head off the bed and looked sleepily at me and laughed. Pushing the fringe off her eyes she continued, "I bet I look a right state." I said nothing. I was dumbfounded and still living my reverie. "How long have you been standing there?"

"Not long. It's time to get back to work, I'm afraid."

"Poo! I was just dreaming of those chalets at the top of the valley. It was beautiful… so beautiful, wasn't it?"

"Sure was." 'And so are you!' I shouted silently.

"I'll be down in five, okay?"

"Okay."

I turned to go.

"Steve?"

"Yeah?" I spun around, seeing her standing by the open door to the bathroom, hoping it would be an invite into my dreamy world.

"We should talk, shouldn't we?"

"Yeah, I guess." I coyly looked at my shoes; I didn't know where else to look. I didn't want to have this conversation and I couldn't stop thinking of her lying on that bed, and that fantastic arse.

"Soon," she said, grabbing hold of the doorframe and swinging into the bathroom with the confidence of youth, the confidence of a beautiful young lady who had the pick of two men.

We worked hard all night, stopping for an hour for a fine dinner of local beef and cheap table wine, and the kids didn't pack away until half ten. This meant a shorter time in the bar with us, most choosing to go straight to their rooms for a chat and a flirt, and I noticed Dave II and Jo, the most unlikely combination, sneak off first.

Anna and I managed to ignore the subject of contact on the rock and chatted trivially of colleagues and our favourite TV programmes as kids. Leslie joined us and when Anna took a break to powder her nose, let me have it about the waterfall incident. I hated her for it, all the more so because she was right. When Anna returned, Leslie patted me on the knee, gave me that knowing look and retired to bed.

"What's that about?" asked Anna, a worried puzzlement on her sweet face.

"Us, I think."

"Hey?"

"She's not stupid."

"Oh."

And that was it. The promised talk had evaporated into the realisation of big, bad Mike, who she had most likely called from the safety of the loos.

I felt the first excessively self-obsessed sulk coming on and told Anna that I was fine with the duty alone tonight. If the girls played up, I would wake her so that she could access their rooms; it was unlikely, they were a timid bunch. I strolled their corridor first, pausing briefly outside Anna and Leslie's room to consider deciphering their muffled idle chatter, but shamed myself into a retreat and a slow prison guard amble past the girls' room, silent at eleven forty-five p.m. and down the stairs to the boys whom I expected to still be up and chatting. All was suspiciously quiet, so I retired to my room deliberately loudly to fool them. Sure enough, as soon as I had shut my door, the giggling and banging began, the louder-than-expected thuds accompanied by a chorus of shushing. It didn't take long to discern the higher pitched giggle belonging to a girl, so I sneaked out to investigate.

Scott, Neil and Josh's room seemed still and I thought I heard honest snoring, so I moved on to Dave and Dave's next door. The incongruous couple actually boarded well, and it was here that I heard the subtle higher pitched tone of a girl. I listened closer and thought I heard Jo whisper. Jo? In Dave's room? In Dave's room? Odd on both counts. I listened again and was convinced that it was her laugh. I rapped softly on the door. They carried on talking, a little louder it seemed. I knocked again, with more force this time. They continued to talk and laugh, so I just walked on in.

Dave, the quiet one, was asleep in the corner oblivious to his houseguest. And there on the other bed lay Jo, naked on her top half save her snow-white lacy bra, and Dave II sitting astride her, a bottle of moisturiser in his left hand, in the middle of the process of rubbing white cream across her tight, athletic tummy. They looked up, Jo surprised and with the beginnings of a look of mortification. Dave grinned at first then forced himself to look solemn and contrite. I said nothing, just stared them down and flicked my left thumb towards the open door. Within seconds Jo had wiped herself down with the tee shirt she had rushed on and was standing beside me at the door.

"Morning!" I quietly, but sternly, told Dave, adding an affected index finger point. He nodded with a look of resignation that went some way to redeeming the grin, but not quite enough. I'd always remember that smirk and the context with which he so powerfully used it.

"Oh my God, sir, oh my God! It's not what you think; it's not. We were just… we were just… oh, God, I know it looks awful, but I… I don't really like him that much anyway…"

"Jo, it didn't look good."

"Oh God, I'm sorry. You won't tell my mum? You won't will you? Oh God!"

"Calm down, Jo. Let's just get you to bed and we'll talk about it in the morning."

As we walked up the stairs, tears began to roll down her pale cheeks. Poor kid. It wasn't a crime to be young and have a bit of fun and do what your hormones dictated, but I was in loco-parentis and I guess as a dad I wouldn't have been happy with what I had just witnessed.

I saw her to the door and said softly, "Just go to bed and don't worry too much. It was wrong and you know that but I won't be sending you home and, if you keep your nose clean for the rest of the trip, I won't have to tell your mum either. Okay?"

She sniffed. "Okay."

"Good. Night."

"Night."

It's true. We do have favourites, and this, not-so little innocent, was one of mine.

Anna was probably aslumber by now in the room next door, no more than fifteen feet from me as Jo quietly slipped into a room heavy with sleep. I thought of Anna in that bed and the uncontrollable wild reveries of the dream world where I hoped to be making an appearance. The reality was most likely that she was wide awake, listening to Leslie's rhythmic snoring and texting Mike under the covers, making sure the digital light didn't wake the sleeping leviathan and incur its wrath.

I liked this time of the day. To be the last to bed in a group of people that you had charge over brought out a primeval pride or propriety that I shared with the leader of the small wolf-pack that now roamed the nearby mountains, reportedly crossing from Italy last year. I descended the stairs again and walked slowly past the boys' rooms, hearing nothing now, and got my head on the pillow by one a.m. I thought of Anna and played myself to sleep.

Breakfast was a quiet affair, the hard work, long journeys and lack of sleep for some beginning to take its toll. I was a bit pissed off at Anna's cooling, and she was the last to join us again, though run close by Jo who tried hard to look calm and collected but couldn't dampen the blushes that warmed the room on this cold, fresh morning. I watched her interact with the others and looked to Dave too. Would he have boasted about it? Although my opinion of him was diminishing, I doubted he would have, though Jo acted as though they all knew and she was guilty as charged. It seemed as though she was fighting valiantly to hold back the tears. I tried to catch her eye and offer a comforting smile but she kept her head down now and was being cuddled by a kind and concerned Kimberley: bless 'em. I doubted any of the boys noted anything amiss – girls are into that kind of thing. The rest of breakfast passed without incident, and the quietness of Jo was matched by that of an equally contrite Anna. Mike was clearly on her mind today.

The group was to visit the Les Écrins National Park, home to towering mountains and magnificent glaciers that still scoured the valleys in these global warming days. The natural theatre of the once-duelling glaciers of Noir and Blanc was our classroom, but our guide, Tomas, told of days gone by when they met, clashing like titans of the ice-world and creating thick rubble lines of medial moraine. Moraines are rock debris fallen from the valley sides and transported atop the relentless glaciers. They are called 'lateral' moraines when found along the edges, but if two of the giants met mid-flow, these moraines would join to flow in the middle and then became known as 'medial' moraines.

Today, however, the higher glacier Blanc has retreated by over a kilometre since the days of Tomas's youth and resides over the lip of a hanging valley and its ice-blue melting (or ablating) front is now fifty metres further back than last year already. To get this high required a hike that I completed with most of the boys, half of the girls and Tomas. By the freezing breeze gushing forth from the cave at the lip of the ice-blue glacier, we sat atop a perfectly smoothed roche moutonnée and ran our fingers across this season's freshly scoured striations.

Anna had remained at a lower level with some of the girls and Leslie was back at the car park where she nursed her sore knee and marked the kids' essays. She was disappointed that it had flared up again but had ascended to these glaciers on a number of occasions before so wasn't devastated by missing out this time. So, the teachers were a disparate bunch today and Anna and I had little time to flirt or even consider our fledgling love affair, if indeed that was what it was to become.

The kids enjoyed every minute up there near the clouds, stroking the rocks, feeling the ancient freezing breeze at the mouth of the melting glacier, taking tentative steps atop the white block and just admiring the grand landscape.

"You know what, sir?" started little Tom, one of the few lads that I didn't have to look up to. "We always go to the beach for our holidays. I've never been to the mountains. But you know what, they're awesome, beautiful and I'm gonna tell Dad that we should go to the mountains next year."

"Good for you," I told him, gasping for breath as we clambered over a stubborn outcrop on our way down to meet the littered-to-grey Glacier Noir in the valley below. The crumbling mountainside had showered this glacier with moraine, so much so in fact, that it was hard to discern from the scree slopes above. Small chamois goats skipped across the shattered rocks and the creaks and groans of the ice monster told us of its presence down there, and the boys just stood and smiled, turning their heads into the wind to listen for the groans, the heartbeat of the nature that had sculpted this landscape.

At a major junction in the path, five of the boys and I left the others and diverted up the small track that ran up a textbook-perfect lateral moraine. Halfway up we stopped and took measurements of the small rocks and pebbles that not so long ago were hitching a ride on top of a much bigger and more powerful Glacier Noir. Our results told us of the direction of previous ice flows as the debris tends to align itself in that direction, taking the path of least resistance on top of the ice before it is dumped in a large triangular hill as the glacier recedes.

From here, we climbed a little further to the end of the path that led into the most wonderful of cauldrons where huge vertical mountainsides led up to the pyramidal peak of Mont Pelvoux topping off at 3946 metres (12949 feet). To our left, the beginnings of the glacier, pure-white this high, dripped over a hanging valley and down into this one. The sounds here were magnified a thousand times and the boys whooped and shouted until their lungs could do no more. Off in the distance a huge crack of thunder told of a chunk of ice peeling away from its mother glacier and falling into an abyss.

The walk back down the path turned out to be quite petrifying as the tiny path blended in with the huge valley that opened up before us, and it was hard to discern and quite disorientating. I was fairly nervous, having left Tomas behind at the junction – he had informed me that this path was perfectly safe – and cajoled the increasingly disconcerted lads. A couple took a little tumble, Tom grabbing hold of Vikram as he did so and nearly pulling them both off the edge. This lateral moraine was laid down at a dizzying sixty-five degree angle and the thirty-metre drop onto the littered glacier top might not kill, but would certainly maim. I was minded to tell the lads not to talk of this with their parents; maybe buying a round would do the trick.

Towards the joining path, and beginning to relax now that the worst of it was over, Dave came alongside me, skipping his hefty walking boots to walk in time with me. Talking quietly and leaning in close he spoke, "Sorry again, Mr Jones. About last night."

"Um, hmm."

"I am, really sorry. I know it was wrong. Stupid of me."

"Yep."

"Well, just to say that I really am sorry. I mean it."

"Okay, Dave. We talked about it this morning and you know the score. Let's just leave it at that."

"Good. Thanks. Good."

He slowed and joined Tom behind, and after a brief silence they both laughed. Being slightly paranoid, I thought it must have been at my expense and was reminded of that knowing grin atop Jo last night. I had a sudden urge to turn round and push the arrogant little sod down the remaining moraine, small enough here to give him a graze or two, but of course it only lingered briefly as a thought.

The two ladies took duty that night, allowing me an easier evening which saw me in bed and reading by ten thirty p.m., though the chances were that the lads next door were due a night of debauchery; they'd been worryingly well-behaved so far. It was rare to get a chance to relax and be a proper member of the human race on these trips, and I failed to make the most of it, falling asleep before finishing the end of the first page of my book.

I was wide-awake at two a.m., a not unusual occurrence for me, but had an overwhelming sense that something significant had aroused me from sleep. I lay there for a while before giving into somnolence again. And there it was.

"Fuck, Vikram, No!"

'Right!' I jumped out of bed, ready to blow up at these thoughtless bastards still pissing about at two in the morning. I burst out of the room and three doors down came to Tom and Vikram's room. Again I heard Tom shouting, "No, no, Vikram. Shit!"

I knocked on the door loudly, hurting my bony knuckles on the thick oak. Blimey, this wasn't a cheap hotel at all, I thought. "Boys? What the hell's going on?"

Fairly quickly, before I resorted to a more powerful rap, Vik appeared at the door. A tall but incredibly skinny lad, he poked his head round the thick oak door at me, his bloodshot eyes even more bloodshot than usual.

"What's going on?" I asked, clearly irritated.

"I don't know, sir."

"What do you mean, 'I don't know'?"

"It's Tom, sir."

"I know it is."

"He's shouting in his sleep."

I pushed the door open, forcing Vikram back, not believing a word of it, and saw Tom still curled up fast asleep in his bed, the covers thrown off and hanging over the side onto the floor.

"Stop pissin' about, Tom!"

I was angry and mild cursing seemed appropriate enough with sixteen and seventeen-year-olds on a field trip at two in the morning.

No reply.

Tom flinched and he gave those involuntary spasms that my old cat Benj used to give when fast asleep and chasing rabbits in a feline fantasy. Tom groaned a little and then grunted.

"Vik, careful!" he shouted.

"Blimey. Sorry, Vikram, I thought you were pratting about," I told him.

"No worries, sir. What should we do?"

"We shouldn't wake him. It can be quite upsetting if people are in a deep REM sleep." I almost convinced myself. Vik seemed impressed, though he looked confused at my reference to his dad's favourite band from the eighties.

I pulled the covers gently off the floor and put them over Tom. His breathing, which had been quite quick and erratic, seemed to slow to a steady rhythm and he began to stir from his sleep.

"Hey. What's happening?" he said, rubbing his eyes, temporarily blinded by the main bedroom light shining in his face.

"Nothing, Tom. You okay?"

"Yeah. Umm… yeah. Why?"

"Because you were swearing in your sleep like a trooper. You even woke me up."

"Oh… sorry… I… didn't mean to."

"That's okay. It's not your fault. Was it a nightmare?" I asked him.

"Yeah." He laughed and began to sit up. "Yeah. We were climbing up that moran thing…"

"Moraine," I corrected him.

"Whatever. Anyway, we were climbing up the thingy and Vik tumbled and… and I tried to grab him but I just caught a hold of his sleeve and it slipped from my grip…" Tom was talking excitedly now and told a keen tale, "and then he fell and fell; it seemed to go on for ever and I was just standing there shouting and screaming!"

"Blimey, Tom, that's pretty vivid."

"Yeah, it was quite scary. Sorry 'bout the swearing."

"That's okay. No harm done. Now, let's get some sleep, hey?"

"Okay," reassured Vik.

I turned to leave the room and stopped for one last comment.

"Lads, I would appreciate it if you didn't tell your parents about that walk. I know it was my fault, but that guide told me it was safe. I'll know another year. If they complain, we couldn't take any other groups. Does that sound fair?"

"Yeah, sure. I understand," said Vik.

"What goes on tour, stays on tour, sir," said Tom: a veteran of PE Department jaunts to the south of France for the infamous 'water sports' and Austrian Alps ski-trips which had left their mark, none more so than the rugby-style tour motto that he had just quoted to me.

"Hmm. Night, boys." I shut the door and went to bed.

Chapter 3

I just wanted to have fun with it

Breakfast was a bit later today as we weren't to go far on our river studies trip, just staying in Serre Chevalier and messing about in the Guisane River. Anna sat next to me again and seemed to be back on track with the flirting, sitting closer than one normally would – I didn't complain. At our end of the table, Tom started to regale us with his nightmare tale and insisted that I gave my version, being the slightly more dramatic, so I obliged and hammed it up, as teachers so often like to do. The lads laughed, the tired mood lifted, as did Jo's eyes from her lap for the first time in a day and received my welcoming smile. She thankfully returned it.

Anna sat close and briefly placed her hand on my knee out of view of the others. Although clearly thrilled and excited by this, I felt annoyance at her flippant emotional banter: want me or not want me, but don't play with my feelings; big bad Mike or not big bad Mike and please don't assume I'll always be in love with you. It was a sensible, rational, but ultimately futile take on my feelings for Anna. She could ostensibly do as she pleased, and any positive action on her part, however small, however rare, would be received rapturously herein. She'd got me. She knew it too. Bugger!

Today was our last full day in this stunning setting and tomorrow we would begin the journey home with an added bonus of a stop off in Paris, the idea of Mrs C and enthusiastically received by the kids and their parents as an exciting enrichment activity. Occasionally, the students were enriched – occasionally.

And today was the day for messing about on the river. One of the options the students had back in school was to write up one of the day's activities as a small piece of coursework and the rivers day provided the best opportunity for data collection. We were to compare three sites along the course of a river: one near the source, nothing more than a mountain stream; one a larger tributary, and finally, the main body of the middle course of the River Guisane in the valley of Serre Chevalier.

It was to be a fun day, an excuse to get wet, and a chance for me to encourage the kids to participate in the fine art of stone skimming. Our third chosen location, north of Monetier-Les-Bains, just outside the hamlet of Le Casset, was perfect for skimming. The middle course of the river begins to meander here as the valley starts to flatten and the power of erosion switches from vertical to lateral, causing the river to cut its way through the soft glacial till in beautiful 's' shaped bends called 'meanders'. The inside of the bends have perfectly rounded pebbles, deposited here on the slower side of the meander and make for rich pickings. The outsides of the bends leave deep channels, the faster flowing river here eroding small cliffs and leaving placid pools on which to skim – a perfect combination.

We set off up the D1091 towards Monetier, through it once again, the route we would be taking home tomorrow, and all the way towards the pass at the Col du Lauteret. The snow had gone but not the sheep, so I kept my eyes on the road and joked with Jo about my alleged butchery.

"I still think you killed one."

I laughed.

"No, I do, and it's not funny."

Anna poked me with her index finger and I could see her smiling at me. I thought about poking her, albeit a different version – she was in that coquettish mood where I'm sure she considered it too. So much better a way to conduct a relationship (no room for disappointment), we could both imagine it to be fantastic and all so less messy.

In a persistent drizzle we unpacked the bus, ungainly ranging poles carried by ungainly teenage boys, and took the equipment over the metal barriers and up to the Torrent du Bez, a small mountain stream and tributary of the Guisane River. Splitting the kids into groups of threes or fours, we spread out along a transect of the stream, raggedly 'v' shaped here where the steep slopes encouraged vigorous vertical erosion.

Each group had to collect, measure and record various sets of data on increasingly soggy scraps of paper, once finely printed and pristine river worksheets. First: river width, easy here at a couple of paces with a tape measure; then wetted perimeter (width under water where water is in direct contact with the river bottom and sides) measured with a small chain that I had fun with imagining kinky positions with Anna; then the river speed along a ten metre stretch using an orange which found it hard going, getting stuck behind sharp, angular boulders that had tumbled from the nascent valley side. We used this because it was in our packed lunch and would float two thirds under the surface and therefore would grab the greater flow of the channel. We weren't a private or grammar school so I could not afford the fancy (and pricey) flow meter with attached propeller which digitally measured the stream flow – at a disadvantage from day one, these poor comprehensive kids. Lastly, we measured the pebble size and roundness to hopefully prove that they got smaller and smoother the further downstream they were taken. We used the laminated sheets detailing 'Powers Roundness Index', one of which had helped trap the cockroach days previously in the grotty youth hostel in Dijon.

We quickly took our measurements, took photos of our data collection for the methodology section, and ran back to the bus as the rain came down harder still. Two minutes further downstream we joined a large tributary and in a burgeoning downpour repeated the activities and decamped to the bus. We had a misty picnic in the small car park once we were stationed outside the quietly beautiful hamlet of Le Casset, nestled alongside the River Guisane itself. The heat from our bodies mixed with the damp air to create a pleasant sauna in the back, and we chatted idly whilst eating our very large and comforting sarnies.

The small beech tree glade here housed a caravan and camping site that had clearly seen better days, two dilapidated vans spewing out their polystyrene innards to litter the green grass site. Our guess was that these temporary residents were flood victims of seasons past and were now left to rot. Shame: it ruined the near-perfect location.

Satiated and having almost dried the outer layers and taking advantage of the lull in the rain, we set up along the banks of the Guisane – four groups of students to measure this beautifully clear Alpine water course, the very last piece of work on this week-long study trip. The students were well-drilled and began without much encouragement. We knew the fun would start here, and hoped that their increased knowledge of river regimes would mean greater care being taken as they waded through the water to the outside of the meandering bend.

Aware of the sudden drop in the water depth, we chose the groups ourselves. Opposite the larger of the wrecked caravans lay a small levee made of loose pebbles and grassed-over mud, not a natural deposition from seasons of floods but a pathetic Canute-like attempt to keep the burgeoning flood waters off the site, and here we set up with two of the girls' groups. The river was straighter at this point and the depth was more even, getting to just above the knees on the opposite bank. In two places across the transect, little islands of pebble deposits had been dropped and the girls, barefooted and jeans rolled up to the knees like a picture postcard of Blackpool beach in the 1950s, set up camp with easy access to both banks. Their shrill screams gave notice of the water temperature.

"What do you reckon?" I asked Anna, looking towards the water and holding up the crude (and cheap) thermometer.

"Temperature?"

I nodded.

"Ooh, I dunno, maybe twelve degrees C."

Although not sounding too cold, twelve degrees for water temperature was freezing and would soon leave your toes, feet and ankles in a state of shock and numbness.

"Much colder I reckon."

I plunged the plastic thermometer into the weak flow on the edge by the man-made levee and waited thirty seconds. Mini-waves lapped onto and over my fingers and I knew that twelve degrees was a wild overestimate. I pulled it out and showed her without looking.

"Four degrees! Jesus!"

The nearby yelps and screams confirmed the measurement. It was bitterly cold and the girls giggled and jumped up and down on the cool pebbles to get the circulation going again in their blue toes. They'd only paddled out fifteen feet.

"Sir, you coming in?" asked Jo, in that quaint, innocent and pleading tone that she had so mastered, and until recently I believed was sincere. I still thought it was really, and put the Dave situation down as an aberration.

"Ooh, not sure. Maybe later."

"That's not fair," shouted Kimberley. I couldn't tell if she was laughing or crying; I think it was a combination of both.

"What about you?" I asked as an aside to Anna. "Are you gonna get your feet wet; take the plunge?" I looked at her closely and smiled softly, moving only the corners of my mouth up slightly. She chose not to answer, knowing that I meant more than just joining the students on the pebble islands. Silence was, again, a beautifully inventive weapon – leave both sides to choose its meaning, usually in the most optimistic of ways.

I'm not a strict teacher at all. I tried it but I just made myself look silly. I'm not a strict person, I'm just me, and this me tends to give in too easily to the pleading of innocent young students. I took off my boots and the warming comfort of my thick woollen socks and walked to the edge of the water, tottering like an infant to avoid the sharper stones, 'ooh'ed and 'aah'ed along to the river and into the water. At first, the contrast in the temperature was strangely refreshing but the brain soon received the dire warnings from the feet and the cold stabbed up my legs in a bruising sensation all the way to my crotch.

"Jesus Christ!"

The girls laughed and I ran, unable to feel the pain of knobbly pebbles ripping into my soft, white-collar-worker flesh, and reached the island to a chorus of laughter and a ripple of applause.

"I think Miss Taylor should come out here too. What do you think, girls?"

"Yeah, come on, miss," shouted two of them together, a stereophonic estuarine drawl that rolled off down the Guisane Valley and disappeared into the thinning beech forest. I smiled an evil grin.

"No, I'm not stupid! It's too bloody cold!"

I looked at the girls with an accompanied shrug of the shoulders that said it all – 'she's no fun, not like me' – another small victory in the war of popularity stakes in teaching. Defiantly, Anna sat down on the pebble levee and looked away across the fast flowing Guisane and through the forest on the far bank and on up the wooded slopes to the mist-bound peaks.

"Come on, girls, let's get this finished," I said and helped the group complete their data collection so that I could get back over to be near the girl I was falling for.

Fifty yards upstream the lads had finished as much as was seemingly possible and were skimming stones down towards us. Once again, Dave was the best of the bunch and his well-chosen pebbles skipped up onto the river island, coming to a halt no more than ten feet from our frozen huddle.

"Careful, boys," I shouted after them.

"Sorry, sir!" Dave replied, lifting his right hand up in recognition of his close call.

I kept looking at the lads and my suspicions began to grow. "You finished?" I shouted against the sharp breeze.

"Sort of," came the reply from the melee.

"What do you mean 'sort of'?"

"Well, the last bit of the meander seems a bit deep, sir."

"How deep?"

Two of them shrugged and Dave picked up another sleek pebble.

"How deep?" I repeated myself.

Tom took the metre rule, paddled a yard into the six-yard crossing and reaching out, drove the stick into the rushing water. It almost touched his hand before appearing to jolt to a stop. They all looked at him and then towards me. I shrugged. Dave let off another fabulous skim and turned back to Tom and the boys. He started to take off his top and was soon strolling around the group with a toned, bare torso. He picked up his waders, the ones he usually wore on a cold Saturday morning whilst carp fishing with his dad at the Sutton-at-Hone gravel pits, kicked off his boots and put them over his trousers. The girls were watching keenly, none more so than Jo, who was clearly admiring the sight of his half-naked body.

He picked up the tape rule and metre stick and stepped forcefully into the fast flowing meander. Within two paces the water was up to his groin, and then after another, to his waist. He seemed not to react to what must have been a piercingly cold experience. Brave sod, I thought. We all watched him reach the far bank in no time at all and proudly sit upon the crumbling turf. The girls whooped and applauded. Anna and I joined in, a little reluctantly, and the boys chucked stones towards him so that they splashed his so far dry and well-toned upper body.

"Stop it, you bastards!" he laughed.

He grabbed hold of one end of the tape measure and chucked the bulk of it across the braided meander to Tom, who caught it competently.

"Four point five six metres," Tom shouted, and Josh wrote it down on their limp and soggy recording sheet.

Dave then retraced his steps, measuring the depth the best he could every metre.

"It's too deep here," he told Tom, who passed another metre rule across to him, just about reaching if they both stretched.

"Ta, mate."

Rudimentarily putting the two sticks together, he measured the deepest section of the curve at 1.30 metres, about to the top of his waist. He was soon back on the pebble island and dressing. The girls gave a ripple of applause and Jo was the last to stop clapping. I caught her eye; she blushed, began to pick up the equipment and started across the freezing river back to the bank and Anna and Mrs C.

Within two minutes we were all sitting on the levee and Anna took in the sheets for safekeeping. The rain, which had thankfully eased during the majority of the data collection here, began heavily again and beat out pretty, rhythmic rings on the pools away from the faster current, which turned into subtle white water at the next meander twenty metres downstream.

On the far bank, behind a copse of balding larch, stood a wooden cabin which, although shabby, appeared to be occupied – the half drawn curtains and odd pots and pans left strewn around the plot gave it a lived-in look. On the bank there stood a small square concrete block, apparently hollow inside. It puzzled me, and as the boys began again to skim in that general direction across the best of the still water, it puzzled them too.

"Try and hit that thing," piped up Dave, knowing that he and I would most likely be the only ones capable of doing so.

"Okay," came a reply and a volley of stones skipped off across the Guisane adding concentric rings of chaos to the ordered pattern of raindrops on the water.

"Come on, sir," encouraged Dave with an affable smile that brought me quickly to my feet – I didn't need much encouragement. Blimey, he was a good lad today. Today I liked him a lot. I could begin to see what Jo might have seen in him after all. I picked a handful of decent, palm-sized stones and limbered up with a couple that multiple-skipped across the pool, fizzled out and sank short of the target, though they were in the right direction.

"Eight!" shouted Josh. "Pretty good!"

Dave was a few throws in front and was ranging in nicely on the concrete box. On my third stone, I'd cut down the angle of refraction and lowered my body as I released, lessening the amount of skips and increasing the distance between them. In four long skips it reached the far bank, embedding itself in the exposed topsoil five feet to the left of the box.

"Cool, Jonesy!"

"I thank you," I said and looked across at Anna. She raised her gorgeous eyes to the heavens – I hoped she'd realise I wasn't seriously chuffed with my skim (of course, I was) but only playing it up to the lads. The eyes came back down and she smiled. Great.

The other boys were good, dropping short with multiple skips that they shouted out the number of – "6,7,5,5!" ringing around the wooded valley. No one else reached the bank, though Dave, trying desperately hard to impress everyone, came mightily close. My fourth stone skipped awkwardly at first, slanting to the right, but correcting itself to bounce perfectly five times and come to an abrupt halt inside the concrete box.

"Yes!" shouted Tom (before I could) and a couple of manly slaps hit my back.

"Right on, sir!"

(Location No.3, River Guisane, Serre Chevalier, France)

Basking in my glory, I failed to notice the local farmer emerge from the woods, just a few feet from the bank, brandishing a shotgun, but he soon caught all of our attentions when he shouted loudly across the river at us.

"Hey?" asked Tom. "What did he say?"

"Dunno," I said shrugging.

"Is that a gun?" asked Jo, a hint of fear in that sweet voice.

"Yes I think so, Jo, but all farmers have them around here. Don't worry about it." I hadn't convinced her, the others or myself with that reassuring comment.

Still he ranted and we watched, especially me, eyeing the gun swaying at his hip in rhythm with the rant.

"I think we should start to leave," suggested Anna.

Just at this point he raised the gun and appeared to point it at me – I suppose the others thought it at them, but I believed he was upset at my all-too-accurate skimming.

"Pardon, m…" I started to say and was interrupted by Mrs C.

She had strolled out in front of me, placing her body between the aim of the gun and myself, and started to address the farmer in a calm, cool, confident manner and in what appeared to be perfect French. After 'Pardon, monsieur' I did get a little lost as she spoke too quickly for my schoolboy translation. She had lived in France as a student and frequent holidays here had helped her keep the language at a more than competent level, if not quite fluent.

We all stood or sat there, stunned to silence, as Mrs C placated the irate Frenchman with a gun and he slowly brought it down, gestured at the concrete box and grunted, giving a dismissive wave of the left hand and turned to go.

"Let's go quietly," she said calmly to the rest of us and we packed up the equipment and left in a hurried silence.

All we could hear was the gushing Guisane and the sharp breeze rustling through the few remaining yellow and brown leaves, taking a couple of stragglers with her as she did so. They littered our path as we retraced steps across the detritus of the not-long-since flooded caravan and camping ground. Still silent, we loaded the bus, took our seats and I started the engine. As we pulled out of the parking bay and started to make our way up the gentle valley slope to re-join the main road, the silence was broken.

"Mrs C, you're a legend!" Indeed she was.

It was hard to feel affection and admiration for a woman that I had tried to dislike for so long, but I endeavoured. The kids began an excited chatter behind us, the majority extolling the virtues of Mrs C and Dave boasting of his skimming prowess.

"Oh, shut up, Dave!" piped up David. It was the first thing he had said in two days, so the group graciously gave these four words uninterrupted airtime. Surprised to be listened to, he continued. "It was probably your bloody skimming that attracted the nutty farmer in the first place!"

Back at the hotel, we unloaded and gave the kids an hour's free time to shower and relax whilst we did the same and got the last lesson of the trip into some order. I was keen to get Anna alone and to test the waters. I felt she was warmer today and I fully intended to assay those tepid depths. Tomorrow we would be in Paris and home the day after and I might never have this opportunity again. Mrs C managed to get to me first, taking me to one side as I tried to follow Anna up to her room for a spontaneously planned chat.

"Thanks for that today: you were great," I pre-empted. She leaned in close, looking around so as to make sure there were no interlopers.

"I hadn't wanted to say anything about the skimming because I know you boys like that kind of thing."

'You boys', I repeated to myself – could she get any more patronising? "Well, yes, Leslie, I do, I really enjoy skimming stones and thankfully the lads do too. Good old boys together!"

Oh dear, I was riled and was defending weakly with a bitter attack of my own.

"Quite, Steven, but I knew it would… end in tears – well nearly."

"Not quite sure what you mean, Leslie? No one was crying were they? No one was hurt at any time, if I recall correctly."

We were moving closer to each other subconsciously, the matador and the goring bull. I wasn't quite sure which role I was fulfilling.

"But you were very nearly shot, and what's much more concerning is that you put the children in danger too!"

"I p… I what!" I laughed, well snorted actually, with disbelief.

She smiled, raised her hand as if to say, 'enough said', and made to go. My role had been defined, so I let her go. Silence was my riposte, the best action in these circumstances. She had done a brave thing, hadn't she, so maybe this silence was my subtle thank you?

I sat next to Anna at dinner and she rested her left hand on my right thigh under the rustic tablecloth, a red chequered affair that belonged more in a rural gîte or the café in *'Allo 'Allo*. It was possibly an innocent action, but my translation led us down the aisle, or at least into bed for a fumble. She lay it there for what seemed like minutes, but was possibly seconds, whilst I grappled with the thought of how to respond at the same time as pouring some wine, passing the bread, indeed orchestrating our very own last supper in this wonderful valley, as well as thinking away a potentially embarrassing erection. I smiled nervously at her. She patted my knee twice and offered her hand to collect the bread. Anna had my bones, my blood, my heart and my broken soul.

The lesson after dinner was intense, with University-style lectures from Mrs C baffling all and sundry and Anna salvaging as much data as was possible from the Guisane and weather-sodden sheets to use back in class, away from the eccentric geographical ramblings of Leslie. By eight thirty p.m. we were finished and the kids sent away to pack before the long drive north to gay Paris the next day. I'd promised them an hour in Briançon if the week had passed relatively event-free. As it had, I kept to my word, and so at nine o'clock those who wished to gathered outside by the minibus for the short ride along the Guisane Valley to Europe's highest and sunniest town (allegedly). All but three of the students and Mrs C were here, dressed in the only clothes left that passed for reasonable teenage eveningwear. We dropped them in the empty square at the foot of the road up to the citadel and the old town, synchronising watches for an hour hence.

"Don't do anything I wouldn't," was my strained, witty remark as they flew out of the bus and towards McDonald's, a pub, a café, both, all three maybe, and we parked up outside the only open café here, around the town centre car park.

"What shall we do?" I asked, feigning disinterest and fighting back the bursting desire to ask for a snog.

She looked at me, and sighed. "I dunno."

This ambivalence readily referred to the whole damn situation I supposed, and I concurred with a sage nod. I was getting a stiffy standing there.

"Come on, I'll buy you a drink."

"Ta."

We wandered around the base of the ramp to the citadel, passing on the ten-minute hike to the old town, and found a quaint 'chocolaterie' hidden down a side alley, neon light dripping down onto us, along with the remnants of the days rain from overhanging windowsills and awnings. I drank a Kronenburg and she, a hot chocolate, and we shared a pastry oozing with bad fats. The unspoken conversation was tense and we skipped in and out of bed and in and out of a relationship to a rhythm of indecision. I so desperately wanted to hold her and kiss her, but the weight of the leaden skies, hidden above us by ancient tenements of the old town, kept my hand pressed to the beer, watching the bubbles take a chance and race for the surface in their thousands.

"What next?" I said, trying hard to smile nonchalantly.

"I don't know, Steven. I don't know what to do."

She sighed again. I still thought this to be quite cute and endearing at this stage in our friendship.

"Well, whatever. I think you're great," I said.

She smiled. "Ta."

Thankfully, music came on to the obsolete stereo system and we tapped our drinking vessels in poor rhythm: good to keep busy. Gradually the mood lifted and conversation eased into us and we were laughing, recalling the idiocy of some of the kids and the rapaciousness of Mrs C. We strolled through the glistening streets of Briançon, the town painted orange in the puddles beneath our feet, and would occasionally pass a small group of our students.

"Hi, sir; hi, miss," came a greeting from two of the quieter girls huddled together in front of the window of a jewellers, paper bags with large swirling 'M's printed on them and the whiff of stale, greasy food escaping.

"Great cultural experience," I said, pointing to the McDonald's bag.

"Yeah I know, but it is different to ours. They sell beer, you know?"

Soon time was up and we were sitting in the bus, engine running and music playing, trying to scare the stragglers into the back. They were all quite punctual, the last group the obvious boys smelling strongly of cheap booze. An hour, I thought. Surely that wasn't enough to get too drunk? At first, there was animated chat about the bar they had found that served a yellow, noxious spirit (Pernod?) and which, thirty minutes later, they realised was probably a gay bar. The girls laughed at them and gradually, as we headed out past the McDonald's and onto the new road that claimed the title of 'peripherique' (unabashed in this grandiose claim), they all stopped talking. Tiredness, but most likely, the alcoholic breeze had drifted over them and they listened to my music.

"What's this, sir?"

"Sorry, kids, I knew you wouldn't like it. It's olde, quiet, reflective nonsense."

"No, no, I really like it!"

Jo, sitting directly behind me, was the only one who gave the impression of sobriety. It was possible she actually was – that, or a hell of an actress.

"Damien Rice," I informed her, "some Irish chappie: melancholy, woe is me, but I like it. Whenever I feel miserable, I put on this stuff and it never fails to cheer me up. You see, however bad I think my life might be, it ain't as bad as this guy's."

"My dad says that about The Smiths."

"Your dad?" This kind of thing was becoming more common these days. Kids were far too often referring to their parents when talking of cultural references all too familiar to me. It was official: I now belonged to their parents' generation.

"Yeah."

"How old's he then?"

"Oh, he's quite young, really." She seemed embarrassed.

"You don't have to say th…"

"Oh no, it's fine, sir. I'm not embarrassed. He is young, and quite trendy really. It's nice. Everyone else's dad seems so old." She said this last sentence quietly, guiltily looking around her in case anyone was listening. They all appeared asleep, comatose by the freedom of an illicit drink or six in fifty minutes or replete from a gorge on a McDonald's feast.

Anna ordered me to bed when we returned. It was a command I hoped to receive many more times in the future.

"You go on up. You've got all that driving to do tomorrow. Leslie's already gone up. I'll stay here and keep watch."

"No, no, don't be silly, I'm fine. I'll help."

"No, no, I insist. I don't feel like I've done anything. You and Leslie driving… I dunno. I feel a bit useless."

"Don't be…"

"Enough!" she said tersely, pressing her tiny index finger to my mouth. "Enough. Go to bed."

My heart racing at what I interpreted as another tender moment in our exhaustive foreplay, I capitulated and followed the lads up to our corridor and got ready for bed. Of course, the tipsy boys wouldn't shut up, so I dressed and skulked along the floor, waiting to pounce at the worst offenders' door and bark at them all, take out my frustrations. Anna appeared in the dull light emanating from the stairwell and tutted, both at me and the boys.

"Sorry," I said, "couldn't help it. They're irritating me."

"Look, I can deal with this. Please." I looked into those pleading, huge, almond eyes and the face that belonged to a heroine in a Manga cartoon, elfin and oddly exaggerated into what seemed like perfection to me.

She continued, "If they cause you any hassle at all in the night, please wake me up. I'll deal with it. I want to."

I shrugged and dropped my face like a scolded child.

"Please, please..." She placed her hand on mine. "Please knock me up..."

"If you insist!" I grinned and it took her a short while to realise the innuendo. She laughed quietly, a little chuckle that I'd not heard before.

"You should be so lucky," was her well thought-out reply.

"Hmm."

"What does 'hmm' mean?" she asked, on full flirt again.

"It means no comment: thoughts to myself."

She sighed and looked to the floor. An almighty crash shook the corridor and plaintive moans, mixed with giggles, a baritone guffaw, and a succession of 'shsh's' followed, and we rushed to door No. 2, the one belonging to Scott, Neil and Josh.

"Oi, boys! What the hell's going on in there?" Ever more like my dad. The thought both scared and tickled me, equally.

"Sorry, sir!"

We went in and saw Josh sprawled on the floor, arms and legs splayed, face down as though he'd just fallen from a skyscraper. A subtle rhythmic movement of his back signified a steady chuckle. They all stood watching him, then looked at us.

"He's a bit...tipsy, sir."

"Hmm," I said, trying not to laugh at his prostrate body. "The Vetruvian Man," I continued.

"Hey?"

"Oh, nothing."

"Sir, Josh has drunk his glacier water. Do you think he'll be all right?"

"His what?"

"He collected it at Glacier Blanc in a bottle; wanted to keep it. He just drank it."

"Why?"

"He was thirsty."

"Oh. I suppose that's obvious."

They laughed quietly, still wary of our reactions.

"So…"

"So…?" I echoed.

"Will it harm him?"

"Oh I doubt it. Maybe give him a stomach ache."

Anna was laughing.

"It stinks in here, boys," I added.

"Yeah, we know. Sorry about that."

"Sir?" came a muffled question from the tatty carpet.

"Yes, Josh: glacial-water-slurping boy?"

"I think we've exceeded the EU shit quota for our hotel room."

They all cracked up at this, Anna too, and I had to join them. Eventually they settled and Anna walked me the ten yards to my door.

"About the knocking up?"

"Yeah?" she asked.

I so very nearly said it all but silence won me over once more.

"I know," she said and gave me that irritatingly friendly, loving, but ultimately patronising 'you're nice' European-style kiss on the cheek.

"Night."

"Night."

Chapter 4

Interested in the scientific process

The long drive north was uneventful except for a brief detour through a mid-morning Lyon, both Anna and I failing to follow the detour chevron off a rare French roadwork. North then, following the Saône, before turning northwest in Burgundy (Bourgogne), skimming the Loire Valley vineyards, almost bare now, the few leaves that remained shivering in the easterly breeze that promised a lot cooler in the months ahead. As the light began to fade, we hit the easterly projects of Marne-La-Vallée, a succession of verdant new towns that looked too modern and planned for any poor soul to be able to live there comfortably, and onto the Paris Peripherique, a poor cousin of the M25. It flowed almost continuously, leading us in an anticlockwise strip around the eastern fringes of the city. A mauve sunset was the backdrop for a shadow skyline almost as familiar as the view from my bedroom window, dominated of course by the iconic Tour Eiffel. Some of the kids had not been here before and were giddy with excitement at the famous urban landscape that was emerging before them.

Somehow, the trusty old minibus, laden like a full-to-bursting rickety rickshaw on a Delhi freeway, made its way uneventfully through thickening Friday evening rush-hour traffic, under drab tunnels, and over even more dreary flyovers, until we were entering Paris along the northern boulevards. These run in deliberately designed parallel lines from La Defense to the Arc de Triomphe, which we sped maniacally around, unaware that our insurance did not cover us for those chaotic thirty seconds (nobody's does, or so the urban myth goes), along the Champs Elysee, the kids' necks craning at the slightly more upbeat version of Oxford Street, and then we hit the marvellous Place de la Concorde and an almighty traffic jam, or 'emboutiellage', as Vanessa Paradis so cutely put it back in 1987.

"Wow, sir. This is cool."

"Indeed it is, Josh."

We edged our way towards the sister of Cleopatra's needle, our size and ignorance carving a relatively easy line against the smaller, dainty and altogether more chic Parisian vehicles, scratches and bumps evidence of their cavalier attitudes to road etiquette.

On my second attempt, I located the entrance to the underground car park beneath the dusty Tuillieres Gardens, affording the kids another circuit of the Place de la Concorde and a game of bumper cars. "They're dodgems, not bumpers!" I shouted out of the window at a puce-coloured Renault that seemed to want to drive into the back of the bus, much to the chagrin of the embarrassed students, tired and irritable behind me. Again, I was playing the dad role to perfection.

The plan was to leave the minibus with luggage still atop the roof. I couldn't face the forty-minute struggle with the cargo net and the almost Herculean effort of strangled knot unpicking that it took to unpack. We were therefore going to walk with our hand luggage the fifteen minutes along the Rue de Rivoli to the pre-booked hostel.

The car park was twenty-four hour security guarded, so I placed the bus in view of the truculent charge d'affaires and managed, in poor schoolboy French, to explain away our situation and empty my wallet of euros to pay the exorbitant fee. Mrs C watched me struggle from the front seat. I tried an 'au revoir' smile and was returned with a classic, nonchalant Gallic shrug.

"What a miserable bunch of beggars," I told anyone who cared to listen as we gathered by the bus before our tramp through a now dull, wet and windy Paris night. They were all too travel-weary to even register I'd spoken. Anna and Mrs C led them from the subterranean lair onto the surface, emerging into one of the most famous locations on the planet.

Despite their weariness, the spectacle of the Louvre, the Jardin de Tuillieres and expensive-looking boutiques and apartments brought them to life as we headed in a straight line down the Rue de Rivoli. In fifteen minutes we had found our accommodation, splendidly situated in an eighteenth-century courtyard, a former convent and now an industrial-sized youth hostel bursting-to-full with a United Nations of excited teenagers. It felt as though it would be a long night as we took our seats almost immediately at the monastic pews for dinner, just across from the reception, only an elbow's width from a group of sickeningly attractive Viking Swedes.

The boys were in awe at the beauty and confidence of the slightly younger Nordic girls who were squeezed in next to us and even the most confident of the lads, Josh and Dave, seemed to retreat into themselves and recede in school years with awkward glances across the table and coy smiles during the strangely silent meal. It was somehow reassuringly British.

We were all to share rooms on the same corridor, and it promised to be a difficult night judging by the excitement and associated din emanating from below our fifth-floor, garret-like dorms. We strategically placed the kids in the safest room combinations and the teachers spaced themselves willingly (or necessarily) in amongst them all. I hoped the sheer physical and mental exhaustion of the week would win them over and that I could at least grab forty winks.

Leslie took control and ordered Anna and I out for an hour, maybe sensing our need for some time together – or maybe not. Out of the wonderful courtyard and just around the corner, we sat in the front window of a busy bar with views across to the Rue de Rivoli and a procession of in-line skaters protesting against their lack of rights to skate when and where they pleased. They were bizarrely policed by a cohort of skating coppers, giving the impression that they were chasing each other through the lively, Friday evening Parisian streets. We watched them and, between sips of too-fizzy beer, watched each other, waiting to see who would break the silence of facile chat and cut to the chase. Anna did first.

"I need to do some thinking when I get home, you know."

"Yep, I suppose you do."

I looked out of the window and at the stragglers of the demonstration, portly businessmen looking comical in ill-fitting sports gear and odd, tiny helmets that gave them an alien-esque profile, and fat women who wobbled like weebles but didn't fall down, covered in garishly coloured lycra, all followed by the last of the police escort. Through the dark, I could almost see them smirking at their entourage. I smiled too, my heart beating fast in anticipation at the possible revelations from the beautiful girl who sat in front of me.

"What are you laughing at?"

"That," I said, pointing to the window and the skaters beyond.

She glanced at them and then back at me, reaching out to touch my hand.

"This is really hard you know."

"Yeah, I guess it is." I looked down at her hand on mine and then up at her and smiled again. "Yeah, I know. I just hope you make the right decision."

Christ, kiss me, I pleaded and looked at those wonderful almond eyes, chestnut-brown irises and shiny dark hair that fell down the side of her face, and over those slender, fair-skinned shoulders.

"Oh, here," I said and reached into my coat pocket, hanging from the hard wooden chair behind me, and pulled out the pebble that I'd picked up from the top of the Clarée Valley.

"This is for you." I passed her the pebble and she took it slowly from my hand, using the exchange to hold my other hand briefly. "I found it in the river at the top of the Clarée Valley. It's beautiful, isn't it?" Say it, you fool. "Like you." I squirmed in my seat as I said it, but grinned to dilute the impact.

"It really is," she said, turning it slowly in her hand, spinning it between her thumb and index finger. "What is it?"

"I dunno. It just caught my eye and picked it out of the river. I wanted something... We should ask Steph when we get back to school: she'll know."

"Yeah, the Rock Doctor's bound to know." She laughed. "You wanted something, you said."

"Um... yeah... I wanted something to remember the day; it was special."

"It was. It's such a beautiful valley. I could live there, you know, up at the top in those chalets. I can just imagine a cold, snowy day and being all wrapped up warm in front of an open fire."

"You know at the rock?" I asked tentatively.

She looked at me and said nothing. I continued.

"It was... It's just... I... I liked it when you held my hand. It... it just seemed right: perfect, you know."

"It was."

She looked down at the stone again, making a point of not meeting my eyes at this significant confession.

"Is this shaped like a heart?"

"Hey?" I reached for the stone and took it, spinning it round like she had and handed it back. I smiled. "I guess so. It must be a sign."

"Was this deliberate?" she asked.

"Was what?"

"The stone: the shape?"

"The shape? No, no. I've only just noticed it. It's only just a heart: almost round. Why, do you think it's a bit crass?"

"Crass? No, God, no. I love it. I love it." She put it in her pocket and smiled at me. "Thanks."

As I marvelled on those words, something familiar caught my eye, brushing past the window. I thought nothing of it until the recognition hit me full in the face.

"Wait here. I've just seen Josh and Dave walk past."

"You what?"

I'd pulled back the chair, my coat arms swinging idly, scuffing the dusty, cigarette-butt-strewn floor and was gone. I caught a glimpse of her as I skipped by our table in the window, for a brief moment a girl from another world, and I thought her even more beautiful, a mysterious veil of anonymity creating a blank canvas for me to paint on a life of a Parisian longing for love, perhaps mine, on a dank, autumnal evening on the Rue de Rivoli.

I dodged the evening foot traffic, soon saw the boys, and quickly caught them up.

"Oi, you two!"

It seemed their ears pricked in recognition, like a horse being scolded after a poor jump, but chose to move on.

"Josh! Dave! Stop!"

This time they turned, a look of mild disappointment and defeat on their faces.

"Back." I thumbed the direction behind me and they passed by and strolled on towards the hostel, a brief 'Sorry, sir' from Josh as honest a response I could hope for and a cynically sly smile from Dave that I hadn't seen in days and had almost forgotten about.

They skulked past Anna; she gave them the stare and they stooped lower still, the true gait of chastisement. I stood in the window in front of her and smiled, flicking my head toward the boys and the hostel and affected a tut. She smiled too. I felt as good as I did lying on that rock in the Clarée Valley, her hand in mine. I subconsciously stroked the pane with my right hand, down by my side, and searched for any striations scratched across its surface. They weren't there, it seemed quite new, but I could feel them, follow their groove as we looked at each other through the reflections.

The lads wouldn't settle, unsurprisingly, so I spent the next hour marshalling the corridors, bumping into Leslie and Anna on occasion until a semblance of calm had returned to our floor.

"Sir?" came a booming voice from one of the lads' rooms and I entered expecting I didn't know what. They stood by the window, curtains swaying slightly as though we'd experienced an aftershock or a tremor. They were smirking.

"What now?"

"Shush," said Tom, elbowing Josh who was leading the exchange.

"What?" I asked, beginning to get a little impatient, glancing at my watch and seeing the time ebb towards eleven o'clock.

"Well, it's just that..."

"Josh!" shouted Dave, "I'm sure sir doesn't want to know this."

"Know what, for Christ's sake?"

"Well, it's just that the Swedish girls' dorm is across the yard on the floor below."

"And..."

"And they're undressing in the window. We can see everything!"

"Well," I said, "should you really be looking?" conscious of what I'd be doing if I was seventeen and had the same opportunity.

"Probably not," continued Josh, "but they're not doing it by mistake. They're flashing us."

The others were all laughing now and were clearly relishing how I would react to this revelation.

"So, what do you expect me to do?"

"Watch them as well," stumped up Dave. He would.

I smiled and affected a shrug of resignation that they would all understand. What could I do?

"I know, I'll go down and speak to their teachers and tell them that all their pretty girls are flashing my sex-starved boys."

"You think they're pretty?" asked Dave, rhetorically. "Isn't that a bit sick?"

I tried to play it cool, knowing that he wanted more than anything to rile me.

"Well, they are pretty. Do you disagree?"

"No, b..."

"Well then," I said and turned to go. "I'd just enjoy the opportunity if I were you. They'll get bored in a minute."

As I opened the door to go, I heard the swish of the curtains and a disappointed grunt from Tom, telling me that the curtains down below were closed and the peep show was over.

"What was that all about?" asked Anna.

"Oh, nothing really, just the Swedish girls stripping off for our boys and giving them a free show."

"What, in their room?"

"Oh no, sorry; they were looking out of their window to their dorm."

"Blimey!"

"Quite."

We walked back to my room, an odd shaped nook with walls that bowed with age, and Anna came in with me, not giving me a chance to close the door, or even invite her in.

"I want to see this," she said and walked to my window. To access it required a very tall person to lean in and over the recess and unbolt the window, paint-cracked, warped and seemingly eighteenth century also. I could quite imagine myself sitting in the corner of this candlelit, odd and tiny garret, working into the wee hours on a classic French novel – well, I'd try at least.

For someone as diminutive as Anna, it required the help of the rickety desk chair to reach the alcove. She sat her cute bottom on the ledge and leaned into the window, dragging it open eventually towards her, paint splintering off in all directions, showering her in ancient lead shavings and almost knocking her off.

"Careful!"

"Oops."

"Anna, forgive me for asking, but why are you so curious about seeing some nubile and naked Swedish girls?"

"Just curious. Can't believe they've got the nerve to do it."

Product of the strict Protestant upbringing in the provinces I presumed. Still, the thought of naked girls, Anna watching and an arty garret made for quite a combination. There were stirrings.

"The boys seemed to think they've stopped now," I told her.

Leaning out now, quite a way, gave me the chance to explore the perfect curve of her right buttock, her gluteus maximus, and upper hamstring – perfection.

"I don't think so. Come and have a look at this!" she giggled.

I hesitantly stepped on up and squeezed myself between her, the alcove wall and the cracking window frame. It was good to be so close legitimately, the majority of our left and right hand sides pressed together in our voyeurs' pose. However, I did balk at the idea of copping a peek at nude young students, some of whom may well have been under age.

"This is all a bit…"

"Odd," she finished my sentence perfectly.

"Yep."

"I know, but it's kind of exciting. I feel like a kid again."

Our faces were almost touching. I should have kissed her.

We had to lean out even further to get a view over the wide and solid ledge to the cobbled courtyard below. I pointed out the boys' room for reference, whilst she explained what had just transpired.

"Those windows there! See!"

"Yep."

"A girl just opened the curtains and wobbled her breasts and then stuck them up against the window."

"Quite a sight."

"Quite."

I looked over at the boys and saw the curtains twitching – who'd blame them – and then the briefest of flashes of what appeared to be four, pale-white buttocks, also stuck fast to the windowpane and then the curtains closed. I looked at Anna. She was agog. And then we both laughed.

"Is it worth it?" I asked.

"What?"

"Telling them off."

"Only if they do it again."

"What about the girls?"

"Same goes for them."

"Okay."

Then, inevitably, it happened. It's the oddest thing isn't it, that however hard you try to recreate the moment of that first, long, proper, full and passionate kiss with a lover, you can't quite recall the exact instant preceding it. Did I lean in first? Did she? Did I stick my tongue in first or did she? Whatever the culpability, we were kissing, the whole of our bodies now inextricably joined, Siamese twins, stuck fast at the mouth. It was fantastic.

I summoned the orchestral accompaniment to suit such a moment but heard only my heart and her breathing slowly yet firmly through her nose, buffeting my left cheek. We couldn't stop and what was probably only a five second kiss seemed to last most of the night. Our lovers' diary would always claim that this first kiss had no first retractor, as a sharp knock on the door was our interruption.

"Sir, you in there?"

"Shit! They can't see me in here."

"Why not?" We were whispering, as though co-conspirators.

"Because." The look said it all and reminded me, harshly, that this was infidelity (to a point) and maybe not that fantastic after all.

"Mr Jones?" The voice came louder still. It sounded important, so I shrugged at Anna and walked to the door, a little tired of the games we were playing. I heard the curtains close behind me and she disappeared into the alcove.

On my return from the boys' room and the temporary fix of the poorly constructed Ikea bunk-bed, I presumed Anna had gone and lay down on the bed, running my fingers through the remnants of the hair left on my head, and let out a loud sigh. I saw two small legs appear from the gap in the musty curtains, followed by Anna, launching herself off the ledge and landing awkwardly on the cold, gothic floor. I stayed on the bed, hoping she would join me.

"I just wanted to say goodnight."

She walked over, bent down and kissed me full on the lips, briefly, and stood up.

"I've still got to think about all this, you know."

"I know."

"Night, gorgeous."

"Night, sweetness." And she was gone.

The screams of excitable children, some of them Nordic and some of them naked, drifted up and out of the courtyard and over the boulevards of central Paris to be lost in the sirens of a city's never ending crime wave. Up above us all, the stars of autumn turning slowly to winter, dominated by the majestic Orion, burnt in faraway solar systems and warmed me through the cosmos. My almanac spoke of consternation in the constellations and supernovae of the heart. It was going to be a bumpy ride of a year, but one that hopefully consisted of rides with a dark haired girl that I was in love with and who slept guiltily down the narrow corridor.

Chapter 5

And sometimes nature offers little choice in this respect

I thought about her completely for the whole of that half term holiday. I could not forget that delicate contact on the striated rock, her hand on my lap and the kiss on the windowsill, though it changed in my mind on each recollection. I was desperate, for the first and last time in my career, for the holiday to end so I could see her again, confirm my reveries and challenge her to make that decision.

I thought it prudent not to text, to leave her alone at this fragile time, though prayed she would give me a hint, a pick-me-up with a choice missive along the lines of 'thinking of you', 'miss you' or even the more daring consideration of 'I've chosen you', but nothing. It made sense like this, or so I convinced myself.

So the grey autumn fugue of late October, early November, gave way to earlier nights and cool, damp mornings and an almost constant overcast sky pressing down on my soul. The second Saturday of half term saw far too many pints in the drab local with Phil, he intent on scoring with rough-looking and ever-ready girls and me wallowing more and more into the bitter pints.

"Come on, misery guts, snap out of it. You'll see her Monday, have a drink on Tuesday, bed by Wednesday and Thursday and Friday and Saturday; well… you'll be knackered I guess." A true poet of the nation, Phil, though there was a song in there somewhere, I was sure.

I attempted a snap and he had snogged a chirpy, running-to-fat, insurance clerk with a double D breast-cup size, so he gleefully assured me.

"Don't worry, mate, I'll not bring her back; not my type."

"Fine. Anyway, she'd soon leave if she saw your Barbie doll collection. Perv."

Her friends were chirpy too, to the point of irritation, but I kept a brave face in the line of facile chat on a variety of subjects, most of which centred around the beauty of alcopops, Brad Pitt and summer holidays in Tenerife. I tried hard to cling to my youthful celebration of the working classes and anti-Thatcher zeal, but kept drifting into my ageing and more natural middle-class smugness at their predictable and mundane lives.

"Tosser," I chastised myself in the mirror of the loo, smelling sweetly of highly scented bleach blocks, the perfume having been released by the piss of several pints. However, on my return to our little gang, the screeches and alcohol-induced permanent grins made me long for a more meaningful chat with a more meaningful human being, so I thought of Anna.

I slept fitfully on Sunday night. Dave was out with chirpy girl: not his type but most probably enough of his type to sanction their union at her place. At least she didn't have to witness his Papa Doc-esque voodoo dolls.

The drive to work was long, grey and fretful. I was always in school before Anna even though I lived fifty minutes further away, a 'jobs-worth' attitude towards working hours that was not attractive in her, but one that I chose to ignore until our love affair had been decided upon.

Pottering between the two rooms that comprised our department, nothing more than a glorified twenty-year-old mobile, a very British temporary fix to Tory education cuts and school rationalisation under Labour, I daydreamed of her entrance. When at last I heard those delicate steps up the rickety wooden ramp, it was something of an anti-climax, finding myself unprepared, torso stuck inside a filing cabinet desperately searching for a set of worksheets on tourism in Majorca, which I was certain I'd copied weeks before in a fit of September readiness.

"Nice view," she said, standing in the door.

"Are you referring to my arse?" I ventured.

"Yep," she confirmed and was gone in the swish of the short black skirt that I glimpsed lay over thick, black woollen stockings. I imagined I witnessed those slender legs longer than I could've done, those diminutive pins that held up that miniature hour-glass figure – a curious shape that I couldn't help but find incredibly attractive.

She readied herself in the adjoining room, her every step broadcast to me through the fragile floorboards, or panels, that creaked and bowed even with her meagre weight upon them. We soon came together in the small store cupboard that I'd customised into a department office. The electricity crackled in that small space and our pleasant banter skirted around our true feelings and we left each other without confirmation or even reflection on the trip, our holidays and want of each other. I guessed that could wait.

The week seemed to pass in limbo, our pre-field trip casual badinage the only form of communication. In many ways this was fine, as it didn't signal a cooling of our friendship, quite often the fallout of illicit snogs, but at the same time it left an uncomfortable taste, an insecurity that hung in the air like the nearly ever-present mists.

On Friday, the temperature dropped and I had to scrape the first light frost from my car windscreen, a significant event in the natural calendar, though I seemed to be doing this less and less in recent years – I counted only a handful of occasions for the whole of the last winter. The coolness in the air afforded views of the first woolly jumpers amongst the staff, most of them discarded by break as the tepid warmth of the archaic central heating system somehow made its presence felt. Anna turned up, typically, with little time to spare before the staff briefing, in a trendy cashmere top, varying shades of brown horizontal stripes reaching down and over those ample breasts and resting themselves snugly above a short, woollen skirt, again thick stockings giving me a grand view of her upper thighs. She looked fantastic and a greeting grin from ear to ear swept through my heart and lungs, leaving me a little breathless and giddy. My God, was this what it felt like to be falling in love?

It soon passed, the day, as fast as all the others had and with a hoarse voice from five hours of lecturing, chastising, shouting and laughing, I found myself standing outside the mobile classroom on the edge of the school, our forgotten kingdom, the Shangri-La of the campus, facing Anna.

"You going to Barbara's?" she asked me.

"What, tomorrow?"

"Yeah."

"Yeah. I think so. You?"

"Yeah, I think so too."

I couldn't resist. "Mike coming?"

She smiled. It was odd, a combination of a go-ahead signal in those wide-open eyes, with a background of guilt causing her to lower her gaze to the right and to the floor.

"No, no, he's not."

I tried hard not to look too pleased.

"Right, okay." I failed. "Guess I'll see you there then."

"Guess so." She met my parting look as I turned to lock the mobile door and then walked off as I struggled to find the bite in the increasingly warped, weathered and child-battered wooden door. She'd caught up with Tamsin from history, their newer mobile gleaming in the orange glow of a security light stuck high up and opposite on the imposing grey block of the outer walls of the school gymnasium.

It was Friday, the light fading, and most of the great educators had gone home for the weekend. Saturday night was to be the infamous 'Barbara's Birthday Bash', the alliteration in bold embossed gold leaf on the ticket, courtesy of this English Department's Celtic coquette. Her dos were legendary. Last year I had vague memories of mammaries as the hedonistic fest hit its height in the wee early hours, an en-masse strip in her extensive and well-manicured country cottage garden. I don't recall this nudity leading to an orgy-esque climax, but still, it was very seventies and free-love all the same. Sadly, Anna wasn't at that particular party, a memory I'm sure that would have been indelibly etched into my mind; for her size, she wasn't a small girl, and I kept a smile on my face imaging the scene, her ample breasts flying all over the place in a wild, deranged dance on the dew-covered lawn.

That autumn had been long and warm, extending into November, but this year the early cold snap had put an end to thoughts of stripping. This was also a house warming, Babs having upped-sticks from the confines of a comfortable country cottage and hit the nouveau-riche status of renovated barn, snugly (or smugly) sat in the bottom of a glorious downland valley, a quaint little hamlet with privileged neighbours who hadn't yet had the privilege of getting to know our Babs. She reassured us, therefore, that this was to be a quieter affair so as not to display her true colours to the unsuspecting valley dwellers this early in her tenure.

I spent the majority of Saturday fretting over the style and substance of my approach to Anna later that night. No Mike, an offer of a bed at Paul's conveniently situated around the corner from Anna's in town, seemed to allow for the prospect of consummation to fall into place – quite neatly so. It was fate. Tonight we would be lovers. It was written in those unseen stars high above the freezing fog of North Kent.

The truth as yet unknown, this party was to be a triple celebration. Babs, a forty-something mother of three, only worked on a part-time basis, two days one week and three the next, in the school's increasingly more complicated two-week timetable. Too many kids, not enough staff and too many subject options had rendered the old fashioned one-week timetable obsolete. She had extended her summer holidays beyond the three extra days her part-time basis afforded and into the middle of the following week, citing 'women's problems' as the prelude to a surgical procedure that none of us explored in more detail, the men choosing to look awkwardly to the floor when it dared to loom in the conversation and the ladies nodding sagely, so dismissing the subject in an emphatic, but final, way.

So, Babs returned to school in mid-September looking wonderfully healthy, perky and somewhat sexier. An averagely attractive lady, enhanced by her wicked sense of humour, she was surreptitiously climbing the list of the 'most top-ten shaggable members of staff', so crassly run by the PE department and revised every sports trip, or occasional session on a Friday evening after cricket against another, equally inept, staff team in the brief fair-weather summer.

Babs had had an invigorative operation, one that all the ladies clearly wished for, but were too embarrassed to ask about. Paul, ever the diplomat, had managed to get Babs drunk at half term, them sharing a now-traditional holiday trip to London to some art exhibition or other, and the post-viewing tipple had relaxed her enough to divulge to her cultural confidant the nature of her recent procedure. He regaled me with this tale with great enthusiasm, mirth and affectation. Pulling his chair in close, he mimicked her mannerisms to perfection, the upright posture, the constant subconscious preening, pushing those golden locks behind those ears for them to rest there no more than a second, then falling back, only to be pushed behind again. He leaned in, puffed out his chest and mirrored her word for word.

"See these?" He pointed to his imaginary breasts. "Aren't these fucking magnificent?"

And with this, it hit me. The change in Babs, the ten-years-younger spring in her step and bounce in her gait was exaggerated by, and a consequence of, a summer holiday boob job. So, Paul quietly informed me, this was the third and but to a select few, unknown reason for the bash – a celebration of a revitalised and magnificent pair of breasts.

Of course, I could not help but look at them on next seeing Babs, which was as she opened the door to me on the Saturday evening. She hugged me too tightly and too familiarly, granting me a whiff of her expensive perfume along with fresh but sweet-smelling sweat and with a hint of grass taken sometime in the lull of the pre-party afternoon, I guessed. Her breasts made their presence felt, sticking firmly to my chest and not parting to the side and down under pressure as they had done previously in such an enthusiastic embrace.

"Hi, Babs!"

"Jonesy you bastard! Helloow! You gonna shag Anna tonight, I hear?"

She shouted this at me, loud enough for all to catch, which fortunately at this stage was only me, Paul, Babs, her husband and a clearly already stoned record executive friend of theirs. I gave Paul a knowing look and he apologised with a return. He later informed me, during a drunken love-in, that this was one of the choice pieces of school gossip that he had had to trade in for the boob job confession. Fair enough and, on the face of it, I hoped tonight would mark the public outing of my and Anna's tryst. From this, she would have to face up to her infidelity and either end the charade with me or finish officially with big, bad Mike.

By ten o'clock the party was in full swing, the attendance topping fifty souls and the notion of a quiet get-together was fast receding, much to the supposed chagrin of the new neighbours. Babs had not, however, survived many a bash without learning a trick or two, and it appeared that all the neighbours within earshot of the barn were here and happily spliced. There would be no complaints tonight.

So, onto Anna. She was mixing well with the London crowd, having arrived fashionably late and we had managed to avoid each other for the first hour. She glanced across from time to time and even the most pessimistic of lovers could read in those eyes that events would conspire to bring us together soon enough. At eleven o'clock the band hit the makeshift stage in the huge living room and thrashed out eight blaring tunes, the poor acoustics improving the din that rang around the large space that once housed hay and cattle. Anna's sister Ruth sang backing vocals, of sorts, and the record producers smiled at the innocence of the sound. Babs loved this kind of music, another desperate grasp to cling onto her rapidly receding ride of youth. She championed this local band and badgered her husband to get them a deal with his well-connected colleagues. Judging by the quality of the performance tonight, I doubted they would be hitting the big time soon, but what with the hedonistic mix of booze, grass and a suspicion of cocaine amongst the London lot, anything was possible.

Halfway through the small gig I manoeuvred my way to the far side of the room to stand right behind Anna, close enough to breathe in the scent of coconut shampoo. I tapped her on the left shoulder and saw the smile come across her face, an irritatingly annoying recognition of the inevitable – that I would find her and initiate the coupling. She leant back.

"What d'you think of it?"

"You want the truth?" I replied.

"What?" She craned her neck further to hear me through the din. I took the opportunity to place my right hand on the back of her neck and moved closer. I left it there.

"I said, do you want me to tell the truth?"

She laughed. "Yes. I think so."

"Okay." I started to caress the back of her neck; she didn't stop me, moving backwards slightly to make it easier for me to do so.

"I think the band is average. Your sister's not bad, but it's a bit of a racket. I don't quite know what to call it."

I wasn't sure if she could actually hear me, but we stayed there all the same for the remainder of the mini-concert, me massaging her neck and whispering sweet-everythings into her ear. I told her how much I thought about us, the trip, the kiss, our future and I'm sure that she said she felt the same too, though it was hard to tell.

As the last song ended and reverberated around the barn and my head, I led her into the hall and there we stopped. She leant against the wall, resting her bum on the radiator, which pumped out far too much heat for such a crowded venue, and I leant against her. For the second time we kissed, a deep, heartfelt kiss, a public kiss that announced our arrival as a couple. My head was spinning, the room was hot and I felt sick. We parted and she went to the loo to ponder on the state of affairs. I took the opportunity to get some fresh air and wandered along the gravel drive and down to the lane that followed the small brook at the bottom of the chalk valley. I could hear it trickling along somewhere to the side of the road and up above the fog had lifted enough for me to discern the outline of Orion's belt. What should have been a wonderful moment felt nothing of the sort. As I stared at the stars through the lingering patches of mist, all I could sense was a feeling of dread and was sure that Anna was feeling the very same emotion locked in the loo at the back of the barn conversion.

We politely avoided each other for the rest of the evening, Paul and I shooting the alcoholic breeze and chatting to a few of the London types about music and art, though Paul made a much better fist of it than me. They kindly offered us cocaine and I refused. I didn't want the prospect of sex enhanced by anything other than my natural desire and a slash of Dutch courage. I wanted to feel this. I wanted to live this. Things like this happen far too seldom in life to dull any memory of the moment. Paul didn't refuse however, and his inane ramblings and pathetic attempts to chat up Ruth provided entertainment enough for me to almost forget myself, and the likely conclusion to the evening.

At two o'clock, Paul had hit the slump and Anna couldn't find any other places to hide from me and the inevitable. The band's manager (well, he had to have some sort of official title other than that of roadie or chauffeur), Rich, our designated driver for the evening, had exhausted all possible business opportunities with the stoned executives, and so we found ourselves crammed into an old school minibus, the band's stuff, the five members and six others requiring a lift back to town. It was uncomfortable, squashed in between an ever more comatose Paul and various nuts and bolts from a disassembled full drum kit. Anna sat behind and occasionally I imagined her hand creeping through the gaps in the ancient seats to play with the elastic band of my fake Kalvin Klein underpants; perhaps she did: it was all a bit of a daze by now.

We decamped at the wrong end of town, near the cheap rentals of Anna and her sister, Paul and a couple of the band members. The next thing I knew, I was climbing the stairs to Anna's flat, slumped on the old sofa, wooden slat sticking uncomfortably into the small of my back, sipping tea and crunching down on toast, marmite and peanut butter – a student day favourite of mine. Anna looked on in disgust as she devoured plain, buttered bagels and a thick, syrupy coffee. I tried not to think of the melange of tastes that a kiss would create between us.

And then we were embracing on the tattered sofa, slipping down the cheap covering towards the seventies paisley-patterned carpet and I was fumbling with her bra strap. It seemed an uncomfortable, even awkward situation, one that I had never imagined this moment would be. Turned on, yes, but her response seemed so listless that I began to question her desire, my performance, the policies of New Labour and life itself, as my mind wandered from the foreplay.

The kissing was still good though. She had such wonderfully soft lips they almost didn't exist, their presence only known to me through the delicate warmth and security they offered; it was quite intoxicating. But her body remained stiff, mirroring aspects of mine and this was interminably frustrating. Did she want me to continue? Was this just a result of her strict upbringing and soon the right button would be pressed and she would melt into me in an orgasmic fit of athleticism?

I fondled her breasts from up inside the now loose bra, the only evidence of her arousal being the hard, large nipples: still she lay quite lifeless. My hand moved down onto her soft, silky-skin belly, not that of an athlete but comfortably plump and female, and then down and over her short woollen skirt and onto her thighs. Nothing changed, not the kiss, the body, the temperature, not even a whimper escaped her, no evidence of enjoyment whatsoever. In a reckless attempt to garner a reaction I put my hand between her legs and pressed it deep into the folds of her stocking. It felt warm, and here, at last, I got a response. She moved suddenly, sat up, adjusted her undone bra and addressed me with great sincerity.

"This is the point of no return."

What the hell does that mean? Not the words themselves, I understood them, but the intent I didn't get. What did she want me to do next? Confused, tired and frustrated, I sat up too, bashing my coccyx on the wooden slat and made the wrong decision.

"You're right. It is. You're still with Mike. This is wrong."

"Yes, it is," she agreed, not straight away, which was mildly encouraging.

We sat there silently and looking to the floor. *Toy Story* played quietly on the TV in the corner. Why we'd put it on and when, I didn't recall.

"I guess I'll turn in then."

"Okay. Night."

She touched my hand as she stood and I gathered that this was not a sign to follow her up, but that of one to bide my time. Bizarrely, I was quite relieved not to be going up the next set of stairs after Anna to that dingy en-suite room. My feelings of dread under the stars had perhaps been portentous, a warning of the dire consequences of our union. It could wait. It could wait for the right time: the absolute, perfect moment.

I arranged the cushions from the sofa and matching chairs into a neat line on the floor and chucked the sleeping bag I'd luckily bought along in case I stayed with Paul, on top. I picked the two newest looking cushions, sniffed them closely and satisfied myself that they'd do as pillows – not too musty. As I settled down to watch fifteen minutes or so of *Toy Story*, I was pretty miffed that Anna hadn't appeared to make sure I was comfortable enough with the offer of a duvet and a couple of plump pillows.

And so began an extremely uncomfortable night, both mentally and physically. I began to ponder the events of the evening and to dissect the details to the point that I realised I'd blown a wonderful opportunity to start the greatest love affair of my life. I'd reached a form of parity in my head on the blame for the failure of our affair only to find that the main light, a fancy dimmer switch circa 1972, was bust and would not turn off, nor would the TV, the on/off button missing and the plug stuck irretrievably behind a rainforest of cables that led here and there to hi-fis, phone chargers, computers, printers and scanners and the DVD and video players. After five minutes of trying to switch it all off, I gave in, paused *Toy Story* and drifted off to the rhythmic whirr of the spinning disc.

In the morning, after no more than two hours of fitful sleep, I planned to leave as soon as I could, preferably before Anna was awake. Judging by her tardiness at school and any social event, this wouldn't be too hard. The grey morning mirrored my mood and I gingerly tidied the living room, got myself a cup of tea and visited the downstairs loo, which was a mistake. Here I discovered that Anna and her sister were not the most hygienic of girls and it quite put off thoughts of missed sexual encounters with this Irish beauty. The toilet itself was mucky; a forest of fur living healthily under the water line, and there was a toothpaste-encrusted sink that hadn't been cleaned for a good few weeks. I considered this was the spare bathroom and therefore only used by guests and the like, but still it was rather slovenly and a bit of a turn off.

My car was outside Paul's on the busy road that led to the High Street and only a two-minute walk from here. In the newsagents across the mini-roundabout, I bought a paper and some chocolate milk and was soon on the road home, looking forward to a day of dossing and dozing in front of the football scores as they rolled in off the teleprinter. I would try, as much as was humanly possible, to forget about Anna and enjoy a very English Saturday.

She didn't text all day, or me her for that matter, and most of Sunday passed too without contact. Eventually focussing away from Anna enough to attempt some schoolwork, I sat down at my rickety desk to mark a set of Year 9 books well overdue. Luckily, they were a bottom-set group, so half hadn't had the foresight, organisation or nerve to hand them in, and what I saw didn't take long to mark. I was writing my last 'don't doodle, it ruins your book' comment below the gang-style graffiti when my mobile rang. It was Anna. My heart missed a beat and then sped up to match tempo.

"Hello."

"Hi, Steve."

"And how are you, young Anna?" I thought playing it cool the best option. Not the right time to bear my heart and soul and fawn down the phone.

"Fine."

"What you been up to?"

"Nothing."

Monosyllabic. Great. Can only be the confirmation of the end, not a grand act of contrition and a confession of true love. Get it over and done with then.

There was a long silence and I could sense her despondent face at the end of the line. It became a vision of clarity hovering in front of me to the point of irritation the longer the silence lingered. It brought back awkward memories of teenage phone calls to hoped-for girlfriends, phone dragged into the entrance hall (well, cubby hall), cord jammed unceremoniously under the gap in the door to afford the only possible privacy in the days of one phone, landline households.

I recalled the posh girl who'd stalked me around the basement of the old town centre Tesco's on a Saturday, me dressed in an oversized and body-odour marinated company blazer thumbing through polyester knickers as part of the stock taking process. Maybe I impressed her with my supposed lingerie cognisance; regardless, we had swapped phone numbers and the next day we were on a walk in the country near our homes, passing over rickety old stiles and through rotten-blossomed orchards, the heat of the new summer wilting the flowers on the branch. We lay on the damp grass and did what horny teenagers did and, feeling pretty chuffed with ourselves, took a stroll up the hairy-backed lane, fresh, green grass sprouting out of the middle signifying its lack of noticeable traffic, and stopped outside the biggest house in my childhood hinterland. Buoyed by the whole process of having been picked up by a posh girl, I impressed her with my rebellious political bravado.

"Look at these privileged tossers. They've got this huge house and grounds and I bet it's all old money, never worked a proper day in their lives. I bet they're all bloody Thatcherites!" It was particularly seditious to be a socialist in those days and parts, the heartland of the Tory blue. This pretty little thing whom I'd just fondled in a damp, mossy orchard, looked at me and then at the house and then back at me.

"This is my house. This is where I live. And yes, we do like Mrs Thatcher. She's better than that weirdy Labour lot of pacifists. We'd have been invaded by Russia a long time ago if they'd got in power."

And with that she was gone. The memory of it, still fresh after all these years, played out clearly in my mind now, not speeded up or black and white or silent. The political awareness of kids then when matched with those of today was quite something – half the students I teach now have no idea, or even care, who the prime minister is. The next day I phoned the posh girl and the long silences, feeling like a torturer's tongue twister, preceded the unyielding chuck. It hit me hard, the humiliation, and I dreaded these taciturn moments.

"Look, Anna…" I broke the silence.

"No, sorry, Steve, no. I can't do this. I can't do this at all. I made a mistake. I'm with Mike. That's that."

Conversation briefly interrupted the distortion of a poor mobile connection and we parted on sensible terms, agreeing that work would not be affected by this recent intrusion to the norm. Life as we knew it was back on track. I was devastated.

The rest of November at work was awkward but drifted off into some sense of normality as December approached and the thankfully distracting alcohol-fuelled festivities began. My problem here was that I lived a fifty-minute drive from the school and the hub of the social scene, North Kent's most vibrant town, and if I wanted a tipple I would have to stay over at Paul's or not drink and drive home, which usually meant a depressing evening watching everyone else get sozzled and increasingly silly until I gave up and left.

The Humanities Faculty do this year was organised by Tamsin, and it was an event I really wasn't looking forward to. I would most likely be sat next to Anna and being a Wednesday at the beginning of December it meant work the next day. So, I chose the drive and not drink option, partly being afraid of what a loosened tongue might do to Anna. This was the first social event that I would be with her since the kiss and point of no return debacle.

The 'Happy Rat' was the best Chinese in town, allegedly, but could possibly have been the chosen venue due to its healthy pricings and location just up the road from Tamsin's. Indeed, I had always thought the 'Happy Rat' was more likely to be on the menu than on the front door. Twelve of us, comprising the ten-strong faculty and a couple of associated colleagues, Dawn and Trevor, the other citizenship teachers, an odd and compulsory subject that belonged to no faculty, squeezed into a corner with enough room for eight. It was a bizarre choice of seating as no other customers appeared the entire evening and there looked to be at least three other tables that could have easily joined to accommodate us all quite comfortably. Of course, this arrangement was karma as I found myself jammed snugly in between Dawn and Anna, both of us manoeuvring skilfully away from each other before tactless Tamsin ordered us to her chosen seats.

My upper right arm had constant contact with Anna's left shoulder, its fragile bones sticking into my nascent biceps. I had joined a local gym the week after the split in an attempt to control my frustrations and look more buff to make Anna realise the error of her decision – that or an opportunity to meet more women and hopefully get a rebound snog or shag to dull the pain.

However, despite a brave effort, the close proximity to her once again and the subtle scent of coconut that wafted in my direction on occasion, re-ignited the dull ache of loss and my placebo life was crushed to the floor. We talked very little, me preferring to mess about with Dawn, a chubby middle-aged matron who laughed at everything I said, and Anna to sit and quite rudely text friends and lovers all night long. I tried not to look at the content but was sure I glimpsed a reference to 'bored' and 'miss you' at one point. Cow.

The rat was quite tender and the MSG not too overpowering and by ten thirty p.m. the last dessert had been left and coffee drank, so we filed out into the dark, frosty street to say our goodbyes and wander off home. It was very cold outside, the temperature having dropped a fair few degrees since arriving and the east wind swept up a gust and re-arranged the litter-strewn road; news of stabbings and car crashes fluttering by in the Siberian breeze. Anna grabbed my arm, linked it through hers and spoke to me for the first time in over an hour.

"Take me home, Jonesy. I need a lift."

And with that we were in my car, well she was anyway, leaving me to scrape the light, newly formed crust of ice from the windscreen and rear window in the freezing wind. Shivering, I pulled the scraper across the passenger window to reveal her face, dimly lit in the light of her mobile phone, still texting Mike I presumed. She glanced up and smiled and I returned it. She knew she had that power over me – whatever wrongs were done to me by her, a simple look could absolve her of all sins.

"Where to, me lady?" I affected Parker from *Thunderbirds*.

"Home, Parker," replied Lady Penelope.

It wasn't a long journey, but it felt good to be wanted by her again, so much so that I'd got a constant enough erection to worry about having to see her to the front door without walking like John Wayne. No need to fret as it was soon extinguished by quite cruel and malicious behaviour by the girl that I thought I was in love with. She continued to text and I looked over, hoping to glean another sweet smile, but she was engrossed in the detail. I caught the words as we trundled to a halt at the roundabout near Paul's to allow a Sainsbury's lorry a wide sweep around it.

'B home in 1 min. Get in bed. C u there, luv me xx'

Thoughts raced through my head like short-track speed skating relays, not really knowing what the hell was going on, who was who or who was in control and actually winning this bloody race. And then we were outside her house. My heart was pounding and I had a knot of nervous tension in my stomach that risked bursting out like an alien and tearing her to pieces.

"Cheers."

I said nothing: could say nothing. I was dizzy with anger, resentment, envy, fear and tiredness. And then she leaned across and kissed me, full on the lips, deigning to even flick her tongue in enough to make contact with mine. The door slammed shut and she was gone.

Incredulous, it was a scenario that I recalled in detail to Phil, Paul and Babs (an almost perfect rendition) at least twice each in the following week. Luckily, they seemed equally incredulous at her behaviour, but Babs had the sense to put a woman's perspective on the whole affair. It was not, she calmly pointed out, a deliberate attempt to court power over men, though she conceded it could be construed as such, but rather a somewhat desperate attempt to keep her present relationship alive in the ever constant fear of being a young modern women without a boyfriend. It was odd to consider that such supposed obsolete values still held some women in their grasp, this terror of being single, but Babs assured me it was alive and well amongst many of her friends. This odd behaviour, she continued, was to keep alive the alternative life, just in case, a possible existence that was altogether much more exciting and thrilling, but it was, at the same time, unknown and frightening, especially the prospect of having to start all over again with someone new. Thus, this confused state of mind pursued an ever more confusing agenda.

Paul, a good looking son of a gun, forced me into a couple of worthless dalliances bringing sexual relief (of sorts), but more importantly designed to engender jealously through careless banter in the staffroom, though ultimately these encounters were fruitless in raising my spirits. I felt that every time I met Anna's eyes at school she could see right through this charade and took pleasure in her power. This both irritated the hell out of me and turned me on to the point that all sexual encounters, whether with a Paul cast-off or self-inflicted, were imaginings of her, so much so that I knew it was frighteningly unhealthy, but like a cocaine-sniffing, nose-cartilage missing pop-star, I was addicted.

The Christmas period came and went, and a two-week break without the prospect of seeing Anna and being reminded of my lustfulness and failings was clearly a good thing. New Year's Eve was typically depressing and had been a morose affair ever since hitting my early twenties; at least it had been for me and my peers, all equally peeved at having to celebrate a year that had invariably been crap, or average if lucky, and the prospect of having to survive January and February before even a hint of spring was to arrive – yuk.

So, I joined Paul and a few of his mates for a North Kent celebration, just for a change of scenery, especially as Phil was away and the local gang had disappeared to in-laws or expensively rented country cottages to try and pretend to enjoy the occasion. Paul promised me a wild time with his band of merrymakers, encouraged by the presence of Babs, her friends, and an entourage of new acquaintances from the happy valley.

We started in a pub somewhere in amongst the frost bitten North Downs and the evening began as I had expected it to: little conversation and badinage and no one, apart from Paul and Babs, to click with. The drinks came and went and a strange and unexpected sense of serenity followed as we neared the dreaded hour back at the barn. Maybe the fact that Anna had so dominated the last few months meant that now, without her, I could breathe again, and even dare to enjoy a New Year's Eve party.

I kissed Babs at twelve (she insisted), no tongues, and moved on around the room hugging people I'd never seen or met before and would never do so again. The very last hug was from Clara, an old friend of Babs', a neighbour from the little village she'd lived in before the barn conversion. She was pretty, Clara, though painted a bit too enthusiastically. Her blonde curls, darkening towards the roots, fell across a very cheery countenance in a carefree manner (not unlike Babs), and her near perfect teeth seemed to sparkle in the glow of my alcoholic haze. We hugged quite a while it seemed, before she turned to me and said, "You gonna kiss me or what?"

Charming. So I did. And there began an affair that was ill-suited but very well-timed: Clara, my tender, blonde-curled, happy, dentist's assistant lover.

It was a good kiss, the taste of ash that she gave me not too unpleasant after all. It had been a long time since I had kissed a girl who smoked, the derision it seemed to engender large amongst the ever-increasing anti-smoking fraternity. Indeed, the lost tribe of puffers were pushed more and more into the last refuges of emancipation, such as the tiny, old and dilapidated pavilion, now the only place in the school where a teacher could go for a smoke. It took five minutes to get to, stuck away on the very edge of the grounds, and five minutes to get back, allowing for only the briefest and deepest of lugs at break. It was alleged to be the unhealthiest of spaces, constantly shrouded in a fug of free radicals, tar seemingly dripping from the flaking walls. There could not be a better anti-smoking advert than the sallow-faced, yellowed-fingered shadows that appeared through the fog at the sound of the buzzer signifying the end of break.

The ashtray comfort her lips and tongue afforded me was one of nostalgia too. The very first French kiss I experienced was from a Parisian girl called Sophie on my parents' sofa at a teen party, faces hidden behind a cushion, the scent of which (smoke and cheap perfume) I had the pleasure to breathe in again and again as I lay on the settee night after night until the odour of the house won through once more.

Chapter 6

The lowest translational velocity for a rebound

Clara: my ashtray-tongued, teeth-polishing salvation. She was my rebound, so much so that I bounced all the way beyond the acceptable realms of bounce-back-ability. This trampoline propelled me into the stratosphere and Anna couldn't even see me up there, let alone pull me back down into her web of yearning.

Clara now lived not far from Anna, and I longed to be spotted coming and going at the times of day that could only signify a clandestine visit. And it happened quite wonderfully one bright and crisp, early February morning. I took a stroll down to the little parade of shops to the newsagents-cum-grocery for milk and a paper. Anna was sleepily stalking the aisles near the bread and tea when she looked up to come face to face with a self-satisfied me.

"Oh, hi, Steve!"

"Hi, Anna. How are you?"

"Good. Good thanks."

She looked a little rough and for the first time I saw a chink in her armour of desirability. Perhaps she wasn't so perfect after all. Perhaps I could get over this and fall in love with someone else. Clara and I had been having sex all morning and a post-coital glow shone from my ruddy cheeks and alerted Anna to the possibility that I might not have been staying with Paul.

"You and Paul been out on the town then?"

"No. Um, no," I stumbled like a guilty, philandering husband. "No, staying with…another friend."

"Oh, I see. Anyone I know?" She was blunt, going straight for the required information. She'd have been great in the Gestapo.

"No, just a friend of Babs'."

"Right. A girl friend?"

"Um, yes, yes. Clara." God, this was surprisingly awkward and not at all the liberating and vengefully pleasant experience I'd dreamt it would be.

"Oh. I see." She was hurt. She was wounded. We said goodbye and she sluggishly dragged her feet home, laden with bread, milk and the same paper as me. Home to Mike, I guessed, so I decided to stop feeling guilty for my innocent deeds and to just feel good about the whole damn thing. Clara was pretty, had a good body and was a lively girl in bed. I was a lucky man.

***

We got an expensive takeaway from the best Indian in town, a quality establishment amongst a throng of others in this very sub-continental of places. It was a quiet meal, mastication drowning out the DVD she'd put on – a foreign flick and a tragic love story, something I'd wanted to see for a while and something I knew she wasn't that fussed about. Did she think me a snobbish prig, I wondered, as I chomped on the delicious lamb rogan josh and popadom I'd saved to crunch along with it? I knew it felt achingly middle-class to like these movies, but I did; they were well made, full of beautiful and doleful women (many who resembled Anna; a fact, no doubt, we both managed to notice and conveniently ignore) and were overwhelmingly miserable. Something about the tragedy of love and art had stuck with me since my student days of The Smiths and Joy Division – Damien Rice was my newest companion now; beautiful, self-indulgent misery.

The film finished somewhere above us as we made passionate love on the floor: well, I suppose it technically was only half-love/half-like, and full-on lust. It was incredibly emotional and somehow I knew it would be the last time we'd do this. I clung on to that post-coital leg like a drowning boy to a buoy.

"Steve?"

"Yep," still clinging. She sat up in a manner that told me, without confirmation, that this would be a very serious conversation.

She continued, "I knew this had all the hallmarks of a rebound event…" Event! She'd been watching too much Oprah, "…but I hadn't planned on it being quite so… well, good!"

"That's nice," I said, trying to wrap my arms around the safety blanket of her right thigh, tighter still.

"No," she pushed me away and sat up further, elevating the status of the impending kill. Trouble was brewing like a category 5 hurricane sucking up the warm, moist tropical seas to the east of the Caribbean Sea.

"What I'm trying to say is that I've fallen head over heels in love with you and that it's completely the wrong time for this to happen to me."

"And?" awaiting the slamming sea to crash over the levee protecting my cosy life.

"I'm saying," she continued.

"That this is a chuck scenario," I finished the sentence.

She laughed, mournfully.

"Yes, a permanent chuck scenario," she said, joining in my irreverent game. It made me even sadder at the demise of this very pleasant affair. I didn't argue, plead or lie my way back onto that leg. She was right. Timing, that little fucker of a party-pooper, had got it wrong again. I stayed the night in a bizarre embrace, a melancholy compounded by the sad songs she played on her stereo as we drifted off to sleep.

***

And across the brick backyards of a North Kent town, another love affair was finishing, this time fate conspiring to such perfect timing that the possibility of two star-crossed lovers to eventually find one another was never nearer.

"Mike?"

"Yes, Anna?"

"I don't love you any more."

That was what I liked about Anna and it terrified me at the same time: her bloody brutal verisimilitude. Mike argued and pleaded and lied in a desperate attempt to keep his pretty girlfriend. He told her that he loved her dearly, not knowing if he did or not and realised, too late for this decisive lady, that it was possibly the first time he'd said it out of safe text and sexual intercourse. Bugger, he thought, I'd let her slip from me, assumed it was all fine, and now she'd found someone else. It must have been that, what else could it be?

Mike, fatally wounded and limping, blood pouring from his heart, fell straight into the huntress's trap, accusing her of infidelity. Of course, she denied it, because truthfully, she had not slept with anyone else. Her emphatic response convinced him of the fact and thankfully for Anna, he didn't press her further on the snogging front. She doubted she could lie about that.

But Mike was at a loss as to why it was over. He knew that possibly he'd taken the foot off the pedal on his attention to her, to them, but that worked both ways didn't it, and aren't all long term relationships like this? It can't be flowers and chocolates, violins and endless sex all of the time... can it? Damn it, it must be someone else.

"For Christ's sake, Anna, this doesn't make sense." He was fully dressed now, not quite sure where he was going to go at this late hour – he lived and taught in London and had come by train but it seemed a dramatic enough gesture in the circumstances. His heart was pounding and the butterflies were having a drug induced rave in his shrinking stomach. He doubted if he could ever eat again. It felt as if he'd been punched in the guts a thousand times and the bruising would never heal.

"Tell me why? It must be someone else? It's… It's Steve, isn't it?"

Why he said that name he didn't really know, couldn't think of another man of shagable age that she spent any amount of time with. Anna didn't bat an eyelid, choosing to ignore the mention of her boss's name, and, unfairly irritated at Mike's reluctance to accept that it was over, was going to tell him exactly what was on her mind that very second – the reason why, now, looking at him, she no longer found him attractive and with that, the love was gone too.

"Your bum is too big."

"What?" he said, incredulous at such a petty but nasty comment.

"Your bum, it's too big. I don't like it."

His rage took him out of the room, slamming the door and pounding down the stairs, out of the front door, leaving it open and out onto the streets of a cold, damp, early morning. He didn't know what to do, where to go, what to think even and walked the streets for the rest of the night, too confused to notice or be afraid of the returning drunks from the cheap nightclubs and late, late bars that had eventually turned out their pissed clientele.

Sometime after three o'clock in the morning, a teary-eyed young man stumbled past Clara's house, dragging his feet as though trudging through hardening concrete. Fifteen feet up above him and to the right I lay, wide awake, feeling ridiculously sad about the end of a nice affair, the end of a happy friendship, the loss of a sturdy leg, the ending of a healthy distraction, and plumbing the depths of memories of Anna until sleep lapped over me like a slow rising tide, gradually, imperceptibly, until it was at my feet, then all around me, lifting me up and drifting my sad soul into the dark waters of my restless mind.

Anna sat up in bed, faded Snoopy tee shirt clinging to her ample breasts and stared at the walls. A tear found its way down her pale left cheek and into the corner of her mouth. It exploded across her lips and the salty taste was licked away before the others, a cascade soon to follow. 'I'm a bitch,' she thought, whilst sobbing, but didn't really know what else she could have said to him.

"I don't actually like you very much, Mike. You're not really a particularly nice person. You ignore me most of the time. You smoke far too much dope. You spend more time with your football mates than you do with me – and you're crap at football. I haven't enjoyed sex with you for months. I think of someone else when we sleep together. I think of Steve. Shit, I always think about Steve. You're right!"

Chapter 7

The most ancient recreational activities of humankind

The first day back after half term was an INSET day (in-service training) or Baker day, as the older teachers still referred to it. A good start to a new term as it allowed a brief lie-in, but a dull-as-ditch-water day, listening to the senior teachers blab on about targets, differentiation and adding value. Bizarrely, we longed to see the kids again and to just get on with the business of teaching.

I'd decided not to tell anyone about Clara; the news would soon enough seep through to those that cared, and Anna had decided to do the same, so our world continued unabated, the odd flirt here and there as before, but both believing the other to be unavailable.

The first clue came with a new haircut a week into term and a revealing conversation in the office-cum-storeroom of the geography mobiles after a particularly rowdy Period 5 with a bottom set Year 10 class.

"You've had your hair cut?"

"Very observant of you."

"It's nice."

"Ta."

I was curious, recalling what she'd said about her hair in France.

"You only get you hair cut when something's up; something's amiss. You told me. You okay?"

She almost told me, but didn't feel ready for the... whatever reaction it would be. She hadn't yet formulated a life after Mike plan – it needed time.

"No, just fancied a change."

"Oh."

"Yeah."

"Cool."

It was, unbelievably, another month until the news broke upon us both, and when it did, it wasn't a revelation, more a slow reaction and a gradual realisation that the world was now a very different place with very different possibilities.

So, a few of us were standing in The Watermill pub, the only pleasant enough 'olde-worlde' venue within walking distance of the school and town set amongst grandiose mercantile four-storey town house terraces, the type of which only the senior management team could afford, and revelled in that Friday night feeling, two lie-ins ahead and forty-eight hours of complete rest. Broad grins were struck across our faces, pulled upwards by the buzz of alcohol that had replaced the adrenalin of effectively being on stage for five hours that day, and kept there by the news that was sinking in, recklessly seized upon by an already drunk Babs who'd guessed by our demeanours, our scent even, that we were both single again.

She had playfully quizzed us on our movements for the weekend, picking up on the emptiness of ideas or plans and then back-tracked over the previous few weeks until she just came out and asked.

"You not seeing Clara any more?"

"I thought you might already know the answer to that." Babs shook her head, looking at me with wide and curious eyes, the way entertaining gossips do when hunting.

"No. I take that as a 'no' then?"

"'Fraid not."

"Oh, I'm sorry, Jonesy. Why'd it finish?"

I shrugged.

"'Cos," was the best I could muster. Although unwittingly looking forward to a future with Anna, I was still upset at my newfound bachelorhood.

"Ahh," she leant across and kissed me. "I'm sorry." It was a little patronising but it was Babs and she sort of meant it in a kind way. We stood together a while, next to the flashing fruit machine. I stared into it like a hypnotised addict. She leaned in again.

"You not heard about Anna?"

My heart skipped a beat at the prospect of the next line.

"No, what?"

"Her and Mike. Nada, finito, caput." She lifted her head, motioned a forefinger across her throat, a pleasant image for a sad end to a love affair.

"Oh, blimey. When did that happen then?"

"'Bout a month ago."

"Blimey, she kept that quiet."

"Yeah, but there were signs."

"Hmm… like the haircut I suppose?"

"Yeah, that and the slavering after you."

"Don't be daft," I said, wishing her to be right. I hadn't noticed it though.

"No, you don't be daft, Jonesy. Go and bloody bag the girl."

She placed a cool hand that had been holding an iced drink on my arm and said, "We've all been waiting too long for you two to get it on." And she was gone, off into the crowd to glean more news on other people's sad little lives.

I slept well that night, and indeed for the next few weeks, just enjoying the thought of Anna until I made a move and had the reality of her to ruin my fantasies.

Easter was fast approaching and Anna and I sparred in the office, taking occasional jabs at each other, sizing up our adversaries like two punch-drunk heavyweights in the early rounds, awkwardly bouncing off the ropes, neither wanting to be the first to land a heavy blow and start the fight proper. Neither of us dared to mention their status, scared of coming out into the open. Softly, softly, catchy monkey, I thought to myself as I brushed past her in the doorway, feeling the soft extremities of her breast and laughed inwardly – not at the titillating contact, but at the stupidity of the situation. If I was a real man, she'd be in my bed this very night, but timidity won through and we drifted into our two-week break happy at the thought of a future together, or so I did.

Oddly enough, I wasn't even sure what Anna was planning to do for those fourteen days, wasn't remotely concerned that she might bounce into another love affair because it seemed as though fate would throw us together sometime in the blossoming spring.

***

Lawrence was a man mountain, an outdoor expedition leader of immense experience. He was an ex-army survival expert with the body of an Adonis, our very own Greek God. He was in his early fifties, I think, but his tanned, weather-worn and chiselled face, along with his athletic demeanour, allowed him the opportunity of dating girls a generation below him.

To an outsider, he would have been a figure of envy, imagining the entire female staff swooning at his Sandhurst-trained feet. But this was the odd thing about Lawrence: a man who'd experienced a great army career, having travelled the world ten times over, shared the occasional outback experience with the likes of Ray Mears et al, a man who'd found a calling in later life to devote his skills and abundant energy to educating young, and on the whole, disadvantaged kids – a man for all seasons; Lawrence was, unfortunately, overwhelmingly dull. He'd corner new, young female members of staff at some point in their first day and terrify them with his looming presence – those endless days sharing canvas with adventurous souls had given him an unhealthy sense of personal space and leaning in towards the girls with that dominant frame was quite intimidating. So they would keep their distance and when the booming baritone entered the staffroom, these new girls would sink into their seats, as though practising a covert operation in camouflage, with such success that it seemed Lawrence had been teaching them on the secrets of outback survival already.

And, oh, how he educated us. I believe that if some natural or political catastrophe were to befall the Gravesham area, the school would continue to stand, governed by this hirsute and imposing general and his army of well-honed survivors. And indeed, a tipsy Lawrence recited this very sentiment to us on many occasions. He would often sing, after a few G and T's, his old school song, "That while the merry world goes round, the school will stand forever!" At this point, we would look for somewhere to hide as he burst into the chorus, a eulogy of big cats and Victorian values, liberally sprinkled with a dash of Latin mottos, all washed down with a rousing crescendo of an Empire call-to-arms: bless him, he was a prat.

But somewhere along the line, Lawrence and I had reached an understanding, toleration on my part to the point that I actually found brief excerpts of his company quite endearing, charming even; somewhere along the line we had struck up a sort of friendship.

He taught business studies, occasional stints of PE and ICT and spent many hours trying to convert the ethos of the school to that of a private institution, putting forward grandiose ideas for military cadet groups and Saharan expeditions. The head humoured him and eventually gave in to his outdoor demands.

Lawrence had a cousin, who knew a man who had a friend who owned a farm on the foothills of Mount Snowdon, a small mountain in global terms, but a potentially inhospitable place for six months of the year. The nearest town, or village, of Capel Curig boasted 2500mm of rain a year, turning the most settled of anti-cyclonic August scorchers into a monsoon-like torrent in the blink of an eye. This extensive hill farm spread up the valley from the outskirts of Capel Curig, including the small ribbon lake of Llynnau Mymbyr, before hitting the first gentle rock-strewn and treeless slopes of Cwn Clorad.

If one were to follow the pastures along the valley floor, gradually tipping up into the hills of Cefnycrrig and Ceunant Mawr, they would spill down into the spectacular Afon Glaslyn Valley that is dwarfed by the extinct cauldron of the volcano of Snowdon behind.

Lawrence often said that although the farm buildings were no more than three miles from the peak, he rarely, if ever, saw it from the shack that he rented for his outdoor school expeditions. For five years now he had been running a Year 7 'Introduction to Wild Britain' trip in the darling buds of May half term. He always took the two school minibuses and four members of staff, but in these more energy-sapping days he found it hard to recruit volunteers who were prepared to give up their time outside of the school terms. This year I had no girlfriend so had no plans other than that of catching up with old college friends and extended family, so I put up my hand, quite fancying a tramp around the misty hills and vales of Wales: a portentous decision, as it unfolded.

Anna too, still pretending that the world had not altered and that there hadn't been a seismic shift in her opportunities, dawdled into the half term break like a café owner in Vichy Lyon, occasionally curious at the change in clientele with their sharp uniforms and brusque manners, but blissfully unaware of the monumental change their presence would have on her life. Not a neat simile but something life changing was to fall upon her sooner than planned as she opened the global addressed email from Lawrence.

'*Oh good folk of this dear educational establishment.*' It was so Lawrence, he didn't need to sign it off, '*I am sending you an SOS. Kate Staniforth has, as you may have deduced by her extra appendages, torn a ligament in her inexplicably fragile and tender ankle and can no longer accompany the intrepid few to the Jack London-esque wilderness lodge of 'Floreat Sodalitas', thus jeopardising the entire expedition.*'

Of course, the majority of 'good folk' had deleted the missive by this point, in fact when they saw it was a global post from poor Lozza, but Anna, bleary-eyed and too beaten to remove her gaze from the mesmerising screen on this penultimate Friday of the half term, having only just removed the irritatingly but equally adorable A* swots from her extra revision class (the GCSE exam was on the following Tuesday), read on and on.

'*I am pleading, therefore, imploring and throwing myself upon your tender mercies for a sweet saviour of the female variety to come to my aid and volunteer of themselves to be our new Kate Staniforth!*'

He was a bit of a prat sometimes but hell, I quite liked his idiosyncratic waffles. At least he cared and was a little different.

"So," said Anna to herself, actually speaking aloud, "you want a replacement for Kate?" and chuckled. She clicked on 'Reply' and wrote:

'Lawrence, I've found myself unexpectedly free this half term and am nervously offering my services – Anna Taylor. P.S. Do you know who I am?'

And yes, he did. Lawrence had an eye for the ladies, but only certain ones of a definitive disposition had an eye for him. They, quite wonderfully, found each other out with unerring ease and a trip to the pub with bachelor-boy Lawrence would unearth a feisty, thick-skinned, often non-lesbian rugby playing ex-public school girl sporting a telling nickname of Jammy or Sturdy Girl, someone who liked to roar with laughter and give an accompanying slap on the back, invariably spilling at least two pints worth of Lawrence's drinks in a quiet and oddly enchanting evening of courting. Needless to say he would, and I quote, "jump their saucy bones," and often not see them again.

Recently, Lawrence had decided that he would see a particular lady more than once. She fitted his required mould pretty much to perfection, but this specific model was slightly different – not only did Lozza actually want to see her for a second time, even after having known her carnally (quite repetitively he happily told me) but also she actually wanted to see him again. This was all the more surprising, as she had seen his infamous home in the daylight.

I never knowingly smelt Lawrence, so was assured that an unnecessarily male odour did not emanate out and beyond his personal space, but he looked so damn scruffy that he could have walked off the streets rather than down the steps of a rather sizable town house in a posh part of town, as he did every morning, courtesy of a pleasantly large inheritance and a hint of blue blood, just enough to course a subtle mauve through those large veins. On one occasion I'd had the misfortune to wait in his lobby prior to the Sixth Form prom, an event regularly hi-jacked by staff celebrating the arrival of spring and the removal of Year 11, 12 and 13 from their timetables for the summer ahead. The lobby was disgracefully untidy, but not dirty, and I couldn't wait to get out and away from that claustrophobic detritus-filled space.

So Julia, an England B hockey international in the not-so-distant past, and still a captain of a particularly good local team, came into Lawrence's life and home and remained there for longer than was the norm. She had also been a PE teacher in a couple of girls' independent schools and was police-checked to work with young people in Kent. Although Lawrence said that she displayed all the attributes of lesbianism, on the CV at least, he assured me that she was most definitely not one.

"Bi, possibly?" I enquired in poor taste.

He looked at me quizzically, and then smiled.

"Goodness, I jolly well hope so!" We laughed.

Julia had been staying for longer periods in the urban jungle that was Lawrence's ancestral home and he had managed to persuade her (with the Head's permission) to accompany him on the annual North Wales expedition. Add Anna and myself and he had the required, risk-assessment-demanded, four members of staff. It was on.

The weather had been calm and unseasonably summer-like through late April, into May and beyond, and by the time Whitsun was approaching the ground was bone dry and the land heated sufficiently to augur the prospect of a pleasant week's camping in the foothills of Snowdonia National Park.

Lawrence and Julia were to drive the fourteen boys in one minibus and Anna and I the fourteen girls, allowing the two spare seats in the front to make it an adult only space – me, the driver and my pretty little Anna, the passenger. Wonderful, sanguine thoughts of the French Alps trip warmed me along the M25, M40, M42 and briefly the M6 before hitting the M54 to the Marchlands, the beautiful Shropshire countryside that borders North and Central Wales. The drive was long, but relatively easy, and even the incessant chatting, shouting, giggling and singing of fourteen little girls couldn't spoil the mood and the moment of me and my ex-paramour driving into the western sunshine.

At three o'clock, after making especially good time around the usual bottleneck that is Birmingham, we decided to stop for an extended break as the M54 came to a halt and rural Britain took over the far side of Telford new town. We swung around countless roundabouts, the roads hidden in verdant dips thanks to the unusually enlightened urban planning of the 1960s and '70s developers, and fell sharply into the Severn Valley at the UNESCO World Heritage Site of Ironbridge and the birthplace of the Industrial Revolution.

The tranquillity of this short stretch of Britain's longest river valley belies its history. It is almost impossible to imagine the noise, filthy stench and choking smoke that must have dominated here, stuck in this vale, a Dante's Inferno with the hundreds of furnaces that blasted Britain to the top of the then developed world and laid the foundations for the economic system that still (shakily and unfairly) dominates today. Ironbridge in the twenty-first century is peaceful and echoes of its past stand in between the bus loads of school parties, miserable in their worksheet-yielding day trips, trudging around the empty chambers of derelict kilns and smelters. The valley turns away from the past to be rudely interrupted by the giant towers of the modern coal-fired power station, brutal and ugly but somehow belonging to this historical landscape.

The kids buzzed around the popular ice-cream parlours and olde-worlde tuck shops, altogether missing the majesty of the iron bridge, the town's eponymous feature, the first in the world, stunningly engineered and bolted together Meccano-style in 1778, eleven years before the birth of the first French Republic. A lot of water has passed under that bridge since then, I pondered, as Anna and I stuffed our faces with double-choc, double-cone ice creams, sitting on a bench dedicated to a once-great industrialist and watching the kids jostle for superiority, the hierarchy of cool rapidly forming in the warm, late spring sunshine.

"Forecast looks good," I thought out loud and Anna smiled a reply. 'Great,' it said. We sat there sunning our faces, heads cocked slightly to the southwest and enjoyed the prospect of a week in the hills, a week with the kids and a week with each other, no more distractions. The aura of comfort that sank on us like an autumn evening mist, knew that the forecast looked good in so many ways – a portentous omen for our relationship. It was to be, once more, another wait for the inevitable, but this time it was uncomplicated – just her and me.

From the borderlands, we followed the A5 through increasingly wooded countryside and the road meandered along with the river systems that would empty out into the Irish Sea.

"This is really pretty, sir," spoke little Emily softly through the cacophony of thirteen noisy schoolgirls. She was sitting behind the driver's seat, a blonde-plaited haired angel who was so tiny that her legs hardly touched the floor and she swung those little limbs in complete joy at the whole occasion and the prospect of the adventures ahead. Anna turned and smiled at her.

"Yes it is, isn't it, Emily? You never been to Wales before?"

She looked puzzled.

"Wales?"

"Yes, that's where we are."

"Oh, I don't think so, no."

"You did bring your passport, Emily, did you not?" I asked, looking at her in the rear-view mirror by craning my neck up to the left.

"No. Did I need to?"

"Oh," I said, trying hard not to laugh.

Emily glanced at Anna and a terrified look came across her face.

"Miss, do I need a passport because I don't think I have one?"

Other girls in the vicinity had started to tune in to the conversation and the giggles faded as they listened to the outcome of the dialogue.

"Now don't panic, Emily. They probably won't keep us in the passport control office too long: maybe just a few phone calls."

"What?" asked Morgan. "Do we need a passport? I haven't got a passport. No-one said anything about a passport." She continued protesting, a diatribe that came out of her mouth like a Bren gun spitting out leaden bullets. The whole bus had now joined us. Anna spoke up.

"Now listen everyone. It's nothing to panic about, but did you bring your passports?"

"What?" "Hey?" "No", came a barrage of replies. Anna looked across at me and grinned but awaited some kind of approval or nod to say 'that's enough now'. I stared forward at the winding road, dusty golden sunbeams flickering through the thick foliage that bordered the babbling river, more white water occurring here, the higher we motored in towards Snowdonia.

"Miss, what's going to happen?"

"Miss, you didn't tell us to bring our passports."

The joke had now reached the point of revelation as a collective panic began to grab hold of them all. We both started laughing in a ridiculously animated way to make it clear that it was just a joke and I spoke up.

"Ha, ha!" theatrically. "Had you going there, didn't we?"

The whole bus groaned, "Oh, sir!" and a large wave of relief crashed over them too and some started to laugh aloud, Jodie pretending that she knew it was a wind up all along.

"You don't need your passports, you silly billies," I said and then paused, "just a photocopy."

The brief buzz of relief fizzled out.

"Hey?", "What did he say?" They were unsure what to do.

"Sir?" asked Jodie tentatively. "You are joking aren't you?"

I couldn't keep up the pretence. "Doh! Course I am!"

"Oh!" shouted Emily and giggled, swinging her legs, tapping them against the back of my seat, a large smile splashed across her sweet face. "How long to go?"

We had passed through Llangollen half an hour before and were no more than twenty-five minutes from our destination. We continued to follow the A5 all the way to Betws-y-Coed, sweet and lonesome in the off-seasons but swarming with tourists, mostly day trippers, on hot summer weekends, the few that it gets that is. Quickly passing through, the road rises towards the hills and mountains, catching up with the steep valley sides until they begin to level out at Capel Curig (at 195 metres). The river to our right, Afon Llugwy, twists and turns through the varying degrees of rock types and faults and plunges at points of weakness to create rapids and waterfalls, none more so beautiful than Swallow Falls, just a few hundred metres upstream from Betws. I pointed them out to the kids but thick-foliaged trees, still young and lime green at this early stage of the season, blocked our view.

"I promise I'll take you there sometime this week," I told the bus. "It's only a few miles from our hut."

"We nearly there, then?" asked Emily, almost shouting it out with excitement.

"Yep, we are, Emily."

Amandeep grabbed her arm and squeezed it and they both giggled with excitement.

"Girls?" I asked.

"Yes, sir?"

"You do know about where we're staying, don't you?"

"Yes, why?"

"A hut."

"Yeah, a hut," they repeated.

"With no running water."

"Yeah, so?"

"No flushing toilet."

"Yeah, and?" they said stoically.

"Well, just wondering why you were so excited about that?"

"'Cos it's like… camping, innit," screeched Amandeep. "It'll be fun!"

"Right," I said and looked at Anna. She smiled back. Bloody hell, she was sexy. I couldn't wait for this adventure to begin.

At Capel Curig, infamously one of the wettest places in the whole of the UK, the sun was still shining though fading to the west and heading quickly towards the hills that blocked the way to the Irish Sea, and we took a left towards Snowdon itself on the A4086.

"Look kids!"

"What?"

"Look straight ahead. It's Snowdon!"

"Where," "What?", "Where is it?", "I can't see!", "There it is!"

And indeed it was, sitting majestically at the end of the valley, a cauldron-shaped mountain of legends, an extinct volcano from the Cambrian era, topping out at 1085 metres, the second highest point in Britain after Ben Nevis.

"Wow! It's high, sir!"

"Are we going to climb, like, that?" pondered Amandeep, her index finger shooting out over my shoulder as she leant forward as far as the loose fitting seatbelts would allow – it seemed to point exactly at the summit.

"Yes, we are, the day after tomorrow, weather permitting."

"Cool."

"I hope not," I said to Anna.

"Me too," she nodded.

"Now then kids, see this valley here, with the flat floor and two lakes, just here ahead of us?"

"Yes," some replied, led by Emily.

"Well, this'll be our home for the week."

"Yes!"

"See the farm and there, the hut next to it?"

"Yes, yes, I can see it," shouted someone from the back with the eyes of a bird of prey, just like the one that circled to the east in the rising thermals at the end of a warm spring day. Only little Emily could see it and she smiled to herself.

Within minutes we'd turned off the main road and onto the track that ran to the farm, juddering across two cattle grids before coming to a halt by a small stand of gnarled trees hugging an outcrop of rock. Three sheep grazed beneath the leaves that bristled in the slight breeze that passed along the valley floor. They were peacefully oblivious to the cacophony that would erupt from the bus at any moment. They sensed it first, skipping down the outcrop and out of sight towards the farm buildings that I knew nestled some hundred metres away, down below on the valley floor. But in front of us, to the left of the trees, was our hut, no bigger than a two-roomed bungalow, our home for the next week, and I could see the quizzical look on the faces of the girls as they poured out of the bus. Some were running around, others already sitting on loose boulders and waiting, presumably for me to get up onto the roof rack and untie the luggage. Anna and I had done this before so our practised military precision had the bus unpacked within ten minutes.

Lawrence and the boys' bus was standing empty next to the hut, but there was no sign of life in it, or around. They'd probably gone for a stroll to the lake and I thought it a good idea to follow.

"Sir?"

"Yes, Emily?"

"I thought you said it always rained here?"

"It does a lot, so just make the most of this sunshine; it won't last."

"Oh-wah!" A look of disappointment briefly came across her face before she looked to the sky and spotted the bird of prey, almost overhead now.

"Look, sir!" she said, pointing with her right hand and shielding her eyes with the left. "An eagle!"

"Where?"

"There."

And I saw it, a magnificent red kite.

"He's beautiful but he's a red kite not an eagle," I said. "Now, Emily, you must keep your wits about you because you're only little, no bigger than a lamb, and kites have been known to take them."

"Hey?" she looked at Anna, waiting for us to crack a smile or laugh, but we remained stony-faced.

"Ah, stop it!" she said, a big beaming smile on her face, and ran off to find Amandeep and the others.

The luggage was put in a pile outside the hut and we marched the girls down the footpath created by wandering sheep to the lakes. From the road it looks like two small tarns, but from here it was clear to the eye that, by virtue of a small passage running behind a lump of granite, it was only a single body of water.

I still couldn't see the boys, imagining Lawrence yomping them up the short, sharp hills at the edge of the U-shaped valley. At the lake, I encouraged the girls to take off their shoes and paddle in the shallows, which they did with the shrill accompanying shrieks when met with the chill of the water.

"It's freezing!"

"Get used to it!" I shouted. "We're swimming in it tomorrow."

"Aarghh, no way, sir!"

Their laughter filled the valley, and the breeze, stiffening now as the sun signalled its intent to dip under the brow of the surrounding hills, took it on up to the magical cauldron of Snowdon and swirled it around until it merged with the thermals that held aloft the two red kites which majestically soared above us.

Dinner that night was a basic affair, splodgy pasta and tomato sauce all round and a ton of bread all washed down with squash for the kids and a drop of vino for the adults. The light faded slowly this far north and west, less than one month away from the longest day of the year, and as the kids ran wild around the hut, knoll and down to the lake, but not allowed out of sight of the duty staff, I took a walk to the passageway that linked the two halves of this beautiful ribbon lake, scoured out by the mighty processes of glaciation millennia ago. It was reassuring to think that the lake preceded the arrival of any peoples to this green and pleasant land. Indeed, it wasn't separate from Europe when the ice retreated from this valley; you could walk to France or Denmark, if that's what took your fancy. Fittingly, it was the very melting of these glaciers that filled this and many other valleys to inundate the basins of the Channel and North Sea to create the British Isles themselves.

Kneeling down, I plunged my right hand into the beautifully clear water and gasped at the temperature contrast.

"Whoa, that's bloody cold!" I said quietly to myself.

"Talking to yourself is the first sign of madness, you know?" came a familiar voice from behind. Anna took a seat on a perfectly formed granite couch and crossed her legs, as though settling down to watch me on TV.

"I'm way past the first sign," I said without looking back.

"We probably ought to chat," was her casual refrain, and thoughts buzzed through my brain like a disturbed wasp nest.

"Yeah, we should." I said no more, not wanting to make a fool of myself, or her, or get my hopes up too high.

"I can see clearly now the rain has gone," she continued, as though I was on the screen and hadn't replied.

"Hey? It didn't rain today?" I was a little confused at her odd comment.

"Oh, you know, from the song. You know the song?"

"Yes, I do, but…" I thought about it a while before carrying on. "I can see all obstacles in my way," I said and looked up. "But there are no obstacles."

"Exactly," she said and got up earnestly and knelt down next to me, putting her hand in the water too.

"Don't you think for a minute, matey, that I'm gonna swim in that," and kissed me full on the lips. She stood up, wiped her hand on her jeans and walked back over the small granite-pocked knoll that had hidden us from the playing kids and disappeared. The light was all but gone now, clinging tenaciously to the surface of the lake, afraid to let go, still mindful of those long, dark winter nights.

The hut, cottage, or barrack-style Stalag Luft, was quite cosy, a roaring fire at one end where the kids huddled in friendship groups drinking cups of cocoa, as ordered by Captain Lawrence (it cooled quickly here with a clear sky) and the basic field-kitchen at the other end. A crude mezzanine floor above us made the sleeping quarters, and an array of different coloured foam mats was strewn along either side, girls on one, boys the other, and an even cruder sheet of MDF created a teachers' sleeping quarter, our feet permanently visible to the children. I had bunked next to Anna, aware of Lawrence and Julia opposite and prayed that I wouldn't be able to discern any fumbling: I was a light sleeper.

Anna slept close that first night and I took pleasure in her bodily rhythms, the unconscious movements of her breathing, tossing and turning and the little hamster-like murmurings that told of stories unfolding in the hidden world of her restless mind. I hoped to be making an appearance there and making a good impression at that.

The kids were thankfully very quiet, shattered by the excitement of a long day and drive, and as the early morning dawned in the still-middle of the night it seemed, I watched the pale milky light inch its way across the makeshift dorm and onto the face of Anna. I saw the shadows play with her tender features and smiled at the twitching of a dream that reminded me of my long gone cat and his rabbit chasing reveries, accompanied by increasingly violent twitches until a mini-fit rudely woke him up. But sweet Anna slumbered on and I closed my eyes not three feet from hers and slept as the sun crept over the hills and began to warm the eastern flanks of Mount Snowdon.

Breakfast was quiet, filling and completed with military-style efficiency, the kids washing the pots, pans and cutlery in the streams that fed the lake, not more than fifty feet from the front door of the hut. They were quiet this beautiful morning, the pale dawn being replaced at remarkable speed by a strengthening sun, more golden by the minute, and shadows shrank at tropical speeds as they raced back towards their hosts and sometime soon after seven thirty a.m. the first golden rays found their way onto the valley floor and our faces.

I took myself away from the barracks, Captain Lawrence in full command, to do my ablutions. I'd taken advantage of the pre-reveille quiet to use the pit latrine the other side of the oak tree knoll and now wanted as thorough a wash as I could muster away from any prying eyes.

The passageway between the two halves of the lake had two, small, clear and crystalline streams that sprang from the foot of the hill to trickle into it and I saw these as good a place as any, behind the granite-pocked knoll, and therefore out of sight. The freezing water tingled the skin at a touch and made me gasp as I washed handfuls over my head, leaning almost too far over the stream. I'd taken my top off and the breeze that was forced through this gap from up valley cooled me and goose bumps appeared.

Unaware, Anna had followed me here and saw it too as a safe and beautiful spot to wash the tough night's sleep away. Through the soap of the herbal shampoo that ran over my face, I saw her take a place on the rock not more than five feet away.

"It's pretty invigorating," I said through the suds and plunged my head into it, just the very top and scooped handfuls of water up to my neck to wash the shampoo away. I resisted the temptation to gasp aloud, trying to remain manly in this delicate situation. I was soon clean of soap and drying my head – it didn't take long with my number-two haircut. I put the tee shirt back on as quickly as possible, tensing my stomach muscles just a bit too much in case she was watching, which she was.

"Been working out?" she asked, a cheeky smile on her face, the sun lighting the edges of her dark hair like a corona during an eclipse (or a post-Ready Brek glow). The colour, until now a dark, deep brown, almost indistinguishable from black, sparkled in the light, iridescent shades of deep red, chestnut and blonde flowing in the breeze until it fell to her shoulders as she moved towards me. The light fell away too and her hair was dark and luscious and hers again.

"No," I chuckled, almost snorting in my over enthusiastic self-ridicule, "just tensing up so you didn't see the flab."

"Looked firm enough to me." She was within touching range now and poked my midriff to confirm her observations. I tensed just in time and she made an odd grunting noise that supposedly meant 'See'. It was rather sexy.

"Can I borrow your shampoo? I've forgotten mine... sorry."

"Yeah, of course." I bent down, grabbed it from the cool grass, still wet from my splashing, and handed it to her. Our hands touched and one of us held the position just that little bit too long until it became uncomfortable.

"Sorry," we said in unison, not knowing which of us had made the faux pas.

"Steve?"

"Yep?"

"Can you do me a favour?"

"Depends," I said, resting my hands on my hips but a bit higher than normal, for theatrical effect.

"Can you wash my hair for me? I'm not quite sure how I'll manage to do it properly in the stream; I'm all fingers and thumbs."

"Umm… yeah, no, okay, yeah." I fumbled my line and fumbled out of the way too as she took my position by the stream and knelt down, knees digging into the wet bank until two patches had quickly soaked into her dark jeans.

"Oh!" she groaned as the wet came through.

"Here," I said, offering my towel and she thanked me, putting it gently under her knees.

"Better. Ta."

She leant over the water and pulled her hair away from her neck and over her head, the ends dangling into the babbling brook. She offered her head to me like that of Lady Jane Grey on the block to her executioner, and this one gave her fair warning.

"This will be cold."

"Okay, okay, I'll be fine."

I scooped up a big handful of fresh water and trickled it onto her neck and let the main body fall over the back of her head.

"Jesus!" she shrieked but held bravely still, awaiting her fate, and I repeated the act three more times until her hair was wet enough to apply the shampoo and work up a decent lather.

"I'll try to keep it from your top." She'd placed a flannel into the neck of her tee shirt to soak up any errant splashes.

"Ta."

I kneaded the liquid into her hair, the contrast of the heat on her head and cool water tingling my fingers. It was an incredibly sensual act and I massaged, suds gathering at the ends of self-forming bunches creating large globules of lather that fell in splodges into the stream, to immediately disappear in the eddies. She tried not to, but a groan or two of pleasure, a volume slightly above a whimper, escaped her lips and added to the moment. It took a lot of scoops of water to rid that beautiful hair of the last of the suds and she gasped each time I splashed it over and across, ruffling the scalp and bunches to pass the water through.

I touched her shoulders after the last rinse and said, "Should be ready now." I picked up her towel and put it onto her head as she started to stand up.

"Ooh!" she said. "That's good."

It was hard to ignore the sexual thoughts that raced through my head and body but I kept it together and nothing was embarrassingly visible in my trousers.

"It would've been easier with your top off," I informed her as she gathered her things together.

"Cheeky bastard! That kind of revelation can wait."

"I'll look forward to it."

It seemed as though we were back to the days of France and the party but as she so eloquently (or confusingly) put it, there were no unseen obstacles in the way. The ease with which this could now develop was somehow disappointing; the challenge was less complicated.

She laughed, reached out with her hand to touch me again, and let it flick my tee shirt, resting it there, again for longer than a mere friend would do. It was nice.

We were blessed with fair weather for the next four days, allowing us the opportunity to swim in the lake (Anna absented – shame), hike the surrounding hills and vales and ascend Snowdon itself. The sun shone that day, was glorious and ever-present, and if anything we got too hot, our paranoia smothering the kids in over concern and consequently suntan cream. We walked the Miners' Track, an easy three-hour hike from the Pen-y-Pass youth hostel car park, and I was joined by varying throngs of overexcited little kids, sometimes me leading the way and at others rounding up the stragglers like a mothering sheepdog. I didn't see Anna much that day, spending the majority of the splendid walk making childish jokes with Emily and her friends.

We all ate heartily that evening; a makeshift barbeque down by the lake and the kids played themselves into exhaustion.

"Hey, Steve?"

"Yes, Lozza?"

"Remember I told you that my mates were coming over tonight – the teachers from Chester?"

"Yeah, yeah. What time?"

Lawrence looked at his watch, the type that did everything including self-destruct if the Russians ever captured him, I supposed.

"About an hour. Anyway, I was thinking."

"Oh, unusual."

"Shut up, plonker." He threw the remnants of a charcoal-burned sausage and it hit me in the forehead leaving a burnt smudge on my pate. The others laughed. He continued, chuffed with his accuracy; he'd always claimed to be a crack shot.

"Well, maybe you and Anna want to go out? We're just gonna chill here by the lake; let the kids play or bunk-up early. We don't need six of us. They're teachers, CRB checked and all that, and we're the ones with the first aid."

"Um," I looked at Anna. It seemed like a good idea and it would be good to get away for a few hours, feel like a human being again.

"What d'you think?" I asked her.

"Sounds good," she said and smiled, slightly awkwardly.

"Agreed then!" declared Lawrence and slapped his thighs, standing up with the momentum the arm swing gave him.

I took the minibus and suggested we drive into Betws-y-Coed, the nearest village of any size with anything of interest to see and do. Anna seemed happy with the plan. As she sat there and watched the scenery pootle by, it was clear that she was happy just to be here, next to me.

The road followed the Afon Llugwy, a tributary of the Afon Conwy that empties out into the Irish Sea some twenty miles north of here. It falls rapidly from Capel Curig to Betws-y-Coed, the river tumbling over faults in the rock to create white water and on occasions, pretty waterfalls.

Betws, as the locals refer to it, but in an almost indistinguishable North Wales brogue, is a linear village, falling in a straight line along the B2360 until it hits the Afon Conwy itself and the flat-bottom valley floor. It is surrounded by wooded hills, some natural deciduous species that sparkle their May-time lime green in the evening sun and others, dark green and menacing, impenetrable stands of pine, planted as a response to the rising demand of wood during the Great War and managed here ever since.

The bed and breakfasts and middle-of-the-range hotels give way to outdoor specialist shops, a couple of pubs and souvenir shops in its heart, and a left turn would take you immediately across the slate-walled bridge bestriding a pretty waterfall where in the summer visiting teenagers down beers before courageously jumping the twenty feet into the dark tea-coloured plunge pool. The foaming water churning at its base creates a frothy scum that is often blown hundreds of feet downstream. Although forbidden, the jumping is exciting and all of the tutting OAPs secretly enjoy it and yearn for those days again when they would consider being so reckless themselves.

A hundred yards downtown, the valley floor emerges and with it the space for a church, a recreation ground, camping site, a nine-hole golf course, hotels and a quaint Victorian railway station, its attendant buildings updated into boutiques and a snazzy Tourist Information Centre. When not crowded Betws is beautiful, but it needs its human throngs to survive, and tolerates these weekend and seasonal invasions: without them, it would be dead.

I'd been here many times, once as a child myself, and its fairy-tale setting and charm had endured in my memory. In later years, I'd come here to test-drive my first bought car, taking advantage of a rare anti-cyclonic heat wave to camp at the caravan site and hike in the hills, ascending Snowdon in twenty-six degrees and gaining incomparable views across the whole of North Wales, North-West England and Anglesey. My first teaching school had taken students to Snowdon for geography fieldtrips and we'd stayed both at the Pen-y-Pass Youth Hostel and Rhydd-y-Creau Field Studies Centre the other side of the river and golf course. I knew the place well.

We parked by the station, the pretty renovated Victorian standalone clock pushing the hour arm to seven, and with the sun still quite high in the sky we took a stroll through the empty train station, over the single track via a footbridge, past the ancient chapel and down the path to the suspension footbridge that spanned the calm-flowing river. The iron and peat in the water, dragged down from the hills, was responsible for the tea colour and we swayed softly on the bridge, watching large fish pop to the surface to feast on unsuspecting flies and insects. It was incredibly serene.

We retraced our steps to the chapel and followed the road around it and along to the entrance of the caravan and camping ground, quite full for this early part of the season, people taking advantage of the unusually clement weather. The road finishes at the ground and a well-trodden footpath takes you to the edge of the river and alongside the nine-hole golf course. A few stragglers were left playing the last holes in the extended twilight of the long, early summer evening and we avoided them, twisting in and out of vegetation between the course and river. The path followed a wide sweeping bend and on the bank, large river beaches of beautifully rounded pebbles had collected, deposited as the waters slowed near its edge.

Little tracks slipped off the footpath to these beaches, and remnants of open fires, charred driftwood in untidy bundles, showed this to be a popular night-time location for the village youths or more soulful campers. We found an untouched stretch of pebbly beach exactly opposite the site I'd measured with a group of students' years previously, and sat on a conveniently placed log. The flies didn't bother us here thankfully, being happy to take their chances on the calm river surface amongst the gorging fish. Birds joined the massacre too, the swish of air preceding the graceful swifts who danced in mid-flight to catch the minute insects and at times flicked the surface of the water for nothing other than fun, it seemed to me. The patterns they created with the feeding fish and landing flies were an eternal clashing of ripples in the still pools.

"Beautiful isn't it?" I said quietly to myself and hoped that Anna would agree.

"Yeah, it is."

She snuggled into me, putting her short arm around my waist and we sat and watched the show the river put on for us. Soon, we were kissing, softly at first, then heavy-petting and we rolled onto the uncomfortable blanket of stones, somehow melding our bodies into bearable positions, the clinking stones bumping together like marbles in a child's fist, until equilibrium was reached.

I was on my left side, Anna her right and our bodies linked together in a passionate synergy. I fumbled with her bra like a schoolboy, pinging the clasp apart and roaming my right hand across her fleshy breasts. It was an incredible turn on. Fish jumped in the evening light, the golden rays of the sun diffusing through the woods on the valley sides until it touched the horizon and threw a shadow across us, and this section of the river. Her hand found my belt and deftly unbuckled it and then undid the jean button and gently pulled until the flies had come apart.

At first on top of my pants, then quickly underneath the elastic to push and pull at me until she grasped my penis in her hand. I moaned like a porn-movie star and she giggled, all the while stroking it in a full grip.

I found my way quickly to her trousers in response, pulling impatiently at the flies until I could get enough purchase to manoeuvre my hand over her knickers. I was soon inside, pulling awkwardly at her pubic hair until I reached the soft, hot and now very wet target. I plunged my fingers inside and this time she groaned and I laughed. This passionate sixth-form fumble intensified and I was soon pulling her knickers away from her body, getting enough purchase to push them over her fine hips and with that, a few inches of her trousers too.

Oblivious to our location, outside in full view of… well, flies and birds and fish, we moved on; it had an inevitable momentum. She moved, pushing her hips off the floor and pulling her trousers and knickers down to her knees.

I had full control of my hands now and reached in and out and round and about until my hand was wet and so too her whole crotch.

She stopped me in full flow and attempted to stand, finding it hard to balance on the shingle with her feet bound by discarded clothes. She bent down and quickly removed her plimsolls, revealing pink-and-blue-dotted ankle socks, the kind worn by pre-pubescent schoolgirls. She left these on and kicked away the clothes. As she did this, I sat up and pulled my trousers and pants down to my ankles in anticipation of our next position.

Anna quickly looked about her, seemingly satisfied enough that we were unseen here on our little picnic spot. I listened closely, just in case any evening strollers were headed this way, my senses heightened by our activity but dulled by the intensity and passion of the moment; I doubted we would have clocked a herd of elephants.

Within seconds she was standing above me, my bum cheeks hitting cold stones, the uncomfortable angles making no impression on my senses, but a big one on my skin I was later to see. She smiled down at me, an angel from above it seemed at that very moment. I reached my arms up to meet hers and our hands clutched tight, guiding her down onto her knees. She winced briefly as they banged the pebbles into an awkward position of support and settled just above me.

She removed her right hand from my left and grabbed my very excited penis, pre-cum wetting the tip in anticipation, and guided me in. We were both so aroused and ready that it slipped in easily and perfectly, an animated gasp accompanying my entrance and I wasn't quite sure which one of us gave it.

It hurt, but at the same time felt good: glorious in fact. Time was suspended, as it is when one is lost in the moment, and I couldn't tell you how long we stayed like that, Anna riding me, but it was long enough for stones to dig in and leave hefty bruises on my behind. My hands held her hips, moved up under her tee shirt and rubbed her breasts as they wobbled with her gentle rhythmic movements. On a couple of occasions I pulled the top over them and leant up to take each one in my mouth. We didn't speak at all, it didn't require it, but I thought about asking her if her knees hurt, guessing they did, and then lost my train of thought as my hand moved again from hip to breast then to neck, to hair which I grabbed in a tight fist and pulled, not hard enough to cause pain but enough to move her head backwards, a primeval act of supremacy; I'm not sure, but we both enjoyed the sensation nonetheless.

And then, in one of life's rarely perfectly choreographed moments, we came together, Anna grabbing at my wrists that were now by her hips. She didn't scream in ecstasy, like they do in Mills and Boon, but shuddered on top of me for a few seconds as I jerked repeatedly, a little less powerfully each time, until she half collapsed on top of me, pushing her face into my neck and breathing heavily. She sighed contemplatively and took a deep breath, as if to say something, but held it for a while.

I stroked her hair and began to feel the shooting pain of pebbles ramming into my backside, spine and shoulders. She let it out, accompanied by a whisper into my right ear.

"I bloody love you, Mr Jones!"

I held her tight as a response, this time not as a weak avoidance tactic, but a deliberately passionate acknowledgement of the most wonderful sentence I think I'd ever heard. Maybe I'd never reciprocated before; well, not quite like this anyhow. To have said it back, post-coital, would have been wrong, smothered in this sexual glue sticking us together at this very moment – inseparable. If I was to confirm my love for Anna, it would be away from this toying emotion. I did love her back, and my tightening grip said that clearly.

I grabbed her hair again, deliberately but not hard, like a tigress would pick up her cub in those powerful jaws, and pulled her head so that her face met mine and we kissed a long, intense lip kiss, no tongues, but somehow more beautiful and passionate for it.

I fell out of her before we moved, the sticky mess left more on me than her and she slowly, and painfully, got to her feet. I hadn't yet experienced the desperate low of post-coital depression that had so plagued me before, praying that the high I felt, its physical presence still coursing through veins and laying on my midriff, was what love really meant; was physically represented by it. Anna's knees were red but pinched white at points of severe pressure and she marched on the spot like a curious stork in a bog.

"Ow!" she laughed through the pain. Her movements were laboured and exotic to me, those careful and delicate sexual dances replaced by this matter-of-fact closure. She stepped her right leg over me, dripping blobs of sex on to my stomach.

"Urgh!"

"Sorry," she said, embarrassed now at our sudden and unnecessary nakedness. She quickly located her knickers and hurriedly put them on whilst I did the same, 'ooh'-ing and 'ahh'-ing aloud like an old man climbing the stairs. As I dressed, she stood facing the water, lost in the sudden realisation of our brazenness. She looked so sweet, like a china figurine on a mantelpiece, and I photographed the moment in my mind and placed it in the family album.

I stood too and joined her, wrapping my arms around her waist from behind and resting my cheek on the back of her head. We stayed like this for a while, until I eventually let go of her with a parting peck on the top of her head, the silken hair itching my nose which I scratched before bending down to pick up a handful of perfect skimming stones. I caught a whiff of her as I scratched: a deep, earthy, basic, human smell, a mixture of sweet sweat and iron, a peculiarly unique scent that would remain engrained on my hands for a few days or so, I noticed, despite the ablutions.

"I see, dumped for the stones already."

"Never, just a little aside before I find you again."

"Show me how?" she asked, bending down to grab a pebble. It was a poor choice.

"Here, try this one." I handed her a gloriously slim, well-rounded, palm-sized pebble. "Place your index finger around the edge... like this." I showed her. "Hold firmly," and I squeezed her finger over it.

"Ow!"

"Wimp."

The gentle evening breeze shot through the trees and ruffled her hair and on it I caught her scent; it was still intoxicating and I had rumblings of another sex session, quite excited at the thought of it.

I let a stone fly, raising my right hand backwards, a slightly curved arm's length and level with my head, and sprang it back towards my hip, letting the stone come loose in my hand and its fine and thinner edge roll over the inside of my now open index finger, and with an imperceptible flick of the wrist, it shot off the end, spinning instantly as it did so.

"Blimey," she said, still counting the skips. "Ten... I lost track at ten; it dribbled out too fast."

"Dribbled?"

She laughed.

"Go on then, you try?" I repeated the routine, this time more slowly for her to follow and she copied. At the end of the back swing, I flung my arm fast and she did the same. My stone skipped out across the calm pool of the bend and reached the other side of the river, coming to a rest on the short bank there. Hers plopped unceremoniously into the shallow of the meander, not three feet from where we stood and sank in just enough water to cover it fully. We both laughed out loud and then hugged. The lesson continued, repetitively flinging stones across the pool, its calm surface disturbed by our constant barrage until Anna finally skipped a stone three times to sink it more than halfway across.

(Location No.4, Afon Conwy, Betws-y-Coed, North Wales)

"Hooray!" We attempted an awkward high-five, as younger kids do, and I picked up another stone.

"This is how you throw," I mocked, putting it in my left hand, left foot forward, and arcing the stone three feet into the air, a weak trajectory that fell very short of even reaching the edge of the beach ahead.

"No I do not!"

"You do! You throw like a girl."

"I am a girl."

I did it again, this time affecting a tennis-ace grunt and she stopped laughing.

"Please don't do that again," signalling with her arms the whole 'throwing-like-a-girl' thing. "You look so stupid. It's quite disturbing how naturally you look so weak."

"Charming!" I grinned at her, waiting for the smirk, smile or any obvious sign that this was indeed a joke, a quip of a statement, but nothing. I waited, assuming this to be an example of a teacher practising faultless acting, an Oscar-winning cameo role. Alas, she simply turned away, picked up another stone and failed to skim it, the plopping sound sinking the pebble into the pit of my stomach.

Anna had managed to throw her steely cold side into the midst of a jolly moment, exploding her ice cool to shower shards of spitefulness into my heart. She did have an uncanny knack of misjudging her reactions to japes. Somehow, on occasions, it was an attractive quality, but at times, her lack of sensitivity was just disappointing.

We'd been here a while now and the light, fading fast in the valley around us, was clinging to the surface like a lovesick teenager holds on to his girlfriend on her parents' doorstep, dreading the thought of a night without contact, without touch, without confirmation of desire. Despite Anna's foibles, I did the same.

We silently made our way back to the footpath that ran around the edge of the golf course, holding hands tightly, and soon found it back across the railway track and into the station buildings.

"I need to pop to the loo before we head back," she said and kissed me on the cheek before letting go of my hand and skipping over the road to the municipal toilets that stood beside the recreation ground. I needed to freshen up too, pulling my pants away from my crotch to stop them from sticking to my willy. The town was fairly quiet now, a few couples chatting outside the hotel bar by the church under crude and cheap awnings, and the occasional dog walker.

"Hello, young man," sprang a voice from nowhere, a thick Welsh accent that seemed to fall on me from the trees above. I turned to find a wizened old man, slightly stooped over a shepherd's crook, an old border collie loyally and obediently by his side. I laughed inwardly at his stereotypically, Old Father Time, Welsh-shepherd get up.

"Saw you down by the river skimming stones just now."

"Oh!" I must have looked startled.

"Don't worry none, I didn't see anything else if that's what's you're worried about!" He laughed, a short snort, showing perfect teeth that almost glinted at me, Hollywood style. "No, just you skimming there. You're good."

"Oh… yeah… um, ta. I er… like a good skim. The stones are great down there."

"One of the best places in the world," he said, leaning in close as though to keep it a secret.

"I'm Steve," I said, offering him my hand, forgetful of where it had been.

"Merlin," he replied. "Oh, don't worry; it's what they all call me around here. I'm not magic, but I'm a wizard with a skimmer." At this, he laughed that snorting laugh and continued to talk. "I've skimmed all over the world you see: Australia and New Zealand, Europe, South-East Asia, Canada, Russia even! I think I've probably skimmed stones in the most beautiful places on earth."

"Wow. That sounds fantastic." It was true that I was humouring the old guy, but I was also very interested to hear about his skimming adventures. I'd always harboured a dream to travel the world in search of the best skimming locations and now, here in front of me, was someone who had done just that. I needed to talk to him.

"Did you do all that for competitions, or, I dunno, a guidebook, or… for what really?"

"No, no, just pleasure mostly. See, I'm what you call an itinerant. I've farmed my way around the world and whilst in those places I chatted to people and found the best places to skim. There's a lot of us out there, you know."

"Cool, I'd love to know more about where you went. What kind of farming did you do?"

"Oh, just a farm hand. Grew up in the Nant Ffrancon Valley," he said pointing across the hills, "on a farm, but couldn't wait to leave when I grew up, so I farm handed my way down to Oz. It was a very different place back then, you know."

"I bet."

"You two in love, I see."

I looked around and could see Anna coming out of the loos. "Yeah, yeah, I think so; yeah, definitely."

He slapped me playfully, but with an incredibly firm hand across my back. "But not forever, old boy, not forever," he told me.

"Hey, I'm sorry." I looked around to see that Anna had stopped across the road and was on her mobile phone, not wanting to interrupt my chat with a mad, old local, I expected.

"No, no, don't take offence. I can see it in your eyes; you're an itinerant too, a wanderer, always looking hey, waiting for the right one." He'd placed his hand on my arm, the dog looking distinctly bored, as though used to his master chatting to all and sundry all day long. However, there was something mesmerising about this old guy. He had a charm, a charisma that was enthralling. He continued, "Waiting for the right moment, perfection, like the perfect skim. Well, let me tell you now, no such thing, just pretty good ones… and she seems pretty and good to me."

"Yeah, she is. She's great!" I smiled at him, and looked across at Anna and she gave a coy wave.

"You staying up at the lakes in Capel, I see?"

"Yeah, with some kids."

"It's lovely there. Say hello to Lawrence for me, will you?"

"Yeah, thanks, I will. Nice to meet you… Merlin."

And with that brief exchange, he was gone. The dog wagged its tail, happy to be on the move again and he crossed the road, nodding to Anna as he walked past.

"Always attracting the nutters," she said on her return.

"Yep, that's why we're together." She slapped me playfully, but it hurt, hitting a bruised section of my hip.

"Together, hey? Yes, I think we probably are," she said and hugged me.

It was getting dark by the time we'd had a drink in the pub and driven back to the farm. Lawrence, Jules and their two guests were sitting outside the hut, two of them smoking, the kids presumably tucked up in bed above them. The smoke drifted up, still visible in the dying light of eleven o'clock in North Wales in late spring. It swirled around, creating pretty patterns of dancing dragons, the blue tint of toxins grabbing a thermal and then being sucked into the lower pressure of the hut through an open upstairs window. I should have said something in defence of the kids' lungs but I'd never met these two and didn't want to appear too rude.

On introduction, they extinguished their cigarettes, and we sat down for a chat and a glass of wine. We talked for a while and, satisfied the kids had settled sufficiently (I couldn't hear a whisper), we decided on turning in. The ascent of Snowdon had clearly taken its toll and we looked forward to a quiet, and as comfortable as was possible, night.

I took a stroll down to the stream, just enough light for me to remember the way across the knoll and down to the babbling trickle that sounded so innocent and lost in this giant theatre of geographical processes. I stripped down to my waist and washed quickly, rubbing away the cold water on my warm skin, then a quick check that the coast was clear before pulling my trousers and underpants off. I stood in the stream, briefly naked, and, at one with this incredible nature, washed away the sex with handfuls of cold, fresh water.

"Ah, ooh, ah, ooh," escaped my lips, followed by a manlier 'Brrrr," rolling the r's to myself for theatrical effect. I laughed at the thought of getting caught in this position and turned to see Anna, barely visible, standing at the water's edge.

"Bloody hell, you scared me!" I said, covering my private parts with my hands like a footballer in a wall before a Ronaldo free kick. She laughed.

"I think I've done more than just cop a peek, don't you?"

"Yeah, but… still." I walked to the edge and she handed me my towel. "You gonna watch?"

"Yep."

"Great."

I towelled down, too cold to garner a reaction in my groin, despite the love of my life watching me rub myself, naked.

"And just remember this, Miss Taylor."

"What?"

"It's very cold and I'm nervous, so no… size comments."

"Oh, no complaints there, Mr Jones!"

I dressed as quickly as my still-wet legs would allow my jeans to pull over, and sat next to her, 'brrr'ing involuntary this time. She put her arms around me and rubbed, a kind thought and action that made little difference to my body temperature.

"Steve?"

"Yeah?" I wondered what could be said at this odd and surreal time in our relationship.

"That was pretty fantastic tonight."

"Yeah... it was, wasn't it?"

"Bit of a problem though."

"Yeah?" Here it was, the rebuttal, the very quick end to my long, and often, unrequited love affair.

"I'm..." she hesitated, "not on the pill any more."

"Oh! Oh, right... um... blimey... um, sorry."

"It's not your fault, you didn't know," she said.

"Yeah, but I should've... could've... you know."

"Yeah, I do, but it was really my responsibility. I could have stopped you."

"Why didn't you?"

"I dunno. It was... the moment, I suppose. It was too good to stop. I know that's a ridiculous thing to say. I'm a responsible adult, well, supposed to be, but..."

"I know exactly what you mean. It was too good to stop. Don't worry, I'm probably firing blanks anyway."

She laughed and continued a close hug.

"If anything happens, we'll just have to deal with it," I said authoritatively and as we pondered on the idea, I began to think how emboldening the 'dreaded' scenario might actually be. If she was pregnant... if she was pregnant, it would be... great! My God, it was at last confirmed. I loved this girl. I didn't tell her this – I was sure she wasn't thinking the same thing.

She let go of me after a short while, my involuntary shaking having finally subsided, and reached into her pocket.

"Here."

"What?"

She placed a stone in my hand.

"A skimmer?"

"No: that's the stone you gave me in France."

"Oh, right." I smiled. "I can't really see it." The light was now dark grey, falling towards black.

"Feel it."

I did and picked out the slight indent that gave it the subtle heart shape.

"Oh yeah, I can feel the heart."

"Not only is it a beautiful stone: it's also a heart shaped stone and I think it represents my feelings for you better than any words I could think of," she said.

"Blimey!" I held it in my palm and enclosed a fist around it: how beautiful…this moment, this action, and these words.

"It's gneiss." Anna pronounced it correctly as 'nice'.

"Yeah, yeah, I know it is: beautiful in fact; but what type of rock is it?"

She laughed. "No, it's gneiss, you know with the 'g'… gneiss: metamorphic granite. I asked the Rock Doctor. She says it's called banded gneiss, found in the Clarée Valley… and other places of course."

"Like where?" I asked.

"God, I can't really remember… all over the place… it's a pebble."

I made a note to go 'all over' one day and get her another stone, a partner to join this one. We kissed and stood up, I put the stone back in her hand and we headed gingerly back to camp, stumbling over rocks and most probably sheep until we came to the hut.

The commotion hit us before the light, an angry Lawrence chastising a group of boys and on turning the corner of the building, we saw six semi-naked lads standing in a line under the weak security light at the back of the hut. Lawrence was standing behind them with a bucket of water and was in the process of tipping it over each one in turn, waiting for their gasps to subside before dousing the next one. We were both quite stunned at the sight, and took them all by surprise.

"What's going on?" I asked, not as another angry teacher wanting the kids to explain, but directed it to Lawrence.

"These little twerps were in the process of keeping us all up!"

"By doing what, exactly?" still at Lawrence, the kids unsure as to whether they should be explaining to me.

"Talking, giggling, throwing things across the room at the girls, despite…" at this he raised his index finger and shook it at the now dark night sky like a biblical character angry at God's betrayal, "many warnings!"

"All right," I said, unsure of what to do next. "Right," I continued. "Well, I think they've learnt their lesson now, don't you, sir?"

"Yes, I think so!"

"Well, go and get your towels and dry off boys, and get to bed. I'm sure you know that we'll be expecting not a single peep out of you for the rest of the night?"

"Yes, sir", "Thanks, sir", "'Course, sir," was the mixed reply, with a muffled whimper from the more sensitive boys at one end. Lawrence followed them into the hut and Anna and I looked at each other.

"Jesus Christ!" she said. "Did he really just do that?"

"I think so. What a bloody fool! He'll get sacked, and we'll bloody well get in trouble too."

"Shit! How we gonna explain it all away?" asked Anna.

"Oh, I'll think of something. Try not to worry, I'll sort it out."

We went in and helped the boys to bed and Anna went up after them. I motioned to Lawrence to follow me outside with a nod of my head. He followed. In the faint glow of the security light, I spoke.

"Lawrence, mate, much that I appreciate your efforts in setting all this up year after year, and much that I appreciate that the kids were being annoying little twerps, but you just can't do that to them any more!"

"Well, I just have."

"I know and I saw it and it was, well…" I struggled for the right words, "it was, well, pretty nasty. If any of them complains, there could be a hell of a lot of trouble."

Lawrence smiled like a kindly old man to a passing simpleton. "Now look here, old chap," he said, grabbing me by the shoulders and leading me away from the guarding light and out of earshot of the others. He continued, "What goes on tour, stays on tour." (Oh my God, not another one.) "I've already made that pretty clear to these lads; they're all on the rugby team. They'll be fine."

And he was right of course, the lucky sod. Lawrence had lived a charmed existence in many ways and that, inexplicably, kept him gainfully employed and able to be a responsible guardian of kids. But whatever his many faults, I never did see him put a child in real harm's way on any of these quite adventurous trips. He truly was a good, old-fashioned maverick, the last of a dying breed in an increasingly serious and sterile profession.

The kids didn't say a word all night, probably too bloody afraid to even draw breath. I slept fitfully, but close enough to Anna to elicit a risky fumble, dozing off in the small hours, hand still on her naked waist below her tee shirt; the same one she'd worn on top of me just hours before. I dreamt of her, school, skimming stones and sex by the water, a place and person familiar to me, but not quite the same, as reveries often are.

In the morning, the drowned-rat boys played and laughed as though nothing untoward had transpired in the night, as though it had been nothing but an odd little nightmare, long since forgotten. Lawrence, it seemed, had got away with it, the lucky sod.

The last two days passed peacefully enough, games and canoeing in the lake and rounders and hide-and-seek in the surrounding fields of the flat valley bottom floor. We spent an evening in Betws, wandering up to the Swallow Falls and watching the local lads jump off the bridge to rounds of applause from our kids; they were reminded to stay way back from the edge, though I was unsure as to whether Lawrence would pick one of them up and throw him over the side, just as an example to the others. I bumped into Merlin again, the dog still looking bored and he gave me his email address and said that he'd update me on any skimming news if I ever decided to take off with my rucksack and world skimming guide; if one didn't exist, I should write it he told me, grabbing my hand and shaking it warmly.

All too soon, we were on our way home, the kids quiet and subdued, the weeklong activities and uncomfortable nights taking their toll and sending them off to sleep for the majority of the seven-hour drive home.

Chapter 8

Can't break free

And Anna and me? Well, this was the beginning of the beginning, and our summer blossomed into a haze of dates and sex and walks and sex and day trips and sex. It was as love should be and I looked forward to a lifelong partnership with this very special girl.

I'd almost forgotten the fact that I could be a father, the events of the everyday controlling me, guiding me through it, enclosed in thoughts of actions before those quiet, calm, all-too-brief moments before sleep when the outside world would drift in.

"Shit," I whispered to myself, "she's not had her period yet."

My calculations, which weren't particularly mathematically taxing, put it at thirty-five days now; that's seven more than expected of course, a whole bloody (well, not bloody as it happens) week. Not to panic just yet. I had heard from girls I'd known, dated even, that sometimes, just sometimes, for some of them, it was not like clockwork, and the lunar cycle was not always to be trusted. I kept my fingers crossed and pushed the thoughts away, at least for another few hours.

On Day 38, she phoned me just before bedtime, instead of the usual endearing text.

"Hi sweetness."

"Hi."

"You okay?" Please, please, please.

"Yeah, I'm fine." There was a palpable sense of relief in that now very familiar voice.

"It's started," she continued.

"Right… good… great! Just like you said, nothing to worry about."

"Nothing, no."

"Great."

We chatted idly about work and finished the call.

"Great," I said, but not in a confirming enough way to convince myself that a small part of me was actually disappointed. In those days since the act, and indeed since the missed deadline, part of me had been gearing itself up for the possible reality of a pregnant girlfriend, and that part of me bloody loved the idea. I was, quite unexpectedly, experiencing my first case of brooding. I wondered if Anna felt the same, but by morning had forgotten my worries and would never ask her – perhaps a mistake.

The summer soon passed, all too quickly for us poor old teachers, and we started the new academic year as a solid couple, open to teachers and soon enough to kids as they cottoned on to our body language and bloody ridiculous happiness. Autumn was long, mild and beautifully colourful, the leaves choosing to sprinkle the pathways in slow dances in the absence of a slaughtering frost or Atlantic storm. All was calm, the weather, work and us, and I was sickeningly upbeat and jolly.

Christmas brought us past the sixth month and people hinted at more permanence to our relationship. Without saying it outright, this intimation was that of moving in together or even the dreaded 'M' word; I wasn't sure I'd ever do that and the thought of such a commitment brought to mind the words of the magical Merlin – "an itinerant", "a wanderer" and I had, for the very first time in this burgeoning love affair, a pang of real doubt.

We spent the festive season at Anna's parents, the first time I'd been to the province of Northern Ireland. The dodgy budget-airline-flight touchdown was, well, twice, as it bumped to halt courtesy of a lowly paid and most-likely inexperienced co-pilot. I had images of a pimply-faced, greasy-haired kid, not long out of flight school, and I even listened closely to his name and accent on the intercom in the fear that it was one of the first students I had taught made good. His lazy Aussie drawl confirmed his cheapness, a jobbing pilot on an extended jaunt in Europe based out of London and Dublin.

The runway at City of Derry airport is short, and the empty seats at the front and back of the plane frightened this nervous flyer as the camp steward explained that they needed to be empty so that the plane could break in time on the tiny patch of concrete. I was scared enough to be thankful that if I was to die, at least it'd be with my one true love; even this morbid thought brought little comfort and another pang of doubt – how much did I love this girl?

Her family were good enough company and the food and drink kept me sedated. We ventured out in the car to pop into the Republic and took a spin around County Donegal, even more northern than Northern Ireland, and also along to the windswept coast of the Giant's Causeway which I didn't get the chance to see through the mist and fine rain, the sort that soaked you in seconds without you realising that it was actually raining at all.

New Year's Eve we spent in a local village hall, the most vivid memory that of Anna's golden lamé trousers that she said she wore as a joke, though enjoyed the moment and attention it brought a little too much for me to believe. I later enjoyed tearing them off and silently fucking her in the games room basement of their country cottage – Happy New Year!

I'm not sure you could describe what was happening to me as happiness because it is an emotion, or a state of being, that I find hard to define or qualify. Surely all of our states of emotion are based on a yardstick experience and as an indecisive bugger I couldn't quite fathom where that yardstick began, or indeed, what it even was. Thus, I enjoyed moments of great pleasure through sex and laughter, sport and TV, film and books, music and always learning something new, but many of these experiences were away from Anna and many occurred when I was alone. And so, as winter bit hard (it was a particularly nasty January), I began contemplating my happiness and my quality of life and how much my relationship with Anna enhanced both.

The sex was good and at times, lost in the moment, my heart exploded with love for this girl but as the endorphins slowed and the buzz subsided, I daren't mention that word in her ear, felt it physically impossible to do so in fact. The key questions were, as I lay next to her, sweat gathering in the folds of skin on my stomach and neck and she glowing, a slight pool forming in her belly button (the heating was too high; it wasn't so much our energetic love making), was this love and was this as good as it could possibly ever get? I didn't want to answer this myself because all I felt at that moment was an odd sense of irritation. I wanted to put on some music but she hated the latest CD I was playing, so I didn't bother. I wanted a cup of tea but she didn't want to move, snuggled tightly into me, her legs entwined with mine and causing me to sweat even more and I could feel myself beginning to stick to the sheets. I was too bloody hot and she always complained of being too cold. I wanted to watch *Newsnight* and catch up on the latest worldwide disasters but she said it was dull and for old people. The dreaded realisation was that this wasn't love after all or, more worryingly, that I just found it impossible to enjoy loving someone.

We staggered through to half term and booked a cheap flight to Italy. We argued over the destination, of course, me having already been to Venice twice and her Rome; she'd said she hated it but my brief experience of the ancient capital was one of total enchantment. As a compromise, we plumped for

Bologna: it was the cheapest flight available and neither of us knew enough about the city to argue for or against. The hotel, which looked sharp, clean and comfortable on the website, was a bit drab in the flesh and our economy deal left us stuck in the only room available, an attic box with a dapple of light coming in through a broken skylight; it dripped condensation at night with the heat of our bodies and archaic central heating system.

Having the change of scenery and culture was refreshing and it pepped us up enough to enjoy each other again. The sex was rekindled towards love and I found a rare Smiths CD in a flea market that cheered me up and out of the winter blues. We wandered the medieval streets, drank syrupy strong Italian coffee and ate stodgy cakes, runny pizzas and polished off a few bottles of cheap vino. The Giordini Margherita let the sun shine through its trees and it was warm enough in the early afternoon to lie in the weak and watery sunshine and read, the slight heat it threw on our faces a glorious hint at the end of winter and the beginning of spring. The tramp up the tower (Torre degli Asinelli at 97.2m) was terrifying, the rickety stairs and non-existent handrails causing me to come out in a nervous sweat, whilst Anna laughed at me reassuringly. When we eventually got our feet back on solid ground I found it hard to see the funny side and a half an hour grump followed until a cool beer in a very trendy bar thawed the ice.

"Why do you find my fears and insecurities so amusing?" I asked her, sipping the froth off the cool beer.

She tutted, raised her eyes to heavens, which irritated the hell out of me, and spoke. "Because you just sometimes seem so weak and well, unmanly. I find it funny, that's all."

"A heart of gold," I said sardonically and gulped down some Perroni.

"Oh don't be so bloody dramatic!"

I always knew that she was a tough character and I admired that in her; it meant for no prisoners in the classroom, but sometimes I wanted her to be just a little more soft and giving and, well, caring.

We flew back on the Thursday of the holiday week and into the teeth of a cold snap. Despite the occasional irritation and heart of stone, there were times when I could lose myself in Anna and this was what I had always hoped a relationship would bring. On Saturday, we took a day trip to the coast, a final fling before we dusted off the books and started thinking of school again.

The wind whipped up from the Dungeness Levels, the largest shingle spit in the world and home to the isolated nuclear power station, across Winchelsea and Pett beaches, seasonally battered by the winter storms and protected for the meantime by newly renewed groynes and revetments, and on up over the sandstone heights of Cliff End to swirl in the dips and vales of Fairlight Country Park where we stood, facing out to sea.

If the wind is from the spit at this time of year, then its origin lies far off to the east, across the North Sea and onto the continental plains of a frozen Siberia. I held her tight from behind as we watched the winter sun disappear behind a grey-tinged cumulus cloud and with it any semblance of warmth that we felt vicariously through our stars' stiff resistance in the face of this eastern chill. I nuzzled my head into her neck and sniffed that fine hair and breathed in a mixed aroma of shampoo and the intoxicating scent that was hers.

The cloud had robbed us of a proper sunset. I felt relieved. Often this most beautiful of nature's shows would leave me in a melancholic mood as the last of the crimson ball disappeared beyond the horizon and ushered forth the cool night with all of its secrets and demons. I didn't want to face this fear tonight. Tonight, a happy Anna was in my arms and tonight I wouldn't let her go.

I'd been here before, to Fairlight, with other lovers. I'd listened to the muffled sound of the crashing waves way below on the rocky beach in all seasons. I'd cuddled with Rebecca just across the track one fine summer's day but had wished she was just a little more kind and sweet and a little less hirsute below the nose. I'd walked these paths with Cath in spring and laughed in the rain but wanted her to be more than just a friend and I'd skimmed stones with Clara but knew that she just wasn't quite right. But now, now I was really here for the very first time. I sheltered her from the cold Siberian wind ringing with nuclear particles picked up from the barren spit and held her tighter still. I was here for the first time; I was feeling a new way and I was terrified that it was love.

***

Winter morphed into spring and the sun came out and didn't go away from the middle of April until the beginning of Wimbledon and the arrival of the little known but depressingly familiar North-West European monsoon, whose deluges bring a halt to tennis games and family barbeques. School was school and the kids were kids and our relationship fluctuated between love and like and like and love, punctuated by moments of deep desire for each other and irritation where space between us was warmly welcomed. Phil would often tell me that this was what it should be like; no one could ever find true and everlasting love.

Anna stayed with me regularly throughout the winter and on into the spring but this dwindled as familiarity pushed our old lives back towards us, and our stifling closeness at work and at home made us yearn for moments of solitude and for the company of old friends. I spent more time with Phil and she with her sister and the Gravesham set. I had occasional emails from Merlin where he told me of skimming chat lines and places he'd been to that I should visit, and the more we communicated the more his ideas gave me itchy feet. The seed of travel, of wandering the world whilst still young enough to not look too foolish, was planted and it began to germinate and grow and flourish in my brain with every contact with the Welsh wizard until the plant sprouted from the top of my head and it became impossible to ignore as just a wistful thought, and indeed, hide from others.

I began to think about the logistics of such an adventure – the house and the selling of it, the thought of chucking Phil and his Barbie dolls out on the street, and Anna…? Blimey, would world travel, a sabbatical from my career, be better with or without her? Would we grow to hate each other together; would she wait if I travelled solo? My God, these thoughts were dangerous and frightening but they were real and would not go away. I started to make serious notes of Merlin's skimming destinations and planned a tentative route around the world in search of the perfect skim. When I logged into a spurious skimming website, I knew things had likely gone too far. If I did go, I'd skim as singularly as was possible in order to write my own skimming travelogue, so made a point of avoiding these odd sites – there did appear to be too many hirsute and scruffy bearded middle-aged men for my liking. My skimming would be mine alone and hopefully more extreme than these part-time accountant stone-chuckers.

Of course, Anna could not read minds, or so I supposed, but my reveries and consequent insecurity seeped from my pores and unbalanced our already fragile arrangements. Spring was beautiful, just like it says on the tin, and we enjoyed each other but she could quite easily sense my distractions. It was hard to tell how she read them but the fact that we slept together less and less suggested she suspected me of going off her; to an extent she was right but I had not, to any definite degree, made a decisive choice and these were just my own little mind games.

Anna made a particular effort to stay over at Easter and the clement weather meant we risked a homeland holiday, a good gamble as it turned out. One Tuesday, after a pleasant evening in a pizza restaurant and a bottle of red later, we found ourselves in bed earlier than normal; sex the intention. It was a mechanical affair that night, nothing too emotional, and my insistence on her keeping as quiet as possible so as not to alert Phil to our actions was perhaps the last straw; her frustrations sizzled and then boiled to the surface, erupting in an odd display. We finished with me on top, and I rolled off to face the window, away from her, and couldn't even muster the energy to remove the condom, it fitting warmly and comfortably on me.

The first thing I noticed was a strange wet sensation trickling down my neck and back and onto the sheets. For a short moment, my mind was scrambled and confused, unable to make sense of the situation. Blood? No, I wasn't in pain. Rain? No, I was indoors. Water? Leaking? Possibly... possibly. Oh, bugger, a burst water pipe! I sat up at this point, putting my hand to my neck, just to make sure it wasn't hot and sticky blood and I wasn't in the process of being bludgeoned to death by my lover. The truth, however, was nearer to that than I would have ever imagined.

Anna was sitting up, holding a glass of water at a forty-five degree angle and had been tipping it onto my back.

"What the hell are you doing?" I asked, still somewhat bemused.

"Bastard!"

"What?" I racked my brains for evidence of infidelity I might have carelessly overlooked, but could find none. I was baffled at the reason for this attack.

"Bastard git!" she hissed.

At this, she poured the remnants of the water onto my head and waited for a reaction. I had a choice: get very angry and shout, get violent or calmly lie down and pretend that it hadn't really happened and hope she would come out of whatever it was and explain herself. I couldn't be bothered to shout, I wasn't a violent man, so chose the third option, lying down again on the wet sheets and turned to the window.

Fully naked still, she too lay down and rolled onto my back, putting her whole weight, which wasn't a lot, on to me and covering me as much as she could, like a hero in a bomb-blast shielding the innocent from shrapnel. She somehow managed to increase her weight as she lay there, turning gravity up with the frustrations that coursed through her veins. She whispered in my ears, her lump of a limp body slam-dunking me onto the wet sheets.

"Why don't you show some fucking emotion towards me? Why don't you fucking want me? Fucking show me you want me!"

I had many sensible, logical and understandable responses and arguments to this, ones that many friends would agree with wholeheartedly, but, lying there, they all seemed kind of pointless, so I said nothing. Needless to say, this irked her further and a string of invectives swam into my left ear, each one adding force to the questioning of my lack of emotion and commitment towards her. Clearly this had been bottled up for a while and her volcano of feeling erupted in a continuous cloud of insecurity for many minutes, an almost constant pyroclastic flow of disappointment.

Sometime in the middle of the night, she climbed off me and we drifted into sleep and in the morning, the beautiful, light, hopeful and safe morning, we woke and the events of the night before melted into our minds as bad dreams to be forgotten and we didn't talk of it. In fact we had a very pleasant day, but a warning had been served and I had, at some point, to respond to it if I wanted to save this relationship. If I wanted to…

And so to spring, and what a glorious season it turned out to be. I was clearly in a state of flux over love, fulfilment, commitment and wanderlust but in amongst this most male of maelstroms I found myself loving Anna still. And in amongst my confusions she fashioned a life that suited us both and, although I pissed her off and she had bouts of coolness verging on ice-cold nastiness, we drifted bizarrely in the right direction. Perhaps I could ride this wave of procrastination and come out of the tube in love and definite.

We took a day trip to get away from the north of the county and reminders of school, tough as it was proving to be at times, and an historic tour of 1066 country, or six minutes past eleven as I so drolly put it. Anna just stared at me. Well, the kids found it funny when I taught the odd history lesson to cover the ever-increasing number of stressed half-to-death colleagues.

We ended up in Battle, perhaps a suitable pun of a place, and there we stood over the spot where poor old Harold got one in the eye; a stone plaque marked the spot.

"Aye, aye, what we got 'ere then?"

"You know, Steve, you are particularly unfunny at times." I think she meant it; she had that look she gave naughty Year 8s when they interrupted the register.

"Well, my Year 7s find it funny!" I said.

"Yes, well, there you have it," and with that she began to walk away from Harold's alleged death site.

"You know, Anna?"

"Yeah, what?" She stopped and looked at me, this time with great affection; talk about me being the confusing bugger.

"Harold probably didn't die here," I reliably informed her.

"And how do you know, Mr History Man?" She took a few steps towards me, put an arm around my waist and waited, somewhat impatiently, for my reply.

"Well, it's not definite that he got an arrow in the eye at all, and it wasn't that which killed him anyway."

"Oh." She seemed vaguely interested.

"No, William sent four of his best knights into the melee – the Saxons were losing at this stage – to bump him off."

"Oh, I didn't know that."

"Yes, well, they found him, injured or not and pretty much hacked him to death; a jumble of arms, legs, head et cetera."

"Oh, nasty!"

"Yep, and thereon hinged the future of this great nation," I said, mimicking an irritating history teacher that used to work with us and spoke a different language.

Anna laughed, let go of me and wandered off, probably in the direction of the fleeing Harold. Her jeans were quite tight around her bum, a bum that I knew from pretty much every conceivable angle, but today it looked different, belonged to somebody else, it seemed. The curve of the glutinous maximus was gone, there being little definite shape to the cheeks, and the whole bottom seemed to sag into the upper leg without any real definition at all. My goodness, did it always look like that? It struck me, quite vividly, as resembling a baby elephant waddling after her mother along a narrow pathway in the riverine jungle of North Kenya; an odd analogy, I know, but that National Geographic picture seemed to snap its negative over the image in front of me today and it was a perfect match. How strange, and as she walked away all I could see was that sweet little elephant wandering into the thick bush. And right there, on that spot, my mind assassinated the sexual image of Anna, quite brutally, and I didn't think I could see her naked in quite the same way ever again.

Spring slowly, imperceptibly, turned into summer, the bluebells wilting and the dandelion seeds filling the air, and Anna and I continued as before. Our anniversary of the coupling in Wales passed without much celebration but we happily muddled towards mid-summer.

***

140

On that beautiful sunny summer's morning, the slaughter of the cows a distant low, we lay together. I touched her slender left shoulder and felt the wonderfully smooth, baby-bottom skin, carefully nurtured to feel this way by bottles of moisturiser that she would unpack from her bag on the occasional days that she stayed over, less now than in the depths of winter. Her hair was short, not long and silken as it was when we first met, when I fell for her. I'm not sure I liked it, or the significance of the recent cut. She had told me on our very first field trip together that she grew her hair long when happy but always had a drastically short cut when insecure or a great change was pending. Well, perhaps I was the guilty party here and my indecision the catalyst, but it still unsettled me nonetheless.

I touched her hair, lightly, and pushed a wayward clump of strands behind that beautifully elfin ear and leant in close to kiss her on the cheek, the heat and warmth that the snug of her sleep produced radiating on to my lips, and I just watched, waiting for that 'Emily' moment: a song that made me happy, made me believe that this is how love should feel 'For Emily, wherever I may find her' by Simon and Garfunkel played in my head. But I didn't love her any more, despite wanting to and Anna must have known this.

And with Wimbledon came the rain and the monsoon and the grey clouds that pushed down on our heads left a heavy heart, and it unsettled us both.

Chapter 9

Losing momentum and sinking

Sometime in the night, in amongst the sex, the doldrums, the fear and the deep sleep, I had made a decision: a definite. Anna slept next to me, a rare incursion into my night-time world these days, and the sun was trying hard to burn away the clouds, although it was still too early to get up.

Merlin had been in touch more regularly recently, bombarding me with more locations for my skimming travelogue. This had now become my definite and somehow, someday, I would have to break the news to Anna and to Phil that, come January, I would be packing my bags and be taking leave of them, the house, the school and my odd, confusing little life here.

I hadn't planned on waiting quite this long, but once we'd returned from camping in France for our summer holiday, (a pleasant time was had by all) I had decided that it was now or never – Anna had to know, but how the hell was I going to tell her?

We took a few days off from each other, pottering around at home catching up with the mundane, and met again at Bluewater for a spot of shopping to blow away the 'back-to-school' blues, and maybe a trip to the flicks.

I was there early, nervous about the forthcoming revelations, as today would be the day, and took a turn around Waterstones where I bought a guide to tramping in New Zealand. Across the wide and naturally-lit boulevard of the upper-floor from the bookshop, was Starbucks coffee house, its open-windowed frontage a favourite people watching spot of ours, and a tanned Anna sat in her usual seat watching the throngs until she caught me looking across at her. A sweet smile lit up her face and I was soon sitting down and sipping a frothy latte.

"Hi, kiddo."

"Hi. What you bought then?"

Bugger. Straight to it. No messing. I passed the black plastic bag, gold-printed lettering of Waterstones adorning it, and waited.

"Oh. Present for someone? Who's going there then?"

I went straight for the kill. No use dwelling on it. I pointed at myself, somewhat awkwardly.

"Hey?" She looked genuinely puzzled. "You?" she asked after a brief pause.

"Um… yep."

"Oh."

She looked at the book, opened it and gave a cursory flick through the pages, stopping at the occasional colour picture, using the time to factor a coherent response, I supposed. I said nothing, not because I was too cowardly to do so, but I just couldn't figure out what to say. What could I say?

"When?"

"Um, January I think."

"Hey?" It took a little while to sink in that this meant leaving school, leaving her.

"January?"

"Yep."

"That means you're leaving school then?"

"Uh, yeah, I suppose it does."

"What the f…" Her sentence fizzled into a difficult silence.

"Look, Anna, this isn't definite. It's just an idea that has kind of grown over the last few months."

"Few months! And you didn't think about possibly mentioning it to me?"

"Well, yes, of course."

"When?"

"Well, now, I suppose."

"Only because I bloody found out!"

"No, no, I was going to talk to you about it anyway."

I wasn't sure if we were having a very loud conversation or whether this looked like a heated argument or not. It shouldn't matter, should it, what people think of us at such an important, life-defining moment, but it did of course. I looked around awkwardly, shuffled my bum cheeks to move closer so as to be a little less loud.

"I was going to talk to you about it today."

"You were." She didn't look convinced.

"Yes, honestly." I placed my hand on hers as a confirmation of my probity. I continued, "And I wanted to discuss what it would mean to…" I didn't know how to finish the sentence.

It was her turn to shuffle on those elephant cheeks, but away from me, and she removed her hand from under mine; for a split second it looked as though she was going to slap it back down, like in the game, the name of which I don't think I ever knew, it hovering there, ready to play or possibly slap or retreat. It did the last of the three and she put it under her thigh, a childish act of security at a very insecure moment.

"Are you gonna ask me to go with you?" I think she already knew the answer but wanted me to suffer, quite rightly.

"Of course I thought about it, but…"

"But you didn't want me to."

"Yes, no, oh, I don't know. I just wanted to do the travel thing before I'm too old to want to do it. Everyone I know has already done the gap year thing, you included, and the more I thought about it, the more it seemed the right thing to do…the right time."

"The right time!" she said, a clear tone of incredulity this time. "The right time! What about us, you little fuckwit!" It had taken longer than expected but we had reached the vitriolic stage. "Well, what about us?" She didn't give me a chance to reply; maybe it was rhetorical. "You want me to wait?" She made an odd, guffawing, 'grumpfy' sound that suggested she wouldn't be cheapened by that thought; she wouldn't wait. "That's just very bloody good of you, isn't it?" Still rhetorical, she continued almost without a breath. "Go off swanning around the bloody world, skimming yer fucking stones and shagging around, no doubt, and then expect to run back into my arms. Fuck off!"

I had a chance to speak now. She expected me to but I genuinely could not find a response, the correct words.

"Speak, shit boy! I'm not playing the doting fool, waiting for her master to return, so, the logical conclusion is that this is, as you so drolly put it," (and then she did the dreaded, awful, speech marks with her fingers), " 'the permanent chuck scenario'." A pause.

"What do you want me to say?" she asked. I really was very confused over the status of these questions.

"Oh, I don't know, Anna. It's shit, I know, I'm sorry."

"Do you want me to say that I love you, beg you to stay, to marry you?"

"I…"

She interrupted. "Well, I do fucking love you, fucking loads and I do want you to stay with me. There, said it."

We both sat silently, shattered by the intensity of the conversation. She leant forward and put her hand on mine this time.

"Shit, Steve, maybe I haven't shown you enough that I do love you. I always said it was the other way around, but maybe I'm just as culpable?"

"No, no, look, Anna. I'm just a confused idiot. I'm so sorry. It's crap."

This was either tragically sad, or an incredibly clever twist on events to make me shrivel with guilt. Anna was now doubting herself and it killed me to see her question her role in our failing relationship but...but it wasn't all my fault. The inconsistencies sprang from both of us, so I should not take all of the guilt on board –just the main body of it.

So, this odd couple, these young lovers who had taken so long to come together, held each other from falling apart and continued to gaffer tape the cracks into autumn. We didn't, bizarrely enough, finish with each other. In fact, the autumn turned out to be rather melancholically beautiful, and it harboured some of my fondest memories of Anna. Meanwhile, I arranged the sale of the house, easier and quicker than I had ever imagined. Phil and his Barbies found lodgings near his chubby office-clerk girlfriend and I began to book flights, hotels and excursions for my trip of a lifetime.

Leaving school was surprisingly easy too, my resignation accepted with a terse reference to career suicide from the deputy head with no solid offer of an official sabbatical and the same position on my return. Nevertheless, I was given an excellent send off from teaching staff at the local Wetherspoon's, attended by some sixth-formers who drank along with us, and I nursed a heavy head at Anna's, both of us becoming more and more aware of the days, and more importantly, nights, ticking away. We made love with a greater intensity, almost desperation, in the knowledge that, more likely than not, we wouldn't be together on my return. I guess my selfish act did not deserve such loyalty.

My inconsistencies and indecisiveness made perfect sense to me, the change of emotion and desire as natural a phenomenon as the changing tide, but to Anna and those in her world it just seemed cruel and careless, thoughtless and heartless. I seemed to them, at least, the very embodiment of a commitment-phobic man, and they urged her to see the light and push me away. But she couldn't because she loved me, and in amongst this maelstrom of thoughts, I loved her too; I just couldn't rationalise it enough to give it form, give it a body I could hold on to, cling to for salvation in this drifting current of life.

I did, of course, think of her and our future a lot and I did admit to myself that this was love of a fashion, or at least a fashion I had not experienced before, but not enough, not quite enough. Christmas came and went, as did we, and the day of departure dawned, or tried to.

Anna dropped me off at Heathrow airport at seven thirty a.m. and went to find a place to park whilst I checked in. It was dark, that mid-winter black that forbids the day to begin, holds the sun to ransom and demands melancholy. It was mild for the time of year, perhaps topping ten degrees, but a stiff so' westerly brought horizontal rain that lashed against the Terminal 4 windows like a car wash on a windscreen.

Gradually and begrudgingly, the black gave way to the faint grey of dawn and we were hugging goodbye at passport control. I had a lump in my throat, partly out of trepidation for the monumental change I had imposed upon my life, and partly because I felt for her, the time she'd invested in me and hoping that we'd maybe settle down and start a family. She hadn't expected this; that instead of packing up and moving in with her to start the rest of our new lives together, I'd was packing up and heading off to the sun, following a childhood dream of seeing the world, skimming the world and hopefully included amongst the wonders I'd see, I'd come across myself and get to know and like me and then, if all was well and good, I'd fall into the arms of the most beautiful woman in the world in the most beautiful place in the world.

That's why I was close to tears as she pushed a letter into my hands and told me not to open it until I was on the plane, and then, opening up my sweaty palm, placed the heart-shaped stone that I gave her in the middle and enclosed her fingers around mine.

"Look after this for me, will you?" she said.

Reluctant, excited, terrified, hopeful and tired, I kissed her goodbye and headed on through the passport control gate. I saw lovers and husbands and wives and children all saying hello and goodbye and felt the thrill of moving on that airports always give me.

I sat on the plane as the day tried hard to dawn through the thick, grey, ugly clouds and we were delayed for over an hour as the vicious wind refused to let me leave and forget all the adult decisions that I'd avoided for so many years. Eventually, Mother Nature eased and let me enjoy a still rather scary take-off, a gentle reminder perhaps that life was not that easy and that these insecurities may still be waiting for me on my return, but somewhere above Belgium we reached the sunshine.

Part 2

In search of the perfect skim; the perfect something

Chapter 1

There are unlimited frontiers yet

The skimming route had brought me first to the North Island, New Zealand and the busy tourist (well, as busy as it gets here, that is) haven of the Bay of Islands and the hub town of Paihia. Was it sad that a man of my age was waiting on the quay, scanning the incoming crowd for a pretty face, like a hormone-crazed teenager standing in the kitchen door at a party watching the pretty fresh-faced arrivals for the one he would attempt to snog? Maybe this was the problem: the boundless opportunities of youth; the unlimited frontiers that you sadly do not appreciate at the time disappear once in your thirties, but my heart still lived there, and every day since leaving I hoped for a new adventure, a fresh face and possibly a brand new love to worry about. It was becoming an addiction.

Along the pier came a short, full-figured, blonde, shoulder-length haired and hazel-eyed young lady. Her ample breasts lay comfortably in a bikini top with a thin, cotton shirt over them, but unbuttoned enough for keen eyes to notice. She smiled a sweet smile at the waiting couples and looked past me to the yacht, the Gungha II, which would be our vehicle for the day. We'd both booked a day of sailing in the Bay of Islands and the sun graced us with its presence, intermittently between the fair-weather cumulus clouds. However, although they skipped by gently on the upper winds, not a puff, not even a breeze was discernible at sea level: and so, our sailing became a gentle motor around the bay and all we could do was laze and chat on deck and just enjoy the scenery and the surreal realisation that this was the beginning of a fantastic adventure on the other side of the world.

For indeed, as we chatted and got to know each other, I discovered that Elaine too was on a sabbatical, albeit shorter than mine, was also at the beginning, and planning to take in both the North and South Island, though I doubted skimming stones was one of her motivations. She was rather jolly, her eyes quite entrancing, and occasionally, when the sun shone through and it warmed up, she would remove her chemise and sunbathe on deck, those pale-white, delicate, but slightly stubby fingers pushing her blonde waves behind those pretty little ears and closing her eyes, face angled to the sun, resting now on her elbows, and without her knowing I could gaze upon her slim waist, ample breasts and contemplate a future love affair. Unlike many friends, I always had the skill of looking at girls discreetly, so was safe in my maritime voyeurism.

The longer spell of sunshine gave me the opportunity to put my new acquaintance into perspective and, although quite pretty, I'd decided that she was, facially, just a little too similar to an irritating former colleague, so I put the love affair on hold and decided to just enjoy her pleasant, upbeat company: let's face it, I could do with that. Anyway, deep down I still harboured thoughts for Anna and hoped to find my way back to her at some point in the future.

She was quite the mermaid, Elaine, and after having had to swim back to Gungha II from a small island, and not having the least bit of energy to return to the water, Elaine looked after me touchingly on a thirty-minute enforced group snorkel. She could sense my distress and unease at this point and expertly guided me through the basics of not drowning and, although my mask leaked and snorkel inhaled almost as much seawater as air, I managed to actually enjoy myself in spotting the odd fish.

Elaine was a diver, a former junior international swimmer, and I think quite liked my incompetence off terra firma. She was easy to talk to and I soon discovered was open to gentle ribbing and our safe and comfortable friendship began the way it would always be – we were easy company for each other and it suited both our travel personas: thirty-something, unsettled, still searching and, although adventurous in the soul, a little reluctant to just let go and wholly embrace the experience.

The day trip lasted around nine hours and we clocked up an impressive fifteen minutes of actual sailing time. On our return to the quay at Paihia, we stopped to watch a local big-game fishing competition returning with their spoils, witnessing a surprised and chuffed teenager take the first prize having landed a huge blue marlin that was winched way above his head for the weigh in, the applause and the mantelpiece photo.

At the pier café we sat and had a beer and realised that although we'd chatted the entire trip we knew virtually nothing about each other. After an hour we parted, she to the horrendous hostel that I'd left the day before and me to my decadent double at the Mousetrap, agreeing to meet later in the evening to go along to the karaoke bar with her fellow Magic Bus tour buddies. Great! A week on the road and at last I was making friends. Maybe this travel lark wasn't going to be so bad after all.

The bizarre little group that gathered in the student union-type bar that so represented the scene here watched and sang along to the karaoke but none dared to volunteer and in the early hours we wandered back to our respective digs. Elaine, Sian and I walked the stunning Australian, Angie, back to the most isolated of the hostels, affording us rare glimpses of the southern night sky away from the town lights, and strolling back to the centre I caught my first glimpse of the iconic Southern Cross.

Sian and Elaine were off to Rotorua, via Auckland, on the Magic Bus (a cheap touring option), which was a two-day journey. On telling them that I planned to go there next myself but as I had a car would do it in just one day, they asked if they could join me. They did, and the very next morning the three of us headed south on a warm and sunny New Zealand summer's day and my adventure was born.

Sian was eighteen, just out of school, and as we chatted along the road south she sat in the back, Elaine next to me in the front, and we felt like two parents touring with their eldest, especially when the conversation turned to music, film, TV and other such cultural references that emphasised the gap in years between us.

Rotorua was warm, sunny and smelly, the sulphur that emanated from the cracks and fissures in the splitting ground beneath the dominant memory. I saw the girls occasionally once we were camped in the grounds of the youth hostel, all of us drifting off into separate activities that these backpacking honeypot towns demand you do. But I found myself spending more and more time with Elaine, sharing a hot tub in the posh spa in town along with two elderly New York Italian, American ex-gangsters. We laughed at their stereotypical phrases and stories of fifties life in the Big Apple, but I found I could not take my eyes off this Irish beauty, the water bubbling up around her armpits and across those white and fulsome breasts. Sitting here, slowly cooking, and turning an unhealthy shade of crimson, Anna and North Kent seemed a long, long way away.

I made friends with a Viking of an Argentinean called Martin, a tent neighbour of mine, a blond giant who spoke immaculate English and who introduced me to the fine art of drinking 'mate' tea, a south American delicacy: a smoked tobacco, green-tea flavoured infusion drunk through a bong-like pipe placed into the mash of tea in an ethnic gourd. It was a wonderfully charming etiquette-filled ceremonial experience, always passing it to the right, always sharing it and everyone else's cold sores. As we talked, this 'Porteño' (resident of Buenos Aires) charmed his way into my plans, both keen to trek some of the Great Walks of this beautiful land and both, bizarrely, sharing a passion for skimming; he'd even read some of the same, sad blogs as me and we both hoped to experience some sublime skimming locations.

Elaine and Sian took the Magic Bus tour to Taupo and I gave my new buddy Martin a lift to the same city, planning to meet up with the girls at a youth hostel there. We took the attractive Route 5, skirting the Paeroa Range and hit the lakeside resort, again home to countless backpackers and thrill-seekers, many planning to throw themselves out of a plane and skydive down into this ancient and still-steaming volcanic landscape, but most to trek across and around the active Mount Tongariro in its eponymous National Park. Having arrived before the girls, we set up camp in the small grounds and donned our walking boots, planning an amble along the Waikato River all the way to the spectacular Huka Falls.

We walked out of town, which didn't take long in a settlement of twenty thousand or so folks, across the parkland of Taupo Domain and onto Spa Road, and then followed the river all the way to the footbridge to Cherry Island at the beginning of a large meander. The river wandered through spectacular scenery here, high sandstone cliffs to our right where a rickety metal platform housed the ubiquitous Kiwi bungee jump that plunged reckless fools one hundred and fifty feet towards the emerald-coloured river below. We had to climb up to it to access the next part of the river path and watched a rather nervous Scandinavian throw himself into the river on the end of a large rubber band, a quicker way to the water than our ascent from it, that's for sure. Soon enough, we were past the last of the houses in the small suburbs and into true, verdant North Island countryside. The river that gushed out of the huge lake was a beautiful emerald green and we stopped on occasions to take tourist photos perched precariously on overhanging trunks and branches.

At a wide bend, an untidy tributary of small falls emptied into the river and in amongst its pools were groups of people bathing. The steam that rose indicated that this must have been the famous 'Hot Water Springs'. The quiet babble of the brooks mingled with the babble of the bathers and it couldn't have been a more serene place.

"I didn't bring my swimming trunks," I told Martin.

"No, me, no as well. But that is not a problem." At this, he skipped off the path and behind a few low boulders and started to undress, save his underpants.

"Come on England!" This wasn't a statement of support for our troubled national football team, but an attempt to cajole me into stripping off too and jumping into the hot springs.

"What the hell," I said and tentatively undressed, leaving just my tatty pants, dark enough not to look too foolish and tiptoed across warm, mossy grass and into the river and the confluence with the springs. It was beautifully warm and an odd sensation with the eddies of the river mixing hot and cold water in a maelstrom around me.

"This is good!" exclaimed my South American friend.

"Yes, it is," I agreed, a grin as wide as the river as I floated atop the warm currents. Looking out across the generous sweep and the gurgling water I started to ponder on the effect of the mixed temperatures on a skimming stone. I stood up, the river reaching to my waste, and felt around with my feet through the silt until I reached a bank of pebbles. I picked up a few, a little rough, but thin and split across a horizontal plane and skipped them through the bend, away from the bathers. They bounced low, but long, and reached nearly across this wide meander.

"Hey, that is good," Martin said.

"Thanks, big man. You want a go?"

"Yes." I passed a stone to him and watched the large arc of his left arm (he was a south paw), the giant swing and the crack of the wrist and his stone skidded out across the Waikato River, five low and fast skips before it buried itself in the far bank.

"Ha, ha! Argentina one, England zero!"

Bugger. This boy was good.

"Well done! Bloody good skimming, young Martin."

"Thank you!" We attempted a high five, but it was pathetic, his hand far too high for me to hit it with any confidence. The next five minutes were spent in an unofficial World Cup of stone skimming, me trying desperately to match the huge Pampas-bred lad. A small crowd from the springs had stopped to watch and were cheering with each stone that hit the far bank and the success rate was fairly even – Martin would be a good skimming buddy.

Two lads approached the river from the footpath and were watching with the bathers. They came over and introduced themselves.

"Hi, mate, good skimming. I'm Dave."

Dave was tall too; a mop of mousy-coloured curls falling out to create ringlets that fell over his eyes like a Dulux dog. He wore a scruffy and holey tee shirt and was slightly grungy in overall demeanour with knee-length board shorts, which were bright orange and straight from a 1950s Hawaiian surfing movie. On his right ankle, clearly visible with his flip-flops, or 'thongs' as the locals amusingly called them, was an odd tattoo, an elaborately decorated 'If'.

We shook hands with Dave, an affable young lad from Plymouth and a bit of an adrenalin junkie on a trip around the world in pursuit of all things scary and potentially lethal. He did, however, love to skim and this most soporific of pastimes followed him wherever he went.

His sidekick was a diminutive teenager from Oslo called Kim. He was a mixed-race Norwegian-Cambodian whose Viking genes came out not in his appearance but in his outlandish and rakish behaviour, pillaging fun and adventure from everything he touched; he was a wild pup of a young man. It soon became clear that they were inseparable and were enjoying the outdoor life that New Zealand offered to the hilt. Kim too loved to skim, as long as he had chanced his life at some point during the day that is.

We chatted a while, sitting in the warm currents caught in the bend of the river and exchanged adventures and dreams, including my desire to pen the essential skimming guide. It all ended with a skim-off, me and Martin against our newest friends and although a close run thing, a final flick of the giant wrist saw the Argentinian's last stone skip off the fast flowing river countless times and, with the last of its kinetic energy, fling itself upon the far bank. Top marks for distance, skips and artistic merit.

"Cool, Martin," offered Kim, his high-pitched voice almost squeaking with delight. It was indeed cool.

Dave stopped, turned slowly towards the hot springs behind, and then threw his arm across the river in a display of biblical theatrics.

"Location Number 1," he preached. "For your skimming book."

He was right – *No. 1 for these travels so far:*

We left the delicious water, braving the cool wind that whipped down the river valley and dried ourselves with the arms of discarded tops and in nature's slow dryer as we wandered downstream towards Huka Falls. We talked more of the book.

"I'd buy it," squeaked Kim.

"I would too, as long as I got a mention," agreed Dave.

We stopped at another wide sweep of this green river, the eddies and currents colliding midstream to create mini-maelstroms that danced in the bright grey light and seemed to bubble with enthusiasm, mirrored by the striplings at my side. I felt the melancholy of age only briefly, dragged along too quickly by their exuberance to dwell on it, and we found ourselves looking onto the river squeezing itself through a tiny gap of tough rock and disappearing beyond.

We heard the falls before we saw them and our two new friends rushed to the edge to see the water fall into the abyss. They ripped off their daypacks, grabbing at something inside. Within seconds they had donned tatty rafting lifejackets and, holding hands, ran off the edge of the path and into the swirling mass of green river and white water, a peppermint mix of pure peril.

"Jesus Christ!"

Martin ran to the edge and looked back at me with a shrug that said they were either dead or the finest fellows you could ever care to meet. I suspected both.

We ran down the path that dropped the five metres of the Huka Falls. Not a great distance to plunge, but looking back at the sheer volume of water that was forced through this tiny gap, I feared for the two fools. And then we saw them, bobbing to the surface way downstream, ripped along fifty metres or so by the fierce current in a matter of seconds.

"Fucking mental," I said to myself, a broad smile greeting their safe return.

A chorus of whoops erupted around the falls, fellow thrill seekers too scared to do what my new pals had just done but appreciative nonetheless. The loudest screech came from the water itself, a tiny, bedraggled Kim flailing his arms to garner enough force to push through the swirls to get out of the worst of the current. He continued to whoop and screech like a howler monkey until he reached the far bank and stood up, arms aloft in a 'Vitruvian Man' celebration. We cheered and applauded and awaited the more measured stroke of Dave to take him ashore too. Once there, the boys hugged and waved across at us and then performed a bizarre dance, obviously practised and causing a chuckle amongst the onlookers this side of the river.

That night we all drank in a crowded pub, jam-packed full of young travellers, and swapped email addresses with promises of reports of decent skimming venues and further meetings along the well-trodden way. Elaine and Sian were there too and, after one beer too many, we all staggered back to the youth hostel, and me to the comfort of my little tent.

This odd mix of travellers dispersed the next day, leaving Martin, me and Elaine to plan a trip across the volcanic hills of the Tongariro National Park: the reason for our trip to the Taupo Domain.

The first day's trek was hard work; we'd over-prepared and therefore over-packed and when I dropped the heavy rucksacks (worn both front and back) at the porch of the Oturere hut my arms seemed to lift and I felt as light as an angel on the wing. Inside the dark hut serious trekkers were lurking in corners, long-since arrived, fed, and settled down regarding us with disdain, the perceived poorly planned, ill-timed interlopers. Regardless, Martin took the hut by storm with his sheer physical presence and charismatic aura. Female eyes seemed to emerge from all corners of the dark room to admire this Adonis.

He cooked an odd meal of congealed spaghetti goo for us all and, as my eyes became accustomed to the gloom, I thought I saw Rachel whispering in a friend's ear and looking over at us from three crowded bunks away. My heart skipped a beat, but common sense told me that it couldn't possibly be her.

I had met Rachel on my very first day of travelling up in Auckland, chatting in a bar as I tried to drink away the jetlag. She was incredibly sweet, saccharine even, as Americans tend to be when on good form and not at home, and her deliciously soft, crisp, melon twang of an accent grown on the liberal streets of Austin, Texas, (a jewel of a city in the most ugly of states) dripped honey into my stale beer. She talked of film and art, books and music and how she had once sung in a mediocre grunge band at the South-by-South West Music Festival. She was cool, as cool as the proverbial cucumber and fitting of the word for one, rare occasion. I'd taken quite a fancy to her on our next day's tour of the city and its environs.

As we finished our food, a familiar figure emerged from the shadows and said, "Hi." It was indeed Rachel, and we chatted a while as the snores began to reverberate around the room. I had already pitched my tent, glad to be away from the sardine tin-packed hut and was to share it with Elaine. Rachel knew this I could tell and although I really wished to be bedding down for the night with her, she assumed I was now with Elaine and excused herself back to the tiny space that was to be her bunk for the night.

Outside, the wind was blowing a gale and on my return to the tent I was met with a brief hail and sleet storm. Inside the canvas home, Elaine and I settled into our bags and subconsciously snuggled together. It was wonderfully cosy and comfortable after the excesses of the day's trek and we lay close together and viewed the photos of the day on our digital cameras.

"I can always swap with Rachel if you like?"

I answered with a quizzical look. "Don't be so daft," I said, "I'm on the walk with you."

"She fancies you."

"Nah, I'm far too old for her."

Elaine didn't respond but her smile told me she was happy that I'd said that. I briefly saw Rachel the next morning, two hours after I'd risen to the most serene and beautiful sunrise and scampered around the camp taking a million photos, showering in a nearby waterfall and beginning to fall in love with life at last. She'd breakfasted inside and emerged hobbling and grim-faced into the sunshine to tell of knee injuries threatening the success of their group's trek. We parted on terse terms, her glaring towards the tent and my still-sleeping camp buddy. It seemed as though she did like me after all and was a little perturbed at my arrangements with Elaine, though on reflection I'm sure the swollen knee was the root of the poor mood.

Last off on the trek from the hut, we enjoyed a gloriously clear day across the Tongariro crater, most of which I spent chatting to the boy Martin. The long descent brought us to the Mangetopopo hut by four in the afternoon and we lazed around the camp enjoying the occasional sunbursts through the cloud-clad volcanic peaks and bathing in the nearby stream, putting thoughts of exotic parasites aside to wallow in the cool and refreshing waters. Elaine was first in the brook, but we gentlemanly kept away until she had returned.

This hut, only three hours from the end of the trek, was relatively empty, the busy tourists keen to get back to Whakapapa and move on, but we still decided to camp out, buoyed on by our surprisingly comfortable night, and maybe buoyed on by the ease and pleasure of our thirty-something company.

That night the heavens opened and we watched the slideshows from my camera to the cosy sound of the whipping wind through the guy ropes and lashing rain on the canvas. The faithful old tent emerged to a bright dawn undamaged, much to the chagrin of the technically superior Americans and their super-deluxe dome two-man effort that flooded out at three in the morning.

The short trek back to the car was quiet and through uninspiring gorse and thick heather-like vegetation that obscured, for the most part, the views of the Tongariro, Nguaruhoe and Ruapehu volcanic peaks. As we reached the safety of the car park the rain came down heavily again and we quickly packed and drove off to nearby Turangi.

The recent poor weather had driven the majority of the trekkers from the hills to take refuge in town and we consequently found it very hard to find accommodation in this Tongariro base town. We let Martin take the last of the dorm beds available in the industrial-sized hostel as he was on a tighter budget than us, and eventually found a twin room on the edge of town in an ostensibly English-style bed and breakfast stuck in the body of an American motel.

A well-earned fish-and-chip supper was shared with Martin at the hostel, attractive gap-yearers giggling behind dorm doors that would open a little so they could gaze out at this cool, tall, long blond haired hunk sitting with seemingly middle-aged friends and drinking a strange brew from an odd contraption, the 'mate' I had come to really quite enjoy.

We left him early to chat with his fan club, promising a seven thirty a.m. pick up to drop him off at the edge of town so he could hitch a ride on the main road to Wellington, and returned to our schizophrenic hotel, taking long showers, reading and chatting sleepily into the early night that felt more like three in the morning to the both of us. The conversation was lazy, speech-slurred, slumbering and dreamy and the defence that Elaine had so stoically kept up dropped and she began to talk freely about her emotions and past loves. Somewhere around eleven o'clock we both fell asleep, tired, sleepy conversation having flirted dangerously close to attraction. At a critical point she had fallen silent, so I drifted off with a newly considered interest in my pretty little friend. The door had been opened, along with my mind, and I considered how comfortable this all felt, how unusual too, how bloody adventurous the whole thing was, and suddenly Elaine was encamped in my mind in first place, and Anna and Rachel had taken a back seat.

The morning brought more rain and an unease that had dissipated itself by the time we had picked up Martin and began to search for breakfast in sleepy Turangi. We sat outside the one bakery of this one-horse-town and ate traditional meat pies whilst waiting for Martin to return from the bank.

And there she sat, my soft-accented, soft-voiced, soft-faced Irish friend, chomping on her pie in a restless manner. I was going east to Napier and she…? I wasn't sure. I knew that Wellington was her eventual destination but Elaine was showing signs of reluctance to follow the big man to the edge of town and had already missed the daily Magic Bus south. So she timidly asked if I'd mind if she hung around with my throaty car and me for another couple of days. I didn't, and wondered whether the weekend jaunt to the coast might turn out to be a romantic seaside getaway. I wondered whether she was wondering this too.

***

By chance, we happened upon a great deal at the Napier Tourist Office – a lovely pseudo Art-Deco building not long constructed on the sea front with bright, beautiful, sparkling sunlight bathing every corner of the well-designed building – an apartment, two rooms, bathroom, DVD and washing machine, for two nights and the same price as a double in a hostel. We guessed it wouldn't be as nice as it sounded in the blurb as the taxi pulled up outside. It was a pleasant suburban street, road impossibly wide as if expecting the next great quake to rip it up, swallow half of it and still leave enough tar-macadam for two-way traffic. The tatty floodlights of the regional cricket ground loomed above and the taxi man told us that it lay just behind our accommodation.

"Could watch a game from your bedroom window, I bet."

His love of cricket wasn't shared by either of us, though I had enjoyed the odd staff game in the sunshine and watched England for two days at the Oval.

The landlady met us out the back and led us up a metal fire escape to a freshly painted, sky-blue door. She gave us a cursory tour of the apartment and we just couldn't believe our luck; it was beautifully bright, clean, modern, large and incredibly comfortable. A huge double bed dominated the open-plan design and an offset room through an arch housed a futon; my bed, I guessed, thinking of the gentlemanly thing to do.

It was a ten-minute stroll into town and the hub of activity around Emerson and Tennyson Streets. We wandered idly and came across a coffee shop off Tennyson and ordered the ubiquitous skinny flat white, New

159

Zealand's version of a latte. Oddly, our landlady served us, a big, broad, beaming grin to go with her big, broad body. She told us that it was her husband who owned the pleasant café. We drank and chatted at a table on the pavement and watched the world go by.

"So, Steve, what ya gonna do wit yer life?" She did have a wonderfully soft, Dublin accent.

"That's an easy one," I said, shuffling my bum cheeks on the hard seat, reminding myself of when I last sat with a pretty girl at a coffee table and did this; a wistful wave of Anna broke over me and was soon gone.

"Well, any ideas there – at least a dream anyhow?"

"Hmm, a dream job perhaps? Apart from being a professional footballer and playing in Rome, living in a villa in the hills, owning a yacht et cetera?"

"Well, yeah, apart from that, yer numpty."

"Dunno. I really quite fancy the idea of being a writer." A confession I didn't admit to lightly. I waited for the giggle; the jokey put down I'd come to expect from Elaine these past ten days.

"Cool, that sounds cool."

And it did, but required a fair amount of talent, measured with a fair dash of luck, no doubt. And doubt stopped me from seriously following this dream.

"What about you?" I asked, quickly turning the table on her.

"Oh Jeez, I dunno. I haven't a clue. Maybe open up a shop like yer man here."

"That would be great. A nice coffee shop, full of books and newspapers."

"Yeah, that'll do me." She smiled, the sun smiled, the whole fucking universe smiled.

"Elaine?"

"Yeah?"

"Do you skim?"

"Do what?"

"Skim stones?"

"Do what with stones?" She looked cute when concentrating, a confusion knitting her brow.

"You know," and I mimicked the action across the table, almost spilling my half empty cup in the process.

"Oh… we call it skiffing in Ireland."

"Oh, right, I didn't know that. Anyway, do you?"

"Doesn't everybody?"

"Yeah… yeah, I suppose." I left it at that for now, not wanting to freak her out with my skimming obsession quite yet.

The rest of the sun-shiny day we pottered around, making the most of the free washing facilities, a rare luxury on the road, and I went for a run along Marine Parade, weaving in and out of the occasional in-line skaters, forever looking to the east and the beach, grains of sand just a little too big and coarse to be beautiful, and then on to the dreamy Pacific Ocean, that wondrous bit of sea that covers one third of the planet's surface. Wow, what a view.

Elaine had indeed camped herself in the main living room-cum-bedroom and I had the kitchenette with the futon and the toilet, but still far better than a sweaty, smelly and noisy dorm. We showered and dressed, a drill in travelling that assured a very non-sexual routine, avoiding each other in towels, though as she wafted past, that clean, crisp, newly scrubbed scent caught my attention and I didn't need to look. The chemicals that fizzed in the air between us had been charged and I knew, we knew, that the tender night's ramble in Turangi was to come to its logical sexual conclusion quite soon. I awaited it with happy, fucking-magnificent and free-spirited enthusiasm. The sun took an age to set behind this east-facing town and we found ourselves sitting outside the Grumpy Mole Saloon. It was hard to imagine a night-shrouded, wind-chilled Britain from here and the memories of home lost their magnetic attraction by the hour.

Elaine was not a heavy drinker, not even much of a social one, but didn't mind me quaffing the few beers to her one as we chatted idly of life and dreams and future travel plans. We wondered on the whereabouts of Martin and what ridiculously lucky young adventure he had happened upon by now. As dusk turned into night we strolled the ten minutes home, occasionally bumping into each other along the uneven and unlit pavements subtly pushed out of shape and line by the huge tectonic forces at work way beneath our feet that kept the denizens of this fair city in a constant state of subconscious angst.

We chatted through the archway until sleep took us, her first and then me, almost, until a strange sensation came over me. It shook me from the nether world of dozing, just before deep sleep, enough for me to wake and look at the digital clock on the electric cooker – 12.05 a.m. I had imagined the bed shaking in my dreamy slumber, thinking Elaine had walked across the mattress to get to the loo, but she still lay asleep next door. A quake perhaps, in this most seismically active of places? I laughed inwardly at the thoughts of sleeping with Elaine and asking if the earth had moved for her.

Whilst brushing her teeth in the loo next morning, me still lying in bed and reading, I asked if she had felt the quake.

"Fuck off, there was not!" she said.

"There was, honest to God, cross my heart." I did, dropping the thriller I'd been picking through, signalling time to get up. "I'm off for a run. You coming?"

"Fuck off!" Again.

"Charming."

"Yeah, don't ya just know it."

I liked Elaine, very much indeed.

In the afternoon, we'd booked ourselves on a wine tour in the surrounding vineyards and wineries of Hawkes Bay. The Sileni Estate showed us the best of its Chardonnay and Cabernet Sauvignon, the three stereotypical Essex girls with us on the half-full minibus downing the butter-sweet white like it was a bottle of pop; still, they were fun.

The weather was overcast, a dull light penetrating every corner of the day and we toured the low-rolling and geologically-new hills of this verdant wine country, well-suited to viticulture in the dry rain shadow of the volcanic mountains to the west. By three thirty p.m. we were all quite drunk, the girls and I, Elaine even, and the odd trans-global alliance of Canadians and Swiss. We were dropped off in the afterglow of five wineries and an all-too sickly aftertaste of good, but predominantly white, wines. The alcoholic breeze threw us on to the big double bed in the living room to snooze the late afternoon away.

Both lying on our stomachs, the afternoon sank into evening, the quality of light not changing a dot, still some hours from sunset at this time of year. I put my left arm over Elaine, across the small of her back, almost unaware that I had done so. It usually took a girl throwing herself naked at me to realise that I was in with a chance, so this was forward stuff. My heart beat faster, louder, so strongly in fact that it seemed to shake the bed to its rhythm.

She didn't react, neither a good nor a bad sign. I found the exposed skin at the bottom of her short tee shirt and stroked my thumb across her nascent love handles; she didn't stop me. My whole hand began to move across the small of her back, strong in muscle, yet soft in its skin complexion. I attempted a squeeze that morphed into a massage, my hand clumsily moving across and up her back, focusing its soft squeezes along the spine. I skipped over the bra strap and onto the shoulders and neck. My arm ached already, but the promising situation gave me a desire to continue despite the pain. She reacted to my neck massage, moving slightly nearer in a quick jump to allow me more purchase. This soft and intimate game continued awhile, my hand pushing further down the top of her bum and to the elastic of her knickers, and then the fingers slid underneath towards the flesh of the cheeks themselves. Still she didn't stop me, choosing the comatose snoozing position she had remained in for some time as a safe a place as any to experience this man and his wandering hands; she curiously awaited the next move.

My hand came out of the knickers and across the whole of her wonderfully full but firm buttocks and squeezed down into the crack at the top of her legs through the fabric of her shorts. She let out a small groan but didn't stop me so encouraged, I continued and upped the ante of the game; it was becoming serious.

Back across to the neck and the spine and this time I stopped at the bra, deftly pinging it open and massaging the back for a few seconds before venturing to the ribs and underneath to hold her left breast in a full grip. She moved a little, raising herself so I could access it and I played with her nipple, teasing it until it became hard and impressively large in my hand. I moved back down the body and quickly underneath her pants and played across the whole of her glorious bum and pushed further down as far as I could towards her crotch.

She was wearing white cotton shorts, so I took my hand to her legs and up into the crotch under the opening at the turn-up of the left leg of the shorts to gain enough access to push the knickers away from her lips and slid two fingers across her now wet crotch. I found her clitoris and attempted to play with it. At this, she gasped and moved abruptly away. Either I had gone way too far or she was an incredibly sensitive girl.

"Sorry," she said, "just be gentle."

My God: a carte blanche to explore. This was turning into a glorious sunshiny afternoon as dusk began to settle a fine, oily-grey on top of the bright grey of the day. I played with her left breast again, my arm as extended as it could be and then down to the shorts again. I took my fingers underneath and to the button of the shorts that popped open easily and I pulled the zip apart. I pushed the shorts off her buttocks and prised the skimpy pants off her until they came to a halt at the top of her thighs, leaving plenty of room for me to play with her, in and out and around.

My hand became wet quite soon and the creamy, wet texture that stuck to my fingers was rubbed across her bum and back, breasts and sheets. I had an incredibly hard penis, now very wet with excitement and still I continued to play until eventually she came, gasping into the pillow.

As she excused herself to the go to the toilet for an overdue wee, I sniffed my fingers and gulped in the scent, the sweet, intoxicating smell of sex and another new, exciting, beautiful lover. Anna was watching me but I chose to ignore her; it was for the best.

We opened a bottle of the Cabernet Sauvignon from the Sileni Estate and enjoyed its crisp palate and sweet volcanic tang; it helped wash down the pizza we cooked in the kitchenette. The DVD player buzzed with The Whale Rider, a feel-good Kiwi movie that explored the Maori legacy and the connection with nature that we seem to lose by the minute. It was a fillip to keep us going toward the whale-watching shores of Kaikoura in the south. I'd be there in ten days or so, a little later than Elaine whose sojourn around this fine land was shorter than mine and so, her tour would be fast-tracked.

We mixed the wine with some bottles of beer, a confused order that left us feeling a little queer. We watched the end of the movie from bed, the finale drifting into our beginning, and in the faint light of the street lamp that diffused its greyness through the kitchenette window, we made love, her on top of me and it was easy and special and close and intense, and a flame had been lit inside us both that would not blow out for a while, we were sure.

The morning was slightly awkward, as it can be when seeing a new lover in a new light and breathing in the enormity of your union the night before. On her return from the loo we made love again, this time more functional, me on top and withdrawing just before I came across her white, soft belly. Like foolish teenagers we'd not talked of safety, of contraception, so I took it upon myself to not come inside; she didn't seem bothered at all, my assumption being that she was protected, though her Irish Catholicism left an air of suspicion that this withdrawal was our safety-valve. What did that website say that I looked at with the kids whilst studying AS Level Population – 60% success rate with withdrawal? Hmm… silly boy.

We breakfasted in the landlady's café with gooey pastries and strong, hot coffee – destination: Wellington.

The clouds had drawn in overnight, filling the sky with a melancholy that couldn't get inside my head – not today. The drive was fairly short, easy in amongst traffic as light as a feather whilst navigating through towns and villages and hamlets unchanged from the pioneer days it seemed. At Shannon we stopped at the sweetest tea house and just enjoyed each other's tender post-coital company, an unspoken understanding in a new relationship that saw us dance in a courtship akin to the albatross that I hoped to see on my way south. As I pondered this careful, choreographed movement around and in amongst each other, I thought of those beautiful white birds and their tendency for monogamy, a trait I envied. I thought briefly of Anna, her naked body on mine, her sweet smile, her smell and I looked at Elaine. Pretty, but not as pretty, charming but not as engaging, but you know, something about the freedom that had brought us here made me gladder than was possible to be next to her, right now, right here.

Wellington was busy; well, compared to the rest of the country that is, and we found ourselves a small and sterile double room in a small and sterile downtown hotel, just off Dixon Street. Elaine would be going south a day before me to embark on her whirlwind tour, and my leisurely skimming search would see us skip into each other again in Christchurch, two weeks from now. So we spent the last day-and-a-half together determined to make the most of our newfound, brazen love. It had not been planned, it was more intense than expected and incredibly sweet, but the transient nature of travel meant that neither of us really thought we'd still feel this way in fourteen days' time. I hoped we would as I entered her again, unprotected, on top of her and those starch-hard sheets. As we lay there afterwards, too happy to clean up the mess on her stomach, flank and sheets, I briefly thought of Anna and compared these two moments; only thing was, that they didn't compare at all. Those Anna days were tense and stressful and dominated by real life and by work and the shitty world that we lived in.

We strolled the central streets and plazas of Wakefield Street, Courtenay Place and Manners Street in amongst the few tower blocks that dared to reach up into these southern skies, stripped bare of ozone, but today blue and open and wide and inviting. It was a café and park day, drinking and eating al-fresco and rambling around the slopes and green spaces of Kelburn Park and the Botanic Gardens, hugging the hills that dominate the city and dropping their unusual and exotic species across walls and paths that wind down towards the sea front.

As evening approached, the keen wind brought in the clouds from the Pacific, at first, light and fluffy and malleable enough to invent fantasy shapes and stories from, but later, dark and low and skipping along on the breeze in this most windy of cities. We wandered the empty halls of the impressive Te Papa Museum, the last of the punters to leave, and were blown along the waterfront, leaning into the wild wind and dodging the spray of giant rollers that crashed against the riprap along the shore. We took refuge in a posh fish-and-chip eatery, seemingly the only customers in this part of town.

The hotel room welcomed us back out of the wind and now spitting rain, and we made love again on top of the sheets in the shadows of the flickering satellite TV. It was intense and dangerous and we came together, and every single minute I spent in the company of Elaine found me sinking deeper into her arms, metaphorically and literally as I buried myself into her. How could it be that I was feeling this way again so soon after Anna? Had I really rid myself of her, a love that had ripped at my very core at times? Was this a holiday romance, or was I just the endless wanderer, the nomad of love that Merlin had so perceptively noticed?

We made love again in the morning, if not at least we made a deepening fondness. It would be our last day together, Elaine catching the evening ferry to the South Island to join up with another Magic Bus tour, so we just enjoyed each other, breakfasting downtown in a cool coffee shop, reading the international papers to catch up on world events and Europe's latest winter storm; a nice dose of Schadenfreude.

The weather was dull; it was windy again and the clouds skipped by on a keen breeze, so low that we could almost touch them if we stretched our arms up towards the antique cranes on the harbour front. Manufactured by Stothart and Pitt of Bath, as it stated on the plaque at the base of these two cranes, a lump of nostalgia stuck in my throat recalling the company name where Mum and Dad had worked in their late teens, fell in love and married in its shadow – a long way away it felt, in both years and distance.

The afternoon felt too much like the last Sunday before a new school term, awaiting the dread of having to get up early the next day. The butterflies that fluttered around in my stomach, thrown about in this windy city, told it all – I would miss Elaine; she was my lover. Both unsettled by the prospect of parting so soon, we went back to the hotel to say goodbye in the way we knew best these last few days. Again, it was a close encounter.

Chapter 2

Beguiling the way with stories

I stopped the car at a sharp bend in the coast road that ran down towards Kaikoura, the super highway that was Route 1, a single carriageway that carried the tiny drift of traffic along the Pacific coast. The parking bay on the corner that seemed to jut out over the cliffs and sea was packed, so I squeezed into the last space to see what all the fuss was about. A platoon of tourists stood, armed with state-of-the-art digital cameras that some fool thought a good idea they recreate the good old-fashioned sound of a 1970s clicking Canon; added to that the beeping that defines the modern era and it was enough to want to throw yourself off the cliffs, a martyr to the brave new world and all its idiosyncratic irritants. And worse still, they all seemed to be German, allowing no room for anyone else to see the subject of such intense interest. Undeterred by the Fourth Reich, I squeezed into a small space, getting a tut in defiance as I brushed shoulders with a terribly-dyed brunette from Bavaria, losing the grey in a brittle coating that gave no quarter in the stiff breeze. I tutted back and puffed out my chest to inch a little further to the car park wall.

Way below, on a seemingly inhospitable outcrop of tough, dark brown rock dotted with pools that were occasionally topped up by huge rollers crashing their surf over the headland, there lived a colony of New Zealand fur-seals. These creatures, not seals at all but a member of the sea lion family, had chosen these rock pools as an attendant nursery for the sweet little pups that played and bleated in the spray that drenched them every minute or so; the bah-ing sound was magnified on the occasion of a gust of wind, soon to be followed by a sprinkle of spray that found its way onto the lenses of the incredibly expensive zoomed-out cameras. 'Ha!' I thought before I quickly snapped opened my cheap Nokia and took a few cute pictures of brown splodges that I later explained away as sea lion pups.

"Hey, Steve!"

I turned, a little spooked at hearing my name in such a remote location, the almost exact antipode of a winter-bound North Kent. I looked hard for the origin, and pushing through the tutting Germans, unwilling to give up their hard fought for and divine vantage points, I saw at first a tall, scraggy-haired Dave and I sensed his sidekick Kim before I saw him, following in the wake of the parted wave that the tall and spindly Dave had created. They high-fived me, inadvertently pushing some senior Bavarians out of the way and jostled into position next to me.

"Hi, mate! How's it going?" asked Dave.

"Good, ta. Good to see you both. Where you been?"

"Trekking the Abel Tasman. It was awesome!"

Dave had already picked up the Antipodean vernacular; the most favoured adjective was 'awesome' in this global neck of the woods. It was overused down here but the landscape seemed to fit its description just perfectly.

"We're off to Kaikoura to swim with seals and then heading on down to the Banks Peninsula and Christchurch. We're gonna swim with dolphins at Akaroa."

"Excellent," I said. "I'm off that way too."

"Cool," said Kim. He was quiet today: the Germans unsettled him – something to do with his Norwegian heritage; I could understand.

It wasn't surprising that Dave, Kim and I were all headed for the same places. There were only so many tourist destinations on this island and this east coast road led to the obvious ones ahead.

"I've heard there's good sea skimming in the Banks Peninsula," Dave informed me, in between clicking away at the cute pups.

"Yeah, me too. Someone told me Le Bons Bay is a great location," I said. This someone was Merlin, who'd kept up to date with my short blog and had hinted at possible skimming stop-offs he'd got wind of in these parts; he was keen for me to write my guide.

"Cool," said Kim again, and then they were gone, barging their way through the crowds towards their lift, a van full of international bright young things. They waved, got in and the van skidded off.

As I returned to my car, it dawned on me that I hadn't a clue where the boys were staying, but guessed that I'd see them somewhere in Kaikoura town a little later; it wasn't that big enough a place not to.

Needless to say, I found myself sharing an eight bedroom dorm with Dave and Kim and an ensemble of other disparate travellers in Dusky Lodge, a large but amiable youth hostel on the edge of town, a mere five minute walk from the pubs and cafés of central Kaikoura and the beginning of the beautiful peninsula that juts its hilly self into an ocean teeming with large marine life. Kaikoura was home to sea lions, dolphins, orcas and sperm whales and so it attracted a similar myriad of tourists.

One of the few pubs in town had a band playing and the whole of the Dusky Lodge had decamped there for the occasion. We mixed with annoying Brits, large north-Europeans, loud Americans, mild Canadians, and odd Japanese and drank the night away. We spoke our own Esperanto, a Pidgin English of sorts, where I found myself slowing my speech down and enunciating unexpected parts of sentences, even slipping into the dreaded AQI and posing an intonated question at the end of each paragraph where there was none. Nonetheless, my non-descript southern England drawl was fairly clear to understand and I enjoyed my odd, global travel club.

Kim slumped down in the corner, having foolishly tried to match Dave pint-for-pint, though half his body volume it seemed. Dave swept through the crowds like a welcome deluge of rain in a parched Sahel millet field, refreshingly sprinkling his charm and humour across the girls (and some boys) before him. It was inevitable, as I watched him woo, then touch, then caress, then kiss the very pretty and sharp Kelly, the twenty-year-old girl who had the weekend shift of House Manager at the Dusky Lodge. They slept together that night and emerged worse for wear the next morning, far too early for young Dave as Kelly started her shift as most of us slept a deep, drunken slumber.

The band was good, well, as good as you get in these lonesome parts of the world and played the tourist favourites of the Crowded House hit list – the only Kiwi band we'd ever heard of. As the clock ticked into tomorrow, the fug of the alcohol coursing through my veins drew me away from conversation and into myself and deep below I found Anna waiting for me, her sweet smile and sparkling hair lit in the golden Snowden sunset; a realisation that the subconscious holds more truths than I'd care to explore and I warmed to these reminisces. I missed her, I missed home and I rued this reckless decision to pack up and travel the world, an early mid-life, stupid, fucking crisis. I was tired and drunk.

'Don't dial drunk', I'd heard in a movie once, which made me chuckle, but I didn't heed the warning and found myself phoning Anna at two thirty a.m., a dull, grey English early Saturday afternoon back home and she was in. I hadn't brought my mobile; maybe a decision I now regretted, but I couldn't be bothered with the faff of charging it up when I found the opportunity; that and the psychological effect of having a permanent connection to the real world and at the beck and call of the normal people back home. If I chose the time and place to call, I remained in control and could continue my fairy-tale existence free from the manacles of 9-to-5.

So, a nostalgic blast hit the nostrils as I pulled open the stiff door of the public telephone box on the poorly lit main drag of The Esplanade. It was quiet, most drunks having staggered back to the variety of hostels, pensions, B and Bs and campsites. The phone rang ten thousand miles away and my heart pounded hard and fast and loud.

"Hi," came a soft answer.

"Hi," I replied. A delay: maybe due to the satellite that was bouncing our emotions around near space, or just a delay of dread.

"Steve?"

"Hi," I repeated, somewhat shell-shocked at my actions.

"How you doing?" she asked.

"Good," I said. Another pause.

"You drunk?" she said.

"Yep," and I laughed. Thankfully, she did too.

"You've not replied to any of my mail," she said.

"No, no. I thought it impertinent."

"Oh."

This was awkward.

"I miss you," I confessed, surprising myself that the thought that had consumed my mind for the last two hours had taken substance in my mouth. Another pause.

"Oh, Steve. I miss you too you fuckwit, but you ran away, not me."

"I know, I know; just wanted to tell you, that's all." The last words slurred together.

She sniggered down the line, maybe imagining the drunken me slumped against the glass wall of a urine-flavoured phone box so far away. I laughed too, for a short while.

"Oh well, just 'hello', I guess," I said.

"Yeah, 'hello' back. And, Steve?"

"Yep?"

"You read my letter yet?"

"No, no." I hadn't. I wanted to save it for a really low moment. "I was waiting," I continued.

"For what?"

170

I didn't tell her. "Oh, I dunno."

"Yeah, that's about right. No fucking clue, as usual." It sounded as though this wasn't said with venom; more like pity. "Well, maybe you should."

"You're right. Maybe I should." A pause.

"Look, Steve. I've gotta go."

"Sure, okay, yes, of course. Sorry to bother you."

She laughed again. Of course it wasn't a bother; it just wasn't a very good idea.

I put the receiver down, missed the latch and it cracked against the window, swinging on its metal link and tapping the side until I gathered it up and slowly placed it properly on the receiver. I smiled at my pathetic performance, feeling sorry for, I wasn't quite sure what, and vowed not to drink so much again. I blamed Dave. He was dangerous.

It was odd that this adjective I'd given Dave should be the first thing I heard in the confusion of a hung-over late morning.

"Dave, you're fuckin' dangerous!" said Kelly, leaning over the reception desk and planting a kiss on his left cheek. It was a sisterly peck, a 'thank you' kiss, our 'one night has been done with' kiss and Dave smiled it away, happy with that scenario.

"Dangerous Dave," I said as we met in the foyer. He looked at Kelly, she laughed back and he patted me on the back.

"You'll never know quite how true that is, young Steven."

I'd booked a midday whale watch, and Dangerous a swim with the sea lions that lived off the rocky banks of the peninsula, not far from Point Keen, on this, the town-ward side. My trip was good, spotting a few sperm whales doing their thing, but the enjoyment was somewhat tempered by the lump of sick that lodged itself in my throat as soon as the boat left the continental shelf only yards from the shore, the incredible drop in depth from twenty metres to thousands, accompanied by an almighty swell and a change in hue from light green to menacing dark blue. Here, the krill were sucked to the surface, followed by their predators and a textbook page of the food chain was laid out before me. The whales took deep breaths, fluked their tails to give a helpful push and dived deep for giant squid. The odd sea lion skipped along the choppy surface and an albatross skimmed its wings along a wave crest with infinite ease and precision. Unfortunately, instead of being overwhelmed by this whole magnificent theatre, I felt nauseous, courtesy of my hangover.

When I returned to land and the relative safety of Dusky Lodge, a crowd had gathered around Dave and Kim, and Kelly watched from the loneliness of the front desk. I smiled a hello and said, "What's all this fuss around our Dangerous boy?"

She smiled. "You won't believe it; the photos he took. Is he one of those guys that adventure just happens too?"

"I believe he is, Kelly."

"Fuck... that's too much of a man for me."

I raised an eyebrow in the style of Roger Moore and she laughed.

"Oh, God, not like that. It's just that life would be much too big to compete with, with that guy."

She made sense. She was mature and wise for such a young and pretty thing. She touched my hand and smiled again.

"I need something a little more steady; feet on the ground."

"Right," I said, clearly blushing and hoping this wasn't what I thought it was. Twenty and thirty-five didn't quite fit.

I took the opportunity of the lull in proceedings around Dave and Kim to wander over and take a look at the pictures.

"What's all this about then, boys?"

"Aw, mate, you'll never believe this!"

"Believe what?"

He thrust a digital camera in my face and I couldn't make out much more than a splodge of black and white and pink, which I guessed was his finger over the lens.

"I've no idea what this is, Dave, apart from a blurry finger that is."

"What?" He pulled the camera back towards himself, looking a little puzzled and hurt.

"No, my friend," he said, pushing the view finder back into my nose, "this is what it is!"

And I saw a very close up picture of a killer whale's head and a shining glimmer of a row of perfect teeth, large and sharp enough to do a lot of damage to the photographer.

"Bloody hell, Dave! What zoom have you got on that thing?"

"This is not using the zoom, my friend!"

"What?"

He then rattled into his, now well-rehearsed, rant and fable of how he and Kim and a couple of other guys were swimming alongside a clutch of sea lions, just feet from the rocky promontory that was their home, when a nomadic pair of orcas showed up with a penchant for a sea lion snack. As the snorkellers treaded water, they witnessed a vicious and swift attack in which

172

three sea lions were taken. It was so quick that they didn't have time to swim for the rocks, hence the front seat view and the nature photographs of the year. The majority of the photos were pretty crap to be truthful, but a few were quite stunningly clear, sharp and gruesome.

"Wow!" I said eventually. "You are one hell of an adventure-magnet, young Dangerous."

He laughed, giddy with excitement at his close encounter, his youth, his trip and life itself.

"Henceforth, you shall be known as Dangerous Dave." I shook his hand at this announcement as though some kind of anointment and he smiled and nodded in agreement of the idea.

"Dangerous Dave... yeah, I like it!" We all did.

He held court for the early part of the evening and we drifted off into town, seven of us including myself, Kim, Dave, Kelly and three dorm mates from Japan; again, a night of a few drinks and pleasant international company. The chat was idle and a bit too young at times, skirting sex and sport and family until Dave began to talk of some of his more unsavoury adventures, the most shocking of which was when he boasted of a threesome with a mother and daughter after a drunken night in a Torbay nightclub.

"Tell me it's not true, young David."

He smiled that big, wide, cheesy grin I'd come to grow fond of and spread his arms, at first a crucifix shape, until his hands curved down and arms bent slightly at the elbow to leave us in no doubt that he was wrapped around two invisible ladies. He looked lovingly at them both in turn, and then affected a kiss for each.

"I don't believe it! You are..."

"A superstar," he ventured. "Troilism!" he continued.

"Hey?"

"Troilism: it's just a posh word for a threesome. I looked it up after the deed." He said this whilst continuing to grin like a Cheshire cat.

"Sick, I was going to say. You are a sick man. That is just not... right!"

He continued to grin, arms still clinging to his mother and daughter pageant.

"Mores to the point, they're the sick ones, the pair of 'em – the mum even more so. How could she?"

"You, my honourable friend, are just plain jealous. It's a definite tick off the list of life's imponderables," Dave informed me. I wasn't sure it was.

A friend of Kelly's arrived and plonked herself down in between Kim and me.

"Hi, I'm Cassandra." She proffered her hand.

"Hi, I'm Steve." It was a warm hand, accompanied with a warm smile. She was a Christchurch girl, but like Kelly was working the summer in Kaikoura – a bar maid at the pub we'd got sozzled in last night that had led to the awkward drunk-and-dial situation.

She was young too, not a day over twenty-three, and very pretty. I pondered the idea that I found her attractive because she was young and not because her face formed a pattern agreeable to me, the constant dilemma to men moving inexorably towards middle age. Did I find these young girls attractive purely because they had the elixir of youth? Would I have found them so attractive fifteen years ago? I decided that I probably wouldn't have as we chatted and I watched her nose move one way, her upper lip the other, a face so malleable that it belonged to a cartoon character, but enjoyed her energy, her vivaciousness, spirit and subtle flirtations; whatever the foibles that our age difference threw into the space between us, she wasn't bothered by it, in fact, found it attractive. So I realised in the wonder of it all that these things can work both ways and didn't feel such an old pervert after all.

Needless to say, it was just a harmless flirtation. I didn't embark on a further complication of my emotions, looking forward to another tryst with Elaine in two nights time down Christchurch way, and in a deeper state of flux over what exactly passed between Anna and me.

The conversations dipped in and out of music and laughter and I found myself chatting to Dave in the corner of our large table.

"It's the look."

"The what?"

"The look." I emphasised 'look' and continued. "You see, both the protagonists know what it means."

"The what?"

"The parties, the two people. What I'm saying is that both of them know the look; they share its understanding and it can be both a wonderful and dangerous thing." I was a little drunk.

"Wonderful?"

"Yep, because it says, 'Yes, if the conditions were right, we could be more than just strangers exchanging a glance. We could get to know each other; we could be lovers'."

"All in a look?"

"Indeed, all in a look and a whole lot more besides. You see…" I leaned in closer, as though to impart some elusive secret known only to those few, the keepers of the key down the centuries. "…It also portrays deceit and treachery which left only in the glance has but a fleeting life. But given a chance to blossom, a chance to ignite, it can spread a wild fire through the lives of the protagonists that can leave a chaotic and charred remain that smoulders for a very long time. It can destroy." I was blabbing.

He looked confused. I think I was too. "Yeah, but how often does the 'look'," Dave left the word in the air in between his fingered speech marks, "actually come to that?"

"You're right. Not that often, maybe one in a few hundred, but when it does… well, blimey!" I sat back and continued. "It also means that the 'lookers' tend to live unfulfilling, transient lives, always looking or deceitfully watching behind the safety of a relationship."

Dave sat back now and pondered on the conversation whilst fingering his pint. "Hmmm… I think I see," he said and then we drifted into other people's discussions.

I gave Dangerous, Kim and an accountant by the name of Lucius, from Andover, a lift down Route 1 to Christchurch, skipping in and out of black volcanic sandy bays and the white fluffy clouds that occasionally obscured the sun; there was a squint-inducing bright-light sun today, not the mellow-yellow of late summer back home.

The crew alighted at various hostels, a shake of the hand or pat on the back as an 'au revoir' before we met again on the tourist trail. In fact, I'd meet them all by chance that very night in a dull sports bar off Manchester Street. As a gentleman skimming-recluse, I'd taken advice and settled on a small four-bed dorm in the slightly more pricey and homely 'The Old Countryhouse' hostel; a comfy retreat on Gloucester Road for the more discerning traveller – well, richer and older anyway.

I stuffed my bag under the bottom bunk of a well-made and solid oak bunk-bed, fresh linen wafting a lemony scent across my nose; the sign of an upmarket hostel, duvets, not sleeping bags and a musty sheet. Above me, the paraphernalia of a young lady's bag was strewn over a ruffled duvet, books and hairbrush and bits of make-up. It seemed a messy business being a girl. Across the room were two single beds already taken by earlier arrivals, their organised rucksacks standing tall against the wall. German, I guessed, or maybe Scandinavian, and both girls too, it seemed, looking at the size of the bags and the various badges of flags and flowers stitched across the front folds.

I did the tourist thing demanded of Christchurch, a very English city, sipping coffees in the pre-quake Cathedral Square and snoozing in the Botanic Gardens, lying under the occasional shade of a weeping willow, its slender and drooping tendrils skimming the surface of the Avon River and sending me in and out of shade at the whim of the gentle breeze. Back at 'The Old Countryhouse', I showered in the late afternoon, enjoying the luxury of a bathroom that had a WC and a shower, relishing the comfort of a long and smelly shit, happy in the knowledge that its pungent scent would be diluted and then replaced with fresh, perfumed smells of ablution. My room, a corner one with large windows that grabbed the best of the southern hemisphere light, was greying in the shadows and as I fiddled with my toiletries, three girls came in.

The liberating joy of travel is that no one bats an eyelid at a 3:1 ratio, unisex becoming a familiar and necessary fact of this transient life. The bigger, North American girl (Canadian, I guessed at her pronunciation of 'right' and 'about', almost a Norfolk twang) was my bunkmate and had a sweet, chubby face. Louise was twenty-four and a medical student on a six-month sabbatical. Her day bag had the ubiquitous Canadian maple leaf flag, the requisite 'I'm not an American' badge of honour for all travellers north of the 48th parallel. We talked small, whilst going about our dorm business, and introduced ourselves to the two single bed occupants: Myra, an Irish girl with a soft accent and a soft face; on first impressions very pretty, but her lack of definitive lines and features saw her melt innocuously into the background fairly quickly, leaving her much taller and striking friend Heather to dominate the room. She was a south London girl, mousy-coloured hair with limbs as long as a Masai herder's, arms and legs dangling all over the room in danger of tripping herself and all of us up and over in this cramped space, but her overwhelmingly attractive trait was the way that she controlled those oscillating limbs with such grace and poise; she had a slow and deliberate way of moving about the dorm that was quite alluring. She had a slim figure that was rudely interrupted by an ample chest that seemed to fill her loose tee shirt quite easily. Her face was odd, sharp, but not cutting, a long straight nose on which rested a secretarial pair of slim, golden-framed glasses. Her hair was clipped up and I could just imagine her untying the mop and shaking it loose in front of the boss; I quite imagined it to be me as I unpacked nearly everything to find my foam earplugs, just in case, and I slid them subtly under my pillow.

The girls were quite chatty. Myra was an insurance clerk of twenty-three who'd had enough of Dublin and headed on out for adventure. She'd met

Heather, a clothes shop manageress of thirty, in Auckland five months ago and they had spent the majority of the spring and summer travelling around New Zealand together. It seemed to me that they'd been everywhere at least twice and were now on their third tour. Heather talked quickly with a south London drawl that was both irritating and cute. She looked at me closely; full eye contact every time she addressed me, as though searching for some clues to my story. In this inquisitive trawl, I caught the 'look'. There was a brief moment of mutual recognition and then it was gone, quickly hidden safely beneath the early rounds of polite dorm conversation.

We all got merry in a pub crawl along Manchester Street ending up in a sports bar to watch re-runs of the Six Nations back home. I wasn't really one for rugby but didn't mind sharing it with others over a pint or two. Inevitably, I bumped into my skimming buddies and a large group of us drank into the early hours, dispersing to our respective hostels along the cool, quiet, city centre streets.

Kim had told me of the good skimming to be had in the peninsula (Merlin had done the same) and we made a cursory pact to meet at Le Bons Bay for a challenging sea skim-off. Dangerous had flirted successfully with Myra and I was sure they'd meet again quite soon to finish their business, which left me and Louise and Heather to chat away across beer-strewn tables and now, all the way home.

As we bedded down, talking and giggling into a slumber, I made a promise to Heather to give her a lift to Queenstown, three days hence. Before then, I wondered, I'd be seeing Elaine again. She'd be here tomorrow and we would head off on a romantic sojourn around the Banks Peninsula. I was nervous. Would there still be a spark?

I spent the late morning, lunch and early afternoon on the beach at Sumner, a short ride outside of the city, surfing the medium-sized rollers on Taylor's Mistake Bay. I couldn't escape the irony of the name as I failed to catch a wave again and again, bowing to the supreme skill of the very young locals. I resorted to body boarding and daydreamed of Anna all the while – me and Miss Taylor and my big mistake.

After a quick shower, I checked in with reception and enquired about the arrival of an Irish lady called Elaine, a friend. She'd been here an hour or so and was bunked up in the adjoining outhouse, an equally comfy and cosy retreat for softer backpackers like us. Nervously, I rounded the courtyard garden, a weak sun casting long, but faint, shadows across the lawn to my dorm building, and entered the outhouse. The communal lounge was empty, a couple of travel books languishing on the big coffee table and a guitar with one broken string resting lazily in the corner. Voices from next door, a kitchen, drifted towards me and on recognition of an Irish lilt, my heart skipped a beat. Shit, here we go! Three people all looked up from their cups of tea or coffee and a sandwich snack. A brief impasse was broken when a huge grin broke across Elaine's face and she spoke.

"Hi there, stranger!"

"Hi there too, me old Irish travel bud."

My neutral smile broke into a very natural, happy grin. It was, quite evidently, great to see each other again. She looked fresh and full of colour and happy and I could just imagine holding her naked body close against mine again soon. The others smiled along with us and I joined them for polite travel conversation, all the while taking the opportunity to look closely at her, size her up, I guess, just in case I had missed something on my first entrance. Occasionally, I caught her doing the same and a clash of eyes would bring a smile to both of us again.

Our dalliance, which seemed inevitable once more, would have to wait until our trip around the Banks Peninsula as we were both booked into separate dorms this very night, so we just enjoyed getting to know one another again, spiritually speaking. We took a long stroll into town, around the Botanic Gardens, along the river and into a quaint, quiet bar, daring to hold hands under the willows and again under the table. She talked and talked of her whirlwind trip around the South Island and I half-listened, half-watched, enjoying the sound of her, the smell of her, and the occasion. I realised for the first time that I had quite missed her these last two weeks.

I left my rucksack at reception, taking just a few clothes in my day bag, and met Elaine at the front, bright and early at nine thirty a.m. (well, early for these heady and carefree days), the brightness though having been replaced by low, grey and threatening stratus clouds, in this, the land of them.

"Hi there kidda," she said, touching my shoulder from behind. I liked that, remembered it and anticipated a close contact this evening – I couldn't bloody wait.

We quickly packed our bags into my hire car and took a right out of town, a long, straight road past nice, old suburban wooden houses, the few with a history around here and, heading toward the shrouded sun, we left the city behind.

The Banks Peninsula is the forgotten gem of the South Island, all the tourists hitting the bigwig honeypots of Queenstown, Kaikoura, Wanaka and

Milford Sound; few take the right turn from Christchurch to this oddly shaped rocky promontory. On the maps it makes the shape of a loosely curled fist, a big, round hole in the middle of the forefinger and thumb allowing room for Akaroa Harbour and a small inlet betwixt forefinger and thumb bringing in dolphins and fishermen's boats into its larger bay. This unique geography afforded a wonderful view as we drove around its tiny roads, many of which were not metalled. On one side of the high ridge that ran round its entirety, lay the dark blue Pacific Ocean, and on the other the glacial blue green of shallow Akaroa Harbour. The height of the Summit Road dropped us in and out of mist and fog, the tendrils dropping the temperature by a good five degrees at a whim and bathing us in a cool Pacific damp that clung to our lungs until a sharp rise or dip blew it away. Only then would we get a view of the dramatic drop to the ocean or the bay and from here, high above this new and exciting and seemingly undiscovered world, we felt like gods peeking down on the mortals way below, the few we came across in this empty place that is. New Zealand is geologically new, being pulled apart, thrust up and squeezed out of the earth's crust, but this place felt old, had the eerie mystique of Celtic Britain and the foggy western Isles; I loved it at once.

First, we headed out on Ferry Road, as though hitting the beaches of Sumner and Taylor's Mistake, but took the 74 onto Tunnel Road and deep underground until we reached the ugly port town of Lyttleton. It was here that the Peninsula was accessed. The metalled road took us around the harbour, allowing the grey port a semblance of beauty the further it melted into the hills behind, through the tiny settlements of Diamond Harbour and Port Levy before the tarmac gave way to dirt track and a hair-raising rally drive took us across the headlands that poked their rocky noses into the ocean, and we settled down into Pigeon Bay, parking up by a small inlet.

We ate stale rolls, one-day old, with cheese triangles topped with poorly chopped tomatoes, accompanied by a bag of expensive crisps that stuck salt crystals on to our olive oil-coated fingertips. The clouds toyed with the coast, rolling in and out with the tides and waves, and a log just off the shore here was both uncovered and drowned in a passing rhythm that gave it life and we skimmed stones across the surface in an attempt to hit it.

Elaine allowed me to stand behind her and motion the art of skimming – 'skiffing' she called it – and I didn't let her go when the demonstration finished. It was a tight grip that felt comfortable, correct, and as though no time had passed since we had said goodbye in Wellington, since we had last slept together. Back in the car, we headed on high into the clouds and I sweated along with the skids at each twisting, slippery corner of the dirt track.

"What's the matter wit you?" she asked.

"Aw, nothing, just a little concerned about crashing off this crappy road and dying. You?"

"Crappy? This'd be a motorway back home, you numpty!" She slapped my knee and laughed.

I didn't recall her sounding so Irish, but gathered from the stories she'd spun that a lot of her trip since Wellington had been spent in the company of fellow countrymen.

Thankfully, the muddy track, giving too much in places and showering the mud-flaps and undercarriage with thick globules of New Zealand earth, gave way to metalled road and we rose majestically into the sky along Summit Road, the sea to our left, the Akoroa Harbour or bay to our right. I slithered to and fro, chasing the ocean to the left and right as I did so, creating a state of confusion in the Tom Tom of my mind – where the hell were we? All the while, Elaine sat beside me, her Irish eyes picking out distant dreams as she squinted into the horizon. In between the motion sickness-producing turns, I had enough time to study her profile closely. Her eyes were more green than I remembered, matching the bay that darted either side of us like a child playing British Bulldog. The lashes above were long and dark, interspersed with flecks of blonde, highlighted in the odd sunbeam that found its way through the mist and hills of this beautiful peninsula. Her nose was small, not too small, but snub enough to endear in me a parental ache and her posture was perfect, that of a dancer and her strong back (I knew about the strong back, had held it close to me on many occasions) held this posture which pushed out at her breasts to fill her tight tee shirt, allowing me the pleasure of watching her nipples rise and fall with the changes in temperature and thoughts of her lover who she saw was watching her closely, inspecting her with every chance he could. She longed to get him into bed, to be close to him again, though she'd never admit to it, and hoped that he longed for the same. Oh, how he did as he watched her on their cruise along the high roads of the Banks Peninsula.

We took the first possible left at a lonely crossroads and zigzagged our way down to the coast, past isolated farmsteads and coppices of unknown pine trees. At a beautifully located bed-and-breakfast on a turn, we glimpsed the golden sands of Le Bons Bay and soon were parking up behind unstable dunes, clumps of marram grass clinging tenaciously to the moving sand.

There was a tatty-looking camper van parked at the end of the rectangular space that constituted the lot behind the dunes, but no one to be seen as we bounded up over the dune ridge to gain our first-hand view of Le Bons Bay. A wide, golden sandy beach spread out before us, a kilometre from headland to headland I estimated, and way out there, beyond the darkened sand recently washed a golden brown by a receding tide, lay the Pacific calmly going about its business, the grey veil of cloud now turning white and threatening to disperse.

Something about these wide-open spaces always makes me want to run, so I did, taking Elaine by the hand and dragging her down the fore dune, toppling newly lodged marram to the bottom as we did so. We performed an odd-looking 'river dance', or 'ocean dance' she called it, skipping and giggling and twisting in this beautiful, untouched, empty space. I felt like the first explorer, or a Crusoe with my Girl Friday.

We eventually reached the ocean, paddling in its tranquil waters, the shelter of the bay keeping the ravages of the Pacific winds at sea. As we tired and turned back to the dry beach, the sea followed, as though our pure joy was dragging it in behind us so we could play without having to take such a long stroll to find it.

Back in the dunes, still alone, we found a comfortable spot, lay out a cheap car blanket I'd bought in Auckland (just in case this occasion should ever arise) and settled down into each other. My view, across Elaine's comforting profile, was of a verdant headland, brightening sky, golden sand and a fast-approaching bright-blue Pacific Ocean – heavenly. We cuddled and snoozed and grew warm in the arriving sunshine. Our serenity was broken by the sound of an approaching car. Within a minute, a noisy gang of lads had topped the ridge a hundred yards to our right and were heading to the sea. It took a while for me to recognise Kim and Dave from my little bubble, but I didn't know the other two. They carried some plastic bags with them and set up camp on the drying sand near the encroaching sea and started to play a variety of games: football, Frisbee and a basic form of cricket. We watched in silence, enjoying the sound of the breeze tickling the thin grass and roaring through our ear cartilage and skipping up a noticeable wave or two, the first rollers we'd seen since we came across the sheltered bay. I kissed Elaine, a long, full smacker on the lips, no tongues, and got up to go and play with the boys.

"I know these lads. I'll just go and say hello. You coming?"

"No, I'm too comfy. You go; I'll just stay here."

I joined them and Elaine watched our greeting, a few slaps and awkward nods and pseudo-gangster handshakes that I neither followed nor understood. From the rug, she watched the taller of the boys, Dave, hand out pebbles he produced from a bag, and then all five of them set about skimming stones across, up and over the ever-growing waves in the ever-stiffening breeze. This wind brought occasional cheers and groans to her ears, some deflected wide of her and up into the hills of the peninsula. She couldn't quite tell, but it seemed as though some kind of knockout competition was underway, at first the smallest of the group (poor old Kim) standing aside, and then the other two, leaving her Steve and the tall ringleader. They skimmed a further three stones until a loud cheer echoed around the bay, rolling in between the headlands on a swirling gust of wind that sent a shiver through her. They shook hands, the grasp turning into a right shoulder hug, street-style, and Steve, her lover, waved a goodbye and jogged up the beach towards her.

***(Location No.6, Le Bons Bay, Banks Peninsula, New Zealand)

"D'ya win then, travel bud?"

"'Fraid so," I said, blushing slightly at my success.

"How?"

"Good question." I guessed she wasn't querying the victory per-se, but the nature of it.

"We kinda made the rules up, but I won on number of skips over an incoming wave; the idea was to skip off its rising crest and continue afterwards."

"Oh, great, well done." Her congratulations seemed genuine enough and I nuzzled down next to her, getting down out of the increasing wind. The emerging sun negated the bite of the now-strong breeze for a further twenty minutes but once the boys had gone, with a shout and a wave and a skid, we found ourselves alone again.

We stood in readiness to pack up and go and find a place to stay in Akaroa and I caught her from behind, placing my arms across her stomach, linking my fingers together. Facing the now-lively ocean, inching ever closer and louder, I rested my chin on her shoulder, nudging my cheek into her neck. I sniffed her hair, a lemony-perfume that tickled my nose in the breeze. We stood there a while, one of those rare moments in life when the perfect silence roared over the ocean and surrounding sounds. I squeezed her tighter as a sign to move and she turned to embrace me – a long, sensual kiss that gave us a foretaste of the night to come.

It was late afternoon when we motored into the tourist town of Akoroa, a small settlement with a service economy much larger than its resident population. The season was late now, so we easily occupied a unit in a motel on the outskirts of town, still only a short stroll from the harbour front. This side of the peninsula was sheltered from the ocean breezes, winds and gales and we strolled into the centre to see what was occurring. Not a lot, so we ambled back along the Harbour Road to the motel. The clouds had gathered again now, skipping in from the southwest this time, across the mountains beyond. We walked closely to fend off the chill and hurried on across the road to the safety of our rented unit.

As light began to fade we lay down for a snooze, the freedom of which I enjoyed daily, away from the hustle and bustle of real life and its irritating deadlines and demands; this seemed such a natural way of living. Soon, we were entangled, an excited and slightly aggressive Elaine fully-clothed, on me, kissing me hard until my lips began to hurt against my teeth, but we continued rolling and rubbing together. It was an intense fumble and I rolled off to freshen up for a bite to eat and maybe a pint or two. Again, the liberation of travel and activity in the open air each and every day meant that a drink most nights was a manageable and enjoyable end to almost every day. I had kept fit throughout, but the easy living was beginning to take its toll on my stomach and love handles; however, my face looked as fresh and ruddy and as alive as it had ever done.

The Madeira Hotel, a little way along the Rue Lavard from our accommodation, the French nomenclature evidence of the colonial discovery of this region, a brief Gallic enclave until the Brits kicked them out and planted the Union flag, was quiet, the sound of the pouring rain seeming to drown out the fifties rock and roll that played on the jukebox and made sense of the décor that fell off the walls. It was quite late by the time we'd sprinted across the road, half-drowning in the process and the landlady umm-ed and ah-ed before agreeing to fire up the deep-fat fryer and fifteen minutes later produced two portions of fish-and-chips, the variety of which, steam cooking under the thick and tasty batter, I'd never heard of. It tasted good, fresh and fleshy and we keenly dispatched the plate, downing a couple of pints in the process.

As the last of the die-hard drinkers finished the extra game of pool allowed before early closing, we forced ourselves off the damp, wooden chairs and bade farewell to the kindly owner, back through the rain, no sign of it easing, this time not sprinting, already anticipating the clothes soon to be ripped off in us finding each other once again. Within two minutes we were naked on the bed, Elaine resuming a contact so close it almost hurt but it made me feel very wanted. And then I was in her and we tumbled and turned into a variety of positions until I grabbed her leg in place on my lap and we made rough love in a scissors position. I recall us slipping to the floor on top of a ruffled duvet we'd long since discarded, and we continued in that position for a while until, at last, she came and I too, over the right cheek of her bum and onto her right flank, over her thigh and onto the duvet.

"Wow, Mr Jones!"

"Wow, indeed," I agreed and we held each other in a messy embrace until a post-coital snooze took me. Sometime in the night, we returned to bed and woke up to a dull light, warm and close together under our sex-soiled covers.

Breakfast was taken in the sunshine, the storm having blown over in the night, on an outside table of a café, looking back to the town and the high hills of the peninsula penning us in. The sun was still warm when it occasioned to bully the clouds out of the way and we bathed in its rays. We took a stroll along the front, and out onto the wooden quay where we sat with our backs to a shed, letting the sun infuse us with its vitamin D whilst trying hard to ignore the fact that Elaine would be gone this time tomorrow, up there somewhere in the sky above Asia, no doubt. My holiday romance would be over and I would once again have to entertain thoughts of reality, of Anna and of my failings as a long-term lover.

But I didn't feel that way, sitting here, arm-in-arm with Elaine; no way was this a failed love affair. Indeed, love did seem the most fitting word to describe what had passed between us these last few weeks: I would miss her greatly.

The drive back along Summit Road was just as scintillating and scary as yesterday, but this time the sunny skies allowed us full views to the ocean and bay wherever they appeared at a turn. As the peninsula petered out and the flat land of the Christchurch plains took hold, we turned off the main road to picnic on a large and luscious green verge next to a white picketed fence behind which there stood two perfectly-toned race horses. They whooshed the flies away with their immaculately groomed tails and their firm muscles twitched in irritation at miniscule bites from microscopic insects. We watched them, admired them through the freshly painted fence and lay back on the rug chatting idly of the adventures we'd shared this last while.

"So, Jonesy," she addressed me, gaining my full attention with a serious gaze, full eye contact. "You gonna keep in touch?"

"No," I laughed.

"Shit bag!" she said and grabbed my arms, pinning me to the rug in a move more akin to the bouncing canvas of a wrestling ring. Looking into my eyes, she asked again.

"I tink you misunderstood me. I asked you, are you gonna miss me, or what?"

"Umm," I smiled at her. "Do you miss someone you think you're falling in love with?" I said.

Shit! I'd done it now. A mild panic gripped me and attacked my throat. I swallowed it down. No, no, hold on a minute. Maybe I meant this. Maybe I did!

"You daft idiot!" she said and placed a delicious smacker on my lips and held it there longer than I'd anticipated. I swallowed another attack down. She didn't say it back, but the kiss was as demonstrative as Elaine was ever going to get with me. The kiss was in agreement – back at you.

We ate in that night, this time bunking together in a double back at 'The Old Countryhouse'. It was a simple pasta affair accompanied by a bottle of the red I'd bought on our wine tour back in Napier: it was a fitting tribute to our romance. Elaine was to fly out at seven thirty in the morning, needing to leave by five, so we went to bed early and made love three more times in our double room. It was close but awkward, as lovemaking tends to be when you know it could well be for the last time. She insisted that I didn't go with her to the airport and my last memory of Elaine was of a dozy kiss goodbye in the early hours.

"I love you too, you daft old travel bud."

I remembered smiling as she told me this, and then hearing the door click behind her, and then an emptiness ran through me like a chill wind and blew away the security her companionship had brought me. God, I missed her already.

Chapter 3

So there is more bounce

No time to dwell, I was on the road with Heather, heading across country, topping the Southern Alps, through Arthur's Pass and on to the relentlessly Tasman Sea-battered west coast. Her company was pleasant enough, allowing me a distraction to keep the wolves of reality at bay and to not miss Elaine too much just yet; that could wait for the night. The low cloud of this poor New Zealand summer, whimpering to a close, had kept views to a minimum and this cloud seemed to follow Heather and me along the tourist route of the South Island. I barely recall seeing the sun shine for the majority of the week we spent as travel companions. At Franz Josef, on that first day, we bunked up in a crowded but comfortable dorm and sipped cool pints in the last glimpse of the sun we'd see for a while, its cheeky rays grabbing me briefly through the eye of a passing depression system.

Heather had large breasts. I'd considered them before, of course, in our short acquaintance, but in a nonchalant manner. However, as I chatted to the young lad from Bristol about football, I caught him looking constantly above me and my bunk and on up to Heather, lying on her front, resting on her elbows so that her loose-fitting nightshirt left a glimpse of her ample breasts for him and me and the rest of the room to see. Strange isn't it, that it takes the lustful glance of another to ignite the very thoughts of that third party in you? I wonder whether I would have ever considered Heather sexually if it weren't for the Bristol voyeur from the self-same city, but the die was cast. However annoying and ignorant Heather may turn out to be (and I'd had hints of that thus far), I'd seen her in a different light through the innocent eyes of youth, and I was curious.

She snored that night, tossed and turned and took several slurpy sips from her bottle of water, crunching the plastic as much as she could to keep the insomniacs from finally drifting off. However, in the morning I first saw her legs, bare and long and silky-skinned, and then her night shorts and pert, firm bottom as she descended noisily from the bunk above. Blimey, what was wrong with me?

Sodden through it seemed, the whole bloody time I knew her: on the glacier at Franz Josef; around the picture-perfect Lake Matheson; through a Queenstown bungee jump and white-water raft; and onto Wanaka and its eponymous lake; the whole time, not a sniff of the sun and the clouds bore down on me, crushing me slowly in their greyness.

I'd come to quite dislike Heather as a companion, but found her curiously attractive, aesthetically speaking. We had not a jot in common, spare our jaunt around these isles, so we kept our daily activities as the focus of conversation; to drift into politics, philosophy and sport was a fruitless exercise and both seemed as exasperated as each other when we did. Our misunderstanding of each other was quite spectacular, but the road kept us together, next to each other in the front seat of a rain-splattered car, under and above each other in mixed dorms across the South Island and ambling along footpaths and pavements when not driving. We had a connection, an odd one at that, but it seemed as though something would need to happen to break it.

I'd been in email contact with Dave, Kim and Merlin and had happened upon a small skimming competition to be held on Lake Murchison, based out of a small trekking hut, a day's tramp from Te Anau, a petit and pretty town on the lonely road out to Milford Sound. Indeed, it owed its continuing existence to the tourist trade that ended up in that iconic drowned 'U' shaped Valley, so spectacularly missed by Captain Cook on his two sorties past it. This was to be my first official competition, and Merlin had told me that it would attract no more than a dozen people; it was pretty much as far away as one could get from anywhere.

Heather and I had bunked in a four-person dorm in a bog-standard hostel in Te Anau, been on a day trip to Milford in the rain, and were now planning our trek into the wilderness. The Murchison tramp is one of New Zealand's most remote Great Walks, the forests and mountains beyond hardly explored. As I read the guidebooks it struck me how recent the discovery of this whole goddam beautiful place was. Out there in the wilderness lived no people, just rare species like the newly rediscovered Tahaki bird, rarer than the Kiwi and just as unlikely to be spotted by two disparate trampers.

The night before the three-day trek, taking in the skimming contest, we had a few drinks in a local bar; a more cowboy joint you could not find. We had learned to tolerate each other at night away from the distractions of wild Kiwi activities involving near-certain death by getting merry enough to not care that we really had nothing important enough to say to each other. As the night drew to a close and the few tourists there began to leave, Heather bought a night cap on the very last ding of last orders and came across with the bizarre-looking cocktails balanced precariously somewhere amongst the jumble of limbs that were her skinny arms.

"What is it?" I enquired.

"Dunno. Some bloke recommended it." She threw her arm back over her head in the general direction of the bar, allowing her tightly clothed breasts to wobble in its lee. They caught my brief attention and she noticed. Heather didn't climb back on the stool next to me, but chose instead to stand in between my freshly placed open 'cowboy' legs. She stood there sipping her pink concoction (most un-New Zealand like, especially here in the macho frontiers) edging closer into me whilst I wittered on about something or other, both acutely aware of the game-play that was unfolding.

"So, what 'bout Elaine then?" she asked, bold as brass.

"Hey?" She had put her left hand on my right thigh, just above the kneecap.

"Elaine. You two an item?"

"Well…" I let out a long breath, not quite a sigh. "Well, I suppose we are."

"Oh." She looked neither disappointed, nor overly curious: just stood close; closer, in fact, and moved her hand further up, mid-thigh now.

"Problem is," I continued, "I have no idea when I'll see her again."

At this, Heather could not hide her pleasure. "You were close then?"

"Yeah, yeah, we were. In a different place, a different life, you know…" I left the consequence hanging there between us, as a buffer, my human shield.

And so began our most soulful conversation of the week, exploring each other's past in a careful and caring manner that was both cathartic and touching. At the end of the conversation, I could have kissed her as a thank you, but I didn't. Her hand was still there; her hips were pushed in close to my inner thighs and she rubbed her thumb up and down the worn denim of my tattered jeans. I was getting an erection.

We managed to get back to the dorm without further contact and quickly went about our ablutions, careful not to disturb our dorm mates, a couple from South Africa. He snored like a trooper, was in full flow, and I knew I'd have an uncomfortable night; noisy, hot and thinking sexual thoughts of a girl I didn't really care for. This crazy travel business: still, it kept Elaine and Anna out of my mind for a short while.

The sun was actually shining first thing but within a kilometre of the National Park information hut, just outside of town, we were plunged into the semi-darkness of a beautiful and fresh, ancient New Zealand deciduous woodland. We would follow the one and only path deep into the forest for the next five or six hours, touching and following the River Waiau at times, before losing it completely in the thicker patches. In the pub last night, a local farmer, part-time tour guide (they all seemed to be) told me how much filming of Lord of the Rings took place here and that the locations for Fangorn Forest and River Anduin were all shot here, and in the first few hours I lost myself in the imagination of that book and film trilogy, keeping the orcs of memory at bay and the wraiths a few feet in front of me.

We picnicked on fruit and cheese and drank from the clear river (we'd been told it was safe) and on our walk Heather refused to pick up a stick and have a pretend sword fight with me. Feigning to sulk like a bored toddler, I lagged behind her and lashed out at dead branches that split into shards in a crack that splintered through the quiet forest and brought a tut and a giggle from the woman, a constant five feet in front. God, she walked fast, too quickly to enjoy the wonder of this mysterious place and I lagged further behind until she noticed.

"Why you so bloody slow?"

"Why you so bloody fast?"

"Am I?" she asked, concerned that I'd been annoyed by this.

"A little bit. Don't know how you can enjoy all this," I swished my stick through the air to identify 'this', "when you're race-walking through it all."

"I can multi-task you know."

"Didn't know walking counted in the list of multi-tasking – unless you haven't got any legs, it pretty much just happens, doesn't it?"

She ignored me, taking the forced-upon-her break to retrieve the large plastic bottle of water from her rucksack and taking a long, loud slurp from it. She didn't offer me any of it, normal protocol for these treks, I'd gathered by now. This irritated me further still as she tramped off ahead of me, keen to get to the hut and away from me most probably. As I watched her go, swinging the stick at a bright green fern along the edge of the path, I saw again the graceful rise and fall of each bum cheek in rhythm with her long and purposeful strides. Her walking trousers were long and tight, a much more expensive pair than mine, and gave her figure an exquisite frame. I sauntered after this bum, seemingly unattached to the top of her; I wasn't really interested in that part of Heather – well, save the breasts that is – and as we walked on and on, I became quite enchanted by her behind. I wanted to see it without the trousers, first in a skimpy thong – no, a quaint flowery cotton pair of knickers – and then naked. I could quite imagine it, and enjoyed the thrill of my X-ray eyes.

The woods thinned towards the river, which we happened upon on occasion, and at one time we sat on a dry bed of moss to watch it flow past, surprisingly quickly. There was not a soul in sight, not a hint of humankind, and I could quite imagine this forest belonging to another world. We moved on when the moisture trapped deep in the free-draining moss had been squeezed up and into our trousers and, at last, came upon a clearing where the National Park hut resided, and to the left we gained our first view of the sparkling and remote Lake Murchison. The clearing widened to the small sandy beach and a deep blue lake lapped upon the shore. There was nobody to be seen.

We took our bags into the hut, dropping them in the corner of the communal area, a few scattered wooden tables and chairs and a handful of basic stoves for those who could be arsed to cook; we'd shamefully stacked up on snacks that needed no preparation – ever the, not-quite-true, traveller.

It was late afternoon; the rare shining sun had spread a golden light across the canvas of Lake Murchison and we were keen to go and bathe in it – the light that is. The foreshore was made of a coarse sand that graded into pebbles, and at two short and low headlands more rounded stones looked promising, big enough to have a bounce-able weight, small enough to fit in the palm of my mother-sized hands – 'delicate and artistic' Babs had called them; 'gay' was the sensitive word that Phil used.

I collected a few in my pockets, bulging my thighs like a pre-Velvet Revolution Bulgarian weightlifter, and shot a couple of experimental skims out across the still waters into the middle of the landscape painting that was the view from here, the picture-perfect mountains framing the multitude of skips across the dark blue lake. I lost count; it was a good skim and a perfect location.

Heather had wandered off to the other headland, skipping in and out of the pine trees that set it into the water. She seemed a tall and elegant lady from here, even with those wild limbs, and I anticipated the fall into bed that would doubtlessly happen soon. We knew; it had been in the look a while ago.

"Let's play, Shithead," she said in a brusque manner that was neither attractive nor alluring, but I still had the pleasant image of her perfect arse in my head, surrounded by orcs and goblins and elves back in the forest. I laughed to myself at the search for the ring, and she stopped and looked up.

"What?" she was smiling sweetly.

"Nothing, just a funny thought."

"Oh."

"Why Shithead, that's a horrible name?"

"No idea, just is, so let's play…shit head."

"Funny," I said and slapped her dealing hand. I really had no idea who was winning this wonderfully named game, a travellers' favourite she insisted, but thankfully, new arrivals kept me from finding out. In from the gathering dusk walked two beautiful young things, a boy and a girl.

"French," I whispered across to Heather and threw in my hand.

"Hey," she said and looked up, disappointed that her impending victory had been snatched from her. Being the only two humans, seemingly, within a hundred miles from here, we felt obliged to greet the strangers and welcomed them to our humble hut. I stood, the chair scraping the floor like an out-of-tune trombone blast.

"Hi, I'm Steve." I proffered my hand to the boy, man; whatever; he was young and devilishly handsome.

"Valerie," he rasped in a Gallic cough that reeked of testosterone. He had a warm smile.

"This is Heather," I said and she remained seated.

"Hi," raising her hand and sprinkling her fingers in a clear sign of irritation – she was enjoying our time together in this forest hideaway.

"This is Natalie." He introduced his stunning girlfriend.

"Hello," she said, shaking my hand limply and awkwardly leaning in to me, giving the European greeting of two cheek brushes, as was now the vogue with coffee morning housewives back in wintery Tunbridge Wells.

"Natalie," she said, reaffirming her identity.

"Steven," I said, formally.

"Ste-fan," she repeated, her Gallic intonation on the 'fan'.

They pottered for a while, claiming the two berths above ours in the rather large and spacious eight-bed dorm. The couple, both in their early twenties, lived in Paris, Valerie a waiter in a touristy café in Montmartre, also a part-time poet (what else could it be?) and Natalie a medical student studying from the Sorbonne. They oozed the air of life's winners, but seemed implausibly nice with it. I liked these two young lovers very much indeed. They, like many

Europeans I had encountered on my travels, spoke exemplary English, though bemoaned the quality.

"I am sorry for my English. It is not as good as it should be."

It seemed fine to me; better than Heather's. We sat around our card-playing table, attempting to teach each other card games translated on the roads of Antipode.

"No, no it's excellent," I said of their English. "It really is." I tried not to gush, or blush, but it was difficult with such beauty sitting so close. I didn't mean Heather.

Natalie had short hair and skin as brown as a toasted bun, suggesting a mixed heritage: the slender face, thin but elegant nose, deep brown eyes and full blush lips spoke of North African descent, the desert sands flowing through her velvet veins and rubbing her skin soft from the inside so that it glistened in the fading light of the evening. As she leant across the table to pick up a winning hand – Heather had successfully explained the rules to our French cousins, which bemused me as I still hadn't a clue how to play Shithead – her long sleeve cotton top fell off her wrists like silk over marble and I enjoyed just watching both of their movements. Valerie had longer hair than Natalie and brushed it behind his ears whilst in deep thought over a puzzling hand. At times of intense concentration he would down his cards and sweep both hands across his forehead, gathering the long locks and carefully, precisely, fold them behind his ears, holding them there with a graceful, slow stroke that ran off the tendrils in a tender flick. As we played, we chatted and, inevitably, talk turned to skimming.

"I'm here to throw stones," Valerie declared, skimming his discarded hand across the table with some aplomb. I didn't mind losing a skim-off to such a charming man. I hated getting beaten by fools, arrogant folk and cruel people at any game – anyone else was welcome to whop me.

"Me too, Valerie. May the best man win."

He smiled across at me and offered his hand. We shook and the girls threw a glance in between us; skimming widows, they didn't get the sport at all.

We took a stroll to the lake in the fading light and examined the stones and water's surface whilst the girls talked, perched on a log behind us.

"Is it just going to be us?" he asked.

"No idea. I think I know a couple of people who are hoping to come here. Maybe tomorrow. The competition begins at two o'clock." I motioned to my wrist, devoid of watch – I'd not worn one since I left work. It was a deliberate snub to my old life.

"Yes, of course."

We both made a point of not skimming in front of each other, as though our skill held a craved-for secret.

Back in the hut, things had changed. The Department of Conservation (DOC) warden had arrived and tapped us for the rent and we paid for the two nights we intended to stay. Also here were seven others; somehow they'd arrived unbeknownst to the Frenchman and me. It was a motley crew of two Kiwis, two Aussies, an American, a Japanese guy and a Swiss man called Antonio; Swiss Tony, I laughed to myself. I tried it out with Heather, but she just looked at me.

"Why's that funny? The Swiss aren't funny. They're dull."

"Where d'you say you come from? Berne was it?"

"Ha, ha, shit head!" She paused and leaned in. "Berne is in Switzerland, right?"

"Yes," I smiled. She did too. That was sweet.

The group sat at three different tables chatting late into the evening, musical chairs that saw us swap around with movements to and from the stoves, the dorms and a lakefront stroll and recce. The DOC warden had a room here, which he didn't always use but tonight he would do being charged with judging duties the next day. The DOC had agreed to the competition last year through an odd request from a spurious stone-skimming association based out of Gore, South Island, New Zealand. I guessed the two Kiwis were members of that group, probably the founders and only members going by their rambler-esque beards.

The temperature dropped remarkably around eleven, so people took refuge in their sleeping bags, a comfort born of a travelling bedroom; smells and thoughts of home. Heather slept next to me, the two bottom bunks of four, her head not more than a foot from mine. She occasionally turned, sighed, and slurped noisily from her crinkling plastic bottle, and at one time checked to see if I was still awake. I was.

"Steve?" she whispered, tapping my shoulder that she found by walking her hand on those slender digits until she came to the warmth of my neck and moved across.

"Yeah?"

"I'm cold. You wearing your hat?"

"No. You want it?"

"Yes please."

I had my hat in the sleeping bag with me in case I needed it, like I had on many cool New Zealand summer nights before, and passed it to her crawling hand.

"Ta." She brushed her knuckles against my cheek, briefly leaving her hand there.

"Night."

There was no response, just a slow removal of the hand and hat, a brief scuffle in the dark and then a silence of sorts amongst the heavy breathing, snorts and 'grumphs' of a shared dorm.

The sun shone weakly through a high blanket of white cloud, spreading the milky-light across the calm waters of Lake Murchison. The mountains shimmered somewhere beyond, too faint to quite discern, but I knew they were there; I could sense them. Everyone slowly went about their travel business and I watched some skim from the safety of the pine tree headland; they were good.

By midday, five more people had arrived and at one o'clock, Kim and Dave appeared, casually, just in time for an official entrance. A rickety camping table had been erected on the beach at an odd and awkward angle, rolling the biros to the far side, and a good-looking skimming pebble weighed down the piece of paper we had to sign.

The final deadline for signing in was one fifteen p.m. There were twelve entrants. The first Lake Murchison Stone Skipping (they used the American idiom) Competition had been inaugurated. Another DOC man turned up, donning a khaki shirt with insignia of kiwi, mountains, white clouds, Maori art and whatever other emblem represented the beauty of this land. Sometime during the morning they'd placed a series of small buoys and ropes to create a wide swimming lane leading from the beach along the side of the west headland, the rocky promontory signifying a slightly deeper channel than that of the east side. The lane reached out maybe a hundred yards and seemed to finish where the headland turned at its zenith.

A whistle rang out at one fifty p.m. and the gathering crowd, who had chatted quietly and skimmed practice stones across the far side of the beach eyeing each other with gladiatorial suspicion, began to huddle around the small table and the two DOC officers.

"G'day ladies and gentleman and welcome to the inaugural Lake Murchison Stone Skipping Competition."

A ripple of applause rang around the group and I shuffled awkwardly on the coarse sand, kicking grains off the end of my sandals.

"A big thank you from me," came a voice from behind us, "and Jim, the organisers, and a great big thank you to the DOC for allowing us this perfect location."

Another ripple. The Kiwis from the night before, one of the Gore members I guessed, was speaking.

"It's great to see so many of you from so many different places and really encouraging to see that word has spread across our little community to allow you to get here. Let's hope this is just the beginning and that each year we can grow in numbers." Another soft ripple of applause.

"Right," he continued, "we'll be playing Easdale rules." I looked at Dave and Kim and shrugged. I had no idea what he was talking about.

"You've got five minutes to gather three stones. Each one needs to be small enough to fit into this." He held up a contraption that belonged in a school woodwork room, and pointed to a block of wood and an attached gauge, two points at five inches apart, the desired breadth of the skimming stone. If it didn't fit in any direction between the two points, it would be rejected.

The competitors rushed to the headland where the best stones nestled untouched in the nooks and crannies of the foreshore. I picked six decent stones that fitted comfortably in my right palm and each had a slightly sharper edge along the longest axis, which I could use as a spinning point on release. None were thicker than four centimetres and as smooth as the surface of the lake, which reflected the milky-white high cloud like a pool of surplus EU semi-skimmed.

Gathering back at the table, pockets bulging with potential winning stones, we listened for further instructions. The tallest of the Kiwis spoke, "Ladies and Gentleman, as in the World Stone Skimming Championships held on Easdale Island in the Western Islands and Highlands of Scotland each September, my forefathers' home, you will each have three skims along the marked lane. Each buoy represents five metres and our judges, Todd and Merv," (the DOC men raised their hands in an awkward acknowledgment) "will be standing on the headland and their estimate of your distance gained is final. The distance is decided on the point your stone sinks or leaves the lane. And please remember that the stone must skip at least three times," (he held up three digits) "within the lane to mark a legitimate throw. Any questions?"

It seemed logical enough to me, and the others looked at each other in agreement of the fact. I had vague memories now of reading about it on the web.

(Location No. 7, Lake Murchison, South Island, New Zealand)

"We will throw in order of registration." I was the fifth name on the list – didn't want to be too keen. The controller took the piece of paper, a clipboard from out of his rucksack and the wooden measuring contraption, to the shore where the lane stretched out before him, and drew a crude square in the sand.

"You will not stand outside the square when throwing, before, during and immediately after each skip. Any questions?" None.

"Right then, guys. Our first contender is Antonio Pizarro from Switzerland!" A ripple of applause.

"Go, Swiss Tony!" I shouted, and he looked across and smiled. A few others cheered and whooped.

His first stone hit the second buoy on the left hand side of the lane and ricocheted off onto the small pebbly beach of the headland. Most laughed; he did not.

"Unlucky, Tony," shouted another.

He placed his second stone in the contraption and got a nod from the referee. Pulling back in the classic skimming arc, he raised his left leg bent at the knee and stamped it hard into the sand, just before the marked line, and the stone flew out at a perfect angle, skipping once at about twenty metres, again, still straight and true at thirty, and a third time at about thirty-five. It was an excellent throw. The fourth skip was slightly askew and the stone quickly spluttered to the left in a shower of miniature skips and sank. A shout from the headland, "Forty-two metres!"

A big cheer rose from the crowd and a few people looked around at each other with an appreciative grin and perhaps with slight relief, realising that to compete with the likes of Tony was not going to happen and that we could all now relax. I was secure in my mediocrity against these fellows. His third stone was equally competent, skimming slightly to the right and exiting the lane at an impressive thirty-eight metres.

"Well done, Tony!" and a loud applause for the cool Swiss man, a possible contender for the inaugural title.

Second up was Valerie. He even looked handsome whilst throwing his body into ridiculous shapes in the midst of a skim. First stone, no throw – he stepped over the line with an embarrassed giggle and a "merde". We cheered.

The second stone sank without a skip, the forceful lunge turning the pebble on its side and it sank quickly into the middle of the competition lane at about twenty metres. We didn't cheer; people shuffled a little awkwardly.

"Allez Valerie!" shouted Natalie from the back of the beach; the nearest she dared get to the throng. She wasn't comfortable with all this male testosterone flying off across Lake Murchison. No girl had entered the competition, unfortunately. I'd tried to convince Heather but she just guffawed at the thought. I'd imagine those gangly limbs would either be totally inept at skimming, or else I would have discovered the next world champion; it had to be one or the other.

"Allez les bleus," I joined in.

Sweeping back that full head of luxurious hair, he wiped his hand on his jeans and picked out a stone from the competition bucket, choosing not to use any more he'd collected. These spares were available to anyone but most chose to find their own perfect stones. Valerie's choice didn't need to be checked in the contraption, as all bucket stones were previously cleared. Composing himself, Valerie swung back his right arm and let go with a beautiful looking skim. The stone span straight and level from his fingers and flew out way beyond twenty metres before barely touching water and rising again for a further ten; the stone barely touched again, spinning off the water with ease and bouncing again another few metres on, at thirty-five. Another skip, three metres, then another two, and another, then one metre, centimetres and it sank. A pause, then an almighty cheer from the ranks. We erupted.

"Forty-five metres!"

He punched the air, rather apologetically, and went straight to Swiss Tony to shake his hand.

An Aussie guy, straight from Bondi it seemed, was up next. Three good stones, all straight, but falling short of thirty-five metres. A cheer and a backslap once in the throng. His mate was next, a compact Mediterranean-looking fellow, Christos something-or-other, whose first stone made a skip out to thirty metres and then turned away on the second at forty metres to bounce outside the lane a third. He groaned and sank almost to his knees. "Bugger!" Had that stayed in, it would've been a winner.

"Disqualified," shouted the referee. The second was disastrous, the stone not even bouncing once within the lane. His mate laughed and shouted,

197

"Loser!" The third looked good, a skip at twenty, two at twenty-five, three within the lane and it sank at thirty-two metres in a spluttering shower. We cheered and he looked pleased enough – God, I would've been.

"Steve Jones!" announced the ref, and it was my turn.

"Shit!" I said and got a couple of backslaps from Kim and Dave.

"Good luck, mate!"

"Cheers."

I fingered the stones in my long pockets and found the roundest one, the best to start with being my plan. I centred myself within the freshly redrawn square and placed my feet in the surfboard position, the best for launching a quality skim. Like a long jumper I swung my pebble hand back behind me, then slowly into my other hand in front, repeating the motion three times as some sort of athletic mantra; it wasn't, I was just avoiding the shot. I cleared my mind, shutting out Anna, Elaine, Rachel and Heather (it was crowded up there) and in the short instance of calm, let fly with an instinctive skim. It shot out, flicking the edge of my index finger perfectly and spinning smoothly. It flew beyond twenty-five metres before ricocheting neatly off the film on the water and continued straight, skimming again at about thirty-five metres (Jeez, this was good!) and then inexplicably, it careered to the right and hit the lane rope at around forty-something metres.

"Ooh," was an audible and collective response.

The DOC warden seemed to shrug and looked over to the ref at the skim pad. Tentatively, the warden shouted, "Forty-six metres!" and a cheer erupted from the throng, led by Dave and Kim and Heather in the background.

"Sorry, Steve," interrupted the ref, "if it hits the rope, it's disqualified."

A boo and an uncomfortable rumble rose from the small crowd. I briefly considered a McEnroe-esque 'you cannot be serious!' before magnanimously shrugging and going for another stone. There was something quite wonderfully British about being cheated at the point of victory, so I enjoyed the pathos. I grabbed the first stone my fingertips hit, as a way of calming my nerves by appearing cool to all else; it was a tactic that worked well at school, especially when delivering assemblies. It wasn't the best, but after heroically failing, I just wanted rid of this one. I composed myself and quickly let it go, a competent enough skim that skipped itself out by thirty metres. A ripple of applause and a palpable feeling of disappointment. I placed my hand deep into the surfing shorts and rummaged around like a schoolboy at a bus stop with no-one watching, and came across a beauty, clearly the best of the four still left there. It was almost perfectly round, fitted into my palm snugly, and had warmed in my pocket. I repeated the nervous mantra of the first throw and, arcing back as far as was possible, snapped my arm across my hip and let it go. Once again, a near perfect release saw the stone fly out over twenty metres before skipping on to thirty, and then thirty-five and again flipping to splutter out just beyond forty. It was close.

"Forty-three metres!"

"Ooh, nearly," I said and stepped back into the group.

"Unlucky, mate!"

"Cheers, Dave."

The other three that followed me weren't that great, but we cheered and laughed as they all fell short of thirty metres, most staying within the lane.

Dave and Kim and two of their friends (I'd not met them before) were the last to throw. First Kim, a no-throw, stepping outside the zone, then another with two skips before exiting the lanes and the final throw a twenty-five metre dribbler. We cheered – it was only right. He was disappointed.

The two mates, Scandinavian it seemed by name and appearance, threw well, but couldn't top thirty metres. So, with just Dave to throw, I lay in a creditable second place, perhaps first if we'd cleared up the lane rule. Nevertheless, a top three finish was definite. I was chuffed. Merlin would have been pleased.

Dave was the tallest competitor, and although technique was the all-encompassing requirement, height, I always believed, was an advantage: longer arc, more speed gained down through the hip and across to release. His first stone was poor, going off the lane after one skip at about fifteen metres. We cheered, and so did he. He took the second more seriously, composing himself, an inward mantra, and arced his arm back, then releasing the smoothest snap I'd seen all afternoon. The trajectory was perfect, the stone seeming to keep a fast, steady speed just above the water; its first contact was subtle, keeping the steady spin and speed. It hit again, heavier this time at thirty metres, but seemed to rise further, allowing another ten metres before hitting again at forty; it didn't wobble or come to a spluttering halt like the others had at forty metres, but skimmed on to forty-five, fifty, fifty-five before calmly coming to rest in a semicircle of close contact skims.

A huge roar erupted from the tiny crowd and in amongst it we just heard the shout of the DOC warden.

"Fifty-six metres!"

Another roar. Like a true champ, Dave declined a third stone, an incongruous combination of humility and arrogance. I wasn't sure which trait was strongest.

Kim and the two Vikings engulfed him in a congratulatory hug and I shook his hand once the melee had fizzled out.

"Superstar, Dangerous Dave!"

"Ah, shucks," he said, a grin beaming across his face like burning space junk across a deep, night sky.

At the big ceremony that followed, Dave received a small trophy, a silver plastic mounted figurine that seemed to be throwing a discus, the nearest gong the organisers could find in the key-cutting shop in Gore. Valerie and I, second and third respectively, received two beautifully-polished Lake Murchison pebbles, a prize far superior to the winner's, but at least Dave would be the name at the top of the page on the weird stone-skimming website-cum-blog that it was promised to grace.

"Next time, let's hope for many more entrants, and some ladies having a go, too."

That night beers were quaffed around a DOC sanctioned fire on the beach, but it wasn't a long night. The cold and insect bites drove us inside and soon to bed to warm up. What a glorious day. Heather wore my hat in bed again, an arrangement agreed on before snuggling into our bags. She reached out to touch my head good night, which was sweet.

The groups dispersed soon after breakfast, the majority onto the mountain stages of the Great Walk having had the foresight to book ahead at the smaller huts up there. I'd tried, but it was already fully-booked, so Heather and I were to walk back to Te Anau and we'd planned to part in Queenstown tomorrow; she flying up north to meet Louise again, and I to continue on my odyssey to the very south and the wild Caitlin coast. We said goodbye to the boys, and to the model French couple, having exchanged email addresses for further skimming contest competition alerts. I looked forward to them.

Our walk back through Fangorn Forest and along the River Anduin was beautifully still but tinged with tedium, Heather keeping her distance with a pace five ahead of mine. I enjoyed her arse on the occasions my irritation subsided and considered the prospect of a drunken fumble to reveal its secrets later that night.

"For Chrissakes, Heather, why don't you slow down and just enjoy it!"

"Oh, sorry, I didn't realise."

An hour out of town, I passed Heather and subjected her to a taste of her own by tramping off quickly ahead. She tried to keep up with me unassumingly, but on a sharp turn in the magical forest I realised that I had left her well behind. Happy at being alone once more, I continued on, secure in the knowledge that she couldn't get lost on the one path here and that the orcs and goblins were just figments of my Middle-earth imagination and that she wouldn't be eaten alive – shame.

I left the forest by a small reservoir and came out into bright sunshine. Sitting on the bank, shaking the last dregs of my water bottle onto my parched tongue, I saw Heather emerge, that long pace striding purposefully towards me. She was smiling. Following behind her was the pretty woman I'd passed by just five minutes earlier, walking her fluffy retriever. Heather waited for her in the sunshine and they chatted as they approached.

"What's with you, speed merchant?"

"Sorry, Heather, just stretching out."

"Oh." She hadn't cottoned on to how peeved I'd been with her solo walking efforts.

"This is Amelia."

"Hi, Amelia."

"Hi there."

"She lives here."

"Nice."

"Yeah, it is. Just moved here from Auckland with my husband."

"Oh right. How long have you been here then?"

"Two weeks."

"Blimey! Quite a change. You like it?" I asked her.

She paused. "Not sure yet. It's beautiful for sure, but it's a bit… remote."

"Yeah, I know what you mean."

We chatted a while; I stroked the dog, and Amelia offered us a lift for the two miles back into town. We were grateful, our water having run out by now.

Outside the small hostel, Amelia wished us a 'bon voyage', and off she drove with a melancholy face that spoke of a lost girl in a land far, far away. I really couldn't understand quite how you could set up your home here. It was remarkably beautiful, but it was so quiet, so isolated, that you had to be a strong unit, a strong minded and resourceful team to survive. I wished her the very best.

We showered and snoozed the afternoon away – nothing more glorious than a well-earned nap after having really worked your muscles. By the time the cloud had returned, robbing us of a wilderness sunset, we'd come to and headed on out for a few celebratory drinks and a bite to eat. I was kind of sad to be saying goodbye to Heather, but I also relished the idea of going solo once more, of not compromising, of selfish travel.

A doughy pizza, and again we found ourselves in the same local bar, Heather invading my personal space in a blatant seduction attempt. I was a single man, half way around the world; I wasn't going to resist. We'd found that bar stool pose and she sank her hips deep into my groin and leant into my face.

"You gonna kiss me?"

I did; it was long and deep and tasted of beer and lemon and sugar. I liked a girl with sweet lips. We kissed for twenty minutes, almost constantly in some form of intimate contact in the corner of the bar until the temptation drove us home to find a quiet part of the hostel to continue our tryst.

Along the shore of Lake Te Anau we played, pushing and wrestling and hugging, a foreplay, a mating dance that involved touch and close contact. Her skin smelt cool and fresh in the breeze, odourless sweat rubbing on my clothes to bond us as we grappled.

At last, we stumbled into the hostel and sank giggling into the small and uncomfortable sofa in the tiny communal area in our wing of the house. It was quiet; the few guests that were staying had gone to bed, including our two South African dorm mates. Our heavy petting continued, two teenagers sparring at a party, and my hand located the clasp of her bra which, when released, let fall her large breasts into my grasp. I played with them until warm and clammy, and then undid her shirt button to let them breathe. I'm not necessarily a man for a larger chest, but I enjoyed these, pushing each one up in turn to take the nipple in my mouth, which I nibbled, sucked and tongued. Sometimes, this was better than sex itself. In between the fondling, we chatted briefly, Heather getting more intimate with every question.

"You had many lovers?"

"A few… more than some mates, a lot less than others. You?"

"Same."

This was an uncomfortable topic of conversation. All the best relationships left the past alone, where it belonged. To talk of ex-lovers was to resurrect them, to bring them into the room; you weren't alone with thoughts of past affairs. I didn't want to think of other men's tongues on her breasts, fingers inside her. Today was my time – me alone.

"You like my tits?"

"I do…very much. A fine pair, young Heather."

"Good." This pleased her.

"Very big for such a tall and slim woman."

"I know. I'm lucky; they just always have been."

I was the lucky one tonight.

I moved my hand down her stomach and on to her trousers. I pressed into her crotch and she spread her legs apart: a welcome sign. I undid the top button and pulled the flies apart. I sank my hand into her warm groin and slipped my fingers deep in between her wet lips. She moaned, a deep hum from her throat as we kissed, tongues deeply exploring our dentists' handy work. She rubbed me, quicker, as I played with my fingers.

"You got a big… you know?"

"I don't think you ask a gentleman those kinds of questions."

"Well, have you?"

"Can't you tell yet?"

"Not through these."

"Well, I don't really know as I haven't really examined many penises, but as they say… I haven't had any complaints."

With this, she unbuttoned my trousers and unzipped the fly. I moved my hips off the seat for her to pull the jeans down a few inches for easy access. She quickly went under my pants and pulled them over her knuckles.

"Blimey, Mr Jones, no complaints from me neither."

Sadly, this confirmation was still a thrill, even for a man of my years. I pulled her knickers over her hips and we sat there exposed to each other and played ourselves into an intense state of arousal.

"You make me want to fuck you," I whispered in the heat of the moment: crass and unlike me to say such a thing, but I did, both the action and the desire.

"You what?" She stopped and I immediately felt the heat of the moment plunge into a deep, cool pool.

"I said, I really want you… now."

"No you didn't. You said I MAKE you," (she emphasised the 'make' with some disgust), "want to fuck me!"

I blushed and stuttered to defend myself. "I only said it in the heat of the moment."

She was re-adjusting herself and pulling up her trousers, indignantly.

"I didn't mean to offend. It was just…you know?"

I wasn't begging so as to rekindle the moment; I was genuinely disturbed that I'd upset her so.

"I'm not fucking easy!"

"I didn't say you were."

"Yes you did!"

"I'm really sorry, Heather, I didn't mean to upset you. I was just getting carried away."

"Arse-hole!" she mumbled as she stood up and headed for the dorm.

Emotions and hormones were running high. We were quite pissed too. A little dumbstruck, I pulled up my trousers and went to the loo. I sat there awhile, contemplating the bizarre situation that I'd found myself in. I considered playing with myself to garner some sexual satisfaction from the moment, but it felt cheap. I waited five more minutes washing and giving Heather time to calm down and get to bed. I felt a bit of a fool. The room was quiet. The two South Africans were fast asleep, sweet snuffling noises from her, and a worrying snort from him that usually preceded raucous snoring. He was a big fellow; it fitted.

There was not a sound from Heather across the room on the top bunk above the other girl and at an 'L' shape from me, our feet the nearest point, still a good few yards away. It felt like she was awake. I sighed, in a manner that apologised, not exasperated, and clambered aboard my bunk.

I slept fitfully, not helped by my fledgling hangover and our dorm buddies heading off on a day trip to Milford Sound at an ungodly hour. We were alone, the still grey light of this poor New Zealand summer, turning to autumn, seeping into the room. It was 7.13 a.m. according to my cheap digital alarm clock. I had no watch, nor phone, but needed some official timepiece for those wake-up call occasions. Bizarrely, I didn't care for the time of day but needed its reassurance at night – a hang up from childhood I presumed.

Heather stirred, took a noisy slurp from her plastic bottle that she kept by her pillow on the bed. I did the same with mine. In the next fifteen minutes, she huffed and puffed, tossed and turned, went to the loo, returned, slurped and sighed once more. I guessed what was to come.

"You awake?"

"Yep," I said.

"I can't sleep."

"Me neither."

"Can I come over there," she asked.

"If you want."

204

I was being flippant. I did want her. I had an erection and the memory of her breasts as witness.

She awkwardly climbed aboard my top bunk, skimpy tee shirt and soft cotton shorts that stopped just at the fold of the bum cheek. She lay out on the bed, the vessel creaking and swaying with our movements, threatening to topple us and tumble us awkwardly (and painfully) onto the floor. Her tee shirt was soon off and I was lost in her breasts. Her hands were on my cock, my pants soon being kicked off my feet, and it was harsh and intense. I kissed her nipples, her stomach, and found my head in between her legs. She tasted sweet, always a relief on these occasions, and I licked until she moaned in delight. Her pants grasped her slender ankles together below my knees so I stopped to kick them off. I pulled her legs wide apart and kissed and tongued and sucked. Moving back up, I lay atop her and rested on my elbows to look down at my cock, dripping pre-cum over her Mount Venus. I had an overwhelming urge to plunge it in, but I did not. I could not be a hundred per cent sure of our sexual health, and did not have any condoms. I'd been cavalier with Elaine, but just couldn't afford to be with Heather. So, I resisted and turned her over, placing my cock into the crack of her cheeks and rubbing up and down until her bum was wet with me. Again it was hard to not just let go and fuck her from behind. Instead, I plunged my thumb deep inside and stroked it as a replacement, pleasing her just as much it seemed. Pushed against the cool wall of the dorm to gain a less painful angle, I continued to thumb her hard.

We soon paused and she looked back at me, straight into my eyes. "I thought you were in love with Elaine?"

"Yeah, well," I said and plunged my thumb back into her, up to the hilt, spreading my fingers across her pubic hair and resting them there, fingertips pushed up slightly so I could pump in and out.

'Yeah, well', I thought to myself, cock as stiff as it had ever been. A noise from the dorm next door interrupted.

"Don't stop," she pleaded, "please, I'm almost there. I find it hard to come; please don't stop!"

So I didn't, and continued, a perfect rhythm, until she finally came, loud and fulsome, shivering, breathing heavily, and then I gently pushed her bum onto the bed, trapping my very wet hand underneath it.

"You want me to finish you off?" she asked calmly, coolly, with experience it seemed.

"Yes please."

"Okay," she said turning round, my thumb twisting easily in the wet, hot and creamy flesh, falling out, wrinkled slightly from its long submergence. She sat up and grabbed me with her right hand, stroking it up and down.

"Don't come in my mouth," she said and was soon on me, lips enclosing me and moving up and down the shaft with some skill, gently, but with authority. I closed my eyes and enjoyed her; thought of no one else but her, a rarity in sexual acts these days. I moved my hips in time with her, penetrating her mouth, hitting her tonsils on occasion and she moaned, as if it was required, whilst quickening the work on the head. It was an incredibly accomplished blowjob, the odd tickle of the tongue and scrape of the teeth to titillate. The pace quickened and I fucked her face with increased vigour, all the time building and building until I lost the rhythm entirely. At this, she guessed it was time to take me out and into her hands, lying down on the rickety and uncomfortable bunk bed and watched me spray a large pool of come over her breasts and up onto her neck and throat. As I emptied myself, the sight of the pearl-coloured liquid on her tender neck, gathering in the hollows between the tendons, was possibly the most erotic sight of my life, until I stopped jerking, empty, and with it my soul departed; a deep, dark, post-coital depression hit me in the pit of my stomach. I knelt there, my cock dripping onto a piece of flesh suddenly losing its lustre; an uncomfortable position, both physically and mentally.

Was I a bad person? Was it wrong to desire something so much from someone you didn't really like? Was it wrong to fuck someone for the sake of fucking? Who did it harm? We had both consented and Anna wasn't here; she was half a world away. Elaine had gone home and Rachel was working somewhere in Wellington. Who had I harmed?

I washed myself vigorously in the shower, scrubbing her off me like I did a smear of dog-poo on my knee as a child, rubbing it away in the lather only to discover that the stain wouldn't go; it was the discovery of a large birth-mark the shape of Greenland across my right knee at the age of four or five, an increasing awareness of my body, of concrete things; and here I was again failing to wash away the stain of lust, an increasing awareness of my infidelity. I suppose it's the dream of most men to have throwaway sex, free from any comeback: no one would ever know; no recriminations. But I couldn't escape myself; escape my disgust at letting my lustfulness take full control of me. I felt weak, paradoxically less of a man. It was no fault of Heather's whatsoever; in fact, I treated her poorly. I was close to hating her; the thought, memory, taste and smell of her were repugnant to me as I washed and scrubbed. It was my post-coital depression at its zenith and I couldn't quite cope with it.

Back in the room, Heather was packing, skimpy shorts showing off her long legs, small tummy protruding over the top of the waist band and breasts hanging free in a loose cotton tee shirt. She'd not put on a bra yet, waiting for the shower to wash me away too.

"Hi. You've been a while."

"Yeah." Washing you off me, you whore, thought my Tourette's alter ego (didn't we all possess Tourette's of thought?). She seemed hesitant around me, wanting touch as re-assurance, but I couldn't bring myself to. What a bastard; I knew it, but I was physically struggling with this.

By ten we were on the road to Queenstown, a familiar and comfortable enough position, me at the wheel, a female companion by my side, and here I relaxed as I watched the glorious countryside pass us by, this time a dapple of sunlight deigning us with its presence; a smile goodbye to our odd little tryst.

In Queenstown we drank a bitter coffee outside the market and watched the pigeons fight over food and sex. I felt as low as them in the pecking order of universal things. We quietly said goodbye, Heather leaving her email contact with me, more out of a matter of principal than desire for future contact; she'd got the message. I said I'd bounce back a mail to get the correspondence under way. We both knew I wouldn't. I just wanted rid of her now and not just because it reminded me of my weakness or of Merlin's astute observations. I didn't really like this about myself. I needed some sort of inner-resilience, a core strength to push away these desires. What was it I'd heard one day on the telly, an American teen soap, but nonetheless full of wisdom? – 'In order to change your feelings, you have to change your actions'. Yes, I'd do that! I could do that most definitely. I'd be a one-woman man from now on – trouble is, just one little issue… which woman?

Chapter 4

After a time, a stone will actually aquaplane

"For Chrissakes, Andy!"

He tossed another stone into the fast-flowing, beige-coloured river and saw it skip across the maelstroms stuck in an ever-present circle above hummocks of rock, or of sunk boats or, who knows, maybe piles of dead bodies stacked up over the years in this far-flung outpost.

"Don't fret, man," said Andy, picking up another stone and skipping it near the armed guards who eyed him with suspicion and a fair amount of contempt, I supposed.

"They're gonna bloody shoot you!" I said; well, nearly shouted.

"What for, man, throwing a stone?" He held another large pebble in his hand, offering it up to the gods as he spoke. Again, he skipped it close to the guards, a little way upstream on the wide curve, and this time they smiled and offered a small round of applause as it skipped innumerable times before sinking not far from their feet. I guess they admired his bravura and skill; for sure, Andy had plenty of skill.

He came from Canada, Vancouver B.C., and had been travelling these past two months since college had come out for the summer. I'd met him in Chang Mai, escaping the midday sun by sipping on an iced latte in the Starbucks opposite the night market. He, like me, had travelled the peninsula all of the way from Singapore and was now hitting the hill-country of the Golden Triangle. I was glad to be out of Bangkok, hot and stifling, and along Kao San Road, the centre of the travel world in South East Asia, love was cheap and seedier than I would have ever imagined. I'd drink late into the night watching football and getting wrecked on beer far too strong for Anglo-Saxon heads. In these bars, I watched boys not long out of school succumb to the charms of Thai and Burmese girls as young as their little sisters and pay for the privilege, and men as old as aged uncles slope off with girls only just old enough to drive back in the UK. It seemed sordid, but was a way of life here that I couldn't fathom nor question – who was I to dissect the macro-economics of modern day imperialism and the desperation of the poverty here that made a career of sex an appealing option?

Andy had been one of the cool, young dudes who travelled light, so light in fact that he had room for his beloved skateboard that almost dwarfed his day-bag-sized rucksack. We'd chatted about travel, meeting at the condiment counter, picking straws out of the tightly packed box.

"You gonna go on the boat down the Mekong?"

"Yeah, in a few days; you?"

"Yeah, in a few days too."

"Slow boat."

"Yep."

So we found ourselves on a minibus, with a motley crew of westerners, headed east towards the border with Laos, towards the Mekong, the thin blue line that for many a mile joins the red dotted one of international borders in a school atlas. The landscape across North Eastern Thailand was that out of a textbook definition of the Golden Triangle; field upon field of verdant green rice, paddies of blowing grass that danced in the wet-season winds, shadows chasing each other across endless acres, and out there, somewhere behind the government-enclosed and funded rice paddies, stood the poppy fields, the cannabis pastures and the gangland banks of Burma and China. The hills rose and fell, little spikes of limestone that clung on to their trees, holding them there despite gravity and erosion's best intentions.

We motored into a small town, Chiang Khong, down the slopes eroded a while ago by the waters of the Mekong, rising far to the northwest in the Himalayan plateau lands of Tibetan China. We pulled into the dusty courtyard of a breezeblock hotel, its existence in reverence to the backpackers and their mighty dollar who follow well-worn paths down the river to Luang Prabang in one of the world's most secretive and penniless nations. We were to overnight here with fellow boatmen and women, all here to experience the powerful waters of the Mekong on the slow, two-day, boat trip to the temple city of Luang in Laos – a communist country; one of the dwindling few, yet tolerant of the Buddhist monks that built the temples and wats of the city that help to make it a Mecca for the traveller.

Andy and I bunked up in a spacious but damp twin room that fronted on to a muddy wall and slope that seemed to suck up the rain like a sponge, waiting for a time to slump over the hotel and bury its guests in a slurry of bygone river silt. The two small holes in the far wall that upgraded this room to one that boasted a river view bore shabby gauze frames that posed as windows. If I stood on tiptoes on top of the rickety bedside table, I could garner a view of the muddy Mekong and a quarter of a mile across the channel was Laos, menacing in its backdrop of black clouds and windblown reeds.

An evening stroll in between showers took us up and away from the settlement and, at the beginnings of a sweeping bend, we found pebbles to skim; whereupon two border guards appeared and watched us, their guns casually falling off their hips. My English innocence of uniformed men wielding guns made me wary of them, but Andy knew they bore no malice.

"See," he said, pointing to the guards, bored now with our stoning and wandering back along the path and into the high grass that matted the levee of the bank. I chucked a couple of stones now they'd gone and enjoyed the sensation of cracking my arced arm across my waist and releasing a pebble into the swirling water.

Andy had been looking for skateboard events on his travels across South East Asia, and me, stone-skimming ones: an odd couple, but surprisingly resourceful in our hunt. Andy had skateboarded in Singapore, though against the law to do so, and again in Kuala Lumpur, winning some cash in clandestine events and I'd won two or three little skimming contests off the island of Tioman in the South China Sea; granted, I'd inaugurated them, but nevertheless, a win was a win.

"There's gotta be some good skimming along the Mekong?"

"There's gotta be some good boarding in Vietnam?"

And so, on we went.

In the morning we wandered down the un-metalled and pockmarked road, its level washed clean in monsoon rains past, and joined the queue at the immigration office. We were summarily processed in a quick and efficient manner and put aboard a long boat that would deliver us to Laos, a quarter of a mile across the river at the border village of Huayxai. We were dumped on a concrete jetty, sloping like a recreational reservoir boat club launch, and joined the gathering queue of travellers atop the slope who murmured quietly amongst themselves whilst they waited for the slow boats to Luang Prabang.

Andy had already disappeared amongst the crowds but soon emerged boarding down the rough concrete slope, skidding to a halt in a shower of sparks that put themselves out in the gently lapping Mekong at his feet. I sat on my rucksack and looked out across the river bend, a meander so large that the boats floated like matchsticks against the wooden jetties, some scraping their hulls rhythmically on the concrete launch. A few girls watched Andy repeat his boarding feat down to the river, this time turning in a shower of sparks and flicking the board up into his hands. Obnoxious, but cool, he smiled, swept back his long, greasy locks and headed back up towards us.

"Cool, heh?" he said to me, making sure others around us heard.

"Yeah, sure," I said, squinting into the sun that was trying to break through the low grey cloud behind his haloed head.

"Fancy a go?" he asked me, placing the board at my feet.

"Why not," I said, regretting the acceptance of the invitation as soon as I stood atop the bloody thing. Memories of early childhood, shaking wildly out of control down our steep road, which now seemed unbelievably flat with the hindsight of thirty years and two more feet: it's odd how the world shrinks the further your childhood floats away. I'd come a cropper then, and things didn't look much better this time as I buffeted over great big bumps and crevasses I hadn't noticed on wandering up here. Nearing the water, I jumped off and stumbled to a stop, misjudging my steps and landing my right boot into a foot of water. Andy laughed, as did the few others who'd watched out of boredom.

"Hey, Jonesy!" came a shout from the crowd.

I looked for a familiar face, Dangerous or Kim, the only people who used that moniker on my travels, but couldn't spot them. Beginning to imagine that I'd misheard it, or was entering some phase of psychotic delusion, I kicked the water from my boot like a disgruntled wet dog in a park and pulled the board up from the shallows. I didn't bother to try and flick it up with my soggy boot.

"Oi, Jonesy!" I definitely heard it; two people, a boy and a girl.

"Mr Jones!"

'Bloody Hell, students', I thought. And from the crowd, parting an idle Scandinavian couple, emerged Jo and Dave, ex-students from my geography class a year or so ago; the kids I'd shared the last French Alps trip with.

"My God! Jo, Dave!" I said and offered my hand. We were genuinely delighted and surprised to meet in such unusual circumstances, here on the banks of the Mekong in northern Laos. To be honest, I'm sure they'd never even heard of the place last I knew of them, let alone be able to find it on map, and then actually, physically get here.

"Wow," I said, standing back and looking at them. "Small world hey? I thought you'd gone to Uni?" to the both of them.

"Yeah, yeah," they said in stereo. "Birmingham," "Leicester," two particularly good establishments for our sixth formers to end up at. I remembered being surprised at Jo's grades; a sweet but slightly dim girl, she'd conned us all by grabbing a B in geography (a miracle) and an A in English and psychology. Dave, to give him credit, was a bright, if occasionally snide lad, and was a solid three Bs candidate.

"God, of course," I realised, "it's June now; you've finished for the year. How was it?"

"Easy," said Dave, sincerely.

"Great fun," said Jo.

"You too still mates then, I see. That's really nice. It's difficult to keep in touch at such a crazy time."

"Well, a little more than friends, sir," said Jo, grabbing Dave's hand.

"Oh," I said, "oh, great, cool. Well done!" Not quite sure why I sounded so surprised, or concerned, but then my memories of France flooded back of the two of them and the moisturiser incident. "Ah yes," I said, "I remember now!" I smiled, and Jo blushed.

"Yeah, sorry 'bout that," said Dave, and kissed her hand, a little bit creepily. I laughed, and so did Jo.

"Still skimming, Dave?" I asked, throwing my arm across my stomach.

"Sure; I even entered a couple of competitions back home."

"Really?"

"Yeah, just local, like, but fun. I won them both."

We chatted about my skimming experiences and I could feel he was keen to pit his wits against me once more.

"Well, Dave, maybe we can enter a comp here on the Mekong? You never know, they're in the most unexpected of places."

"Yeah, cool, Jonesy, I'd like that."

Our boat, moored in amongst a flotilla of long, narrow craft tied together, was pointed out to us by a very disinterested-looking pilot, and he led us across two bumping boats to access ours and fingered in the direction of the rear where we gratefully dropped our rucksacks. His co-pilot stuffed them unceremoniously into a tight pack, covered them with tarpaulin, and expertly tied it down. Andy looked at them with the propriety of a dad over his teenage girl on her first date with a punk, and they carefully put his board to the side, tucking the canvas neatly around it.

Once full, we pulled away into the strong current of the muddy and mighty river and were off in a southerly direction along the Thai border, where hours later we would turn east and into deepest Laos. Aboard the craft, which topped off at forty feet in length, sat thirty travellers, all of them European, excepting Andy, all of them white, and all of them extremely middle-class.

Deep we motored into one of the poorest countries in the world, in the Guinness Book of Records for its tonnage of bombs dropped upon it per person thanks to the Americans', largely fruitless, attempt to cut off the supply of ammunitions and men along the Ho Chi Min trail that ran down the Laos side of the Vietnam border. The legacy, of course, is still millions of undiscovered and unexploded devices, waiting patiently to maim and kill unsuspecting farmers, kids and hikers.

I sat with Andy, behind Dave and Jo, and we chatted as we watched the mesmerising Mekong River valley pass us gently by. The swirling muddy waters were banked by luscious green levees which rose high above us, indicative of its wet-season power and strength when it would top them to flood the villages and fields with life-giving water and silt for rice growing. Behind the banks rose lofty limestone peaks that came and went with twists and turns of the middle course of the river. It was still wide here, maybe fifty metres across, and the migrating meanders were hardly noticeable in this majesty: and always there was jungle, sometimes thick and lush and riverine, but occasionally it would ascend the limestone peaks and be seen deep into the horizon, peak upon green peak.

Every two hours or so we would magically come across a little village, the banks worn bare where its only line of communication was constantly in use. As we approached, scores of little kids brightly clothed and screaming with excitement, would greet us. Waiting patiently were their parents, armed with cold Cokes, water and the state-owned beer, BeerLao, the only one available, but, thankfully, bloody good and offering excellent merchandise in printed tee shirts, which, of course, were bought too as souvenirs.

Dave and Jo were travelling with a group of students, also in their teens and early twenties, friends who'd attended schools in Norwich and now, the redbrick Universities. These four girls and one boy were excellent companions, full of vivacious energy and a pleasure to talk to and share crisps and beer with. The sole male of the group, Charlie, was a beautiful chap, in looks and manner, and was travelling with his girlfriend, one of the Norwich girls.

After the second village, and five hours into the eight-hour journey of Day One, I found myself sitting next to Jo. We talked about Uni, about school and what she hoped to do.

"I'd like to teach, too," she told me.

"Great, Jo, you'd make a great teacher. Primary or secondary?"

"Oh, the little ones. I love the little ones. I couldn't do what you do."

"Oh, I dunno, it's like any job; you learn how to cope, to survive and enjoy it wherever possible."

"Still, all those horrible spotty kids and their hormones." She talked with maturity and a maternal nature well beyond her years, not long since a spotty teenager herself. As we chatted, and I enjoyed this adult version of one of my sweetest students, I was distracted by a black log floating down the river at a slightly slower speed than our 'slow boat'. I looked back at Jo as she reminisced about the French Alps trip, minus the moisturiser, and then the time delay in my slow, slow brain clicked in.

"Shit!" I said, gaping wide-mouthed at Jo.

"What; what is it?" She instinctively looked at her shirt, brushed at her shoulders and patted her jeans. "What; what is it? A bug?"

I had looked back at the log, now forty-five degrees behind my right shoulder, and had seen it transform, like a magic-eye picture, into the body of what looked like a local farmer, dark trousers flapping in the current and surface breeze, his tree-trunk arms held rigid above him, his fingers spread like winter twigs. His bloated body gave him ballast, the decaying meat giving off gases lighter than water. He floated serenely behind us, ever onwards and towards Cambodia and the sea, and hopefully, some sort of Nirvana and not just a silty-brown Mekong delta.

"Oh my God!" said Jo, mouthing it more than the sound escaping her. "Is that…?"

"Yes," I interrupted, "it is." I smiled; not too sure why, but the sight of my first dead body since working as a domestic in an ICU at a local hospital as a student didn't seem as shocking as I would have imagined. There was something quite serene about the theatre in which he played out his final role: better to die by falling into a mythical river than in a sterile hospital ward stinking of piss and death. Granted, the poor man may have had a bullet put through his brain and been dumped, but somehow I felt as though this was a pleasant finale, an epilogue of natural cadence; well, that's what I convinced Jo of, at least.

"See, it's not sad really, Jo; it's really quite beautiful."

She looked at me with a smile a timid girl would give a potential mugger and looked away to the forest to have a think about it. Damien, a photojournalist from Ljubljana, Slovenia, was gutted he'd missed the body as I told him about it at the makeshift bar, four feet by four feet, located just in front of the well-packaged luggage.

"Oh, man," he said, puffing on a very strong-scented joint, "I wish I'd seen it. I'd have taken a great photo." He spoke English with the laconic ease of a white middle-class Californian drug dealer – with the accent too.

"You not worried about the law here?" I asked, fearful of the rumours of the death penalty being given out to careless westerners caught smuggling drugs in this neck of the woods. He laughed with the confidence of a man having seen the heart of darkness, and offered me a drag.

"No thanks." I was a little wary.

"Wait 'til we get to Vang Vieng," he said, "and then you'll see just how serious they take drugs in this country."

Unsure as to his meaning, I left it at that and returned to my friends and we passed the time by playing a quasi-ignorant version of University Challenge. We spent ten minutes coming up with various genres of questions and then fired them at each other, giggling at our lack of depth of knowledge on a wide variety of subjects. The sun fell behind the thickening clouds long before it set and rain sprayed the wide river bends with squalls that rattled this way and that, a dance that came and went with the breeze. Evaporation gave way to steamy trees that added layers to the lowering skies, and just before six we docked at the transport hub village of Prakbeng. Planks upon jittery planks made a makeshift jetty and we stumbled to shore, Andy tripping on his baggy trousers, treading on them to keep his balance and stay dry but baring his arse to an amused slow-boat crew and a bemused gang of accommodation-touting locals.

Within ten minutes, the whole of the boat had somewhere to stay and was being led in small groups up the muddy main street (okay, the only street of this forest village) with its bamboo shacks tumbling up the hill, and concrete foundations that sometimes spilled into the street to improve the road surface which bore evidence of a burgeoning economy. It seemed as though this little place had hit the jackpot as the half-way house to Luang Prabang, and the grateful westerners paid top dollar to stay here so the villagers thought. To us, it was still peanuts.

All along the road locals came to see us, and it soon became apparent that this was not out of idle curiosity but out of the Golden Triangle economics. I'd never had so much puff stuffed into my hand, never seen so much opium and heroin or tabs or mushrooms in one place as I saw on that short stroll up to my bamboo lodge. The majority of the kids bought something, clearly not heeding the travel book and Foreign Office website warnings – 'Drugs kill here and not just in the body fuck-up way; it could lead to execution or, if you are lucky, life imprisonment in a rat hole with a pot-pourri of Laotian criminals, some hell bent on being bent with you,' or words to that effect.

Being a cautious traveller, I avoided the hawkers and watched the open bartering with amusement. The Norwich girls bought a few bags of weed, Charlie a cocktail of Golden Triangle allsorts, and then we followed our host to the lodge; Andy and Damien stayed and comparison-shopped for a while. Money had granted our landlord a foundation of concrete and a basement of open shower rooms and toilets that worked and could be washed clean each night, the Mekong water trickling unassumingly into the public sewer that ran down the middle of the high street.

The two-storey shack housed four bedrooms and eight of us. I was to share with Andy or Damien, but they'd been left in the streets, eyes lit up like toddlers in a candy store at the potential of chemical cocktails. The girls: Emma, Imi, Clarice and Clare, would share, I was sure; leaving Charlie, Damien, Andy and myself to fight over the remnants. We played an assortment of card games, drank some BeerLao and then went for a bite to eat.

It was surreal indeed to be chomping on a slice of pizza margherita on a bamboo veranda overlooking the Mekong, but real it was. We drank enough beer between us to empty the generator-driven fridge and eat into the warm storeroom surplus. We had been told of a curfew that had you locked in your lodgings by midnight and, being new to this unpredictable land, we decided on an early-ish night, leaving the pizzeria by eleven. Well, the owner was politely asking us to go, turning off the lights and refusing to serve any more beer.

The card games continued in the landing hall of our shack and the chemicals fizzed around the room, shutting eyes and popping them open alternately. A little local man joined us, squeezing in between two of the Norwich girls and swaying to the music that played in his head. After a round of snap, or some other interminably boring card game, he livened up the room by grabbing Imi's left breast. Indeed, although a mighty fine boob, it was something of an intrusion and, after the initial shock, he was bundled out of the lodge unceremoniously; not too difficult a thing to do as we were all twice his weight and considerably less stoned. The owner appeared, as if by magic, and informed us that it was now twelve o'clock and, as we'd been intruded upon, he would lock the front door so keeping us safe and comfortably curfew-ed. The cards cadre fractured into smaller and smaller groups as the day, the beer and the drugs took their toll; Charlie and Clare disappeared first, then Emma and Clarice, then Damien and Andy to revel in a drugs-addled fug no doubt, leaving Imi and I and a hard-core game of pontoon, a childhood tipple I was much more fond of.

It took me a while to realise that this meant we were the last two and therefore to share the last available room, but my head was somewhat spinning with passive pot-smoking, and it took a rather more sober Imi to point the fact out as she peered over the rim of her glasses, her nose peaking above her fanned-out cards.

"Looks like me and you and the rat room, Jonesy."

"Indeed," I said, casually fending off her even more casual reference to our sleeping arrangements. She was a cool customer.

"Jo likes you," she said in between twists.

"That so," I said, equalling her cool, cool poker front.

"Yeah. Twist… Five card trick!"

"Bollocks," I said and threw down my measly banker's nineteen.

"She talks about you more than she does Dave."

"Just reminiscing on her school days that's all."

"Yeah sure. You see the way she clocked you on the quay. Nearly came in her pants."

I looked up at Imi. She was smiling. "Quite," I said.

"That's why she and Dave stayed elsewhere. She couldn't stand the thought of you both in the same accommodation."

"Imi, don't be daft."

"Don't deny it, Jonesy; given half the chance you'd sleep with her. I can see it in your eyes."

"Imogen, now listen. I think you're being wholly inappropriate." I gave her my best teacher stare, which was poor, at least compared to Anna and her evil Unionist pout.

"Don't try that teacher stuff on with me." She was still smiling.

"My God, you must have been a bloody scary kid to teach."

She pondered a while. "Yes, I think I was."

"Thank God I didn't stay in Norwich to teach then. I could've been the poor old bastard that you crucified."

"Oh yeah, you trained at UEA; that's why you know Norwich."

We'd all given potted life histories on the boat. Imi was studying Physics at St. Andrew's, and was quite the scientist according to her school friends. Now, let's take a little look at this extremely confident young lady, my roommate for the night: a tattooed chest, a robin redbreast poking its head through the loose canvas of a large bra; a pierced eyebrow and lip; red hair streaked purple in a handful of strands; a short cotton dress, flower prints from a Laura Ashley catalogue, and sturdy thighs that led to smooth calves, tanned olive in the tropical sun. Her eyes were large, enclosed by naturally luscious eyelashes that seemed permanently mascaraed, and a delicate right ear poked through her thin shiny hair as though to tempt the sexual devil. It made me want to nibble it, press a hand upon her robin breast and run the other up her sturdy, soft, apple legs. Indeed, it had been the robin tattoo that had caught the attention of our Laotian friend; maybe he thought he'd catch a bird in his drug-addled brain, and it had been, after all, an innocent and misinterpreted grope. I suggested this to Imi.

"I don't think so; not the way he grabbed it."

"Oh, sorry; did he hurt you?"

"No, it was just… let's just say it was a more-than-friendly grasp."

"Ah, right."

"Bed time, methinks; a long day on the boat tomorrow."

"Indeed; we're in here, I guess."

Inside the room, which backed on to the sloping forested hill that surrounded the village (and when I say backed onto, I mean that I could grab a handful of foliage through the open window without stretching out my arm; and when I say window, I mean an opening in the bamboo hut without a pane of glass), there was just about enough room to fit in a rickety old queen-sized double bed. A clean duvet and clean-looking pillows sat atop, a pleasant flowery pattern all the way from John Lewis, Bluewater, it seemed. We looked at each other and I pulled out my sleeping bag.

"I'll lie on top in this; you have the duvet."

"You sure?"

"Yeah, of course."

It wasn't too embarrassing, both being used to the unisex world of travelling, of sharing closely with strangers, of trusting pretty much everyone you meet; it was a nice way to live. As I sorted through my things, the usual bedtime routine that would organise my toiletries, water and clock within a hand's grasp in new and unfamiliar places, Imi went downstairs to the loo and I took my time to read the graffiti scrawled across the newspaper-print wallpaper, not John Lewis, I guessed:

'Beware the rat!' I laughed. 'The rat will come!' 'It's the biggest rat in the world!' 'Hide your cheese!' 'Hide your tackle' 'Mein Got, ein rotten!' 'Sleep with one eye open – the rat will come!' and on it went. I continued to read, the smile turning into a grimace and I considered the endless scribbling in front of me. Granted, it was funny to put the travellers ill at ease and I even thought about adding to the wall. But hang on; this was one hell of an effort for a late-night joke. I looked again and followed the warning words across the lintel of the door and onto the ceiling, leading still to the far wall. It was now taking on an epic proportion: a Hollywood serial killer wouldn't have taken so much time with eight pints of his victims' blood to tell the detective who he was in tantalising clues.

Imi returned, dressed in a long tee shirt, a sweet improvised nightie with a picture of Pooh Bear swatting at honeybees, his left paw stuck in their hive. It was cute and incongruous with the piercings and coloured hair. Her breasts, unsupported, filled the shirt and her nipples pulled at the cotton; it had been cool in the concrete basement. I pointed to the wall.

"At what point do rumours get so big that they become the truth?"

"Hey? Yeah, I saw it earlier." She looked at the wall, and I could see her mouthing the words of warning, a smile spreading across her full lips.

"I'll leave you to it," I added and went to the loo to do my ablutions as best as was possible in the basic surroundings.

On my return, Imi was in bed reading a D. H. Lawrence novel, *Sons and Lovers*. 'What a cool young thing,' I thought, 'a Physics undergraduate but still in touch with contemporary literary classics'. My pomposity of thought made me smile.

"Enjoying it?" I asked whilst squeezing in between the duvet and my sleeping bag zipped open to act as a blanket.

"Yeah, love it. You read it?"

"A while ago. Can't really remember what happened, but I remember enjoying it."

"Mm… I know what you mean. I'm like that with films."

"What you reading?" she asked, yawning then and displaying a pierced tongue and a couple of silver fillings.

"This," I said, and picked up *Middlesex* by Jeffrey Eugenides, a book I'd had recommended in Oz, finding a copy in a hostel and swapping it for a dull Dan Brown. It was good.

Our torches followed the words across the pages until sleep took us, quite quickly tonight. I woke to the pitch black of a jungle night, sensing the event first and listened briefly to the forest noises, seemingly bloody close, if not in the room by now. Imi sat bolt upright and let out a breathless, "Shit, shit, fuck, fuck…", her heart pounding so hard that I think I heard it, or at least felt it through the mattress. The panic quickly seized a hold of me too. Shit, the rat!

"What, Imi? What is it?"

"The worm, it's fucking glowing!" A little louder this time, but still rather breathless. I hoped the others wouldn't wake, thinking I'd freaked her out somehow.

"The what?" I asked.

She was shaking, sitting up straight. I slowly and carefully put my hand on her arm and brought it down to her lap. She was still shaking.

"The fucking worm, it'll eat us all!" this time whispering and slightly muffled. A bad dream; I was mightily relieved to not find the rat scampering towards me, its jaws aimed at my soft, white Caucasian throat. I didn't want to wake her, fearful of how she might react, so I held her arm and spoke softly.

"Go back to sleep, Imi. It's a bad dream. There is no worm. Go to sleep. Shh."

She mumbled something about being eaten again, but slightly less convincing in its warning this time. Within a few minutes she was asleep, pushing herself deep into the duvet and I scrunched up into a foetal ball, just in case. My heart rate slowed, returned to normal, and I thought of my travel girls and which one I might marry to pass the seconds, minutes, almost an hour until sleep took me. I nodded off, though I had managed to master the art of snoozing with one eye open; you never knew.

The village woke first, forced out of bed by the increasingly loud screeching of the forest animals and domesticated pigs that wandered the streets and feasted on human shit. I was up before Imi, having showered in tepid water and taken a stroll, along with the pigs, to watch the river flow by. I wondered what had happened to my farmer and if we'd pass him during the day, stuck fast in a tangle of forest flotsam.

The bamboo hut was stirring when I returned but I came in on a still slumbering Imi, and quietly sorted through my things.

"Morning, Jonesy."

"Morning, young lady."

"Did we fuck in the night 'cos I've got a hell of a backache!"

"No, Imi, just a fight with the glowing worm."

She rested her head on her right elbow, red hair falling into her mouth. She spat it out of the way as she got up.

"Shit. No way! You dreamt of the worm too?"

"No, no, you did. You just… shared it with me."

"Is that all we shared?" She placed her index finger in her mouth and gently bit at the end, baring her pretty white teeth.

"'Fraid so. If anything untoward passed between us, it was only in a dream…or possibly the rat in the night."

"Ah shucks, Jonesy, self-deprecation fits you just fine. Not such a bad dream, I bet."

I let the kind words hang between us and smiled at her. The thought hadn't seriously occurred to me until this conversation; surely not another love complication, but it had been discovered now; it existed, and I would play with the idea for the rest of the day to help pass the time.

The boat was loaded and off before ten, the mist lingering on the river like a ghostly shroud and we quietly motored east into the rising sun, visible comfortably to the naked eye in its full glory through the milky mist. All was silent – the river, the forest and the boat. People slept against each other and one or two quietly smoked at the back, thoughtlessly flicking butts into the river. Damien was one of them, camera hanging around his neck, alert and ready for the shooting of my dead farmer. I sat with Imi and she nodded off on my shoulder smelling of youthful hope and I enjoyed being her travel pillow, soaking up some of that lust for life.

As we continued, I entertained thoughts of our union and watched the sun burn away the mist to unveil a sticky, humid jungle that grew thicker and more impenetrable by the minute. The sun grew higher and hotter and triggered the growth of thick, grey clouds that gave off sharp showers as the afternoon floated on. It was a more subdued boat today and people either slept or chatted quietly in twos or threes. Imi and I shared imaginary snapshot profiles of the characters around us, assassinating all but a few with childish jibes and of course, we assured ourselves immunity to these attacks. She was a lot of fun and kept me smiling all of the way into the busy docks of Luang Prabang, this heavenly city, temple upon temple tumbling down the central hill to the confluence of the Mekong and its tiny neighbour, where it sat sublimely.

We found a suitable hostel in the backstreets, large enough to accommodate a band of us brothers and sisters, and we divvied up the double rooms as sensibly as possible. Before I even suggested a union with Andy or Damien, the gentlemanly thing to offer, Imi had reserved us the downstairs twin, spacious and with an en-suite but dingy with a frosted windowpane that backed on to a dark back passageway.

"Me and Jonesy'll have this one," she insisted grabbing the key, a flimsy metal spindle attached to a roughly hewn block of balsa wood, a pocket-unfriendly object that would be an awkward reminder of our partnership. It wouldn't fit in her pockets, and if jammed into my jeans would make me look very pleased to meet her.

The humidity hung in the room like a sauna and ate away at the fabric of the curtains and bedding. "Nice," I said and put my backpack next to the bed jammed up against the slimy wall.

"You sure you'll have that one? This one has a firm mattress." She sat on the edge with her legs pushed out straight and bounced on it like an excited toddler in Ikea.

"No, you're fine. You take it."

"We can always share it," she said, her smile turning into a devious chuckle.

"Stop teasing me, young lady. You're being very unfair."

"Oh, sorry, Jonesy, just having a bit of fun; no harm intended."

"None taken. Now, you showering first, or am I?"

"Well…" she looked towards the shower and placed her left index finger in between her ivory white teeth once more.

"Ah, ah," I said, raising mine in a mock warning.

"Sorry," she mouthed and grabbed a towel and was in the en-suite, locking the door after herself. I sorted through some clothes for washing and lay back on the bed, hands linked behind and shut my eyes whilst listening to the dribble of the shower, the shriek of Imi as the water slowly came up to a bearable heat and then the gentle hum of a pretty girl washing away a day's sticky perspiration. She was a sweetie and she made me smile. I liked sharing with Imi and although, of course, attracted to her, felt secure in our mock flirting: it was going to lead nowhere and we were both quite happy with the idea of that. I wondered what her story was: mine required no more complications, of that I was sure.

***

Strolling the streets of Luang Prabang at night was a beautiful and serene experience; soft street lighting and a paucity of bars and cafés led to a downbeat sense of relaxation. The curfew took us out of the bars by eleven and to bed by midnight. I chatted with Charlie and the girls, occasionally sharing a thought with Dave and Jo. Although the senior party member by a good few years, I was gratefully accepted, feted even, as the wise old owl and they listened kindly to my safe advice when requested. It was an interminably comfortable few days and I could have stayed right there in that situation, in that Shangri-La, for eternity.

Down by the tributary that flowed through the hinterland of Luang, ever increasingly rural and poor and primitive but yet peaceful, we found a quiet bar with tables tumbling up the hill and affording views of the few lights that ran along the quay, their flickering reflections interrupted by the occasional punt taking a local worker home.

Andy had disappeared for a day or two, but found us once again in that bar.

"You, you English bastards! I can smell you a mile off!"

The girls laughed, charmed by his New World bravura. We sipped a local cocktail, beautifully entitled 'Pink Gays', tart and fruity and frighteningly quaffable, and the others smoked odd combinations of cannabis and flakes of opium. I declined with the wisdom of having been there, however briefly and unpleasantly. Imi linked arms with me as we hit the quay and we picked up pebbles to throw over the long boats parked up for the night; they threw circles of light across the water that shimmered with the impact of stones, until they gracefully fell back into a gentle, swaying reflection.

"Good shot, sir," she said as I pitched the stone into the reflection she chose, shattering the image into a shower of pixelated light.

"Thank you. You know, it's about the one thing in life I'm really good at; well, the one thing that I believe I'm truly good at."

"Lucky you. I haven't an inkling of what I can do well." I liked the way she spoke to me; like a scatty Home Counties aunt – apart from the swearing that is.

She snored quietly that night, a sweet little snuffling that felt wonderfully reassuring as I lay awake and day-dreamed of success, somewhere, somehow.

***

We'd planned a mass exodus of the enchanting Luang Prabang for the day and hired as many mopeds as the desperate vendor could muster from friends and relatives and neighbours, clearing the street we lived on of any transport that day, and headed out of town. Destination: a mythically beautiful waterfall a few miles out of town and glorified in the guidebooks.

The A13, the main artery from here to the capital Vientiane, was metalled and as good as any B-road back home after a hard winter, and we swerved with ease around the numerous potholes, pigs, chickens and naked children.

Rising into the hills, chugging slowly up towards the mist, our path was crossed by busy farmers and the occasional camouflaged local bearing an AK47 casually slung over shoulder: described as bandits in the guide book, but rather friendly in reality, smiling and waving nothing but flesh at us as we pootled by. It was a rare sight, a Quadrophenia of sorts, heading down the A21 to Hastings on a bank holiday but instead of stopping off at a Little Chef, we would park up by a bamboo gazebo, lazily built and situated on a bend that afforded glorious vistas into ravines, valleys and terraced paddy fields – when the mist cleared with a puff of a light breeze that is. These open and hastily constructed shelters were most-likely drying platforms for harvested crops but today were a place for us 'easy-riders' to relax, smoke and chat away. A few locals looked up for a second from their back-breaking work; it must have seemed an odd sight for them to behold but one they were becoming more familiar to – with increased tourism and contact with westerners came increased indifference; quite right.

By noon, we had passed through a couple of bustling towns, investigated a thriving market, soaking up its sounds and smells and had descended deep towards the jungle-river that led to the falls. Toothless, inanely grinning ladies gave us a sheltered bay to park our rides, a small fee charged for the privilege, and a boatman beckoned us onto the river. Eight of us clambered aboard the long boat hewn from local trees, the chipped marks still splintering into my shorts, and we wobbled across the river to the far side of a long meander. Looking back to shore, little children ran along the bank waving, a couple of them jumping in and trying to swim out to us before being beaten back by the increasingly fierce current as the bend progressed. Three girls sat on their haunches fanning a fire with banana leaves bigger than themselves, tending a boiling pot that looked big enough to hold the remains of a Norwegian tourist or two.

The rich minerals in the limestone hills all around, dressed luxuriantly in riverine forest, ran down to the falls and deposited themselves into pans that gathered pools and created a cascade of falls befitting of a fantasy movie. Overhanging tree branches made for strong diving platforms and the more competent swimmers were back-flipping before I'd found my swimming trunks in the backpack. The young things bared their bodies with pride, not yet ravaged by years of indolence, and I quietly slipped into a pool by myself and watched their frolicking.

Dave, of course, was fearless, diving like a gannet off the highest branches and appearing from the depths, Adonis-like, a wide grin sweeping across his face, a look so natural that you couldn't fail to smile at his pure, unadulterated joy. Imi joined in as coolly as it came naturally to her, diving unnoticed off the lower branches and floating beneath the umbrella canopy, taking in the beauty of it all. I watched her and saw her young body twist and turn in the pools like a playful young seal pup – it was enchanting. She swam over to me, still stuck in my corner, arms stretched out across a crusty rim to support myself as I trod water horizontally.

"Oi, perv!" she said, splashing water in my face from three feet away. "You been watching me for ages."

"Oh, sorry," I blushed, "it was… I just kind…" I really didn't know what to say, so stopped myself, shrugged and raised my arms above the pool to exaggerate the action and said, "It's a fair cop."

She smiled and sat down in the shallow water next to me. "I don't mind at all, you old soak; I'm flattered. Does that mean you fancy me then?"

I thought carefully about my reply. "Well." I stroked my chin, "I guess it does, but… I'm probably a little bit too old for you, so it's best just to leave it at that and apologise. I won't ogle again."

"Oh." She sounded disappointed. "Why you not swimming with us; diving?" She mimicked a dive with her hands, a praying motion that sank her down into the pool and gathered water around her breasts.

"Not a great one for swimming, I'm afraid."

"Oh. What about diving?"

"No, even worse. It always seems to get up my nose however hard I try to avoid it. I'm useless."

"Oh."

"Not very manly, is it?" I said, paddling my legs out like a four-year-old in a toddlers' pool.

"No, not really, but I find it quite attractive; makes me want to mother you." She planted a big, wet and slobbery kiss on my balding pate and splashed away back to the others.

***

"Will I ever learn?" I whispered to myself, heart pounding like a jackhammer on concrete, standing ten feet above the largest pool and clinging for dear life to the wide trunk of the beautiful tree I had foolishly climbed to follow a beckoning Dave. Imi had tried to talk me out of it, but I wanted to try and overcome a double fear, namely heights and plunging underwater. Ten feet didn't seem so high from down in the pool but up here, an extra six feet thrown in from my viewpoint, it seemed a hell of a long way and I found it hard to take my grasp from the safety of the tree trunk.

"Look, Steve," said Imi, speaking softly and calmly, "it's a bloody lot easier to jump than clamber back down; just do it!"

"Okay, okay," I said, heartbeat ripping at my throat and wobbling my voice. I stepped tentatively along the branch, still holding onto the trunk, shuffling like an old lady towards a waiting bus, "okay, okay!" I let go, and a rush of adrenaline shot out in all directions from the pit of my stomach, pushing me over the edge until it hit my toes, which grabbed on and pulled me back.

"Okay, okay." I couldn't hear the shouts of encouragement and derision at equal measure: another rush volleyed across my bows and I was suddenly in thin air, legs dangling, trying to run on oxygen, a paddling duckling fledging the nest from a first storey window ledge. "Shit! Fuck!" and then I was underwater, a swirling, gurgling world that imploded in on me and sucked me down, down, down. Pushing hard, desperately, with my legs, I kicked and kicked and eventually broke the surface, gasping for air and coughing up the mineral-rich water that had forced its way up my nose and down my throat. I heard a muffled cheer as I coughed up the last of the water and gingerly swam to the edge of the pool to gather myself. Imi was soon over, grabbing my arm as I pinched water from the corner of my eyes twixt thumb and forefinger.

"My hero," she laughed and her grab turned into a full hug.

"Never, ever, ever, fucking again!" I gasped into her neck.

By three in the afternoon we had tired of the pools and diving off each and every available trunk and branch; I even tried once more, with equally foolish consequences. The river boatman was nowhere to be seen, the pot still bubbling away with Scandinavian long pig, but no kids tended it. The river was too wide and fast flowing to consider a swim across, so we waited. Ambling slowly along the sweeping bend, I came across a collapsing section of bank briefly forming a muddy beach and exposing small, sharp, angular rocks that came away at the slightest tug. I'd soon collected a handful of pebbles and, pleased with their flat and straight-lined bedding, a perfect horizontal sandwich of geological eras, I threw them across the river. They spun awkwardly along their sharp edges, a one or two on the Powers Roundness Scale, but skipped effectively enough, sinking after several skips in the middle of the bend. Gradually, the others joined me, and inevitably an impromptu competition evolved. It was clear that the old sparring partners,

Dave and I, were the most adept skimmers and our makeshift final saw me skip a stone nearly to the far shore.

"That's over twenty skips, man!" shrieked Imi with delight, jumping up and down, clapping then spinning around, her full breasts wobbling in her loose-fitting top. Dave swung over a big skip but it veered towards the end and sank way before my best throw. It pissed him off and I was pleased that I could still beat the auld foe. He offered me his hand but shook grudgingly. I returned a wide grin and a "Bad luck, mate." It plunged the knife in just that little bit further.

"Hey," he said, tapping me on the shoulder as we mounted our bikes once across the river half an hour later, the boatman returning from his poppy-seed-induced siesta, "I'll take you tomorrow. We'll go down by the river; you know, where the two join up – there's good stones there."

"The 'confluence', Dave," I reminded him, a geography lesson a year or so late.

"Yeah, that," he spat. I smiled back at him.

The motorcycle gang ate together in the wonderful night market that sprang into life along the narrow Thanon Chao Phanya Kang and decamped to a variety of bars, meeting again on the way home from the curfew. Imi and I were holding hands, the others considering us a couple, and we enjoyed our innocent friendship, letting them think their seedy thoughts. A sharp shower hit as we got to the hostel and we sprinted in past the stoned Norwegians and their American groupies, two Texan girls who wouldn't leave the three boys alone: granted, they were tall, handsome and charming but I hadn't had a sober conversation with any of them to date despite their near faultless English – their pupils dilated wide and dark even in the mid-afternoon sunshine.

Imi was a little tipsy and lay next to me on my damp and musty bed. She sniffed at the pillows.

"Hmm, smells of you," she said, nudging her nose into the fabric like a little hamster into wood shavings. We were soon kissing, in between fits of giggles, not quite sure if this would make or break our unique partnership.

"Hey," I said, in between slow, soft pecks, "let's call this a one-off, so that it doesn't ruin anything."

"Sure thing, bub," she said, hiccupped, and blew a raspberry into my neck.

Ten minutes later, we were clamped together, the giggles having drifted into gropes and she had her hand on my boxer shorts. She was in her underwear, red, spotty knickers, and a pink bra that I soon unclasped. Her breasts fell into my hands and I explored with fingers, thumbs, lips and tongue. She was truly a unique young lady, and I considered my options as she took a break for a long overdue pee.

Was this the right thing to do? Was it sensible? Was I taking advantage? Was she too young for me? She returned, breasts swinging in rhythm with her soft gait, and all those concerns were banished in the pure beauty of that sight. I rolled on top, pinning her to the bed and kissed down her body to the spotty briefs. I pulled them over her hips and quickly down to her ankles. She raised her legs to allow me to pry them off, giving me a fine view of her slightly shaven Mount Venus. Her pubic hair was short to the sides, and thick and black over the bone. I kissed along the inside of her right leg, down to the crotch, and then repeated the action on the left leg. As I neared her lips, she shook with excitement and I teased until she pushed me, gently, into the middle. It didn't take long for Imi to come, which she did with gusto, grabbing my head and digging her nails into my scalp whilst muttering some obscenity under her breath. I didn't stop, and she came again, quicker this time, and once more until she couldn't discern one orgasm from another.

"Fuckin' Hell!" she gasped, "Fuck... in... Hell! You fabulous bastard!"

My face was wet with her, and I breathed in her luscious scent. I was dripping myself, with excitement, and waited for the next phase with great anticipation.

"Steve?" she spoke softly.

"Yep," I said, hovering over her, not more than an inch from entering.

"I'm," she hesitated. "I'm, a..." She laughed.

"A what?" I asked, kissing her neck and pushing myself onto her lips, waiting for the invitation.

"I'm... a virgin."

I stopped, and moved myself back. "Oh, really?"

"Yes. Don't sound so surprised."

"Oh, no, no, it's just... you know?"

"What?"

"Well... you're, what, twenty-two, and so pretty and fun."

"Charmer."

"I just assumed..."

"Well, to assume makes..." I finished it for her.

"No, seriously, I am. I just haven't... I dunno... wanted to do it with anyone... not yet."

"Imi, I don't think I'd be your best bet; holiday fling and all."

"I know, I know, I don't want to put any pressure on you, on anyone. If you did… we did… if you wanted to, I think… yeah… I think I would… I feel ready. I trust you, but if you don't… you know, I'm cool with that too."

"Blimey, Imi, this is big," I said and knelt up.

"Don't flatter yourself, love," she said and grabbed my pecker, the conversation having taken its toll, and pulled me back up to attention.

I lay on her, two sweaty bodies together, and she played with me in between our stomachs until I came, shooting a lot of come over her hand and onto our midriffs. We lay there a while, enjoying the hot sticky glue and I considered that sometimes you don't need to have full intercourse to have one hell of a time. The smell of us drifted in the sticky breeze coming in through the fly-meshed window high up above the side of the bed.

"Do you know what a Linden tree is?" I asked.

"No, no idea. Is it green?"

"Yes. Good start – does narrow it down slightly, but still a wide choice left I'm afraid."

"No, I have no idea. Is it English?"

"Well, yeah, kind of. It's indigenous to North-West Europe."

"Ooh, hark at the geography professor."

"Well, it is; that's the proper word," I defended myself. "Anyway," I continued, "it's kind of like a horse chestnut type of tree; a bit like a conker tree."

"And your point is?"

"Well, in the summer, about July, about now in fact, it flowers a kind of long white tail of small flowers and seeds." I measured the average Linden tree flower stalk in between my right hand thumb and forefinger. "Anyway, it lets out a really… I dunno… pungent smell… really strong, really distinctive."

"Yeah, and…" Imi was watching me closely, so closely that I felt my vision begin to double as my eyes crossed over trying to focus on the sweet freckle on the end of her nose in the dim light.

"Well, it smells exactly the same as…" I lifted off her slightly, the sperm sticking in long white stalactites between us, "…this." A waft of come hit our nostrils.

"Yes, yes!" she said excitedly, slapping my arse. "I know what you mean. It does, it really does!"

"My brother and I call it the 'Spunk Tree'."

She laughed, then added, "I've never mentioned it to anyone in case I was a bit wrong or mad... well, it's a bit pervy to say, 'oh that fragrance is exactly the same as'... you know."

It was warm in that room, but somehow we slept for an hour or so, me on top of Imi, a wonderfully comfortable mattress. I showered whilst she still slept and crawled under the sheet next to her and slept an unusually long and sound sleep.

***

By four in the afternoon, a small group had gathered down by the confluence of the two rivers. It wasn't as easy to get there as we first thought, having to cross the smaller tributary of the Mekong over a ridiculously rickety old iron bridge into the outlying village suburb with its dusty track, bamboo houses and loose pigs, none of them savvy in the Laos green cross code, as they dodged over-laden trucks leaving Luang Prabang for some unknown outpost. A few curious locals followed us with their rheumy eyes until the daily grind brought them back to pig-watching, nose-picking and opium-smoking; older men, all of them, the women nowhere to be seen, most likely out tending the fields or running a market stall.

We clambered down an overgrown footpath to the bank and looked over the confluence of the Mekong and its unknown little sister, the brown silt of the latter refusing to mix until well downstream from here and creating a two-tone Mekong that ran south from Luang Prabang. If I'd had taken science more seriously in school, I might have known how the change in density would affect the skim of a stone, but I didn't; I intuited it.

There were to be five competitors: Dave, myself, Andy and Bjarny and Lucas, our Norwegian drug buddies. The two Vikings skimmed well, threatening to reach half way across the Mekong here, but not quite reaching the change in colour and density with their two skims. Andy skipped with effortless ease, his gangly body moving in simple animation to skip the stone easily two-thirds of the way across, the jumps taking a discernibly lower trajectory in the clearer Mekong flow. Dave was next, his first stone turning uncomfortably on its side quite close to shore and dunking itself deep into the river.

"Shit, fuck!" he muttered, but loud enough for me to hear five metres away. He took his time, felt the second stone betwixt thumb and forefinger and let loose with an almighty throw that spun the stone in endless skims way out into the more opaque Mekong and falling just a few metres short of the far bank.

"Way to go, man!" shouted Andy and high-fived young Dave. "Awesome!" Jo's eyes lit up and she kissed him with girlish pride.

"Go, Jonesy," he goaded. So I did.

The first stone skimmed beautifully out beyond half way and came to a stuttering halt just beyond Dave's.

"Ah thank you," I said and bowed, just to piss him off. I took the second stone and repeated an equally perfect skim, this time the extra effort bringing a stutter that saw the stone desperately skip up onto the far bank. A little cheer erupted, the odd whoop from the North Americans, and I'd won the inaugural Mekong Classic.

***

Vang Vieng was a bit of a haze: drink and drugs and rock 'n' roll. A lot of the group departed from there, many east across the prehistoric pot-laden plains to Vietnam, whilst the more discerning took the road to Vientiane. Dave and Jo had gone east, Andy and I down to the capital and Imi asked to come along with us, and later with me, on the short flight to Siem Riep and the Angkor Wat complex, ancient and stunning capital of the Khmer in present-day Cambodia.

We had a spacious double at the front of the once-upon-a-time palatial Lane Xang Hotel in Vientiane. It had, so the guidebook informed, once hosted the top party apparatchik from fellow Communist states, back in the glory days of the first Cold War. Since the break-up of the Soviet Union and the fading away of Fidel into wrinkles and dementia and China's cheating capitalist-communist model, it had rusted into an enchanting parody of itself. It still boasted the biggest swimming pool in the land, albeit crumbling around the edges of the deep end and infested with happily breast-stroking crickets, along with a snooker club with five tables, the musky-green baize tending to rot in the tropical air.

Our room was large, the bed seeming somewhat lost pushed up against the centre of the back wall. This wall was thick and marked the end of the hotel, our room being the last on the left hand side on the second floor corridor. A rusting French window led onto a dilapidated balcony that Imi tentatively placed a flip-flopped shoe upon.

"It seems safe enough," she said.

Buoyed on by the false security of the western traveller, a confidence instilled only by the presence of dollars in a wallet, we sat out on the balcony and looked across to the trees that rustled their dry leaves in the warm tropical breeze.

"Ten dollars, man!" Andy had screamed, flicking up the board coolly into his hands. "Too steep for me bro. I'm off to find a cheap room and a Laotian masseuse." I expect that was where he was right now, as we tried to locate the wide sweep of the Mekong that the guidebook insisted was no more than one hundred metres away.

"I can smell it," she said, lifting her head and flaring her nostrils to suck in its scent. I tried it too, but could only discern dust and heat and an odd concoction of cooking smells that wafted up from the kitchen somewhere around the corner.

"Nope; can't get a whiff of it, I'm afraid. Odd though, 'cos I can usually smell the rain on its way."

"Freak," she said, still flaring those cute nostrils in the direction of the trees, and probably, the river.

"Hey, I'm not the one who can smell an invisible river."

"Well, I don't know why you can't. It's pretty strong."

And then the breeze shifted, pushing the broad leaves up over themselves and displaying a lighter shade of green, and the rustle rippled across them in an odd symphony of foliage.

"Um, hold on." I sniffed the air. "I got it, I think." I sniffed again. "Yeah, a kind of, I dunno… cabbage smell."

"Yep, that's it – the Mekong stinks like a cabbage; well, here it does anyhow."

The Lane Xang Hotel was the second tallest building in the city; the other showing itself a half a mile to the left rising just above the trees. Its skeleton dominated the low-rise capital and its emptiness threw a shadowy ghost across us all. Started sometime in the nineties on the banks of the Mekong, somewhere over there, it never came to fruition, the foreign company that promised its financial security dive-bombing in the Asian crash of '97.

Imi drank from a bottle of water retrieved from the tired-looking mini-bar that also housed two small cans of Coke and two bottles of BeerLao: unlikely shelf-fellows.

"There a price list for that stuff?" I asked.

She shrugged and pulled away the stray hair strands that had been blown across her face and had stuck to those luscious lips, before raising the bottle and taking another swig.

"So," she said, looking still to the invisible river, "you wanna make love?" and took another swig.

"Sure," I said, stood up, took her hand and led her to the bed. It squeaked to our rhythm and we both came quite quickly, sweat lying in a thin sheen between us. I stayed inside her, and felt myself shrink in the sodden condom. Eventually, after drifting in and out of an odd reverie, I pulled out, carefully holding the end and moved off her. The air was cool on my stomach and I lay there, flicking the puddle of sweat around my belly button.

"So?" I said.

"So what?" she asked.

"You know, how do you feel?"

"I don't know," she said, sighing heavily and turning on her right flank to face me. Her breasts sank towards the bed, lying atop one another and I kissed them one at a time. The nipples became erect. She played with the bristles of my short hair, flicking a fine mist of sweat across my brow.

"I don't feel much different." She paused. "I never really expected to." She saw the look of disappointment on my face. "No, it was good and all... great, it was lovely." She kissed me to reassure. "It's just, I dunno." She sat up. "I just never thought I'd enjoy it. I just haven't ever felt very... sexy."

"Well believe me, young Imi, you are very sexy indeed."

"No, I don't mean it like that. I mean, I've never been much bothered by it, so it's never been a pressing issue."

"Oh right, I see," I said though I couldn't really. I pretty much always felt like sex though did love the idea of love; it was fascinating and comforting, cathartic even.

"Can we do it again?" she asked.

"What, now?"

"Yeah, if you don't mind?"

"Hell, no," I said, and rubbed my hands to warm them and pressed them firmly onto her breasts.

"Oh, you fucking pervert," she said, and I was soon on top of her.

"Don't use a condom. I want to really feel you this time."

"Oh, right, but won't that be a bit careless... dangerous?"

"No, I don't think so. My period's due any day. It should be safe enough."

Again, I ignored the advice I'd given scores of students regarding safe sex and sank into her and it did feel different and we both gasped. Lying there afterwards, in another round of sweat, we spoke softly as the tropical sun began its hasty descent, burning the dust orange and filling the room with an amber light through the gap in the drawn and musty curtains.

"I can smell you," I said.

"Ta."

"No, no, I can smell that you're nearly... you know."

"On the blob!" she said in a monotone and deep bark, pretending to imitate the typical crass bloke.

"Yeah, I can smell it. Maybe it's in the hormones or something."

"You can, can you? And pray, Mr Jones, what does my period smell of?"

"Baked beans."

She laughed.

"Baked bloody beans!"

"Yeah," I said. "I really like baked beans by the way."

"Good thing," she said. "How do you know that it's because of my 'time'?"

"Well, I've smelt it before."

"Oh." She looked away.

I hadn't thought about the reality of this situation hard enough; the realisation that I was the senior partner, the experienced one and that all her love making from now on had an initial point of reference – me. It was quite an honour and I felt unworthy of it. We lay there quietly, letting the night draw in upon us, and I think we slept.

Getting ready for dinner, Imi sat down on the bed, letting the damp towel fall around her like a discarded skin and spoke.

"I'm sorry, Steve."

"What for?" I asked, spraying the near empty deodorant onto my pits and, with a final fine mist, across my buttocks. I shook it, and with a shrug tossed it toward the bin that it hit on the rim and ricocheted in.

"Shot," she said.

"What for?" I sat next to her and became her towel.

"For making you feel guilty about sex; about not being a virgin."

"Hey, that's okay. You didn't. I don't." I kissed her paternally on the forehead and suddenly saw myself for what I was – a bit of a cradle-snatching chancer and briefly shuddered at myself. Then, as we hugged, I reappraised the scene: I hadn't taken advantage of Imi, far from it; I hadn't pushed her; it was on her suggestion and it wasn't going to be a one-night stand. I was incredibly fond of her. Granted, I'd been fond of quite a few girls in recent months, but it didn't make it any the less truthful. Imi was, for the time being, my girlfriend and we would do what boy and girlfriends do as consenting adults.

We didn't go far for dinner, just out the back of the hotel, past the snooker club and cracked paving of the swimming pool. A diffident security guard wafted a hand in salutation, or maybe it was a Laotian two fingers, and we were in the dark streets of the capital. Across the empty and wide two-lane boulevard was the small rotunda of the Namphou Garden, Vientiane's Piccadilly Circus, with its broken and dried-up fountain and three restaurants kicking out what seemed like half of the country's lighting capacity, but still only a flicker. The smallest eatery looked the nicest, set back slightly and fitting snugly between two bakeries closed for the night. It was French cuisine, run by two Parisians, so the blurb advertised in good English on the sandwich board on the cracked pavement outside read. We ate healthily on snails, beef and crème caramel, parting with $10 for the pleasure. It was the most expensive meal I'd had in months, but it was worth every cent as an odd celebration of Imi's newly found womanhood.

The next day was a lazy affair, rising just in time for breakfast, and we explored this oddest of capitals by foot: the markets; the wats, and just before five o'clock we stumbled upon the river the other side of the plane trees. It was wide here, swinging off to the east in a haze, and the rotten stink of cabbage was all-pervading.

"Told you," said Imi, and linked arms with me. "Now let's go back to the room and fuck like rabbits."

"Such a lady," I said and got an immediate erection.

Imi was learning fast and, as we screwed into the night, all the inexperienced awkwardness left us – it was quite the perfect occasion. Our flight to Siem Riep was to leave at four in the afternoon and we breakfasted lazily enough, catching a cheap cab to the nearby airport (everything seemed nearby in this quaint little capital). We were sad to leave.

Chapter 5

Get as many bounces as possible

Siem Riep was much hotter and the rain had returned; buckets of it sloshed over our heads every twenty minutes or so. It seemed that the sun would dry us just in time for the next deluge, the water cycle in perfect harmony as the steam lifted from our sodden brows.

"You're on fire."

"Cheers, Jonesy; you're not so bad yourself."

We picked a reasonably cheap hotel, booking in by six, the first hint of evening in the crimson sky.

"Red sky at night, fucking wet," said Imi. I looked across, puzzled. "Blank verse," she continued. I laughed and followed her into the empty swimming pool and courtyard bar. We drank bland European lagers – no BeerLao here. I missed it already, but had the tee shirt. We were the only two customers in this ghostly complex it seemed. The hotel was situated on the road to Angkor along the long boulevard of brand new and empty chain hotels, all awaiting the longed-for and predicted rush to witness the wonder of the jewel in the Khmer crown – it hadn't quite arrived yet.

"We could go into town, or eat here?" I asked, tired and hinting at the latter with my intonation, and eyes.

"Let's eat here and give the fuckers something to do," she said.

"Right, let them earn their measly dollars."

We clinked our glasses, a toast to western decadence and almost enjoyed the hedonism we mocked.

"I'm not quite sure what this is," I said, picking at the rice and...

"Me neither." Imi lifted the plate to her nose when sure the waiters weren't looking. Three of them stood nervously, attired awkwardly in the hotel company garb and they waited impatiently for their two customers to finish each course. At a time, they would disappear outside, a trail of wispy smoke the evidence as it swirled around the courtyard unable to mix with the

236

thick and humid air that blanketed this part of the world at this time of year. The smoke would hang in clouds of silvery white, palling at head height and dancing in tumbles and pirouettes.

"It's nine thirty, Imi. I'm tired, and we've a long day of temple tramping tomorrow. Let's go to bed."

"Can we take the wine?" Imi grabbed the half-empty Aussie white and followed me out into the courtyard, parting the smoke like Moses did the Red Sea.

"Did you pay for the meal, or charge it to the room?" she asked as we rounded the pool, a menagerie of dead insects floating atop. She'd gone to the loo whilst I'd sorted it out a short while earlier.

"Paid, in dollars, and gave a big tip. Felt a bit guilty at spoiling their easy night."

"Quite," she said, taking my hand and leading me through the empty lobby and on up the two flights of stairs to our room, 201: sex in another country; that was four on this trip so far. My atlas of amour was fast filling up.

"I guess this'll all be a holiday fling memory for you one day," said Imi

I leaned towards her. "I guess all shags are just a memory at some point."

"True," she said. "But I think I'll remember this more fondly than you will." She touched my sweaty brow.

"What makes you say that?" I asked.

"Apart from the fact that you're my first lover? That's always pretty special, hey? It always will be to me. I'm just another girl to you."

"Not fair, Imi. I'm here with you now; that means you're the girl." I emphasised the 'the'.

"Okay," she said, sighing melancholically.

"Look, Imi," I grabbed her arm and held her gaze, "who the fuck knows what will happen? All I know is that we're here now and being with you is wonderful. I'll never forget these days. How could I?"

She smiled. "Silly me," she said. I climbed on top and showed her what I felt and it was great once again.

We hired a moped from our friendly bellboy who knew a man who knew a man who had one to rent, and off we motored, slowly, anxiously down the road, east of the city of Siem Riep and back six hundred years into Angkor Wat.

"You driven one of these before?" asked Imi.

"Yep."

"When?"

"What, apart from our trip in Luang Prabang?"

"Oh yeah. I mean, apart from that time, of course."

"In Italy and in Greece."

"Right."

She didn't seem convinced as I wobbled around a pothole the size of Belgium; neither did I. We stopped at the tollbooth entrance to this UNESCO World Heritage Site and parted with a larger amount of dollars than we were truly comfortable with. It would be nice to think that these cents showered their way through the fingers of the elite and into the pockets of the townsfolk of Siem Riep. We doubted it by the greedy way they grabbed the notes.

Back on the moped, across the ornately carved Dragon Bridge and back in time to one of the most glorious spectacles of man-made history, Angkor Wat. The ancient city spread itself over a vast expanse of semi-cleared secondary rainforest and we sat agog in awe of it all, chugging our way along the tree-lined avenues, past ancient tumbledown structures and scores of locals who smiled and pedalled tourist trinkets or washed in freshly-filled pools along the verges.

"Guess these guys didn't pay," I shouted back at Imi.

"Hey?"

"Never mind."

"Hey?" she said again and we carried on until we swung the bike around a large curve to come face to face with the temple of Angkor Wat itself, the eponymous structure of the ancient city, a view reproduced a million times over across the globe. We sat in silence and watched the grey clouds gather above its highest wat, sprinkling holy rain over the random monks that sat atop burning their smelly incense. I parked up, locked it as instructed by Anders, the owner, and we walked across the moat bridge, laughing at the little kids that dive-bombed in, splashing their friends and giggling inanely in the process. It was an idyllic sight and one quite forgot the one-legged and one-armed beggars, legacy of a war-torn part of the world struggling to survive in the twenty-first century.

"Hey, mister, hey, mister?" A little girl tugged at my shorts: beautiful almond eyes and a smile to sink a thousand hearts. "You won buy pos car?" She held up a tattered pack of Angkor Wat postcards, sun-bleached along the edges.

"Later," I said, pointing at the entrance to the temple complex.

"No, now! Onry one dollar. You give prease?"

She looked smaller than a doll in a toy buggy but could converse in English with me quite adroitly.

"One dollar? For how many – all of them?" said Imi, smiling at the little ragamuffin.

"No! You rob me. One dollar for two!"

"Two! That's very expensive." She kept a hold on my shorts with some considerable strength.

"Hey, mister. One dollar, okay?"

I gave in, the capitulation of a weak man, and handed over a dollar to receive two tatty postcards of Angkor Wat in return, a deep blue sky superimposed over the usual grey fug. My mistake was obvious at an instant as a horde of Khmer kids rushed me, waving trinkets and postcards and tee shirts. It took me a while to break free, with loose promises of returning.

Thirty minutes later, Imi and I topped the highest wat of the main complex, a frightening ascent up steep and long steps that threatened to topple you at any moment. I pondered on how many tourists came a cropper each year on these stairs. The view across the treetops of Angkor is at once stunning; a green canopy spreading to the horizon, interrupted in occasional places by turrets of temples and jagged tumbledown towers. Some are surprisingly intact, looking as complete and new as a Wimpey Homes estate, whilst others resemble a post-Reformation abbey, buttress roots of mighty forest trees splitting walls into twos and threes.

"Hey, mister?" – a tug at my shorts again. "You said you buy my poscar."

"I did." She looked up at me, a well-rehearsed gaze of confusion. "I have." I took the two postcards from my daysack. "Here." I held them in front of her nose and wiggled them. She grabbed at the edges.

"Thank you, sir," she said and skipped off down the steps. I stood, mouth agape, and watched her zigzag through the crowds to disappear in the second storey of the complex.

"Bloody Hell! Did you see that?"

Imi stood with her hands on her hips, and was laughing.

"Hey, mister?" It was a different little girl this time. I eyed her with suspicion; the sweethearts were fast turning into scheming urchins in my mind. "Hey mister?" She tapped me on my soft belly – I hadn't worked out properly in a while. "Where you from?"

"England," I said.

"London?" she asked excitedly.

"Well, near." She looked at me. "Yes, London," I reaffirmed.

"London is capital of England, popuration ten milryon."

"Well done," said Imi. "How did you know that?"

"England has popuration sixty milryon!"

"Wow, you're a clever little thing."

"You wan buy poscar?"

"How much?" asked Imi. She'd been suckered.

"One dollar for four." She held up four postcards.

"Okay," she said, pulled out a note from her back pocket and took the cards with a 'thank you'. Imi gave me a look – you know the one – that shot through me like an arrow. However innocent, that superior sneer would always rile me; a weakness, I knew, but one that still catches me off guard on occasions.

Like a Pied Piper, we led the gang of children off the summit of Angkor Wat, away from the peace-searching monks and their impromptu shrines that wafted sweet incense across our noses with a turn of the tropical breeze. We briefly stopped at a vast wall of bas-reliefs depicting images of hell, torture scenes which Pol Pot had gratefully reconstructed. Out into the main courtyard, the kids drifted away, pinched at the edges by more affluent groups of western tourists. Children still performed acrobatics into the moat as we remounted the moped and chugged along a wide boulevard, a wall carved with life-sized elephants to our left and a series of towers to our right which we read were used for tumblers and acrobats to perform for the king over the decades that the Khmer ruled from here; it was incredibly impressive.

The Bayon temple, the one with the giant stone faces akin to those that populate Easter Island, was as photogenic as the guidebooks promised as we rattled out a ream of digital polaroid. Imi was a fine model, fronting the huge smiley faces with hers, the edges of her birded tattoo showing tantalising glimpses of breast if I zoomed in. Most of our lovemaking had been in shadowy rooms, curtains pulled, or at night, and I'd only traced the outline of her glorious body art without properly appreciating its beauty in full, natural light atop me. I planned to rectify that when we returned to the room later this afternoon. We chatted with fellow tourists, all equally smiley as the Bayon faces, and left forty minutes later, sad to leave the monument behind.

Macaques screeched from the trees along the road and we motored further into the huge complex, touching as many of the temples as was humanly possible in a long morning. By two o'clock, we had explored the majority of the site and weighed up our options. We had the bike for another four hours and the map showed a myriad of temples outside the main Angkor complex a good few kilometres out towards the Tom Le Sap Lake and its water villages. With the moped, we could reach some of them today and see the others tomorrow.

Leaving the Dragon Bridge, we swerved along the road into Siem Riep and eventually found the correct road, still metalled here, that led to the Royal Baths: a must-see recommendation from fellow travellers. The city disappeared behind us in its chaotic rumble and the green of leftover forests and paddy fields took control. All around, the peasant folk of the Khmer went about their daily business, oblivious to the tourists that gawped at them like a painting in a museum; one day, the crowds would be so large and the city so developed that one would be hard-pressed to find a Starbucks from a Costas.

Chickens pecked at invisible corn in the shadows of stilted huts placed high to avoid the monsoon floods; pot-bellied pigs rolled around in mud and lazy opium-puffing men swung on rickety old hammocks slung from the floorboards of the hut above, some sleeping deeply despite the clucks of chickens and squeals of piglets. At times, the forest would clear and a view to the horizon would drown us in the vibrant green of the rice fields, the long grass dancing in waves to the tropical breeze that had no definite idea of where it originated from or where it was going. A humid indolence spread itself across the land and if it were not for the dire poverty of the colourful characters we passed, it would have been another Eden.

The metalled road soon ran out of funding and a dark red tropical earth track took us further away from the city. A turn of the track led to a huge opening in the forest and here before us, hiding behind a tangle of roots and creepers and seasonal shrubbery, stood the vast pool of the Royal Baths. The site was larger than two football pitches, the water an opaque marble glass, trimmed by ornately carved steps and scattered crenellations where local women scrubbed at brightly coloured cotton clothes. Time had defeated the Khmer, but not its structures, not yet, and the old social order had crumbled along with the dynasties. Today a Utopian world of sorts played itself out, the poorest of the poor, the most dispossessed, doing their laundry in the pool of the living gods.

We embarked on a stroll around the perimeter, nodding and smiling at local girls who scrubbed at their clothes on the steps, soapsuds speckling their faces.

"Do you think they'd mind if I threw a stone across?" asked Imi, a thin pebble in her hands. "I want to make pretty patterns on that water. It's so dark, it doesn't look real."

I looked about at the odd groups of girls doing their chores. They didn't seem bothered by our presence and didn't much sanctify the place by the act of washing their sweaty briefs in it.

"Yeah, go on. If they looked pissed off, we'll just apologise."

"Okay."

She ran down the steps and hurled the stone into the pool. It hit some twenty feet away, shattering the surface and sending perfect concentric rings in all directions, the first of which hit the steps by our feet in seconds.

"No-one seems bothered," I said.

Imi picked up a loose stone by her feet, no bigger than a conker, and chucked it high into the air and then, with the help of gravity, into the pool. The same beautiful pattern again, like in any body of water one knew, but the stillness of the bath against the blackness of the water was quite breath-taking, a perfect mathematical symmetry created by the ripples. Again, the women didn't look up from their hard work so we scrambled along the ancient steps looking for stones and flecks of masonry that looked too neglected to be redeemable in a future Time Team quest to these ruins, until we had collected a good handful of potential skimmers and stood on the first step above the shimmering black water.

I'd not thrown for a while, so took it easy with the first stone, skimming it gently out, ten skips painting a complex web of semi-circles and Venn diagrams that filled this section of the pool. After two or three throws, a couple of the girls stopped their work and looked out. They seemed to be smiling, not squinting at the hesitant sun that had found a hole in the threatening clouds.

"They pissed off?" asked Imi, stopping short of lofting a bigger flake of masonry into the water.

"I don't think so. Think they're just curious." I raised the tone of my voice at the last word, not mimicking an Aussie, but as a sort of rhetorical question: a hopeful validation. "Let me try another and see what happens."

By now I was warming up and I tried a competition-style skip, watching it bounce gracefully, deep towards the middle of the pool where it scuttled into infinite bounces creating a fantastic mess of almost constant ripples. A round of applause rang around this part of the Royal Baths from the now-watching local girls. Two of them shared a joke at our expense and giggled amongst themselves. I threw another three stones across the pool, making one bounce high into the tropical sky before it turned sideways and crashed deep into the black tar.

A small group of girls had gathered now and were making their way along the steps towards us. They bowed as a salutation and we returned the address.

"Steve." I pointed to my chest.

"Imi." She did the same to hers.

The girls giggled and just stood there looking at us both. I bet we were quite a sight to behold.

"Here," I said, and handed a stone to the girl standing nearest me. I say 'girl' because it was what they had looked like from a distance, but closer up it was harder to tell. I put their ages at somewhere between fourteen and forty, a deduction as accurate as a Year 7 student guessing a teacher's age. She took the stone with a subtle bow and watched me closely as I let fly with a pebble that dutifully skipped a dozen times. They applauded. Our friend took position on the bottom step and threw the stone with some skill, it skipping five times before disappearing into the abyss. Her friends screamed with delight, bouncing up and down on the spot and clapping between shrieks. Within a minute, we had a skimming school in operation along the banks of the Royal Baths, young Khmer girls competing for screams and skips across the dark pool. It was a highlight of the trip in this part of the world and I noted the location as a possible world skimming championship venue; it would definitely go in the book.

*(Location No.9, Royal Baths, Siem Reip, Cambodia)

By the time we had navigated through the manic rush hour of Siem Riep, the sun was a lazy orange, its edges dripping crimson and injecting the clouds around it with a mauve sheen.

"It'll be dark soon," prompted Imi, shouting loudly into my left ear, the slightly better one she had deduced from our daylong tour of Angkor atop a clatteringly noisy and half-dead moped.

"Can you remember the way?"

"Yeah, I think so." I wasn't sure. A busy restaurant with red plastic chairs spilling out into the street looked familiar, so I swerved down the pot-holed track that ran alongside it. Within a minute, the bustle of the city had become a gentle hum and we were tracking through the narrow streets of the suburbs. The sky was a translucent blood-orange now, a light that turned the road in front of me sepia brown as though we were chugging through an early daguerreotype of colonial French Indo-China. The big house on the corner, a colonial-looking edifice, marked the end of the street from which we had picked up the bike, brought here by Kim, the brother-in-law of the owner, Anders.

The young man greeted us with such enthusiasm that it seemed as though he had never expected to see his bike again, or more likely the fact that it had got us back here without conking out. We were invited in to his apartment (well bedsit), a kitchen-sized ground floor room adjacent to a garage full of junk. The room was musty. The double bed, lacking a duvet or sheets of any kind, dominated the space and against the back wall stood a rickety bookshelf full of travel guides, garnered second hand judging by their wrinkled spines and thumb-crumpled edges.

He cleared a bundle of clothes from the small sofa that he gestured for us to sit on.

"You like the motorcycle?"

"Yes, thanks… it was great."

"Good, good." He sat on his hands on the edge of the bed, leaning in towards us in anticipation.

"You like Angkor Wat?"

"Beautiful," said Imi, spreading her hands above her head, in some kind of jazz-hands pose. This was her version of sign language, a thesaurus of phrases that I had come to understand over the last few weeks.

"Sorry for mess." He did his own sign language too, a matador-like throw of the arm to mean his apartment.

"Oh, no, fine. This is fine."

"No, it is not good. It is my home." This, clearly, was an uncomfortable statement for the two moneyed westerners to deal with. "So, where you come from?" he asked after a suitably chastened silence.

"England." "Britain," we said at the same time, and laughed awkwardly.

"London?" he asked excitedly.

"Yes," I said. "London."

"Now, that is fine," he said and stood to shake our hands. I hadn't the gumption to disagree with him and reveal the geographical shift in my patronage of thirty miles or so.

Anders gave us a bitter cup of black coffee, but sweetened enough to ease its acidity, and we talked. His life opened up in front of us and slapped us across the face. He was not christened Anders, but Lim, soon to be orphaned as a consequence of the last throws of the Pol Pot regime. As a young boy, he spent many years in a refugee camp in Thailand where he had caught the eye of a Swedish charity-working couple; indeed, his almond-shaped, chestnut-brown eyes were quite engaging as he talked. Looking more closely at the bookshelf, I could discern a photo or two of a young Anders and his (quite-shockingly opposite-looking) foster parents: tall, blond and thickset. His parents educated him both in Thailand and Cambodia, very keen for him to keep in touch with his roots here in this very city. Although still a young man, twenty-five he told us, Anders had a limited time left on earth. At some point in his late teens, he had contracted HIV and could no longer be granted the visa he required to join his parents back in Sweden where they had returned after his marriage to Kim's sister. His frankness was humbling, and he made it quite clear that his wife was not HIV and that they were very careful that she would never be. I studied his face throughout and a sadness beyond our understanding shone out of those beautiful eyes. We wished him well, making a point of shaking hands and Imi kissing his cheeks and swapped email addresses; he had a Hotmail account and could use the hotel computers if he asked kindly.

Our walk back through the streets to the hotel, a good twenty-five minute stroll, was a quiet one and we just held hands and watched the hustle and bustle of the early evening pass us by. We didn't make love that night; it didn't seem quite right, but instead cuddled ourselves asleep. In the morning, the fug of travel kept us quiet until we had breakfasted alone in the courtyard of the ghost hotel, still seemingly the only guests attended to by a host of hotel employees.

Tomorrow, we were flying on to Bangkok and the day after Imi would be going on to Hanoi, and I on the long flight back home a few days later. It hit me like a brick that within a week I'd be sitting... where, exactly? In a friend's flat reading the newspaper, drinking proper tea, eating peanut butter on toast and listening to bands on the radio that had been made famous long since my departure? And then another brick came in through my window of consciousness, shattering my thoughts into a million shards: Imi would no longer be sharing my bed and I would be attending two weddings in August that would also be attended by Anna... Anna, my God. Although we'd kept in some kind of spurious contact through email, there'd only been the one conversation by phone, a drunken ramble in South Island, New Zealand. As the year had progressed, the emails had become more perfunctory and less frequent. She did enter my thoughts on occasions and, being a man, I did recall her sexually, but Anna now seemed a very long time ago. I still had the letter she'd penned, but had never opened it. Why? Fear, guilt, who knows, but maybe my impending return would bring me to break the seal and read her innermost thoughts. Anna – my goodness!

"You're miles away," said Imi.

"Yeah, just dawning on me that we only have two nights left together."

"Yeah, I know." She put her hand on mine on the breakfast table, strewn with crumbs from the stale toast.

"And I haven't really seen your tattoos in a natural, bright light... whilst, you know? I want to see the robin bouncing on the twigs when you're on top."

She took my hand and led me up to the bedroom, a cursory nod to the waiters who pounced upon the breakfast table. She walked the short distance to the curtains and opened them, flooding the unmade room with a bright, tropical light. The net curtains swayed in the lee of the swish and she was naked in seconds, pulling at my belt and yanking my trousers and pants down to the ground and I hurriedly ran on the spot to kick them off. She took me in her mouth with force and performed with some skill. Before I came, I reciprocated and she ended up on top and I saw the light play with her breasts as she quickened the pace on me. It was an explosion of emotions when we came, me just before her, and it was sad to think that this could be one of the last times we would be like this, comfortable like this, intimate like this in each other's nakedness.

Part 3

Rediscovering Anna

Chapter 1

Falling sideways into the water

It was grey: the sky, the clouds, the light, the general mood aboard the plane as we bumped through the dew point and down into an arc over the city of London. Even though the weather was shit, the city looked peaceful, looked new and seemed to sparkle in my eyes along with the Thames, twisting and turning to the west towards Heathrow. The knot of homesickness exploded in my gut and I realised just how bloody glad I was to be back in Blighty, if only for a few weeks. As the pilot plonked the plane down on the north runway, slap bang on the painted line, I looked across at my fellow passengers, most short-term vacationers and a few lucky fellows returning from Bangkok with a Thai bride far too young and beautiful for them. The girls looked nervous. I saw my face briefly in the reflection of the small cabin window, seat 23A, and it was tanned, but tired. I needed a good sleep.

Phil was living in a shared house down near the High Street and had offered me the spare room and a futon until I'd decided what to do next. I'd promised him I'd be gone by September whether to a new job or away again, the latter most likely despite my present glee at coming home.

It was early August now, but everywhere seemed very green on landing. It had been an averagely crap English summer to date and its verdant hue was impossible to ignore, just like the ridiculously over-sized number plates on the 4x4s that pulled up for the gap-year returnees in their throngs opposite the Terminal bus stop.

Within three hours, I'd stepped off the train onto the Victorian platform, eerily quiet for a working day, and was just minutes from the house. Phil had left the key under the bin at the back of the property and wouldn't be home for a few hours yet; time enough for a nap and a dream of the girls I'd left behind. It was odd to be back home after seven months on the road and, once I'd upgraded my phone and received a hundred or so texts from people unaware that I'd not taken it with me, I felt a pang of normality, of the mundane, of routine that I'd missed these past months.

Phil hadn't changed; literally still sporting the same torn jeans and tattered tee shirt combo from the last time I'd seen him the weekend before I left.

"You look well, mate," he said as we sat sipping pints of local real ale in the historic quarter. I quizzed him on his affair with the chubby clerk. Two months, tops, he informed me.

"Yeah, ta. I feel well," I said returning to his opening gambit. "Ta, you too," I continued. He didn't. He looked knackered and had lost some weight, courtesy of endless nights of sex with a girl he'd met in the gloomy drunken vapours of a post-World Cup defeat back in June. He told me that he almost felt okay about England's pathetic exit as a consequence. This was big news indeed.

"You'll meet her tonight. She's great." He rubbed his hands across his thighs, almost unconsciously but uncomfortably salaciously – the thought of Phil romping naked in the next bedroom with a pretty young thing made me feel a little sick and a tad nostalgic for... Anna, Elaine, Imi... I didn't know what: nostalgic for someone to pretend to love; nostalgic for the intimacy.

"Fab!"

I did meet her; she was surprisingly normal, nice and pretty and I did have to listen to them shagging for most of the night. She was a screamer.

The weekend of the first wedding arrived mid-August, and I took my ablutions very seriously, anticipating the meeting with Anna, keen to impress, despite my hapless abandonment. I sprayed on too much of the expensive cologne I'd bought tax-free in Bangkok and was parked down by the river by seven to pick up the boat for the wedding reception.

All of the old crew were there, teachers I'd had the odd contact with through email that seemed pleased to see me but unchanged by a world that had turned me upside down. I drank heavily, having downed my first pint by Tilbury and already feeling light headed by the time we cruised underneath the QE2 Bridge.

I'd seen her at the bar, looking as beautiful as ever, and we were exchanging awkward smiles out of courtesy: hard to read the true intent behind those almond eyes. I'd missed her I thought as I sniffed in the estuary air, a pungent cocktail that swam down the Thames bringing with it London's daily hubbub and a scattering of high-level clouds, a mackerel sky that promised rain from the west by midnight. By the time I was face to face with my ex-lover I was merry and couldn't hide the excitement and fear in my countenance and voice.

"Hi," I croaked, clearing the frog at once with an awkward hawk.

"Hi," she said: ice cool, not a twitch in that piercing stare. "You look well," she continued. "Hear you've been having a ball."

"Yeah, yeah, it was great. Thanks." I took a sip from my beer and looked into her eyes as far as she would allow. It wasn't a long way, not even breaking the film of the cornea.

"You didn't write much."

"No, no, um, I wasn't sure you wanted me… to… um." This was a poor performance.

"To what? Hear you talk about fucking other women?"

"Um, well, not exactly that, no."

"Then what?"

"I… Christ, Anna, you know why."

She took a long swig of her large glass of red wine, keeping me in her stare. God, she was attractive, perversely more so when her blood was coursing thick with ire.

"Think I'd wait, didn't you?"

"No… God, no, course I didn't."

"Good, 'cos I didn't. I met someone." Fine, I could deal with that; I expected as much. "I'm engaged. Regardez la rock!" She waved her tiny left hand in front of me as though to wake me from a daze.

"Oh, great, um, congrats," I said. Shit, how come I'd not seen the rock; poor observation.

"You wanna know who it is?"

"Um, yep, no, uh, yeah, I suppose I do." I braced myself.

"Mike."

"Right."

"Yep." She took another sip.

"You, er, cool with that?" I asked, not quite sure of its intention. She waved the hand again.

"What you think?"

She turned, brushed her hair across her forehead and weaved through the crowd of ex-colleagues. It was pleasing to note that her arse still resembled that of a baby elephant.

It was a good night, and it wasn't until I was driving home, badly hung-over, in the morning, that the realisation of Anna's permanent unavailability began to sink in. "Shit, that's it," I mumbled to myself in between slugs of chocolate milk that soothed my throat from an uncomfortable night of snoring twixt bouts of waking nausea.

The next wedding was the following Friday and I spent four days catching up with family before heading back up the A2 for another night of drunken debauchery; well, I was sure I'd drink too much again especially if, as expected, Anna came with Mike. I wondered if he'd pick a fight with me and considered the equation of his height against my dexterity: I was quick; he was big.

The 'Lodge on the Water' was the kind of wedding reception venue that low-salaried young teachers would choose more out of affordability than aesthetics; it had often been a venue for school proms – cheap, efficient and ultimately soulless.

Jennifer and Aaron were young science teachers, had trained together at the school, gone off to cuddle orang-utans in Borneo and returned engaged. Judging by the increased girth that Jenny wore in that simple wedding dress she was carrying the next generation of good-minded scientists too.

Anna was there, but no Mike; he'd turned down the invitation. He probably didn't fancy another night of Anna and me playing spurned ex-lovers. I didn't blame him.

The nineties soundtrack to Jenny and Aaron's childhood played along in the background whilst we ate, drank, danced and laughed politely at the nervous speeches. Towards nine o'clock, as the last of the finger-food was being cleared from the tables, Anna plonked herself down on the vacated seat next to mine.

"I'm extremely cool with it."

"Hey?"

"Mike, and the…" She waved it at me again, this time more subtly, almost under the table and in between our almost touching legs.

"Oh yeah, sorry about that. I didn't mean…"

She delved into her handbag, a small black number to match her dress, and picked out what looked like the invitation. She passed it to me. I took it and strained my eyes to read the writing in the dim light of the disco.

"I think I need glasses," I said and smiled.

"It's addressed to you."

I looked closely, trying really hard to rejuvenate my ageing lenses.

'Steven Jones, Poste Restante, Queenstown, New Zealand', with a large pink 'UNCLAIMED' stamped across the middle of it, twice, neatly bordered to make two pretty rectangles. I flipped it over, 'Par avion' and 'Return to Sender' embossed on the index finger of an inky hand that pointed across the world from the Queenstown delivery branch. '16th April', the date read.

"Shall I…?"

"Open it? Yeah, sure."

I carefully unpicked the fold of the envelope. The postmark on the date of delivery to New Zealand was '2nd February'. Inside, it felt like a card. Shit, I hoped it wasn't what I thought it was. Anna's neat little penmanship gave her address in the corner just beyond the pointing finger. Two cartoon robins danced on the front of the card and pecked a kiss at each other that showered little red and pink hearts to the edges.

"A little bird told me…" I mouthed the words in silence as she watched me. I closed it, returned it into the envelope and stared at her.

"I didn't know you'd sent it."

"You did. I emailed you."

"Oh, sorry." I stared at the card, fingering it, contemplating what to say next. Anna abruptly broke the silence.

"So, how many girls did you screw?"

"Aw, jeez, Anna, I…"

"Well, you did though, didn't you?"

"Clearly you didn't stay celibate." It was a crass thing for me to say, considering. The venomous vapour drifted off as the music cranked up high enough to muffle our bites and we sat across from one another in a tense silence. I looked closely at her through the middle-eights of nineties dance classics, tapping my foot and waiting for the ice statue to melt or at least shatter into tiny pieces across the beer-splattered floor. Instead, she smiled, fiddling awkwardly with the necklace that sat in the hollow of her neck.

"Nice necklace," I mouthed, pointing to my throat.

"Hey?" She leaned in closer until I could discern that coconut shampoo smell that fronted her familiar scent.

"The necklace." I pointed at it, stabbing my finger too far and too fast, tapping the stone with my fingernail.

"Ooh, sorry," I said.

"That's okay."

There was a pause. I drank in her scent whilst I had the opportunity.

"It's gneiss."

"Hey? Yeah, it is."

"The stone; it's gneiss." She gargled on the silent 'g' to make her point. "Banded gneiss."

"Oh, right." I shifted uncomfortably, remembering the heart-shaped stone I still had back in the spare room at the bottom of my rucksack. It had joined me on my travels, a totem of our love, a lucky talisman, as was the thick envelope she had stuffed into my hand at the airport back in January. I hadn't opened it to this day; to break the seal would have been to surrender to the reality of my situation, and I had escaped to put reality on hold for as long as was possible.

"Where d'you get it?" I asked.

She looked at me, pausing, clearly thinking carefully on what to say next, how to phrase it.

"Clarée Valley."

"Oh."

"Yeah. I went back there in the spring… with Mike."

"Oh, I see."

"Found this stone."

It was perfect, almost an immaculate sphere, beautifully polished to reflect the shimmer of the cheap glitter-ball flickering above.

"And Mike had it made into a necklace." She pulled it up off her milky-white flesh, just to make sure I knew she meant 'this one'. I couldn't help but look like a lost little schoolboy refused a Mars bar on a tedious shopping trip.

"Ah man, but that's our place, our valley, we…" I stopped myself.

"Was," she said. "You're the one who pissed off…"

"Yeah, sure, I know. You're right, but…" I stood, slapping my thighs to help me spring up and went to go for a pee. "I need to…" and pointed to the gents'.

"Okay, but don't disappear. Come back; I need to say something to you."

I stood in the loo, uncomfortably stuck in the middle pissoir of three. Two elderly men, the grandees of the two families joined together in holy matrimony, struggled to force urine around their inflated prostates as I found it equally impossible to pee, the sheer fright of such a social unbuttoning too much for my bladder to relax enough. One of the old guys sprinkled a tinkle at the porcelain, shook vigorously, zipped up, and with a grunt was gone. I noted that the dirty git failed to wash his hands.

"Twat," said the remaining pops.

"'Scuse me?" Oh God, I was now going to get into a fight with an OAP; would probably lose too.

"Oh, sorry, sir, not you. That bombastic old fart!"

"Him," I said, pointing my thumb in the general direction of the door behind me.

"Yeah. Father of the bride."

"And you are…?"

"Father of the groom."

"Oh, well, the kids love each other sure enough."

"True," he said, patting me on the back as he left and with it, releasing the dam.

I tried not to think about Anna whilst I checked myself out in the mirror, scrubbing my hands far too long, a slightly disturbed OCD sufferer in training, and let the water flow between my fingers. It was cool; felt good. Anna was still there, waiting as she had intimated she would. There was a lull in the music.

"You've been ages. Did you have a shit?"

"Charming. No, just a little chat with the fathers of the bride and groom. Seems they hate each other."

This greatly pleased Anna. She smiled; it was nice to see those teeth, bared not out of distress or anger.

"So…?" I said, holding my palms up and leaning in, a Paxman-esque pose of impending interrogation.

"I just wanted to tell you something. We might not get the chance again."

"Okay." I held the pose, my heart hammering at my chest like a wino at a closed bottle-shop door.

"Well, I just wanted to say that… that, I didn't say it enough at the time, but just wanted you to know that…" She was struggling. My heart pounded still. "…that I really, really did love you, you know."

I sat back. "I know. And I did you."

"Did what? Say it? You can't can you?"

"I can… hold on." I leaned in close again. "I loved you too, and I never really told you; loved everything about you…" a slight exaggeration but I was getting tipsy and getting further intoxicated by her confession of true love. I was just about to launch into an exhaustive list, one that I'd practised many a time, usually in the wee small hours of a sleepless night in the months before we had consummated our friendship, when her phone rang, and she bloody well answered it too, bringing our purge of love to a shattering halt; it was Mike.

We smiled at each other occasionally across the dance floor, and I found myself at Phil's flat, on the futon, courtesy of a drunken ride home in Emma's huge people carrier driven by her erstwhile reverend husband, who hadn't had a drop; it was a big sermon on Sunday and the rumour was that the Bishop of Rochester was paying a visit.

"You and Anna seemed to get on well," Emma observed.

"Yeah, I suppose." It was a very non-committal, teenager-in-the-backseat, answer.

"I think she still has a thing for you. Talks about you a lot at work."

"Really?" I watched the dark fields of the Greensand Ridge dissolve into the pitch black of the night away from the orange glow of the main road. "If that were really true, Emma," I said, talking to my ghostly reflection, "then she wouldn't be marrying Mike now, would she?"

"She doesn't really want to. Oh, Steve, it's so obvious," she said, turning back to look at me as she did so. The Reverend Father kept his peace and stared at the road ahead. He knew his advice would not be fitting in this modern and most agnostic of messes.

The futon awaited and I was soon dozing off to the sounds of sex in the next room and the subtle bass of Bob Marley's 'Legend'. I didn't dream of Anna that night, but the restless REM brought forth a heart of darkness as lovers appeared, mocked, stripped and teased before me, and I couldn't touch them, I couldn't have them, despite having the mother of all erections, which I awoke with. I played myself off to the erotic images of the dream, still fresh in my head, a collage of Elaine, Rachel, Heather and Imi, but I came into the image of Anna. She had a habit of timing it just right up there.

Chapter 2

That boy claimed to be conqueror

It was mid-September and I was on a bus heading north onto the German Plain. I planned to stop a couple of nights at a campsite just south of Aarhus, Denmark's second city, where I would meet up with Kirsten, one of the crew I travelled with across Western Australia back in April; she was studying there, a Masters of some sort, I'd forgotten. Immediately on hitting Denmark it became cloudy and the coach was soon drowning in an almighty thunderstorm which left inches of spray on the roads and made passing the juggernauts the scariest of activities for the driver, and for us. Even on super swipe speed, he would drive blind for seconds as the articulated trucks threw bucket-loads of spray across the windscreen. I chose not to look at times and sank my head into a book.

The thunderstorms that had accompanied me through Denmark thus far swirled in circles around the city of Aarhus on my arrival and I somehow managed to find my way across the south side of the city on a local bus, lugging my rucksack and rudimentary camping equipment, including a borrowed tent, and then along the wooded shore of the Kattegat in amongst the downpours.

Five kilometres or so south of the city limits, past the youth club jamboree encampment and the very big mansions that sported the national flag atop proud poles, the forest began and the coastal cliffs lifted from the flat port zone. In the middle of this small paradise stood the Blommehaven campsite, my pre-booked accommodation, courtesy of Kirsten: the University digs were still on holiday lets and booked out to spurious conferences and the extortionate hotel prices pushed me under canvas. It was a good idea and I was excited about it, despite the extra luggage; Kirsten was to arrive the next morning from Copenhagen.

They had a few spare pitches, although mine, 431, was not marked and therefore very difficult to locate and seemed to be the only site on an odd camber. Unfortunately satisfied that this awkward pitch was indeed 431, I quickly set about putting the tent up, fearful of the arrival of the thunderstorm that seemed to be rolling around the bay just out to sea from Aarhus. Luckily, it stayed off land for the time being and, although the ground seemed to be baked hard, I managed to pitch the tent with little fuss. In celebration, and in defiance of the storm, I sat outside it and drank a couple of warm beers from the bottom of my rucksack whilst reading my book.

The coach journey north from Hamburg had taken just over four hours and having pitched the tent and relaxed a while I couldn't be bothered to hit the city, so decided to stroll down to the nearby shore and explore. It wasn't exactly the dream beach, with brooding clouds to sea, sharp pebbles underfoot, and to the north the industrial landscape of Aarhus, a small container and ferry port with a couple of belching chimneys in the background, which I later found out to be the Ceres Beer Company Brewery. However, to the south, the woods stretched as far as the eye could see and dripped into the sea at a headland, and across the angry-coloured but bizarrely calm-looking Kattegat stood the islands of Denmark, some blurred behind dark purple strokes of sharp showers and others burnt brown in the late summer heat wave that now seemed to be nearing its end. I wandered along the shore past remnants of campers' fires, sat on a rock and watched the storms out to sea wondering how long it would be before they came this way and tested my pitching skills and the durability of the tent which had only thus so far endured a weekend on a cold cliff-top on the Isle of Wight, according to its owner, Phil. A small jetty by the beach entrance to the campsite was now attracting some early evening adventurers and brave families stripped off for a bracing dip.

Back at camp, I ate an unimpressive John West tuna meal bought cheaply from the camp store and opened one of my lifesaving bottles of wine, bought in Hamburg and designed to stave off the steep prices of Scandinavian booze. A wasp joined me as I lay down reading and refused to budge. The long resisted storm eventually hit as dusk finally turned to night and with it the wasp settled down somewhere in the tent for a kip. I failed to locate him and decided to settle down too, listening to the sound of the storm through and over the music from my earphones.

I wasn't here to hide from the onset of another year, it being my birthday, but travelling alone helped me forget the inevitability of the ageing process and to wake alone in the tent on such an auspicious day was an odd feeling. Luckily, I felt loved as a few text messages bleeped in felicitations (I'd capitulated to modern life and had packed my phone this time), including one from Anna, which got me thinking about her again. In the dull light of another dawn, the wasp appeared as if from nowhere, the drowsing-induced tempest and dusk having long gone, and he buzzed me a few times before I lost patience and swatted him. I felt a little guilty at my indolence in not trying to open the flaps and cajole him out.

I began this year in the manner I meant to go on, and put on my running shoes for a brief jog along the shores of the Kattegat, grey and uninviting on this special morning. After my ablutions, I hired a bike at the reception and headed off along the coastal bicycle path into Aarhus. The girl in reception was somehow convinced I'd only booked the one night here and was keen for me to leave and free up a sloping pitch. I played the confused and ignorant Englishman card and she gave up and waved me off.

I followed the coast road into the city and along to the harbour where I found a bicycle park near what looked like the cathedral. The back view from the port was unimpressive but, when I emerged at the front, the dark red brick building rose high into the concrete sky and made its presence felt on the city and I enjoyed a brief tour of the Dom. From here the streets of the old town spread out in a triangle and I followed one, the Rosengade, to reach a quaint cobbled medieval square where I breakfasted at the popular, but rather expensive, Café Jorden. Posters on the street lamps across the square advertised the 5th World Orienteering Championships and I wondered which of the jolly souls who breakfasted with me were to run later on that day.

The waitresses were young, blonde and stunning. They all spoke perfect English, just like every Dane I have ever met. I'd read in some magazine article that the Danes are supposed to be the biggest busted and blondest nation in the world, and nothing I'd seen this morning could possibly disprove it; all of the girls that passed me as I sat there eating my eggs and bacon seemed to fit the bill, and every one of them was beautiful. I'd reached the Nirvana of street eye-candy. As the day wore on and I became accustomed to this near-perfect beauty, I began to tire of it almost and to wonder whether the auburn girls with small, pert breasts were the most sought after by the young men of the town, as they would be so exotic.

I strolled the medieval streets of the old town and then down the central shopping streets to the station and the nearby town hall or Radhus, a 1940s structure of grey marble that dominates the skyline at this end of the town, but I was unsure whether it was a wonderfully designed and built piece of modern architecture or just plain ugly; maybe both.

Across the road and open parkland lay the city's concert hall, new and pleasant enough and the rather striking ARoS, the new art museum, a seven-storey gallery of thrilling design inside and out that housed a varied collection of Danish art that could wile away many an hour if the weather dictated so. I thoroughly enjoyed it and the sumptuous loos, which I would always take advantage of when travelling – no one does clean and attractive free toilets quite like the museum fraternity.

As a birthday treat I found a table on the now busy riverfront of the tiny Aarhus A River; a small pedestrianised area that attracted the beautiful people of the city who were finishing their working day and relaxing into the evening. I ordered a pizza and a beer and kept an eye on the steel-grey sky that seemed impossible not to be raining from, the clouds bulging at the seams like a water-filled balloon grotesquely swollen to the point of bursting. Graciously, the rain stayed away and I walked back to the Dom and found my bike for the ride home, expecting to get thoroughly soaked in the process.

The ride back was long and uphill as the road followed the gentle rise of the cliffs into the forest and on toward the Blommehaven campsite and pebble bay. Miraculously I stayed dry, the storm repeating its path from the previous evening, heading out over the sea and on towards the islands. Just before the jamboree youth camp, I saw the first of the throngs of returning orienteers, a ramshackle bunch of all ages, sizes and shapes, and followed the long line back towards the forest where our paths diverged. I returned the bike to reception and, with two ice-cold bottles of Ceres in tow, headed down to the bay to celebrate my birthday looking out to sea. It was seven o'clock now, and Kirsten was due here before nine according to the dissertation-length text that had accompanied my birthday greetings.

I walked a short way from the small wooden pier, past the families gathering around the large pile of stones that was later to host a marshmallow-toasting fire, took a seat facing east out to sea and supped on the Ceres. My legs began to cramp so I stood and stretched, exercising by selecting pebbles and skimming them out over the small waves that hit the shore at reassuringly steady intervals, the squall out in the Kattegat not yet affecting the size and force of the breakers at my feet. To the north, towards the city and harbour, families were now bathing off the tiny pier and, as the dusk slowly, almost imperceptibly, began to settle, more people strolled onto the beach to sit in and around the large stone circle, awaiting the evening fire.

A middle-aged man began to skim, twenty metres away from me, and his young daughter copied him, her stones barely reaching the sea and plopping unceremoniously into the small waves. However, her father was a seasoned skimmer and whooped at an effort that produced nine or ten skips before dunking neatly into the dark grey sea. My best to date in this venue had been eight and he looked across, both of us aware that he was clearly the unofficial skimming champion of the Kattegat. In a few minutes he and his little girl had scoured the beach towards me in search of the perfect skimmer and he approached with a kind smile.

"You are a better skimmer than me," I said, confident that he would understand me; after all, he was Danish.

"Yes, I think I got nine or ten. And you?" Oh, the international language of the skim.

"Only seven or eight."

(Location No.10, Kattegat, Blommehaven Campsite, Aarhus, Denmark)

A jovial lorry driver, who liked the English a great deal, we chatted about the Germans, the war, the weather and compared our tans, his evidence of the recent Indian summer; he was a more sun-baked chestnut brown than me. Maybe the Danish skies have less ozone than back home. There was definitely something in the air, as virtually all of the Danes were wonderfully tanned. He spoke of the flying fish that come out at dusk, though we saw none that night, until he bored of me and went off with his daughter.

I strolled back past the now roaring fire and the marshmallow-toasting campers and on up the hill to pitch 431. As the last of the northern light faded through the thick beech trees, I turned in for the night and awaited the rain that was waiting just out to sea, and with it, the arrival of a good friend, one that I'd known only well through cyber-space, but remembered as a kind, pretty and happy countenance on the end of a supple Viking frame. I was a little nervous at our meeting, but excited all the same: travel and freedom, and love and laughter; it had to come to an end soon, crashing down on top of me like the storm that raged and fell upon the islands of Denmark out to the east.

The muffled chattering of families settling down for the night, like a flock of roosting starlings atop a telephone wire, sent a soporific fug over me, and my eyes grew heavy upon the novel I was nearing the end of, the denouement not thrilling enough to keep me awake.

An approaching car's headlights swamped me in an alien-green canvas light. It came to a stop nearby, the engine choking itself to a halt, and a door slammed loud enough to wake the little ones who'd probably just dropped off after much cajoling. And then a rap on the canvas, followed by a 'Halo?' booming from an operatic frame it seemed, announced the presence of Kirsten.

Although email contact had included photos of us travelling through the never-ending dangers of Australia's outback, I found it hard to fix a live image of Kirsten in my head. I scrambled with the zip of an unfamiliar tent and spilled out onto the dampening grass, fine dew settling down upon the outskirts of the city now. I laughed at my awkwardness, my knees pushing hard into the damp grass to push me up, and we stood and greeted. My goodness, she was larger than I'd remembered and the bear hug that welcomed me left me quite breathless: I thought I heard a rib crack.

"Steve, it's good to see you after all this time."

I saw her teeth glowing in the last light of the northern skies, and we both scrambled into the tent, Kirsten in quite a dextrous manner, despite her size. I pondered on her likely position in the scrum of the university rugby team, settling on prop as I followed her through the half-unzipped hole.

Once inside, barely enough room for both of us to sit with my luggage and all, I put some light on the situation and Kirsten's pretty face emerged opposite mine. Yes – that was what she looked like: a photograph was accurate enough but it didn't possess life; it didn't have a beat, a breath. Although big enough to squash me mercilessly, and not necessarily fat, Kirsten was a very attractive girl. We tried an awkward hug again, across my rucksack, and she slapped me hard on the knee.

"Steve, it is so good to see you. How are you?"

"I'm good, Kirsten, and it is great to see you too. You look very well."

"I am, I am; we have had a good late summer here in Denmark. Look!" She pulled up her tee shirt and pushed down her waistband to reveal a two-tone body, milky-white beneath the knicker-elastic mark, and a beautiful Mediterranean-bronze above. She clumsily pushed the waistband low enough to offer me a glimpse of pubic hair, an auburn brown that suggested her blondeness could have been false; it was hard to tell but was surprisingly titillating.

"Wow, an excellent tan."

"Well, thank you." She looked around the tent; it didn't take long. "Is this it?"

"Yep, 'fraid so," I said, spreading my arms wide, well as wide as the canvas would allow, to reveal its spaciousness.

"Hmm," she said.

"What?"

"I think I was too optimistic with my luggage."

"Hey?"

"Come."

She squatted in front of me, her jeans riding down to reveal the tan line and with it the top of a garishly pink thong, and popped out of the tent. I followed. By the time I'd awkwardly got to my feet, Kirsten had beeped the boot of the car open to reveal her treasure-chest of camping paraphernalia. We stuffed the duvet into the tent to plump up the base, nice and comfy, and she threw in her sleeping bag and a couple of pillows, covers freshly laundered and smelling of a Provençal lavender-field.

We propped ourselves upon an island of duck feathers, room made by my rucksack finding a home on the back seat of her Skoda, and shared a bottle of sparkling wine.

"Skol!" We clinked glasses, albeit plastic ones.

"And, oh shit, yes, happy birthday to you, Steven!"

She planted a slobbery wet kiss on my lips, tasting of sugary pears, and we giggled our way quickly through the bottle. The fizzy wine sat atop the Ceres beer I'd quaffed earlier and a pleasant fug buzzed my head. I thought for a split second that it was the ghost of the poor wasp I'd swatted that morning.

Kirsten was fun, more so than I'd recalled. I suppose I was too busy chatting up Edi at the time in Australia to notice her, but I began to regret the time I hadn't spent with her. I don't recall when sleep came, but it did at some point amongst the dizzying laughter.

***

The storm stayed away that night and in the morning it was dull, overcast but thankfully not raining, so we packed up quickly, leaving the fly-sheet bunched up in the back seat to allow the morning dew to dry off on the drive to Skagen and Grenen, Kirsten's planned-for destination. At reception I paid my dues, including membership of the Scandinavian Camping Club, and we shared a huge, decadent chocolate Danish pastry and a bottle of chocolate milk for breakfast, which we ate in the car watching the newly arrived drizzle making pretty, random patterns on the windscreen. The locally searched-for Eurobeat FM (or it may as well have been) played the worst selection of middle-of-the-road music imaginable. James Blunt was a radical choice for these people. I made the dial search for another station and found Danish rap that had never heard of the watershed, a cacophony of Euro-accented English swear words of the worst kind to give it that gangster edge.

"What the hell is this?" I asked. Kirsten laughed.

"We may be the happiest people in the world, but our music is shit, yes."

We said goodbye to the Viking settlement of Arhus and headed north, still on the E45 through the, at first, gently rolling and slightly sun-kissed wheat and dairy fields of North Jutland, through another ridiculously heavy downpour fresh off the North Sea with an intensity unfamiliar to a rain-shadow dweller from the south-east of England. Indeed, it was so bad at one point that Kirsten drove completely blind past an absurdly long HGV, sitting bolt upright, head pushed to the windscreen in a vain hope of a safe passage through. She just put her foot down and shouted, "Shit, shit!" as the wall of water that sprayed from the lorry drowned us.

"German," I said, pointing behind us as the wipers worked frantically to clear the flood.

"Fuckers," she said, her nose still inches from the clearing windscreen.

Under the Limfjorden, an inlet which separated mainland Jutland from the top of Denmark, through a long new tunnel just north of the city of Aalborg, advertisements telling me that I could fly here for £25 via some unknown dodgy carrier from Stansted or Luton, and here the landscape changed. Here it was flat, a sandy soil that exposed itself at the slightest scratch, hardy pine trees and dunes topped with marram grass and dwarfed willows in the slacks that rolled on to the horizon and the three seas that surrounded this land's end; the North Sea to the west, Skagerrak to the north and Kateggat to the east. It felt like the end of the world but, as we neared tiny Aalbeck and Skagen, tourists began to gather.

On the increasingly crowded roads north until suddenly we were on the outskirts of Skagen and diverting west toward Grenen. We somehow missed the planned campsite and ended up down the road in Poul Eeg's, a pleasant enough family-run affair where the majority Danes, minority Swedes, uber-minority Dutch and uber-uber-minority English families with pre-primary age nippers were enjoying the death-knell of the summer.

We pitched expertly in place 246 and were soon off to hire bikes, my bum still sore from the brief Arhus excursion. A right and then a left turn under the leaden skies, though seemingly just out to sea as is the pattern here in Denmark, and we were battling brisk northerlies, weaving in and out of armies of pedestrians and cyclists on a dark road to absolutely nowhere. Past a grey lighthouse that was hard to discern from the Kattegat skies beyond and then, far sooner than I'd expected, a flick to the right and we were there. The beach had a reception centre, a posh cafeteria and an artist's grave, plus the familiar-looking pillbox defences built by the Germans in the forties no doubt, fearful of an Allied invasion from the north but which eventually came much further to the south and west on the Normandy beaches.

A short rise over the first busy and fully-vegetated dunes and ahead of us was a spit of fine white sand set off to the north east, its tip maybe a kilometre away discernible by the throngs of people that paid homage to the meeting of the two seas on a Danish pilgrimage. We walked to the shore arm in arm, took off our feet (well, that was what Kirsten suggested in her normally near-faultless English) and paddled the swash and backwash all along the Kattegat sea front, zigzagging the screaming children as the suddenly fierce swash surprised us all and drenched the trousers and skirts below the knees.

They were all so happy, these holidaying Danes. Was it the last hurrah before the autumn and long winter, the intoxicating and mesmerising venue of the two clashing seas, or was it that they were just a happy people; mature, satisfied, content with their lot? Who knows, but Kirsten's fixed grin hinted at the latter.

And there we were at the edge of the bounding main, the two seas colliding, the Skaggerak flowing east towards the Baltic and the Kateggat west towards the North or Norwegian Sea. The stiff breeze further rattled and unsettled the duelling neighbours and the clashing sound drowned out the noisy throngs and the chugging of the bizarre tractor engines that pulled the passenger carriages as they plodded the north shore from the car park. For the briefest of moments we were alone with them both (the seas) and we marvelled at the scene and the light, and perhaps this was why Skagen and Grenen had become the Picardy and Normandy coast of nineteenth-century Scandinavia, attracting a prolific artists' colony.

And then we were back at the car park, unlocking the bikes and speeding off into Skagen town. Once again, far sooner than expected, we hit the centre parked under a stand of oak trees (the climatic climax vegetation here away from the dunes) and wandered the pastel coloured house filled streets.

"Hey, Kirsten, you ever been to California?"

"Yes, I have. Why?"

"Well, there's this place called Solvang…"

"Shit, yes, I know, I have been there!"

"Don't you think that this is just like Solvang?"

"Yes, it is. Cool."

We both stood and watched the tourist families.

"It's sad," she continued, "but I wanted to come here because I've not been here since I was a little girl."

"Really?"

"Yeah."

From the Solvang-like quaintness of the artists' quarter we walked down the main street, past ice cream shops and posh boutiques. The wider streets here let in an abundance of light, enough to remind me that this was really the end of Denmark and nothing lay beyond except sea and sky. The rain began to fall out of an oddly bright sky and accompanied us to the end of the street where we took refuge in what must have once been a rough sailors' bar, now a mock English pub that sold pricey pints of ale. We drank and talked until the rain eased enough for us to venture on to the port and harbour, bigger and busier than the map suggested, and beautiful yachts from across Scandinavia and northern Germany docked here to enjoy the light and the seafood. We did too, Hastings-style in a harbour-side boutique with plastic cutlery and sitting in the now pouring rain with a beer, sharing a wet trellis table with a smiley old couple from Copenhagen. From these seats we observed and the holidaying Danes that mixed with us seemed a very happy and peaceful people. I felt it too, briefly, in between daydreams of fucking Kirsten from behind.

We wandered back through the now quieter and emptying streets as dusk began to approach and hopped on the bikes to work off the fish supper. We speeded back up to the end of the Danish world and, on an almost empty beach, strolled up the spit to the meeting of the two seas. All alone at the very point where the two clashed, we paddled out and joined them. To the west, the sun was trying to set beneath heavy grey clouds, but tiny gaps let forth angelic crimson rays that painted the wet beach shades of pink and red and gathering flocks of gulls danced in the showers of colour before settling near the dunes. The quality of light over the two seas and back across the beach to the dunes was something exceptional, even to the untrained eye, and we just stood and listened to the quarrelling bodies of water. I knew it would be a place to return to one day and must warrant a ranking in the top ten skimming destinations of all time (according to my tome that is).

Sand dominated this unusual spit, pushed back one way, then the other, until neither won and, instead of the traditional curved end seen across the world, it spat itself out in between the arguing seas at a ninety-degree angle. But as fate would so kindly grace me this last year, I looked down at the scuffed-up sand, a condition of a day's trampling by curious tourists, and saw three neatly carved pebbles showing me their shiny bellies.

"Thank you," I whispered to myself. Kirsten was knee-deep in the middle of the clashing waves and screeching with joy at the sight and feel of it: just me and her and these two bodies of water. Sea skimming is tough at the best of times, but these unpredictable squalls made it nigh on impossible. I cracked a stone out to the right of Kirsten and saw it skip neatly off a crest that hadn't emerged when I'd taken aim. The stone spun up and into the grey sky, and it caught Kirsten's eye and she watched it disappear into the depths.

"Hey, let me have a go?" she shouted above the noisy water.

I beckoned her to the edge of Denmark and she splashed out of the sea towards me like a Siren to a lost sailor.

"Here you are," I said and planted a pebble in her large hands. She blew off the wet sand I hadn't managed to remove and launched an almighty throw out into the seas. The stone hit a newly formed crest and bounced high into the sky, hard to discern against the black clouds out towards Norway and Sweden, and then skipped another crest appearing as if ordained by the Viking Gods, and then another and another until it was lost, swallowed by the angry squalls. She stood there rubbing her hands together to flick off the sand and smiled at me.

(Location No.11, The clashing seas, Skagen and Grenen, top of Denmark)

"I'm excellent at smutting."

I'd read somewhere that that was what they called it in these parts, and it made me smile. "I can see," I said. "What you doing next weekend?" I continued.

"At school. Why?"

"It's the World Skimming Championships... um, sorry, Smutting Championships in Scotland, and you," I pointed at her, "should be there."

"And I would win, but I have school; it is important."

"I know: all the more easy for me to win then," and I unleashed the last stone which sank pathetically into the first wave it hit.

Back at camp, once again avoiding the angry-looking storm that just sat still over the Kattegat, close enough to almost touch with an outstretched hand it seemed, and we settled into our little canvas home, listening to the family next door who played cards into the night, still outside and laughing themselves silly. We drank a bottle of wine apiece, virtually sitting on top of each other, reminiscing on our travels and then, curious childhood accidents.

"This one," I showed her my chin, a white slash of scar tissue untouched by stubble all these years, "was when I fell off my bike, aged six, straight over the handlebars and onto my head." I did a diving motion, followed by a slap on my chin, just so she truly understood the scale of the disaster.

"Ow," she said, and placed a finger on my chin to briefly trace the scar, albeit only a thumbnail in length; hard to discern if you hadn't had it pointed out.

"Well, look at this, Steven."

She pulled down her tracksuit trousers. We were dressed for bed, North European camping-style; woolly hats at the ready just in case and comfortable M&S lounge wear. She flung the grey pants down in between us and rearranged herself so that I could see her thigh.

"This," she said, a little tipsy and slurring as she went, "is a scar!"

And it was: six inches long and looking as though a worm had dug its way just underneath the skin, like a tropical parasite from a gruesome Channel 5 documentary.

"Wow," I said. "May I?" – finger at the ready.

"Of course."

She took my hand and placed my index finger at the top end of the scar and then drew it slowly down. It felt rubbery, but not unpleasant.

"How did you do that?"

"A real bicycle accident."

"Oh."

"I was twelve and my bicycle was hit by a car. I broke my leg, and they had to insert a metal plate."

"Wow. You win."

The scar was lighter than the beautifully tanned leg it sat upon and I pondered on how on earth I'd not seen it in Australia; we'd all swum together, but I had no memory of the blemish. I left my hand on her leg and spread my fingers out to cover the scar. Her leg was nicely warm.

It was an odd silence as she looked at my hand and then at me and then moved in for a kiss. It was a hard and passionate kiss, our teeth bumping on occasions and she took my hand and moved it unceremoniously up into her crotch.

"I knew we would do this," she said as she fumbled with my slacks and I with her top, one handed, the other busy sinking its fingers deep into her warm, moist crack.

It was difficult to get a reasonable position for sex, and at one point I found myself, now fully naked, behind her, my bare arse sticking against the canvas and pushing it out nearly a foot. The thought of accidentally treading on a torch somewhere amongst this detritus amused me for a brief while, imagining the scene, a Thai shadow-puppet show, a pornographic cartoon for all to see.

Kirsten's thong lay stranded half-way across her fulsome bum cheeks and I leaned down to take the elastic between my teeth and pulled them down and away from her crotch, and once free from the wide arse, they fell to her knees. I then sank my head in between her cheeks and stuck my tongue as deep inside her as I could from this squashed and awkward position. She tasted of salt and the sea. We pleasured each other orally for a good twenty minutes or so.

Kirsten lay beneath me now and my knees sank into the duvet and then hard into the sandy floor beneath the flysheet. She spread her legs wide and pushed them up to rest on her stomach and I was inside, deeper and deeper until it seemed as though we would both pop from the pressure we put her body under. And once we ascertained how far I could plunge in without an explosion of flesh and guts we fucked hard and fast. On a couple of occasions I came out and stabbed her in the groin; it hurt.

She was a noisy lover and the thrill of the sex banished the fear of embarrassment that our poor neighbours could impose on us by asking for quiet, or those knowing looks in the morning. Usually, I would have asked her to be quiet with a hurried 'shh' in her ear, but tonight I was too enwrapped in the animal sex to be concerned. We huffed and puffed and sighed and grunted for a few more minutes before she shrieked into my ear, accompanied by the digging of her nails deep into my arse to leave a red-raw mark for days. I continued to pump and she screeched more and more until, at last, I came, deep inside, and we both lay there sweating profusely and chuckling at the absurdity of sex the second it's over and the chemicals fall back into their rightful place.

"Fuckin' hell, Kirsten, that was a proper shag!"

"Shag? What, like the bird?"

"No, sex, screw, you know?"

"Yes it was," she said and dug her nails in one more time.

"Ow!"

"Sorry."

We lay there a while until I softened and fell out, lubricated by our juices and slopped to the floor.

"Urgh, it's a bit messy," I said and fumbled around for some tissues, which I knew were somewhere here. "Can I turn on a light?" I asked.

"Yeah, sure."

I found a head torch and punched it on, one click too many, and it flickered into its disco mode, LED lights flashing into my face, setting 'three'. With a flashing image of a naked Viking girl coming and going in my head, I found the tissues and set about clearing up the mess. I mopped up the come on the duvet below her crotch and passed a tissue around and inside her crack.

"Thank you."

"Welcome."

We continued to lie there, cooling off in the Jutland night and listening to our breathing.

"I need a pee," I said and put on some shorts and a tee shirt. "Won't be long."

The elderly Norwegian couples in the pitch across from us were drunk and one of the men mounted his bike as I returned from the loo and said to me, "I am a little drunk and am going for a ride. I am sorry." He smiled a merry smile. "No, no, it is a good thing," I told him and disappeared into our tent.

Kirsten was in a baggy tee shirt that covered her crotch and fell onto her thighs, crumpling up just above the end of her scar. Post-coital conversations were invariably awkward, especially those from a one-night-stand, and more so those with friends clearly not meant to be lovers.

"Kirsten?" I said, pointing my thumb behind me at the zipped up flap of the front door. "Neighbours are too drunk to have been bothered by the noise."

"Oh, good… sorry, but, you know, I was having fun."

"Me too."

"Steven?"

"Yeah?"

"You know that this is not real, hey?"

I looked at her, a theatrical and quizzical mien, with a hint of wronged puppy. I knew exactly what she meant, and she was right.

"Hey," I said, pinching a fold of fat beneath her shirt, "seems real enough to me."

She smiled. "Stop it!" She grabbed my hand. "You understand. You are going back home to England and I am going back to school. You will fall in love with another English girl and you will have children, and I will marry a bespectacled Danish professor and have 2.4 children with blonde hair, glasses and braces. It is how it is meant to be."

I nodded, a little sad at her verisimilitudes.

"And this isn't real," she continued. "It is an adventure, some fun, but not real."

"I know, I know," I said, playing with the soggy tissues like a scolded boy would with his laces.

She put my hand under her tee shirt and rested it on the folds of fat, crushed into synclines and anticlines in this small space, and I moved it up to her breast and lay it there, warming her nipple.

"I wanted you when we were in Australia, but you were with Edi. I was jealous, but even if we had made love, it would not have been real."

I played with her breast; she let me.

"Real life is over there," she said, pointing to the side of the tent, and I followed the beam of light that shot from her finger, miraculously zapping itself across the Jutland peninsula, hitting the North Sea around Esjberg and continuing in a straight line across towards the UK. It would have made landfall just south of Walton-On-The-Naze and then slipped across Essex and over the Thames estuary and on into Gravesham to shatter through the front door of 23 Clevedon Street and on up the stairs and into the bedroom of Anna, and from there into bed with her and Mike, and then it would pierce her heart.

It was revelatory.

I nodded the whole time I followed this beam shining across the sea, and continued to play with her tit.

"Kirsten, you are so right… Do you want to fuck again?"

"Yes, but remember, this is not real life."

She laid back, legs bent at the knee, and I entered her, still a little sore from the rough sex not thirty minutes before. And when I came, I thought of Anna and when I smelt Kirsten's hair, I smelt coconut shampoo and when I kissed her lips, I tasted Anna's.

Kirsten was wise for her years and it had taken her words, an exploration of her body, a circumnavigation of the globe and a silly number of wild flings, to realise that I was, and always had been, in love with Anna Taylor.

Chapter 3

Changes in speed and rotation did not change this fact

The one way flight from Aarhus was cheap but nasty and bumpy and we almost crash-landed into Stansted ninety minutes later. I had crossed myself and said a prayer or two to whatever God was listening and closed my eyes as the paper aeroplane hopped, skipped and jumped to a halt on the runway – never again with this airline.

'So, Steven Jones, what the hell are you going to do now?' I thought, looking out of the window from the shuttle coach that was at a standstill on the Essex side of the M25. If Kirsten was so right, and I really believed that she was, then I must take action now. Anna was to be married, to that bloke, and I knew that she loved me more than him, but how to win her back? How to convince her that I was over my worldly flings, had come through the other side of my early mid-life crisis a wiser, more reliable man? It didn't look good from whatever angle I approached it, from however many rose-tinted glasses I got from Specsavers. This would have to be smart and bluntly honest. An easy start, with a text...

'Need to talk. Are you free?'

I would allow her a twelve-hour window. Anna was the kind of girl who'd reply post-haste, but I had to factor in the 'pissed-off' element that would keep those twitchy little stubby fingers from the reply button. I didn't have to wait more than twelve minutes. I considered this a good sign.

'Unless general chit-chat, not sure wot there is to talk about'

I left it ten minutes, not sure why.

'Not chit-chat. V important... please.'

I could hear the sigh in the almost immediate response.

'Okay – where, when. Some of us have to work'

I thought about it a while.

'Bluewater. Starbucks. Tonight. Six p.m.'

Good. I was impressed with myself. I really was going to go through with this. A delay of eleven minutes. I was still stuck on the M25, though there were hints of movement somewhere ahead; the ambulance and fire engines had been through a while ago.

'*Okay*'

***

I was loaded to the full as I waddled through the Village entrance to one of Europe's biggest shopping malls. A security guard eyed me with suspicion; potentially enough TNT to blow this wing sky high, but I smiled and he saw that I couldn't be a threat to anyone, not in terrorist terms, at least.

It was five forty-five p.m. and the centre was busy for a Thursday. I fell off the escalator and dragged my bags across the walkway to the Starbucks I used to hide in on school trips here that seemed like years ago now, but in reality was only twelve months. It was crowded, the smell of today's brew stinging my nostrils, mixing with sickly spilt milk and greasy pastries. It was hot too despite the open window front and air conditioning units big enough to dissolve an ozone hole the size of Kent pumping out cool, plastic air to the mall. The only two seats available were between the door and the sliding windows and allowed a breeze of sorts to circulate around my sweaty back. I hated those people that grabbed a seat before they bought a drink, excepting the babies, the elderly and the infirm, but saw no other course of action this time and dumped my bags around the seats – sorry.

It was only on my way back with mocha in hand that I realised that these were the self-same seats as those that I'd finished with Anna some months before; karma of sorts, but not sure yet whether good or bad. Perhaps I could use this to my advantage. I pulled out a novel from my rucksack and pretended to read assuredly, lazing back in the chair so far that I nearly put my back out. I tried not to look at the clock obsessively but managed to trace the minute hand by its subtle movement in between the odd word of the book. Six o'clock seemed a long time coming but it passed, and the minute hand slowed down almost to a halt. My heartbeat was quickening, sweat trickling down the small of my back, tickling me and then dissolving into the fabric of my cheap BHS underwear. As the minutes slowed, I began to consider this a poor idea. I mean, what kind of an idiot would have me back after all of this shit? But I did love her and I could show her that.

In the middle of my argument, a tap landed softly on my shoulder, and it was Anna. She had taken me by surprise.

"This a piss-take?" she said, referring to the table choice. I couldn't help but laugh.

"No, no," a laugh, "it really isn't. Truly, it was the only table left. I'm sorry."

I pleaded with my eyes and the supplicant left hand, open and inviting her to sit. She briefly hesitated, then chose to join me.

"You look well."

A good start. I was sure that I looked like shit; certainly felt like it.

"You too." And she did. Well, she'd put on a bit of weight and I could see the down on her lips quite clearly, but her eyes were as divine as ever; divine and encapsulating. She had me again.

It was an impressive five-minute conversation of inanity until she politely cut to the chase.

"So, Mr Jones," she said, slowly, almost like a villain in a Bond movie. I was Bond, she the head of an international drug-running cartel; only this time, I didn't have a Walther PPK or a gimmicky pen that could shoot poison arrows – it was a Bic from Martins the Newsagents. This could be the end of the successful franchise, right here, right now.

"So, Mr Jones," she said again, as though reading my mind and playing along. She didn't look at me, but at the empty sachets of sugar that she now played with; having poured them into the latte that one of our ex-students had kindly brought out once they'd spotted us and asked if they could serve us at the table. I hadn't remembered her taking sugar in coffee; not sure I remembered her drinking much coffee either, more's to the point, but it was a decaf latte with a squirt of hazelnut syrup: it smelt like puke.

"Can't get enough of these," she'd said after Sandeep had handed it over with a cheeky grin. She spilled loose granules of sugar over the dirty chequerboard tabletop. I watched them bounce in all directions, one or two onto the floor, also dirty with coffee-stains and squashed remnants of chocolate-chip cookie crumbs.

"So, Mr Jones. What is so earth-shatteringly important that we meet up the moment you get back from…?" She hesitated and placed her hand palm up towards me, an invitation to finish the sentence.

"Denmark."

"Denmark?" she repeated, eyeing me oddly.

"Well," I said, "it's just that I've been thinking."

"Dangerous."

"Yes, well, umm, I've been thinking that I've rather made a mess of all this... us, haven't I?

"Yes you have... and?"

"Well, I just wanted to apologise."

"You've done that already." She sat back. "Remember; at the wedding."

"Oh, yes, yes, I know but that was, you know, all a bit awkward."

"And this isn't?" She was on form, I'll give her that.

"Well, yes, but there was another thing."

"Go on," she said, burning through me with those bloody gorgeous eyes.

"Well," I coughed, composed myself and continued. "I don't want you to marry Mike. I want you to break it off. I want you to be with me." There, I said it. I sat back now and waited for the fall out.

She sat with her mouth open, a look of incredulity verging on hysteria.

"I know, I know," I continued. "It's crass, shit, crap, blah, blah, but whilst I was away, I couldn't stop thinking about you, about us and about how much I missed you... loved you... wanted you, and how much I made a mistake... fucked it up."

She was still looking impressively nonplussed.

"Look." I took advantage of my stinging assault on her credulity. "I'm going to Scotland next weekend, for the Skimming Championships," (I motioned a rather slow and pathetic skim, rather like her attempts in Wales, the day we first made love), "and I want you to come with me." I sat forward and grabbed her arm, pulled it across the sticky table and held her hand in both of mine. "I don't expect you to change anything, but just give me a shot, give me a weekend away, give us a chance to prove that we really, really should be together. Please, I beg you?" A little over the top, but I was enjoying the pleading now; felt empowered by it, oddly, because at last... at last, it was absolutely the right thing for me to do.

"Steve, for f..." the 'f' drifting off into nothing. "I'm getting married to Mike... I..."

"Please, just a weekend."

"But..." She sat back and moved her hand from mine and looked at me. "A weekend... and then, that's it?"

"Yep, if that's what you want. If you never want me to bother you again, a weekend, and then I'll be gone. I won't take a job back at the school. I'll get out of your hair forever."

"Is that a promise?"

"Yep."

"Can I have it in writing?"

"If you want."

"Fuck sake! You paying?"

"Yeah."

We both just sat there.

"So, that's a 'yes'?" I asked.

"Christ! I suppose it is. I can't believe that I'm doing this. Fuck knows what I'll tell Mike I'm doing. This is insane!"

She pulled her right hand through her hair, her beautiful, silken black hair and laughed. "It's crazy, but I do need to get away for a few days."

"I'll sort it all out. Just be ready next Saturday morning – early."

"Shit," she said, shaking her head. "You email me the bits and bobs?"

"Yep."

"Fuck, this is mad!" She stood up, placed her handbag strap across her shoulder; the leather bag slapped against her small bum. "Saturday?"

"Yep."

"Fuck." And she was gone.

I sat there, considered the parting a 'yes' of sorts and listened to my heart rattling against my ribcage like a crazed lunatic at his cell door. I would win her back. This was karma. We were meant to be together.

Chapter 4

To skip unencumbered across the water

A large part of me expected a no-show, a final indignation that I most thoroughly deserved, but amazingly, at eight thirty a.m. on a cool, late September Saturday morning, Anna Taylor came walking up to me, pulling a small suitcase on wheels. She looked stunning; had clearly made an effort. I kissed her on the cheek and smelt that fantastic coconut shampoo-flavoured hair.

"No mention of home. Nothing. Just you and me and Scotland."

"And the skimming," she said.

"Well, yes, that too." I was already on the back foot, playing defensively.

"It's okay; I'm actually quite excited about it."

About the skimming, or about this, I thought. I didn't ask.

The flight was full, maybe some of them skimmers I considered, and we took off into a crisp autumn sky, that golden light that only September can muster, showering us through the airplane window as we turned north towards the land of the Picts. I held her hand on take-off, still a nervous flyer, but mostly because I could and it might be the last chance I ever get; she didn't mind.

The approach into Edinburgh was swift and exceptional, framing pictures of the castle, Arthur's Seat, the Firth and the Grampians to the horizon. It looked pleasant enough outside, a balmy twelve degrees the co-pilot joked on touchdown, and we were soon on the shuttle bus to the terminal. At a corner, I grabbed for balance at Anna's waist and settled my hand on her plump midriff. I held on to the fabric of her jumper as we swerved the other way.

"Sorry," I mouthed.

"That's okay," she said and touched her hand to my wrist, leaving it there briefly; it sent a shock through my veins back to my heart.

"I've got a reference number," I said to the jolly clerk, a young Scot in his early twenties and seemingly delighted to be checking out rental cars at 10.50am on a Saturday morning.

"Right," he said, dancing his fingers across the keyboard and driving the mouse this way and that on the desktop beside me. "Okayyy," as he continued to tap and click away. "Well, Mr... Jones," he reminded himself with a quick glance at the paperwork, "I'm afraid I can't offer you the car you ordered."

"Oh, but..." I started to interject, not looking forward to the awkwardness of having to complain at a lack of fore planning on the company's behalf.

"But I can give you a higher range model for exactly the same price."

"Oh." He enjoyed the look of surprise on my face.

"In fact," he said, grabbing a chunky key tab out of the drawer below the computer, "it's a brand new Lexus, 4-wheel drive; only seventeen miles on the clock."

"Wow, crumbs, thanks."

"No problem."

I looked back at Anna and smiled. She seemed rather pleased too: a promising start to the most important weekend of my life.

We pulled out of the airport, a little judder as I tried to get used to a new biting point on a car far more powerful than I'd ever driven before. I bet we looked a right old pair of Scottish toffs as we motored off through the suburbs of the capital and on towards the motorway that led to Glasgow and beyond to Loch Lomond and the Highlands and Western Isles, one of which, Easdale, a tiny scrap of rock off the Island of Seil, would host the championship tomorrow afternoon.

I'd booked a B and B in Oban, a view back across the bay to the town according to the website, and a leisurely forty-five minute drive from Easdale. I was excited about seeing the Highlands again; it had been a long while since I camped and hiked here with some college friends.

As we headed further west the clouds gathered like lumps of cotton wool steam over a northern England power station and welcomed us across the country with, at first, a spit of rain and then as the clouds quickly darkened, cascades of freshly recycled Atlantic Ocean lashing across the windscreen and testing even the ultra-modern and fast wipers on this high-end model.

"Nice," said Anna looking to the rising hills, their tops already shrouded in sheets of water, and turned up the music we'd found on a local station – better than Jutland FM, that's for sure. We sang along badly to some nineties dance classics, tap-dancing the brand new steering wheel with my skinny fingers, and I enjoyed the freedom that the road, a car, music and a lover sitting next to you gave. If heaven was a moment, then it was this moment: the moody skies; the adventure ahead, as yet unwritten, and the anticipation of all of this fizzing through the air-conditioning and pouring into our excited faces.

I put my hand on her leg after a cheeky gear change and left it there, a memento of a long-lost love perhaps, and she placed her tiny right hand on mine to gracefully embrace it. I could have talked her in and out of love with me a thousand times as we headed on up the A82 past gloomy but beautiful and mysterious Loch Lomond, but I chose to stay silent, not wanting to put a hoodoo on our weekend sojourn.

By late lunchtime we had crossed the hills and glens of the western Highlands and found ourselves chugging through the relatively busy streets of the town of Oban. Out past the headlands, hills rolled into low clouds, perhaps mainland mountains, some of them Munros, but hard to tell in this dreich – perhaps they were the backbone of some beautiful isle or two out there towards the end of the old world.

The B and B, according to the perplexing map from their website, was through the town centre, past the docks and the idly ticking behemoth of a Caledonian MacBrayne ferry destined for Skye or Mull or Eigg or Rum or some other magical land beyond, and on up a spur of a green headland, the road hugging its flank and rising gradually to give the posh houses that resided there a grand view back across the bay, harbour, town and hills.

Halfway along sat our home for the night, lights already ablaze to warn away the inclement weather with a Highland welcome, and I parked awkwardly in next to a couple of foreign cars, one French and one Dutch, the ubiquitous travellers. I hadn't been to Amsterdam for a few years now, but was always surprised to find any Dutch there at all. Didn't they permanently reside in brown Volvos on the French Riviera, blocking the narrow roads with their trailing caravans, the population exiled and strewn-out across the honeypot sites of Europe?

We booked in with the kindly landlady, she being happy to see this youngish couple in contrast to the senior citizens who sat in the dining room drinking coffee, chatting in Pidgin English and staring out across the harbour from the beautiful large Victorian sash bay windows.

Within thirty minutes we were in town, the rain dripping to a drizzle, and we headed into the hotel bar across from the quay and ordered a late lunch of toasted sandwiches, a pint of McEwan's for me and an orange juice for Anna.

"You not partaking?" I asked, raising my pint as a prop to the question.

"Nah, don't really feel like it."

No bother, I thought; she wasn't ever a big drinker and our sexual adventures to date had not all been alcohol-induced. Indeed, our first time on the banks of the Afon Conwy was a sober affair, if not a little reckless on recall.

I had another pint of the bitter ale as Anna nibbled at the crusts she'd discarded earlier in the meal and I smiled inwardly at the simple pleasure of sharing her company once more. We sauntered along the harbour front during a break in the clouds that rattled in from the southwest on the jet stream and warmed our faces in the short bursts of solar rays that hit the sea wall that we dangled our short legs from.

"This is still fucking mental," she said as a cloud shrouded us in its shadow once more.

"Yep... but it's pretty easy though."

She sighed. "I guess." She scuffed her heels against the granite wall of the docks and looked out to the ferryboats that rested in the harbour. "Yeah, it is easy. That scares me." A pause. "It's big!"

"Thank you."

"Idiot. I meant the boat." She flicked a thumb at the hulk of the Caledonian MacBrayne ferry, bound for Mull.

"Caledonian MacBrayne," I said in a whiny, high-pitched Scottish accent, only loud enough for Anna to hear, scared that I might upset a tough-looking local. She smiled.

"Great name," I continued, dangling my feet at a trot to bounce off the wall in a pretty pattern that sang out a love song in my head.

"Steve," she said, turning to face me and blocking my view of the hull of the boat. "What the hell are we doing here?"

"Watching ferries."

"Don't!"

"Well we are." I sounded like an irritating Year 8 trying to show off to his mates as he back-chatted the teacher.

"You know full well what I mean."

I sighed, picked up the pace on the wall, scuffing, and then patted out a happy-slappy rhythm on my thighs. Jeans always make for a good percussion fabric. I wondered whether Buddy Holly thought the same before he put hand to thigh in a recording of 'Everyday'.

"Anna?"

"Yeah."

"I love you."

She didn't reply; don't blame her really. I smiled a coy apology for bringing up the matter here and now.

"You know what, Steve? I really think you do."

"I do!" I jumped in, far too enthusiastically.

She smiled, picked up my left hand and placed her pudgy little paw underneath; warm to my skin through the thin and fading cloth. It was a blustery afternoon and the clouds skipped past, growing thicker and getting lower by the minute. The temperature seemed to drop quite suddenly.

"I'm cold. Let's get back for a snooze," she said.

"Great idea."

We stumbled to our feet and rounded the harbour, back past the renovated warehouse restaurants and on up the road towards the B&B. It was getting dull and dark, earlier than it should at this time of year this far west, nudged into a premature dusk by the thick blanket of stratus grey that threatened to spill its load across the bay.

The house was quiet, the dining room empty and the lights off, dark and unwelcoming. The faux chandelier from the upstairs hall shone a beacon that we followed to the bedrooms. I sat on one of the twin beds watching the telly whilst she read a book. It was eerily quiet as if something foreboding was waiting to happen and it sent a shiver through me. This was not quite right; in fact, quite wrong, but I soon thought myself around, determined to fix things.

"Anna?"

She slowly, reluctantly it seemed, pushed the book to the horizontal on her knees. "Yes?" She looked across. I believe she had been waiting a while for me to make my move.

"Do you want to make love?"

She sat there, motionless, staring at the telly too now, at the weatherman and his conducting hands that threw clouds and rain across the UK at a whim. She put the book to the side and it fell down the tiniest of gaps between bed and wall. "Bugger," she said, putting her hand down the crack as far as she could.

"Leave it," I said. "I'll get it later." I was keen for the moment to be grabbed at; it may be the last chance and I didn't want it wasted – no regrets.

She puffed out her cheeks and rolled her little legs to the floor, took two steps towards me and knelt on the bed looking me straight in the eyes. I saw her in that room in Paris; smelt her anticipation and angst and excitement.

"Dickhead," she said and kissed me softly on the cheek. What beautiful soft lips she had. I kissed her back and brushed those luscious lips, soothing the cracks on mine: I'd forgotten my balm. The gentle embrace, the teenage pecking, continued for a full minute until my tongue found its way through and wriggled around hers, sharing its moisture and working deeper and more frantically until we sank into a mock Greco-Roman bout on the bed, both fully reclined now.

We pushed and pulled at each other's clothes until we were naked and I raced my right hand across her breasts, in between them to touch the sternum, then down and over the pot belly with its silken milky-white cover and into her crotch and my fingers slipped easily inside.

"My God, you're wet," I whispered into her ear, in between nibbles: she liked that, I recalled.

"I wonder why," she moaned, breathing ever more heavily and erratically.

Before we were lovers, she had talked of how fellatio seemed abhorrent to her and at that time I never thought in my wildest dreams that a) I would get to fuck her and b) she would be bloody fantastic at giving head. It wasn't the first time she'd taken me fully in her mouth but this was the best time. I closed my eyes and imagined her doing the act upon me in graphic detail in my mind. It was an odd thing to do but it took a while for it to dawn on me that I no longer had to imagine that it was her tongue rolling around my head once more. I opened them quickly and watched her slowly, carefully, thoughtfully move her naked body up and down, the knees acting as a hinge to give her the subtle rhythm. She groaned at the pleasure, the memory and the present, and I pushed it in as fully as was possible without gagging her.

My hand reached round the back of her bum and located the wettest hole and sank two fingers as deeply inside as I could get from that angle. We stayed in that position for a while until she came up for air and my arm ached to the point of numbness. Silently, we rearranged ourselves and pleasured each other orally for several more minutes. She slowed the sucking, hesitated as I worked on her clitoris, and breathed heavily across my shaft finding it increasingly more difficult to multi-task, eventually leaving me alone to concentrate fully on her pleasure. I teased, stopping each time she reached towards a climax until she stopped me and said, "Fucking finish it, you prick tease!" It wasn't nice to hear her speak so but I was too far-gone to care; so I did.

She came with a scream, and a subtle tsunami of juice that washed my lips and dripped down my cheek. It was an odd taste of sweat, iron, salt and Anna, the unique ingredient that gave each lover a personal perfume. As she lay on her side, I removed my head, wiped my mouth and moved round the back. She was diminutive, and, as such, easy to move and position to our satisfaction (well, mine I suppose) and I slipped in easily from the side. She gasped, grabbing my arm and made to stop me with a hand running quickly to the point of union. But once there it relaxed and fell away, and she moaned as I pumped hard and quick and like a fucking chimp. It was pure animal lust, but liberally sprinkled with human affection and love.

She came quite soon, smudging my pubic hair with a creamy wetness and I continued to pump, wanting more than ever to flood into her, my beautiful, stunning, one and only, lover. The hand returned and this time pushed down to us and moved me away. Reluctantly I withdrew, breathing heavily and watching the wet between us fall in drips to the clean sheets.

"You okay?" I asked.

"Yeah, yeah, but…" She stopped, thinking hard on what to say.

"Do you want me to stop?"

"Yeah, no, yeah, no… Look, can you put on a condom?"

"Oh God, yeah, sure. Oh, sorry!"

I quickly got to my bag and rummaged around inside for the packet of three hopeful rubbers that I'd remembered at the last minute. Not wishing to ruin the moment, I fumbled with the foil, ripping it open and grabbing at the rubber. It slipped between my fingers but I managed to save it from falling into the juice on the bed. Carefully, I pulled it across the soggy head and over the softening penis. She grabbed at it, keen to keep it up, and helped it fill out to take me fully inside.

She laid back, legs bent at the knee, slightly akimbo and, as in the style of the preaching explorers of the Victorian Empire days, we fucked for a long while. I didn't want it to finish; I wanted to freeze the moment, cryogenically seal the feeling and flavour, the hormones, but all good things… and then I did, just before her and I exploded like I had never done before. As I shuddered to a halt, she came too, gasping into my neck and briefly biting into the skin to leave a small lesion, a love tattoo that I'd treasure for the three days that it stayed with me.

As we lay there hugging hard, so much so that sweat stuck us like glue, I couldn't help but sense an aura of desperation between us; not so much emanating from me, or from her, but our union sparked it into existence and I lay there breathing her in and feeling increasingly desperate, desperately lost and sad. I never, ever wanted to let go.

I watched her shower, slowing the image to half speed to watch with incredible precision the way she ran her hands across her soap-sudsy covered skin. It was an odd arrangement, this room, and indeed us, I thought, the shower cubicle placed awkwardly behind the opening of the door. The room had the shower, but no toilet, which was located along the corridor and shared by the three rooms on this floor. Anna took her time, didn't mind me watching and seemed to enjoy the pleasure that I gained from doing so. She would smile occasionally and run her hand repeatedly across her little potbelly, almost subconsciously. I daydreamed a life for us and imagined holding that belly, nine months distended and holding our child. It was a happy reverie and I smiled back at her.

We cuddled for a while, both fresh and clean. She'd snoozed through my shower, unfortunately, but grabbed a quick look before turning on to her side, right arm tucked across her midriff.

At half past seven we dressed for dinner and took a stroll down the road towards the quay and the warehouse, derelict not long since but now regenerated and housing four quite posh eateries. The clouds had been blown away and the sunset cast a dull purple light here. It was noticeably lighter than in Kent at this time of day, further west than back home, though the equinox that pushed the sun to the south of the equator right about now meant that those beautiful, lingering long evenings were passing.

It was busy, the restaurant, but the maître-de took pity on the young lovers and showed us to a hastily arranged small table in the corner. I found it hard to squeeze in between the wine fridge and the table, but was grateful for the seating and view across the working quay back to the town which began to twinkle in the lighting of street lights, cafés and front rooms.

Anna was quiet; I could understand why but I was keen to keep some sort of conversation going to stop her thinking too much. I wanted nature to win out and bring her round to me, regardless of common decencies and the wronging of a betrothed. I'd make up for it all, I thought, tucking into the fried whitebait that we shared across the tiny table. I finished my beer; I liked to quench my thirst before hitting the wine, and started on the white they recommended to complement the main.

"You sure?" I asked, the bottle teetering over the glass. She seemed to think about it a while before declining, placing her soft hand over the top of the glass.

"No thanks. I like to keep a clear head with you."

"Fair enough. You don't mind if I do?"

"No, not at all. Go for it."

She looked at me with an odd expression, possibly regret, but I was quick to dismiss it. I must stay focussed, stay positive; stay in control. The main course was delicious; locally caught haddock in a fancy jus and the wine washed it down a treat. The edges began to fuzz around Anna and the town blurred into the dark night. We talked of school, of memories and laughed at them. It was good to see her smile, watch those eyes sparkle with a grin.

It was gone nine thirty by the time I squeezed out of the table and it was refreshing to be outside in the stiffening breeze; it had grown progressively warmer in our tight corner as the restaurant filled and spat out table after table. They were clearing a healthy profit, it seemed. The road home was dark, the streetlights badly placed at an interval long enough for a true blackness to engulf us before hitting the next orange glow.

Opposite the entrance to the B and B a gate led to some slate steps, gratefully lit by the nearest street lamp, and they continued down to the rocky beach which spread fifty yards along a concrete jetty covered in a grimy seaweed that was exposed by the outgoing tide. We slid along it comically until we reached the gently lapping waters, here, in the sheltered bay. The town was lit behind the rump of the headland and it was beautifully dark ahead into the bay and the islands and mountains beyond. It took a while for our eyes to adjust and we stood there holding hands like age-old lovers had done for centuries, looking to the sea and the skies. A faint green glow shimmered on the horizon, barely noticeable at first, growing in its luminosity as the dark around us took form.

"Wow," I said, "is that...?"

"Shit, yeah, I think it is!"

I watched the sky swirl above the far hills and pushed Anna in front of me to grab her from behind and place my warm hands over her soft little belly.

"Are you sure? Are we far enough north?" I asked.

"Yeah we are; I've seen them back home – south of here, I think."

"Really?"

"Yeah."

"Wow... it's weird but it's not quite as spectacular as I'd expected, but it's still pretty cool."

"Yeah."

I held her from behind and squeezed as we watched the green fog zap the skies like an opening scene to a 1950s sci-fi 'B' movie.

"You made a wish?" she asked.

"Oh, does that work with this?"

"Yeah, I think you're supposed to."

"Okay."

I made a wish. We were quiet for a while watching the green lights dance a tango across to the darker northeast, visible above the silhouettes of the hills beyond the town. Water lapped at our feet.

"Steve?"

"Uh huh?"

"I'm pregnant."

"Shit, that was quick," I joked, finding it so amusing that I let out a chuckle.

It took a long while, in reality probably only a few seconds, but there, under the dancing lights, it seemed to take forever for the news to sink in. I still had a smile on my face, pleased with my wish-related retort, and it took eons for the muscles to relax, retract and turn into a confused grimace.

"Really?"

I was still holding her.

"Yes, really."

"But we... just now, I..."

"Yeah, I know... I'm sorry."

She was off, up the slippery slope as quickly as her tiny legs could carry her and her unborn without falling. I continued to watch the flickering skies, seeming now to resemble the jumbled-up sparks of confusion that zapped across my frontal lobes.

It was all quite simple really. She was pregnant and going to have a child with Mike; indeed, they were soon to marry, presumably so as not to give birth to a bastard but all this? She did love me, of course she did; that was plain to see, but why all of this if her situation was so... so... unredeemable? We had never stood a chance against such forces of nature; I never stood a chance. The no-drinking made sense now, the stomach tracing made sense, but this... all of this? The whole goddam picture was as confusing as hell.

'What to do now?' I thought and then said it aloud to the Aurora Borealis that danced across the northern Scottish skies. I laughed, more through incredulity than humour, and saw myself, here, as others might view me in a movie, and considered this scene something of a well-deserved comeuppance.

"Fuck it!" I said. The only bloody time I'd decided on some sort of permanent solution to all of my love affairs and this happens. I threw my arms up to the heavens in an awkward display of surrender for the viewing universe and loped slowly back to the room.

Chapter 5

When the heat is on

She wept at times in the night but refused any form of comfort. I pondered on her state of mind and what the tears represented and tried to keep my ego out of the equation for once. She cried for the infidelities with me; she wept for the unborn inside of her, the snot tickling the end of her nose as a reminder of her wicked act; and she wept for me, for us, and the sheer bloody rotten timing of it all. I could not hate her; shit, I quite repulsively wanted to fuck her again and again as though to rewrite the DNA inside of her. I loved her.

I slept surprisingly well, the deep sleep clogging the corner of my eyes and wiping itself across my knuckles as I rubbed them awake. The morning ablutions were cordial enough, though we dressed and washed as acquaintances, towels draped over immodest parts, as now the sanctity of the flesh had banished the view for our wanton pleasures. This was truly the marking of an end to a relationship as awkwardness prevailed.

The late breakfast conversation was surprisingly ordinary and mundane, talking mostly of stone skimming and the approaching competition.

"What time's the flight again?" she asked, pointing to her dainty wrist, the dark hairs brushing themselves in a sweeping caress towards her elbow. I desperately wanted to touch them; kiss them.

"Seven thirty; get in at eight twenty-five. Should be home by ten, ten thirty."

"Good."

'Yep, fucking great,' I thought, not quite sure whether the bitterness brought it spitting out of my mouth at the same time, but she didn't look up. Back to Mike, back to life, back to reality. I hummed the lines into my orange juice.

Out of the silence of the falling crumbs from toasted organic granary, doorstep wedges, she spoke. "Why did you never reply to my letter?"

"Hey?" I wracked my brains for another misdemeanour. What had I misplaced or ignored this time?

"You know," she sighed, sitting back and looking at me with those doleful, puppy-dog eyes, "the one I gave you at the airport?"

Of course, THE letter! The one that I never quite had the courage to finish... well, start reading, open even. It had remained in my rucksack for the whole of the seven months of my travels, a St Christopher of sorts. It had soon become impossible to face; it remained a monument to our love, frozen in time.

"Oh, right... sorry."

"Sorry what...?"

"Sorry, miss?"

"No, you idiot!" But she did smile.

"I know, I know. Do you want the truth?"

"Please."

"I told you didn't I, at the wedding?"

"You did?" she wracked her brains for the memory, lost up in there in the crazy confusion of this mess.

"I never read it; never opened it."

"You what?"

"Sorry, never read it."

"Why?"

"'Cos... I'm not really sure."

"What did you do with it?"

"Nothing."

"What do you mean, 'nothing'?"

"Nothing; left it in my rucksack. It's still there." I pointed to the ceiling, and by chance, straight through to the bag, laying on its side and spilling clothes across the floor.

"Really? But... why?"

I shrugged. "Too scared I guess."

"Of what?"

Of love, of course! I shrugged again.

"You are a bloody mess, you are," she said.

"Yep. Sorry 'bout that."

She finished her coffee, pushed back her chair, brushed the crumbs from her lap, stood and went upstairs. I had an erection on the way. I wanted nothing more than to go upstairs and nail her and tell her that I loved her, open the letter, rip it up into tiny pieces and sprinkle it on her naked body like rose-petal confetti. As it was, when I packed my clothes away, I stuffed it into my jeans' back pocket to rest alongside the heart-shaped stone I found for her in the Clarée Valley: maybe they would bring me luck in the competition.

We were on the road within an hour of breakfast and enjoying the early morning sunshine. The clouds to the west had blazed orange first thing in the morning as I took a peek out across the bay and onto the mountains that hours before had shined an emerald green. She was still asleep and I was quite awake by six fifteen a.m. I had watched her breathe, considered the two beating hearts inside of her, and sighed wistfully onto the window pane, briefly steaming it up with my disappointment.

'Red sky in the morning, shepherds warning' – and indeed it was prophetic; the last of the sun's rays were swallowed by the greedy grey clouds that invaded in vast numbers from the west as we drove on. It was raining by Kilninver on the A85, and it mirrored my mood; I was sad, sad for a lost love, a love that I should have cherished and flourished within. It should have been a bloody gloriously sunny day.

The scenery, in between the tear stains running down the window screen, was still stunning, and we surveyed the landscape in a calm reverence. By Clachan, on the tiny B884, we had reached the beautiful stone bridge across the narrow straight to the Isle of Seil. A troll surely lived beneath it, its rise and fall so exaggerated that it belonged to a fairy tale.

The tide was out far enough right now for the island to feel connected. This narrow channel followed a scar in the crust, an ancient fault, and twice a day millions of litres of Atlantic seawater would rush along its cracks and crags to make the island and separate it from the rump of Britain.

Seil seemed different at once, a magical realm passed into. The geology had changed too this side of the fault line, with rock that belonged to a different era and the road passed along the widening crack, allowing a creek to form and soon, a wide channel, the Seil Sound, separated us from Scotland.

"I'd love to see an otter," I said, looking to the channel and the innumerable craggy inlets that would be a suitable site for a holt.

"Wrong time of year."

"Yeah?"

"Yeah, sorry."

"Oh... how you know that?"

"*Countryfile.*"

"Quality."

"Yep."

I imagined her and Mike and the babe, all cuddled up on a sofa of a Sunday night watching John Craven chase otters around the Highlands. I was jealous.

The long sliver of rock that was Seil headed south and slightly west and we drove headlong into the Atlantic front that lashed rain into us.

"Shame 'bout the weather," I said, pointing to the flood that was led across us at quick intervals, displaced this way, then that by the over-worked wipers.

"Yeah," she said, a sigh of disappointment so deep that it represented much more than just the grey skies.

The road hugged the coast and then skipped inland and, at the last, threw us up over a sharp spine of rock to hit the hamlet of Easdale, a whitewashed homestead of cosy cottages that stood guard here at the end of the Old World; it was quite spectacularly isolated. From here, we would get a small boat to the island of Easdale that rose out of the black sea like a smudge through the incessant rain. Although no more than three hundred metres away, the falling clouds set it in the middle of the Irish Sea, and Sirens washed their screams over the hills to warn me; a little tardy, I considered.

We parked up in the last space we could find in the overflowing car park and spent five minutes suiting ourselves in waterproofs big enough to drown us in Gore-Tex. It was clearly very busy and we trudged in the rain down to the small harbour to catch the ride across the sea. A wet and bedraggled huddle of bodies stood on the quay watching the approaching boat appear from the veil of dark grey cloud that touched the water. The wind had dropped to a whisper allowing the rain to beat incessantly at a vertical and perfect ninety-degree angle. The rush of rain that fell like stair-rods was so overwhelming that it felt like a constant stream of water from a heavenly power shower, and the infinite patterns of concentric rings that filled the sea all around us were enchanting and mesmerising; we all stood and just watched Nature's show.

"It really rains when it rains here," I said to the middle-aged man in a Macintosh cape next to me.

"This isn't rain," he said, smiling into the sky and getting his face soaked in the two seconds that he did so. "This is a beautiful summer's day!" A couple of his friends laughed. The back of his cape bore the name of his brass band. They must have travelled a few hours to get here today, and as I looked around at the gathering crowd I saw the associated baggage that would follow in the caravan of a brass band. I was amazed that I hadn't noticed it before. They joked amongst themselves in broad Central Lowlands accents and asked if we were going to compete.

"Me? Yeah, I hope to."

"Me, no," said Anna, raising her eyes to the heavens to disassociate herself from such lunacy.

"You the entertainment?" I asked.

"Aye, part of it," said the man. "You guys are the headliners!"

The boat had docked and a few bedraggled souls stepped up onto the harbour wall from it, allowing us to waddle down and replace them on the craft. It would easily carry twenty people, but the baggage left a few of the band waiting for the next shuttle with another gathering group of competitors and curious onlookers. We motored quickly into the wall of water and watched the boat parting the infinite concentric rings of the raindrops in front. It was as calm as a millpond and the rain fell harder still, if at all possible, threatening to overflow the ocean and flood the mainland. Easdale rose quickly as it appeared through the wet fug, a scraggy lump of slate that stood high above the sea as if to banish the impending deluge.

We unloaded and Anna and I helped with the boxes of brass up the small path to the green and the village hall that doubled today as Skimming HQ. It was incredibly busy inside, a mist of condensation and evaporation stinging the eyes and the smell of wet canvas, wool, dog and humans stinging the nose. In the ordered chaos we found the traditional trellis table that seated the committee members and housed the now soggy A4 pages of the list, kept safe in the clasp of a tattered clipboard. I flipped over the first full page of names and scribbled my entry, 'Steve Jones' in place number 83. It was going to be a busy afternoon.

"Good luck. Skim-off for the adults begins at one p.m. You can practise in the quarry opposite the lanes."

"Thanks."

"Ney problem, pal." I was sure he put the accent on, as though to please this awkward-looking Sassenach.

We listened to a local bagpipe quartet until the squeal beat us into a retreat. Next door, we crowded into the pub, low beams forcing the majority of the clientele to stoop over their pints and pies. Wet dogs shuffled at our feet, zigzagging between us to wipe themselves dry and we spotted a free seat, squeezing ourselves into a corner next to an antique pianola and a table full of trinkets and trophies, cheap looking medallions spilling out of their tiny plastic wallets and spraying over the table top. Anna fingered a couple of them, as I did my pint, and laughed at the inscriptions.

"Look," she said, "this'll be yours in a couple of hours." She handed me a gong with a genuine smile of pleasure on her pretty face. The bigger trophies, the serious ones, topped the pianola and were quite artistic, arranged around intricately carved and beautifully polished local stone.

"This is great, isn't it?" I said, rubbing my hands up and down my damp jeans like an eight-year-old sitting down to a Happy Meal with a weekend dad.

"Yes it is." Her hand was still playing with the best of the trophies. I took her soft paw in mine and held it tightly. "Don't!" she said. "I can just about do this." She pulled her hand from my grasp and flicked it around her head to explain the 'this' as the whole skimming thing.

"Sorry."

The pub was heaving and, in amongst the comings and goings, I spotted a familiar stoop. I stood and waved across the room in a vain attempt to attract his attention.

"Who is it?"

"Dave. Dangerous Dave! A guy I met travelling. Can't believe he's actually here... He can't see me."

He was gone before I could untangle myself from our stuffy little corner.

"You'll see him out there, don't fret."

"Yeah, sure; you're right."

"Of course," she said.

"Shall we go and have a look at the quarry?"

"S'pose so," she said, and we put the soggy wet gear back on and shuffled past the crowds to reach the exit. The brass band had started up next door and we listened a while in the easing rain.

"Think it might stop," I said, holding my hand out to catch large drops of fresh water.

"I bloody hope so," she said. Anna was tucked up snugly in her expensive rain gear and her little face looked forlorn and blue, squashed and distorted against a tightly pulled hood. I laughed at her, and a deformed and crooked smile was returned.

"Bet you were a miserable kid."

"I'm still bloody miserable."

"Hmm. Come on."

We walked around the corner, following the snake of people in front of the beautiful blue and whitewashed cottages towards the far shore of the island; it wasn't big. The path led over a small summit and down into the cauldron of two disused slate quarries, parted by loose slate slag and filled to the brim with fresh water. The quarry to the right was bigger and enclosed to the sea on its far side by steep cliffs, long since dug out and pockmarked by transient quarrymen. It was here that a lane made of fishermen's rope and buoys had been laid, maybe three metres across and spanning the length of the quarry, some seventy metres or so. The pit to the left of us was smaller and led around the corner, back towards the village and its sea wall was shallower allowing fine views, I guessed, on clear days back to the mainland.

And the people: all around the quarries they stood, hundreds of them, a multi-coloured raincoat of humanity filled the cauldron, awaiting the one o'clock kick-off.

"Crikey!" said Anna. "There's loads of 'em."

An outside broadcast team with BBC badges followed a reporter who mingled with the crowds and interviewed people at random. It was twelve thirty p.m. now and people gathered in and around the competition lane in increasing numbers. Serious-looking skimmers were practising down by the smaller quarry and we made our way down to its shore to do the same. The rain was definitely slowing, allowing the mainland to impose its mountains and glens on a fast-appearing horizon.

"How does it work, then?" asked Anna, watching me rifle through stones on the shore with scores of others.

"Well," I said, head down in amongst the slate and shale, "I can either find three beauties of my own, or use the official bucket-load. They have to be a certain size, not too big, not too small. They've got this measuring thingy if you use your own stones. Someone said three inches in diameter, I think."

"What you gonna do?"

"Dunno. Depends." I rifled through some more loose stones. "Though I reckon the best ones have already gone." I pocketed a few average pebbles and loosened up by flinging them across the water without too much effort. They skimmed well enough, reaching up to twenty or thirty metres and bouncing more or less in a controlled fashion and reasonably straight; it was promising.

"How do you win it?" she asked.

"It's not the number of skims or skips; that's what they do in other places. This is about distance. You have to keep the stone inside the lane and it has to skip at least three times. The longest skim wins."

"Cool."

A couple of guys near me looked on, impressed. I'd forgotten that I could throw a quality stone. I found a few more decent pebbles and Anna told me that she was going on up the hill to get a good view for the competition. "I'll catch you up." I skimmed some more, still pleased with the quality. As I drew back for my last practice, a slap across my shoulders pushed me forward and I splashed a boot into the water. "What the f...!"

"Jonesy, you bastard!" It was Dangerous Dave. We hugged, awkwardly of course, and chatted whilst skimming stones across the water with renewed gusto.

"I'm twenty-third to throw," he said.

"Eighty-third."

"Jeez, it'll all be over by then."

"Perhaps... Kim here?"

"Na, visiting family. Anyway, he's shit at skimming. This'll be between me, you and a couple of other guys I saw throwing earlier."

"Yeah, you think?"

"Yeah, I think. You know of any others turning up?"

"No. Valerie can't make it."

"Good, the Frenchy's too bloody good for my liking... Who you here with?"

"A friend. She's up there." I pointed in the general direction of the hill and the hundreds of people gathered there.

"Oh yeah? Anyone I know?"

"Nope. Just an old friend."

Dave hit me playfully on the arm; it hurt.

"Not my throwing arm, you cheating git!"

"Sorry, man. Just you're always with some chick or other."

"Hmm."

***

***(Location No.12, World Skimming Championships, Easdale Island, Scotland)

We'd begun to gather around the skimming block: an ancient, large and flat stone would stand the contestant in front of the lane. The referee sat next to it, behind a smaller trellis table, with list at hand and two buckets of competition stones at his feet. On the table stood the measuring instrument in case the serious throwers had wanted to use their own stones. Dangerous had found his friends and had gone over to the far side to watch the first throwers. Anna and I stood near the front, a few feet up the small hill, and listened to the banter of the local organisers and competitors; it was good-humoured.

The TV crew emerged from the crowd to stand directly behind us and started to talk to an elderly man who stood with his equally elderly sheepdog. It took me a while to realise that I knew him.

"Hey, Anna? That's Merlin. You remember the old chap we met the day…the day we, you know, by the river in Wales?"

Anna was hiding behind me, looking to the ground and keeping me always between her and the cameraman.

"Leave him be," she said, tugging at my coat sleeve. "I don't want to be fucking seen on TV! I don't want Mike to know about this."

"Doubt anyone will see this, Anna."

"You never know."

True, I didn't, but the chances seemed quite slim.

"Okay. I'll wait 'til they go somewhere else."

"Thanks."

"Yeah, sure."

Soon enough the reporter had gone up the far side to seek out Dangerous no doubt; he had that way with the world.

"Excuse me?"

"Yes, son."

"I doubt if you remember my face, but we know each other. I'm Steve Jones. We've emailed about skimming." I threw an imaginary stone into his groin.

"Yes, of course I remember you." He took my hand and shook it vigorously. I patted the disinterested dog on the head. "I've really enjoyed your emails. Sounds like you had a great time travelling and throwing stones."

"I did thanks. And thanks for the tips."

"You goin' to write that book?"

"Of course," I said, smiling all the while at the old man.

"Did you come here with anybody?" he asked.

I introduced him to a shrinking Anna, still hiding behind me like a shy toddler.

"Pleased to meet you, young lady," he said. "I remember your face."

She smiled curtly and pulled me away, still tugging at my sleeve.

"We're going to get a bit nearer, ready for the action. You taking a throw?" I asked.

"No, just watching. You?"

"Sure."

"Good luck." He winked at us. It smacked of a reminder of his perceptions of me; an itinerant lover. The old bastard was right and I both loved and hated him for it.

We shuffled a little further down the hill stepping in between excited competitors and spectators. It was fast approaching one o'clock and we found a spot near enough for me to squeeze through when the time came for my turn, but still high enough to give us a decent view of the action.

"You see all right from here?" I asked.

"Yeah, okay," she said, straining at the toes to push her little frame up as far she could. I pulled her in front of me to gain a better vista through a gap of Gore-Tex.

The compere announced the opening of the competition to loud applause and North American-style whooping. The first competitor, a girl, took to the skimming block and picked out a stone from the bucket. With some skill, she let a stone skim proficiently along the lane for eight or nine skips before it sank. A voice boomed from the far side of the quarry, a referee opposite the buoys neatly placed at five metre intervals to help with the marking.

"Twenty-two metres!"

A loud cheer erupted accompanied by enthusiastic applause and a splattering of simian whooping. Her next two stones were poor, one sinking straight in and the next skipping out of the lane at around five metres. Nonetheless, she received a rapturous reception on stepping down. The competition had begun.

He was funny, the compere, and sprinkled his script with the occasional profanity to keep the TV editors on their toes, no doubt. The BBC presenter took her turn after a few minutes of mediocre skimming, much to the derision of the crowd. She fumbled around in the bucket and pulled out a stone that she immediately dropped into the water at her feet.

"Zero metres!" shouted the referee, and the crowd erupted with laughter and applause.

"Put that on yer telly box!" shouted the compere. Again, loud laughter.

She blushed, but shrugged it away and picked out another stone. This time, she chose the unusual backhand style, reserved for fools and novices, and threw it flatly into the water just short of five metres. It sank immediately.

"Better. Sort of." A ripple of laughter again.

Her third actually skimmed four times before sinking against the left hand ten-metre buoy. She raised her hands, bowed and received a large round of applause.

It wasn't long before Dave's name was read out, and he stepped up to the mark.

"C'mon, Dangerous Dave!" I shouted from the crowd, and was easily heard by the majority.

"Hold on, a fan," interrupted the compere. "It's not just Dave Cunliffe, but Dangerous Dave Cunliffe. Give him a round of applause." We did. "I hope you're not too dangerous, Dave? If I were you hen, I'd stand back... just in case." A chortle from the women standing nearby.

Dave had picked three near-perfect stones earlier, taking a great pride in showing me them; they looked good. He pulled the first from his pocket and rubbed it lovingly between the thumb and forefinger of his right hand. He stood still, sniffing the breeze like a curious puppy dog, and drew back his long, long arm. The arc he swung was huge and the perfect stone flew perfectly from his hand, spinning at a vast speed, straight and steady. I'd lost count of the number of skips before it sank near to the fifty-metre mark. It was the longest throw of the day by a country mile and the crowd erupted in appreciation.

"Dangerously good, Dave!"

His second was equally skilful, his wiry frame throwing it out straight and fast again, this time passing fifty metres and skipping out of the lane nearer fifty-five.

"Bloody fantastic, Dave!" shouted the host. Another roar.

"Come on, David. You can hit that wall!" he encouraged over the microphone.

Dave stood on the mark once more and prepared himself. This time, he threw the most perfect of skims that flew and flew and bounced and bounced and hit the far wall without seeming to slow or deviate in the slightest.

"Barnes Bloody Wallace!" shouted our host. "Yer very own Barnes Wallis! Sixty-five metres! The first person to hit the far wall today! That could well be the winning skim ladies and gentlemen. Give gorgeous Dangerous Dave Cunliffe a huge cheer."

Skim after skim came and went and although a few were good, topping off at around forty to forty-five metres, most were mediocre or poor.

Competitors number 68 and 69 were brothers, huge Viking types with surnames ending in 'son' was all I could gather through the static attacking the PA system. They were good. Sixty-eight hit the far wall with his first skim and took the applause like a seasoned pro. His brother (I think it had to be by the look of him) threw his first stone almost out of the lane immediately, but his second flew at incredible speed straight up the lane and skimmed to a halt at the foot of the wall.

"Did it hit?" shouted the compere.

"Aye!" came a shout from the referee at the side.

"A family double! Incredible, ladies and gentlemen." Their relationship was confirmed. "This is turning out to be a hell of a competition this year."

Again the competition relaxed into comedy, skimmer after skimmer failing to reach the fifteen-metre mark, the stone plopping unceremoniously into the opaque water without a skip or flying out of the buoyed lanes almost immediately. Soon enough, skimmer number 83 was called.

"Steve Jones! Must be a nom-de-plume. What you trying to hide, Steve? Who're ya running from?" A chuckle from the crowd.

I stood upon the mark, and limbered up, looking to my right to spot Anna in amongst the spectators. She waved, somewhat reluctantly it seemed, keen for me to get on with it and get the hell out of there and on the plane home to Mike and the real world. I nodded.

Picking a good-looking stone from the bucket to the side, I stood straight and felt it between both palms. I swung it back behind me, meeting my left hand briefly, and repeated the action a couple of times. The nerves tingled in the pit of my stomach; they'd been there all weekend, not so much for the skimming, but for the long shot on love that I was failing to perpetrate here.

"Bollocks to the lot of you," I muttered under my breath and flung the stone too deep into the lane, the first loop too long to generate a continuous and steady skim. It bounced apathetically a few times before sinking into the depths at around twenty-metres. I received a splattering of applause, and looked again to Anna. I could see her watching closely, an agitation on her poor little phizog that struck me through the gut like a rapier blade. What a selfish fool I'd been.

I picked up another stone, the first I could grab and let it fly competently along the lane, skipping calmly up to forty-metres, and spluttering to an uncountable stop just to the right of the lane.

"Thirty-nine-metres!"

"Not bad, Keyzer Soze." It made a few people laugh.

"Okay," I said and grabbed the largest of the bucket pebbles that I could see. "This one's for Anna," I said to the compere.

"Ladies and gents. This throw's for a girl by the name of Anna." A cheer. I lost her face in the crowd as I swung my arm back and forth. Leaning back, I lifted my left leg like a star rookie pitcher and let fly with the best skim I'd thrown in a while. It left my hand at the magical thirty-degree angle, spinning off my index finger perfectly and hitting the lane slap bang in the middle at around twenty-five metres, before skipping again at forty. It hit the water only three more times before it crashed into the far wall.

"Fuck me! That'll do," I said, the words drowned in an almighty roar and round of applause.

"Another great throw! Fantastic, Mr Jones. We'll see you in the skim-off!"

I received a collection of back slaps from the crowd nearest the mark and stood to the side to chat with a couple of previous throwers, who were full of kind words. I decided to stay near the action for a few more throws, before heading back to poor Anna. I must have been there a while, chatting, clapping and whooping when the occasion required it.

"Ladies and gentlemen, and the venerable BBC, yet another Dave! Please welcome Dave Cummings." A few whoops. We were running low on our enthusiasm tank for much more than that, though still having a ball. It took me a short while to check the name.

"Dave Cummings! Shit!" I said under my breath, but loud enough for me to distinguish it from a thought. I couldn't believe it was him! And next to Dave stood Jo. They were both still together, it appeared; still wonderfully youthful and sporting the olive-skin tan of the middle class summer break students.

My phone buzzed; it was hard to retrieve it from under the layers of Gore-Tex, jumpers and jeans and by the time I'd pulled it out, the buzzing had stopped.

'Missed Call – Anna'

'Hey? Where is she?' I thought, scanning the crowd in and around Merlin, the last place I'd seen her.

Another buzz. A text message. 'Am at car. I'm going. Get here now!'

What the fuck? I rang her number and waited for it to connect. Third ring, she picked up.

"What's going on?"

"I'm at the car."

"Why?"

"I want to go now!"

"But I'm in the play-off: the skim-off."

"Fuck that. I wanna go now!"

"Why? I could win. World Champion and all that." A brief pause. "Is this just to piss me off?"

"No, you dick head, it is not, though I admit it would have been a good idea. No, I just saw Dave and Jo, our ex-pupils!"

"Oh, right, yeah. Dave's skimming now." His first stone was good, sinking at around forty-five-metres. "Did they see you?"

"No, thank God!" A pause. "But you do know that I still teach Dave's little sister?"

"Oh, right, yeah, no, yeah, shit I forgot."

"And if they see me, with you, it won't take long to get back to school, and to Mike, and then I'm buggered."

"Oh right."

Dave's second stone was poor, leaving the lane soon after the fifteen-metre buoy. I stood, a little dumbfounded, as he geared up for the third with an almighty arc and launched possibly the best skim I had ever seen. There was a tremendous roar as the stone flew perfectly straight, barely touching the surface of the water, as it skipped again and again, without slowing, to crack hard into the slate wall at the end of the lane.

"Another sixty-five-metre throw! My God, that's five now! And two of them by Daves! This is now officially the best World Skimming Championship we have ever hosted! Now, Miss BBC, please put that on yer telly box!"

When I stopped clapping and whooping, I turned on my toes and started up the hill, forced to the right of Merlin by the lapping tide of people, and soon broke free at the summit and found the path back past the cottages and along to the village hall and harbour.

Chapter 6

24-plus-infinity – the Lake Mackinac record skim, circa 1977

She looked sad and lonely when I reached the car and rather than be mightily pissed-off at having missed out on the opportunity of becoming a World Champion, of sorts, I felt her pain, her angst, her discomfort and was acutely aware of my irritating bloody-mindedness since our first touch of flesh on that rock in the Clarée Valley. Anyway, I was at least the fifth-best skimmer on the planet, so was pleased enough. I could always believe that I may have won and dreaming of glory is far better than facing down the reality of losing at the last.

"Come on then, let's go," I said.

She just looked at me, still irked at having almost been rumbled.

"Dave skimmed really well. He hit the wall too." She said nothing but just opened the door and started to strip off the waterproofs whilst holding onto it. She threw the trousers and jacket over the seat and into the back.

The skies were still grey, though a lighter shade of pale now, the dew point having lifted, and the clouds hung there motionless in the non-existent winds.

"Not a breath of breeze, not even up there," I said pointing to the roof and turning the car onto the bridge, topping the summit with a flutter of the tummy and descending back onto mainland Scotland. Anna hadn't said a word since we'd met at the car park so I turned the radio on and pushed the volume way up high to get the football commentary. I didn't have to compromise any more. She'd have to listen to the crackly game regardless.

Coming down the side of Loch Lomond, a last minute goal interrupted the silence. Another United win was a bit irritating, but the commentary was exciting to listen to and it took my mind off the odd situation that I found myself in. The village of Luss was approaching and I calculated that it would be another two hours to the airport from here.

"Should be there in a couple of hours."

She looked across and then down into her lap as her phone started to buzz. She picked it up and answered it.

"Hi… Mike?"

Great.

"Hello… Mike… I can't hear a fuckin' thing."

She put the phone down and shook it; put it back to her ear.

"Hello. Hello. Shit, no fucking signal."

I looked across and smiled – a wry smile.

"Can we stop? I've gotta phone Mike." Pause. "Don't say a thing!" she said, pointing at me. I shrugged.

The huge car park at Luss was perfect timing.

"I need a pee anyway," I said.

I swung the car into the half-empty lot and came to a halt near the toilet block and coffee cabin.

"You want anything?" I asked, pointing to the cabin.

"No. Just want to ring Mike."

I looked at my phone and saw that the signal was strong on my network. "You wanna borrow mine?" She gave me the teacher look. "Fair enough."

"I'm gonna use the public phone."

"Okay. I'm going to go for a walk and get a drink on the way back. I'll give you ten minutes but then we gotta get going."

"Uh huh."

I beeped the car locked and went to the loo. The map inside the tourist office showed a path that led through the tiny hamlet and onto a lakeside track. I decided that I'd go along there for a few minutes and have a quick think.

The fishermen's cottages were a little too quaint, lived in now by retired Glaswegians or second homers, but their lane led to the path and bridge which crossed a wide stream that entered into the loch. A pretty girl was leaning against the railings of the bridge and gave me a beautiful smile as I walked past.

"Hiya."

"Hi."

I took the path a short while along the loch side and then doubled back to the stream to look for some pebbles to throw; they would be my placebo skim-off chucks. I scrambled down the side of the little estuary and skidded on the abundant loose stones at its edge. A few metres to my right stood the wooden bridge, recently renovated it seemed, and I saw the pretty girl still leaning against the wooden rail.

She smiled from the bridge, and her reflection sparkled in the clear, still water, a girl from another world looking back. And it was this girl, the one who lived in the water, that would be my future love, possibly my future wife, I hoped. The owner of the reflection turned slowly, waiting for me to look her way again and scuffed her feet along the newly pinned pine boards; a final flick of her hair, a glance back and she was gone down the lane.

I picked up a perfect pebble, a stone transported down the Luss Water along Glenn Luss, maybe originating from Old Shielings or Coille-eughain Hill, who knows, possibly Beinn Chaorach at 713 metres (or 2280 feet in Imperial). The endless attrition of rock on rock, stone on stone, pebble on pebble had created a well-rounded, palm-sized projectile found in amongst the local boulder clay and fluvio-glacial drift, and I threw it across the pond. It skipped once, twice, three times, each skip a little closer as it lost energy from the ricochets. After six, the gaps between jumps were too imperceptible to count but it seemed to skip into infinity. Just under the bridge it disappeared, breaking the perfect image of the girl and throwing her to the edges of the river in concentric circles. Maybe she would return, reform as the rings hit the banks and bounced back, but I didn't wait to find out. Living life in memories and hope seemed the easiest thing to do.

(Location No.13 and No.1, Luss, Loch Lomond, Scotland)

I walked up the slippery bank, dislodging rocks that would tumble to the river and tens of years hence would be picked up by dreamy fools and skipped across the river to the lake. I took to the walkway that led to the bridge and looked out across Loch Lomond, the sun hitting the far banks through a gap in the clouds, and sighed.

'And the sad reality', I thought to myself, leaning on the rail of the bridge, 'is that all the greatest love affairs in the history of the world are either left undone or unsaid, and remain lost in the melancholy of a lonely mind'.

Behind me the concentric rings of the rebound formed to shape the face of a beautiful girl, for a split second, and then were gone. And if I had seen it, I would have recognised the sweetest smile of the dark-haired girl who lived there.

I felt for the unopened letter in my jeans' back pocket, and pulled it out, fingering it lovingly as I did so. Leaning there, looking for the girl in the water now, I picked at the well-worn edges and got a purchase inside the fold of aged paper and ripped at it. The envelope seemed to disintegrate in my hands and pieces fell to the water, dancing complicated patterns as they did so. I pulled open the folded A4 school paper, still slightly scented from the day she put pen to paper, and started to read.

Once finished, I put the note carefully back into my pocket. I felt for the body-warm, heart-shaped stone of banded gneiss, pulled it out and dropped it unceremoniously into the stream below the bridge, watching it disappear in the wake of a perfect set of ripples.